REVOLUTION 2050

Jay Chalk

DANCING LEMUR PRESS, L.L.C.
Pikeville, North Carolina
www.dancinglemurpress.com

Dedication

To Amanda Hollister, who inspired me and never rolled her eyes (at least not in front of me) when I handed her manuscript, and to Tim Mabe, who, in the many early predawn hours we shared, taught me what prayer and dedication *really* meant...

PART I

November didn't just suck; it *really* sucked.

Samuel Aden Moore dodged teenagers, making his way through the crowded school corridor. The month began with rationed electricity just as an unusual cold-snap hit. Every other day compounded the coldness and the darkness with little cheer in between. Every other night, a diesel generator echoed from a rural home. Sam finally reported the generator and within hours, deputies showed. They confiscated the generator, writing the owner a budget-breaking fine for violating the Law of Acquire: if *all* could not acquire, no one acquired.

A week later, the sheriff's substation was firebombed. The next day Provincial Guard troops patrolled the semi-rural region. Blue Humvees cruised country roads, setting up roadblocks, creating anomalous traffic jams. Soldiers searched for weapons and watched for suspicious activity. A few days later, black-uniformed soldiers surrounded a few farm homes, including that of the generator's owner. They kicked in doors and hauled away people. *Those scofflaws got what they deserved,* Sam had mused. The Law of Acquire was a good law, leveling the playing field for those less fortunate.

Sam paused, leaning a six-foot frame against a cold locker as teenagers passed. Last week, his ailing mother had died. Mourning, according to law, was limited to two days; he had taken both. Now, his first day back from the funeral and the region's new *commissar* wanted to see him.

There were still five days left in November...

"Mr. Moore," a teenage boy said, extending a hand. "Sorry about your mother. Glad you're back."

Shaken from his thoughts, Sam gripped the offered hand. "Thanks, Brian. It's good to be back." He patted the young man on the shoulder, turned, and stepped down the corridor to the commissar's office. The closer he drew to the office, the more his stomach knotted, and he wasn't sure why. He glanced into the principal's open office door. A dark-haired woman of perhaps forty stood inside, talking to the young math teacher, Marna Johnston.

The older woman did a double-take as Sam passed. Then she glanced to the teacher in front of her. "Marna, just a sec."

6

She stepped around the teacher and hurried to the open door. "Sam!"

Sam stopped and turned, eyeing the approaching high school principal.

The woman stepped toward him. Tall and trim, the principal's short hair was brushed back. A blue blouse and khaki skirt hinted frowned-on femininity. She halted, smoothing the skirt. "I tried covering your butt," she murmured, "but someone slipped the commissar one of your student's essays before I could intercept it."

"Terri, you're *too* paranoid."

"You think?" Principal Terri Woodriff shook her head, eyeing him. "Sam, you're deviating from *Directorate* curriculum—again. I can't protect you much longer. I..." the principal hesitated. "I have a family to think of."

"I understand."

Woodriff raised a brow. "Do you?"

"You worry too much," Sam said and sighed. He shifted, shoving hands in trouser pockets. "Besides, I don't know what essay you're talking about."

Yet he did, and inside, he cringed. He should've reported the student's words, but something had kept him.

Woodriff again shook her head. "You're playing with fire."

Sam flipped up the right collar of a blue dress shirt. A gold triangle with an eight-point, blue star at the apex sparkled there. He glanced at Woodriff's collar. The same gold triangle and blue star shone. "I am one of *them*, one of you guys now, remember?"

Seconds passed. The principal chewed a lip. "The commissar says your classroom is an 'incubator.'"

"Oh?" Sam chuckled. "Well, every story has a beginning, a middle—and a vidmail. It's only a misunderstanding." He stepped away. "You know what they say, 'teaching is a *deadly* calling.'"

"Especially in the humanities," Woodriff said, gazing after him. "Sam, you're part of the machine now. Remind yourself of that."

Sam nodded, heading to the commissar's office. Mulling over the principal's last words, he made a left. Several steps and his tall frame shadowed an open doorway. "Mr. Tipton, you asked to see me?"

A thickset, middle-aged man with a shock of gray hair sat behind a rich, teakwood desk. In front of him sat a single sheet of notebook paper. He looked up. Wire-rimmed glasses rested on a thin nose. Thick glass lenses reflected overhead lights, giving the commissar a pasty, walleyed look. Jonathan Tipton reminded Sam of a dead carp he'd seen washed up on the banks of the Santee River.

"Come in, Mr. Moore, and close the door."

Sam stepped in and reached back, gently shoving the door closed.

"Please, have a seat."

Nervous, Sam stepped forward, awkwardly settling into a wooden chair in front of the older man's desk. The commissar's high voice was squeakier than normal. Fear and a strange rush gripped Sam. Twisting around, he surveyed the almost-bare room. Video monitors lit one wall. He turned back; his gaze rested on a portrait behind the commissar. North American Commonwealth President Robert Henshaw's photo struck a noble pose. In his sixties, the president's benevolent gaze was that of a caring grandfather. Sam's thoughts crystallized, and he fought down revulsion. He had to tear his thoughts away lest he vomit. His eyes came to rest on a painting below the president. A silver circle enclosed a silver triangle with an eight-point star in each corner.

"Compliance" was scripted in the left side of the circle between the lower and upper star. *"Awareness"* was spelled out between the stars on the right. *"Unity"* blazed under the triangle's base.

"We've visited before, haven't we?" Tipton asked.

Sam jerked, shaken from his thoughts. His eyes leveled on a *silver* triangle and star on the commissar's gray collar. "Yes, sir."

"The previous commissar was a little lax in his duties," Tipton began, "hence his reassignment." The commissar paused. "Your late father was worthy of his high Directorate position. With that rank came certain privileges. Mr. Moore, your Directorate membership is a result of one of those privileges. Do not treat such opportunities—gifts—lightly." Tipton tapped fingers on his desk. "I'll be frank. If it had been up to me, you wouldn't be wearing that gold triangle." His tapping paused. "Yet, now and then, a fresh approach may be used *if* carefully monitored. Therefore, for now, I'll withhold judgment on your teaching skills." The tapping resumed. "You need to impress *me*, Mr. Moore. A report on you claimed that you had a natural ability to bring young people into the Directorate fold...its triangle of life. For that, *and* for your father's glorious service to the Directorate, you were accepted into the *Directorate Triad.*"

The tapping seized. Leaning back, Tipton placed hands

behind his head. The high-backed chair squeaked, pronouncing unknown judgment. His mouth turned up unnaturally at the corners in what passed for a smile. "You and Principal Woodriff are the only ones in the region to achieve that lofty trust. That trust must be respected and reciprocated."

Sam nodded. "Yes, sir."

"I am sorry about your mother."

Sam nodded again. "Thank you."

The commissar straightened, and a forefinger pushed up the glasses on his nose. Clearing his throat, he touched the sheet of paper on the desk and shoved it to Sam. "This was written by one of your students, that new boy, Mark Thurmont. The infraction occurred in your class, while you were on leave."

Sam reached for the creased notebook paper. Wincing, he scanned the paper.

*They desire the empty mind, yet fear the empty page. A bullet didn't kill my father. A **word** did. My father was called a traitor to the state, a traitor to the Directorate. As he was dragged away in handcuffs, he called the Directorate the "traitors." Knowing he was to be executed, his last words to me were not, "Son, I love you," or "Son, take care of brother and sister." No, his last words to me were, "Mark, fill up as many blank pages as you can."*

And this I will do.

Sam sighed. His insides quivered. He'd taken up this paragraph last month, locking it in a desk drawer. Now, here it was. Laying the paper on the desk, he forced calm. "Mr. Tipton, if I may ask, who was Thurmont's father?"

Tipton removed his glasses and rubbed the lenses casually with a handkerchief. "He was no one." The commissar replaced the thick lenses on his nose. "Who he *was* is of no importance. His name will be erased from history, like all the others."

Moore's throat tightened. His own mother's loss, and that strange something from before, tugged. "Mr. Tipton," he began, "the boy probably still grieves for his father. I understand the kid was dumped on us from the rebellious western region. He has no direction, no Directorate education beyond a halfway house."

"That's no excuse!" the commissar snapped. He glanced over wire rims, staring hard at Sam across the desk. "I deal in the concrete, Mr. Moore, not conjecture. Psychological evaluation reveals the young man is highly intelligent but delusional, therefore, it's not surprising he's...how do you say it in this region?" Tipton paused, gesturing. "The boy has 'taken to you.'"

Sam cringed inside.

"But, we believe the Thurmont boy is a *gift*. We want to keep

9

him." Tipton eyed him. "Mark Thurmont trusts you, Mr. Moore. Feed that trust. Think of it as training a high-bred dog."

I want to punch the man in the mouth, Sam thought.

"Anything the young man says or writes that remotely resembles insurrection, I want on my desk that day."

"Yes, sir," Sam said, nodding, his gaze focusing on his shoelaces. *What is going on here?* He shifted in the seat. The commissar's ever-knowing gaze felt like a dagger to the chest. Something incomprehensible crept into Sam's thoughts: resentment. He forced down the evil concept and swallowed. "I'll redirect thought and closely monitor writing assignments. I'll focus only on Directorate topics."

"Good," Tipton said, reaching for the notebook paper. "To quote a great philosopher, 'need focuses one's thoughts.' You must make your students understand that dissention, even in thought, will not be tolerated. Nothing in life is free, Mr. Moore. Even thought is by design." He paused, scrutinizing Sam. "I swear I just saw a moment of rancor in your face?"

Sam's left leg began quivering. Anger seethed just below the surface. The commissar was trying to provoke him. But why? Sam forced calm. "I'll bring Thurmont into the fold, Mr. Tipton."

"We live in tenuous times," Tipton murmured, eyes narrowing. "Don't supersede your authority and neutralize what other educators have accomplished. *That* could be a dangerous game, indeed." He sighed and waved nonchalantly to the door. "You may go."

Sam rose, walked stiffly to the closed door, and twisted the knob.

"Leave the door open," Tipton said.

Sam non-too-gently yanked open the door and then stepped into the front-office corridor. *Damn that old man—why hasn't he retired!* This new commissar's sole purpose wasn't to oversee Directorate edict but to make life miserable for his subordinates. And lately, Sam seemed to be the target *de jour.* He sighed; he had only himself to blame. Well, it was behind him now. He would follow Directorate rules to the letter—as if there was a choice. Life was easier that way, and more secure...a life with little or no choice. *They* would make life's choices, would take the risks, and if they screwed up, *they* would pay the price. Sam's jaw tightened. At least, that's the way it was *supposed* to work.

He passed by Woodriff's open office and glanced in. She sat hunched over her desk, scribbling on a notepad. Sam hesitated, then kept going, not wanting to rehash the ass chewing. Besides, only five minutes remained in his conference period, and there was something in his classroom that couldn't wait: a quiet moment.

A minute later, he stood outside an empty classroom at the end of a long, well-lit hall. Sam pressed a forefinger to a built-in keypad near the door. A tiny light switched from red to green; the door swung in. He hurried inside the classroom, and overhead lights brightened. "Close door," he said. The door swung shut. His anxious eyes instantly went to a corner near the door. They were just as he had left them.

Golden chrysanthemums radiated from a vase on a makeshift table. The flowers gave life to an otherwise gray sameness, and Sam's sanity clung to the bouquet as a drowning man to a life preserver. He wasn't sure why he was drawn to something so simple. He reached out, reverently touched a petal, and felt guilty for enjoying a fleeting moment of self-identity. He should banish such thoughts; they weren't healthy. The Directorate had the citizens' welfare at heart. *They* knew how life should be lived. He glanced up to a tiny overhead camera. The corner he stood in was the only blind spot in the room. Both he and the students not only enjoyed the mums, but also enjoyed the illicitness of breaking the rules on contraband. If the flowers were spotted, they would be deemed "alien" and destroyed in front of the children. And, once again, he would find himself in front of Tipton.

Ring. Sam jerked, startled by the school bell. With reluctance, he withdrew his hand. Students began quietly pouring in, and he stepped past them and into the hall. Teenagers passed one another in orderly silence. Teacher/student conversing was all that was permitted in school halls. Now and then, murmurs drifted, mostly from underclassmen, to whom *Transit And Meditate Period* or *TAMP* were something new. Freshmen were particularly distracted, high school being their first experience in coed institutions. A frown from a teacher usually silenced the offending voice.

"Good morning, Mr. Moore."

"Good morning, Jeremy," Sam replied to a seventeen-year-old boy sliding past. "The nine-weeks are up today. You guys get to go home for a weekend."

The young man, wearing the school uniform of blue shirt and khaki slacks, halted. A small backpack dangled from bony shoulders. "Yeah," he said, and sighed.

Sam stood outside the open door, brow wrinkled. "Don't be so enthused."

11

The boy shook his head and turned, plodding to a desk.

"Mr. Moore," a girl said from behind.

Sam turned, and a teenage girl gave him a quick hug.

"Sorry about your mother," she said, stepping back.

"Thanks, Regan," Sam said, as other students filed into the room.

Two other girls caught up with Regan, and all three strolled into the classroom. Now that they were out of the hall, they chattered away, heading to their seats.

He loitered near the open door. A few teenage stragglers hurried by and the halls cleared.

Ring. Sam stepped back into the classroom, and the door automatically closed and locked. When the array of monitors entered, the door would swing inside, remaining open, and to Sam's relief—and amusement—hide the forbidden flowers.

Standing over a computer in back of the room, he submitted attendance electronically. Sam forced down internal distractions, swallowed, and stepped to the front of the classroom. The commissar's ass chewing still stung. He'd better get his act together; there was no such animal as an *ex*-Directorate member.

Sam paused in front of the class, and whispers died down. "Today, we're going to cover last night's readings." Sam grabbed a dry erase marker and scribbled on an old-fashioned white board: **"God is dead...and we killed him."** He turned, surveyed the twenty-two students in a pastel sea of blue and khaki, and then hooked a thumb to the board behind. "Whose words are those?"

Throats cleared, heads lowered, and the floor became a focal point.

"I'm waiting," Sam continued. "This was in last night's readings. And, of course, I know all of you anxiously dove in."

A timid hand went up, then another.

Sam called on the first student, a young lady whose long, dark hair was worn in the mandatory ponytail. "April?"

"Machiavelli?" she said meekly.

"April, you are so wrong," a male voice replied from behind her.

The girl turned, giving the boy a snitty look.

"Yes, she's wrong," Sam said, gazing at the young man who spoke. The boy made straight A's and wasn't above showing off academic abilities. "Tell us, Brandon," Sam said, eyeing him, "whose words are those on the board?"

The boy's round face puffed up proudly. "Karl Marx wrote that in the *Communist Manifesto*."

"Wrong," Sam said flatly. "Although, you're getting closer."

Several hoots went up. "Mr. four-point-O, you're O and two!" someone shouted.

Sam chuckled inside. The day before Moore had left for funeral leave, Brandon had also given a rare wrong answer—and no one had forgotten.

Brandon gazed at the boy who spoke up. "At least *I'm* going on to college, loser."

Oohs drifted. "Okay, that's enough!" Sam barked.

Silence enveloped the classroom.

"It was Nietzsche," came a voice off to the side.

Heads snapped around to the voice's source. Sam's gaze fell to a blond-haired boy halfway down an end row. It was the new kid, Mark Thurmont.

"Friedrich Nietzsche wrote it in the late 19th century," he said.

"Very good, Mark," Sam replied, studying him. The boy's deep tan told a story that most of the other students, with their pale skin, probably wouldn't understand. Mostly, though, it was Mark Thurmont's gaze that seemed to separate him from the other children. Sam had seen that gaze before, that haunted look, the look of one who is on a suicide mission to the soul—if there was a soul. Yes, he'd seen that look long before the boy arrived. To see it, all he had to do was look in a mirror.

He recalled the boy's written passage about seeing his father dragged away in cuffs. While that still happened to *certain* people, most of the children here were insulated from it, living in dorms on state-school property.

"Do you think he's dead, Mr. Moore?" the new boy asked. "Do *you* think God is dead?"

Sam blinked, stupefied. How dare the boy question authority. He could almost hear the commissar's chair banging against the wall, scrambling up, dashing to a video monitor.

A girl sitting across the aisle from the new boy leaned across. "How can someone who never existed die?" she murmured.

Sam sighed, gathering his thoughts. "Our society outgrew the God-concept," he said loudly but calmly. He glanced around to the other students. "Just as the polytheistic Romans outgrew the need for their gods."

Most students nodded in agreement. Here and there, a doubtful glance was cast, but those who believed otherwise, remained silent, knowing the consequences of speaking out.

"Test tomorrow," Sam began, "over chapters eleven and twelve. There will be a little something on the test over the Ten

Directorate Enactments." Groans drifted. "Now, take out your notes and let's review."

Forty-five minutes later, students quietly, dutifully, filed out of the classroom.

"Jeremy," Sam murmured to a young man stepping past him.

"Sir?" the boy said, halting and turning.

"That look on your face at the beginning of class...anything change at home?"

"No, sir." The boy hesitated.

"So, *they* haven't released your father yet." Sam paused, allowing the room to empty. He touched the boy's elbow, casually leading him to the corner near the flowers and out of camera view.

"Mom is working two jobs," the boy said with his head down. "I just wish dad had kept his mouth shut. He was leading the protest."

"Shh," Sam whispered, nodding to the ceiling camera. His gaze returned to the boy. "No matter what, be proud of your father. He stood up for what he thought was right."

"I'm proud of him," Jeremy said in a hushed tone. "But now, we have nothing. My going home this weekend will only make things worse." He paused, stammering. "Mr. Moore, I miss Mom and Dad and my little sisters and want to see them, but..."

"Take this," Sam said, slipping something into the boy's hand. "It's not much, but it may ease the guilt."

The tall, scrawny boy opened his hand. In his palm sat a one hundred U.S. dollar bill. "Mr. Moore—sir, I can't...I mean, like, this is *real* dollars!" Eyes wide, he stared at the blue-green bill, incredulous. "Do you know what this is worth?"

"Yes, I do," Sam said, smiling. He patted the kid on the shoulder. "Now, go before you're tardy."

"But—"

"It's a loan. Pay me back when you can." Sam gently shoved the young man out the door. "Get outta here."

The boy cinched his backpack and took off, waving. "Thank you, Mr. Moore!"

* * *

Sam plopped down in a chair behind his desk, unusually weary and drained. Another vacuous day was just tossed onto yesterday, which fell onto the one before, and so on, until a mountain of bleached, empty skulls loomed, blocking the horizon. At twenty-seven, Sam had no answer or cure for the descending bleakness. Yet, it wasn't his job to produce an answer. Acceptance was the way of things, the way of the mouse and the sidewinder. Unscrewing a cap, he took a swig from a water bottle and glanced up, eyeing the tiny, black bubble in the ceiling.

The solar-electric cart hummed smoothly through the small town of Perchance, Carolina Province. The vehicle's mismatched rooftop solar panels glistened in a forlorn, late-autumn sun. White contrails, in a convoluted game of tic-tac-toe, crisscrossed an otherwise clear sky. The cart passed under a large, overhead marquee, and Sam glanced up.

*We will fight the good fight **together**!* it read in scrolling text. Sam gripped the steering wheel and stared out the windshield, knowing what followed: *Compliance...Awareness...Unity...* Over and over the marquee scrolled various versions of the same message until the subconscious cried, *"Enough!"* and became numb.

In the passenger seat sat a thin man in his late 30's, quietly staring out a side window. "What do you think it's like, Sam, on the other side...over in the Western Alliance?"

Sam glanced to his colleague, Zack Zhimmer. The man taught chemistry. In public, Zhimmer was a man of few words. But in private, and if he trusted you, his thoughts would flow. ZZ was gifted with a keen, wary mind, and when he spoke, one listened. His words always held a truth that hit the target, the one swimming just underneath the veneer, the target most feared.

"'Western Alliance?'" Sam scoffed. "Is that what those scum are now calling themselves? They're nothing 'but dogs in need of a master.'"

"They also use another name," ZZ said, "but you know as well as I that even whispering *those* words can get one heavily fined, or worse, fired and black-listed."

Sam glanced to his colleague. "I guess those western provinces think that naming themselves validates their so-called 'cause.'"

ZZ nodded, gazing out the passenger window.

Sam turned back to his driving, the cart slipping past long-abandoned businesses. A once-popular chain restaurant, a car wash, and a large box store sat empty, and, Sam allowed, maybe, just maybe, forlorn. Why the buildings—reminders of the past—hadn't yet been torn down was anyone's guess. The Directorate was particularly efficient at modifying or erasing history, and Sam had no problem with that. Winners wrote history; losers lived with the consequences. A chilling scenario took seed and he shivered. What if...what *if* the Directorate were *not* the victors? He dismissed the absurd.

"I hear those people out west are starving," ZZ said.

"Huh?" Sam blinked, his thoughts broken. "Starving?" He cleared his throat. "Yes, yes, I've heard the same."

"It's all so odd..." ZZ murmured, and his words trailed off. "You and I both have that new boy, Mark Thurmont. He's from the West." ZZ glanced at Sam. "Wouldn't you say he looks healthy?"

"Remember," Sam said, "he was in a halfway house before he came to us. I'm sure he was 'cleaned up' before his release."

"The boy certainly doesn't fit the image of who *they* say lives out west," ZZ continued, "you know, those psychopathic suicide-bombers we're always told about?" He turned a narrow face to Sam. "They say those western rebels are nothing but a psychotic horde bent on taking down civilization."

The cart idled up to a traffic light, and Sam glanced to the older man. "I heard that the rebel leaders keep the populace drugged up."

"Drugged up?"

"Yeah, drugged up."

"I haven't heard that," ZZ said, "at least not about the *entire* Western Alliance."

Sam glanced to ZZ. "What if it were true? That would explain their craziness in not wanting to become part of the Directorate."

"There's no government infrastructure on the planet that could induce mass medication," ZZ said, snorting. "Besides, that would be insane. Imagine trying to control a drug-crazed mob? The mob and the government would turn on themselves, become a feeding frenzy." ZZ paused. "I can see those suicide-bombers being drugged, but...but the whole population?"

The light changed, and Sam stepped on it. The electric motor whirred then changed to its usual dull hum. One hand on the wheel, the other on an armrest, Sam stared out the windshield. "It would keep them docile. Just a small dose...make them easy to control."

ZZ gave an annoyed sigh. "Sammy, I agree with you on most things, but, on this rumor, as a chemist, I just can't see it happening. How would it be administered without the public knowing?" He paused, picking sticky lint nonchalantly from a coat lapel. "It isn't practical."

"ZZ, nothing about those western provinces are 'practical.'"

Silence settled in. The cart hummed down the nearly empty thoroughfare. Decrepit gray buildings rose around them. Now and then, they passed whitewashed brick where someone had spray-painted his or her displeasure with the world. *No,* Sam mused, *not the world, only the Directorate, which made those taggers—those traitors—even more dangerous.* He wished just once he could catch one. And then...

After several lights, the cart made a left onto tree-lined Holly Street and continued for three blocks. Sam slowed, admiring the naked trees. The ancient oaks were the few trees left in town that survived the axes and handsaws during the civil unrest known as the Dark Days in the late 2020s.

Disgusted with the old, corrupt U.S. regime, the people had rebelled. Urban areas were battlegrounds. In rural regions, hunting rifles became sniper rifles. To break the population's will, the government had ordered electricity, petroleum, and natural gas shut off in the rebellious sectors. Trees were felled for fuel. Food was scarce, especially in the cities. Times were dark and grim, and many people starved. There was a coup, more fighting, and then a political party known as the Directorate seized control, restoring order. Sam gripped the wheel, staring straight ahead, as thoughts drifted.

*He was maybe three, standing in the middle of the highway in his underwear, screaming. In a nearby grassy median, momma's rumpled form, along with dozens of others, lay in a growing pool of blood. Daddy was one of the **good** soldiers, and he was gone. A hulking black shape, its tracks churning up asphalt, sped toward him. Frozen in horror, he peed his pants. Without warning, soft arms scooped him up. It was a stranger, a woman. Later, he would call that woman Mother, and her husband, Father. Gripping him, she darted to the side just as several tanks thundered past. Then came the **bad** soldiers...*

"Sam—watch it!"

"Geesus!" Sam swung the wheel, just missing an oncoming cart. He glanced in the mirror. An arm was shoved out the retreating cart's window, as the driver gave the one-fingered salute.

"What's wrong with you, man?" ZZ said. "Did you nod off or something?"

"No. I...I don't know what happened. It was like I had a flashback or something." Sam glanced sheepishly to the chemistry teacher. "Didn't mean to scare you."

"A flashback?" ZZ said, staring. "What do you mean, 'a flashback?' A flashback to what?"

Sam swallowed. "Don't tell anyone, but lately, I've been having these dreams of the Dark Days, and—"

"Nightmares," ZZ said, interrupting. "They weren't dreams. Those days were nightmares. I was in junior high back then, when the Directorate rolled in and saved us."

"They didn't save my mother," Sam blurted. "They killed her, and probably my father, and they killed children, right in front of me, and...and..."

"Don't say such things!" ZZ shouted, glancing around fearfully as if others had heard. "Sam, you're a Directorate member. How can you say such things?"

"I don't know."

"You're right," ZZ said. "You *are* dreaming. The Directorate would never do that. They rescued the country." He paused and looked away. "You know this topic is taboo."

Sam sighed. His jaw tightened. "Yeah, it's just that—"

"Let it go, man."

Sam nodded as he steered the cart around a curve, and ZZ stared out the side window. Quiet, expectant seconds passed.

"I thought your mother just died?" ZZ murmured.

"She was my adoptive mother."

"Oh."

The cart's hum magnified the silence.

"She was the only mother I ever really knew," Sam said.

"Didn't know you were adopted."

"Never had a reason to tell anyone." Sam glanced to the man seated next to him. "And, no one else needs to know."

ZZ gave a sympathetic sigh. "I'm sorry, Sammy. Sorry about everything."

Sam nodded, silent.

Leaving the tree-lined avenue behind, the cart halted at a wrought-iron gate. A guardhouse stood on a tiny traffic island between entrance and exit.

ZZ handed Sam a plastic key. Sam reached through the open window and swiped it through a black box. A tiny red light on the box switched to green, and the gate slid sideways. Sam tossed the card back to ZZ and eased the cart through the entrance while glancing to the armed guard sitting inside. The guard scrutinized the two teachers, then turned back to several video monitors.

The cart wound through the gated edition known as Windward Community. Identical, brown, single-story duplexes surrounded them. Each house boasted a thin sapling rising from a tiny, manicured front lawn. The community opened five years ago to satisfy a new law that segregated *intelligentsia* and Directorate members from the general population. All local educators were housed in Windward; *silver triad* Directorate members were housed across town in Leeward Community. Educators were told that because of their importance—and citizens' personal threats—they were safer in the *Communities*.

Sam swung the two-seat cart into a wide cement driveway, halting alongside another cart. All carts produced since year-before-last were prohibited from seating no more than two adults.

"It's been awhile since Haleana and I worked the same shift," ZZ said, smiling.

Educators were only allowed to marry other educators, otherwise, no marriage certificate was granted. To encourage compliance, a stipend was given to couples who taught at public schools or institutions of higher learning. Most of the public was not directly affected by *Educator Nuptials Laws*. There were exceptions to the nuptial laws: if a spouse was a Directorate member, worked for the government, or was employed as a professional in a medical field, a marriage certificate was granted. The couple could be housed in the Community but without the stipend. ZZ's wife, Haleana, was an RN at the local hospital.

"Wow, and both of us off this weekend," he continued. "Taylor and Jenna home from school. The four of us *together* again."

"I'm happy for you, ZZ," Sam said, grinning. "I envy you, sorta."

ZZ punched a button on the dash, and a gull-wing door swung up. About to step out, he paused, glancing to Sam. "It's the 'sorta' that hurts," he said, suddenly serious. "Sammy, I know you're now part of the clique, and you didn't hear me say this—"

"Then don't."

"The Directorate has no business raising anyone's kids."

"Careful, ZZ."

"We want our children back, Sam."

Sam tapped the steering wheel impatiently. "There's nothing we can do but comply."

"Hell, we're teachers, aren't we?"

"And we would be the first to disappear."

The older man pointed an accusing finger. "One day, our children will turn on us, Sam." He paused. "*They* will be the Directorate. And they'll loathe us, curse us for what we did to them. One thing our children will not do is love us."

Sam stared numbly. That seed of cynicism that he and ZZ were not really teachers but disseminators grew roots.

"You know I'm right," ZZ said, climbing out. He reached back into the rear compartment and pulled out a briefcase. Glancing back in, he planted two fingers to his temple, as if pointing a gun. "We're nothing but worker ants." His thumb came down. "Pow!"

Sam eyed him, quietly alarmed. Why did ZZ trust him? If the commissar ever received word of this exchange, they would be arrested and charged with treason. If convicted, they would hang. He gazed up at his friend, pretending all was well. "Have a good weekend, my man, and say 'hi' to Haleana, Taylor, and Jenna for me."

ZZ nodded, reached up, and grabbed the door latch. "Sam, I'll see you on Monday." He yanked, and the door eased down, clicking shut.

Sam bumped the transmission into reverse, backing out. He glanced to the front stoop. A nine-year-old boy and twelve-year-old girl darted from the door, sprinting to their father.

Sam cruised down the narrow street, the worrisome conversation weighing heavy on his mind. Off to the left, still standing empty, sat his old duplex. Two months back, he was given permission to move in and care for his ill mother. Now that she was gone, he had sixty days to settle his mother's estate and return to Windward. His adoptive father, Jason Moore, had died of a heart attack four years earlier, leaving just his mother and him. The Moores had had a biological son in the North American Commonwealth—NAC—army. Sam never knew him. A year after Sam was adopted, Kyle, twenty, was killed in the Battle of Detroit.

The cart hummed to a stop at the closed gate. Sam swiped an old national ID. The guard inside the shack, a young man Sam didn't recognize, glanced at him then scrutinized a small screen.

"Come on, moron, stop the authority bullshit," Sam murmured. "Just open the freaking gate."

After what seemed like forever, the gate shimmied and began sliding open.

The cart eased through the exit, and the guard eyed the teacher suspiciously.

"And to hell with you, too," Sam muttered.

The cart rolled south down Holly Street. Sam enjoyed the temporary escape from Windward's closed confines. The Community's high, chain-linked fence was claustrophobic. It was designed to keep people *in* as much as out. And, Windward's traffic was closely monitored. Standard National Curfew—SNC— was 10:00 P.M. to 5:00 A.M. There were exceptions, of course. Emergency personnel, military, night-shift workers, farmers, ranchers, etc. held exemption permits. Directorate members had no curfew. Sam could come and go as he pleased. That's because he was *chipped*. All Directorate Party members had an R.F. microchip implanted in a forearm. Removing it was a felony. Party members could be scanned and tracked by several means, including satellite.

Sam swung the cart onto the main avenue, motoring out of town. Without warning, a yellow dash lamp popped on, reminding him he had only thirty minutes of power left.

"Shit!" Sam slapped the steering wheel. His mother's house was six miles east of Perchance. He cart-pooled with ZZ and even allowing for errands, he seldom drove 400 miles a month. The cart's battery pack should last 500 miles with no charge. In addition to the solar panels' charge, the cart was hooked to the school's faculty plug-in rail throughout the day—one of the job's few perks—and was plugged in at home in the evenings. Yet now, the batteries couldn't hold power for one day. He winced; a new battery pack would cost him.

November couldn't end fast enough.

hat new battery pack for your cart finally came in today. Drop by the shop tomorrow morning, and I'll install it.

Sam eyed the half-sized holographic image rising from the living room floor. Leonard Spencer was old enough to be his grandfather. Spencer and his wife, Michelle, owned a local garage and an adjacent convenience store. The store clandestinely sold lots of life's most precious jewels, like real flowers. His wife ran the store and kept reminders of fairer times discreetly hidden. Yes, Michelle's country store sold a lot of other things, if one had *real* money, and knew how to ask.

Sam sighed, both relieved and irritated. "Leo, the timing couldn't be better—or worse. My cart's battery pack won't last another week. And today, you tell me the new ones came in, and it's payday—"

And you'll be broke by noon tomorrow, Leo said, and chuckled. *Is that what you're trying to say?*

"You got it."

If you'll be here by nine, I promise to make it all come true by noon. Leo paused. *I also have a little something to ease the pain.*

Sam raised a brow but dared not say more over the vidphone. "See you in the morning."

I'll be here. Make sure to bring your wallet.

"Later," Sam said, masking eagerness. The holograph crackled and dissolved. Seated on a couch, Sam reached over and unplugged the vidphone from the laptop computer resting on a coffee table. He examined the palm-sized, black vidphone in his hand.

The vid's outside dimensions hadn't changed much in the last thirty years, but that's where similarities ended. The innocent-looking device controlled society in a way never intended nor foretold. Besides a video communicator, the tiny box was also a handheld computer and entertainment center. In addition, it could remotely steer a cart, guide a lawnmower, dispense medications, and accomplish tasks only dreamt of a generation ago.

Sam chuckled. If God wasn't dead, he was living in the vidphone. Humanity's humanness had been immaculately arranged in a two-inch by three-inch piece of plastic. Sam recalled that not so long ago, the vid acted as the personality's extension, or, perhaps, even its replacement. The vid had its own character, social life, and protocols. Warmth had been reduced to zinc, copper, and gold; human heart and intellect replaced with circuits and nano-chips. And all with an on-off button.

When the Directorate began enforcing its political agenda, it had gradually, discretely, erected firewalls, limiting and monitoring Internet access. Yet, the vids' world was all consuming; no one had noticed or cared. Unwittingly, the Directorate had stumbled upon its new weapon: distraction. And they welded it with expert hands. Almost unobserved, Directorate tentacles, in the guise of a caring parent, began strangling freedoms, a few at a time. Before long, the frogs were gathered, tossed into the pot, and the Directorate gradually cranked up the fire.

In 2045, without warning, a Chinese satellite exploded, knocking out 80% of digital communication in the Western Hemisphere. In a split-second, the vid's world dissolved.

Then came the great silence.

Sam was working on his graduate degree at Virginia University the year the faux conversations stopped and reality set in. The long faces, the looks of bewilderment...

"Lambs," his adoptive father had called them. His adoptive father, a commissar-colonel, had said the masses were, "Lambs in need of guidance. And, *we*, Sam, are the wolves who will guide them." The lambs bleated, clueless, searching for direction, and the wolves gave the lambs direction. "The wolves' secret to ascendancy, Sam, is to get the lambs to believe the wolves aren't as bad as the lambs think wolves are."

Sam rose, sighed, closed the battery-powered laptop, and surveyed the living room. In a hurricane lamp's dim light, he could just make out his parents' photos on a bookcase across the room. He thought of the carefree, pampered life he was raised in up in Richmond. They had lived in the most upscale, gated community around. As a member of the ruling elite, his family lacked nothing. He even owned a horse, and it was cared for at an expensive stable. He had loved horses and horseback riding.

Until one day, when he was fifteen, and riding alone, he came upon a strange horseback rider. On a gravel road, a boy around his age sat bareback on an old mare. The mare was harnessed to a rusting, windowless car. Sam had pulled up as the mare trudged past, towing the ancient beater behind. A man and two small children shuffled silently alongside the horse. An infant's wail then a woman's voice came from inside the ancient Chevy. The teenager on the horse turned and glanced at him. The boy's face was grimy, his gaze hollow and hopeless. Sam stared after the sad group until they slowly, painfully, disappeared around a bend. He swung his horse around and headed back to the stable.

He never rode a horse again.

Sam was suddenly in the present. Today was his day for electricity. How could he have forgotten? Blowing out the oil lamp, he brightened the room, yet a strange malaise settled in, and he couldn't shake it.

At two A.M., he woke from the sound of howling coyotes.

* * *

The cart idled into the open garage bay. A yellow warning light glowed on its dash.

An old man wearing dark-blue overalls raised a hand. "That'll do."

Sam shoved the transmission into park. Dressed in jeans, sweatshirt and work boots, he climbed from the cramped vehicle. The odor of electric motor lubricant and battery acid wafted. A blustery wind whipped through the open garage door, scattering brown oak leaves, and Sam shivered inside a heavy coat. A scraggly-bearded, twenty-year-old young man stood at the garage entrance and tugged on a cord. The overhead door rolled down, hitting the cement floor with a loud thud. Sam nodded to the man by the door, a former student. "Hey, Johnny."

"Hey, Mr. Moore," he replied, returning the nod. He stepped to the cart's rear and began flipping up latches.

"Got heat in the office," the older man said, walking up.

Sam turned. Maybe in his seventies, Leonard Spencer was tall and still had youth's exuberance. Deep-set, intelligent eyes held something rare these days—humor. A neatly trimmed beard covered a weather-worn face.

"Any coffee?" Sam asked.

The old mechanic paused, adjusting a ski cap covering a bald dome. "You know where it's at," he replied, while watching his younger helper unlatch the battery pack cover. Leo glanced back to Sam. "Don't forget to stop in next door."

About to speak, Sam did a double-take. The older man's eyes held a strange look...almost a twinkle.

Ten minutes later, clasping a Styrofoam cup of hot, black java, Sam stepped outside the small garage. The bright morning sunshine and clear sky was deceiving. It had to be near freezing, unusual for this far south and near the coast. Summer seemed so far away. He flipped up a collar and hurried down a cracked sidewalk to a nearby red brick building on a corner. It wouldn't be long before dull, gray paint found its way to this block in its never-ending quest to expunge history. In the distance, the Directorate's overhead marquee flashed history's modern replacement.

On the red brick building's side, the words **Harold's Drugs Fresh Eggs & Milk** were still barely visible in huge, faded, block letters. Sam thought of all that had passed since those words were painted and wondered if the Directorate's words would still be read, still have meaning, 150 years from now. It was amazing how history's faded facade could break through the ether. He cursed himself for having such thoughts. Shivering, he hurried past tarp-covered gasoline pumps and the lone, operating diesel pump. The store's entry was a paint-flecked oak door, and he grabbed the worn brass handle and pushed. Bells jingled, and jingled again when he shut the door. *Convenience* store was a misnomer from another era; this was now a dry goods store. Shelves full of home-canned food greeted him. The mingled smell of wood smoke, Ivory Soap, oiled leather, mixed spices, and mold greeted him. His boots thumped on the wooden floor, and he breathed deeply, relishing the innocence. He loved coming here. He always left the Directorate outside. And there it lurked, just outside.

"Can I help you?" an elderly woman asked, stepping from around an aisle.

He smiled.

"Oh, Sam—I was just wondering about you." She smiled warmly. "Leo said you'd probably drop in."

He nodded and sipped coffee. "Good morning, Michelle—Ms. Flower Girl."

She chuckled. "Speaking of, I won't have any fresh flowers before week-after-next. But, that's not why you're here." The woman stepped up to him, tapping his arm. "This time, I have something other than flowers that may interest you."

Sam scrutinized her. The woman's gray hair was held in a tight bun. Unlike her robust husband, Michelle Spencer was frail. Her slacks and flannel shirt hung on her like burlap. Inside, he sighed; she seemed paler and thinner than usual. Sam had heard whispers that she was terminally ill...pelvic cancer. She was over seventy-two, and government treatment was non-existent. Private health care was outlawed ten years ago, National Health Care—NHC—replacing it. Yet, NHC ceased after age seventy. If you were over seventy, and didn't have cash, you were on your own. Medical facilities were prohibited from treating anyone over seventy unless the patient had cash.

Believe it—the facilities were closely monitored. The Directorate reasoned that resources were better utilized for those deemed more able to contribute to society.

"Katie!" Michelle shouted.

Sam blinked, shaken from his thoughts. "Who's Katie?"

"What is it, Granny?" a young woman asked as she stepped toward them.

"Honey, I want you to meet someone," Michelle said over a shoulder.

A slip of a woman, hardly more than a girl, halted in front of the two. Dark, curly hair just covered her ears, highlighting fair, porcelain skin.

What the... Sam swallowed. His gaze instinctively moved up and down, devouring her. Worn jeans and a tight, pullover sweater only enhanced the girl's curves. He grew flush and bit a lip, focusing on a jar of peach preserves on a nearby shelf. *Damn, he had gawked—and they saw it!*

"Sam," Michelle began, "I'd like you to meet our granddaughter, Katie. She arrived last Tuesday."

"A granddaughter?" he murmured. "You never mentioned a granddaughter."

"This is our son's daughter. They live up north, and she attended university up there," Michelle said. The older woman turned to the younger. "Katie, this is Sam."

Hesitating and unsure, he extended a hand. "Sam Moore, ma'am."

The girl shyly reached for Sam's hand, her dark eyes shining. "I'm Katie...Katie Spencer. Glad to meet you."

"You may regret the 'glad' part," Sam said. *Okay, moron, stop with the stupid shit!*

"Sam teaches at the high school," Michelle said.

"Oh, really?" the girl said, releasing his hand. Her demeanor changed, and she looked at him, taunting. "Must be 'interesting' to schmooze among the commoners."

Sam's jaw tightened, strangely disappointed. So, she had an axe to grind with teachers. Who didn't? She was cute all right, but her attitude sucked. The northern accent only refined what seemed a nasty disposition. Just goes to show looks could deceive. Well, he could give as well as receive. "'Amusing' is a better word," he replied, giving a disarming smile. "If I'm taking flak for being a teacher, it must mean I'm over the right target."

"'The right target'?" the girl replied curtly. Her eyes widened.

"What a disaster," Michelle murmured, stepping between them. "Now that you two have been properly introduced, perhaps *I'll* give Sam a peek of what came in. Katie, you can finish stocking."

"But he's a teacher," Katie protested, "and where I come from, teachers can't be trusted."

"Katie," Michelle jabbed the girl's arm, "that's enough. And I think you owe Sam an apology."

"Apologize for what?" Katie eyed Sam suspiciously. "Besides, I don't think he'd be interested in an apology—or what we have—anyway."

"And I think you'd be surprised," Michelle replied, "on both accounts."

Sam stood nearby, nonchalantly sipping coffee.

Tense seconds passed, and the girl looked up. "It's Sam, right?"

"Yeah."

"Come on, I guess." Katie nodded in resignation and turned. "Follow me."

"Apology accepted," Sam murmured, trekking behind. He deliberately looked away, yet, from the corner of an eye, caught the feminine sway of her hips. He swore inside; how can a girl walk like that and be such a bitch?

"Katie," came a man's voice off to one side.

She halted behind the counter, and Sam drew up next to her.

"Where are you taking *him*?" the man asked. Around Sam's age and wearing a heavy coat and cowboy boots, he strode up. "Do you know he's one of *them*?"

"Caleb!" Katie said, surprised. "I thought you were coming by at lunch?"

Sam glanced quickly to the girl. So, she'd already found matching kindred. He chuckled inside; birds of a feather...it figures. Sam knew the man, as did most in Perchance. Caleb Jeffery, one of the local assholes. Jeffery believed himself tough. In reality, he was a bully.

Scattered throughout Colton County, the Jeffery clan was known for their malice. Most locals despised them, some feared them, and the Directorate, surprisingly, looked the other way.

The Directorate didn't fear them. No, not at all. The Jefferys were simply useful idiots, yet their time for usefulness was expiring. Sam shifted, sighing. He had a Jeffery boy in class—Cory Jeffery. Seemed a good kid, though a social outcast. The man facing Sam was his uncle.

Katie touched the man's arm. "Caleb, I'm busy now. Why don't you come back in a couple of hours?"

The man fumed.

Sam shoved out a hand. "How's it going, Caleb?"

Caleb hesitated, then reluctantly gripped the offered hand, shook once, and released it. "I've got business with Katie. If you'll excuse us?"

Katie rolled her eyes. "Caleb, please."

"I'll come back later," Sam said, turning. "It's no big deal."

"No!" Katie grabbed Sam's arm. "*Caleb* was about to leave." She gave Caleb a hard glance. "*He* can come back later."

Caleb's face reddened, and he gestured to Sam. "Katie, that man's not only a school teacher but worse." He paused. "He's also one of those Directorate Party guys."

"I know he's a teacher," she replied, "and they all work for the Directorate. He's also Granny and Papa's friend, and that's good enough for me." She paused. "Now, Caleb, I'm busy. If you'll—"

"Moore doesn't just work for the Directorate," Caleb interrupted, relishing his impending revelation.

Sam sighed, impatient, yet hoping to avoid a scene. "Caleb, this is not the time nor the place. The lady here doesn't want to see this. Why don't you quit while you're still ahead?"

The man gave a sick grin, enjoying his moment in the catbird seat. "Katie, standing next to you is *the* Directorate. He's a full-fledged Directorate boy."

"What?" Katie said, again wary.

Caleb tapped his collar. "Yep. Usually wears one of those triangle doohickeys."

Sam eyed the guy. He wanted to strangle the man, yet kept his cool. There would be another time. He cleared his throat, about to speak, when Michelle Spencer barreled around a corner, arms waving.

"Caleb Jeffery!" she shouted. "You came over here just to start trouble. You get outta here—right now! Don't make me call Leo!"

Caleb stared at Sam, his face ugly with anger. "Moore, just wait until it gets around that an old woman saved you, and you had to hide behind her skirt."

Don't, you idiot! Sam ignored the voice. Setting the Styrofoam cup on a wooden counter, he stepped up. "Saved me from what, pray tell? You?" He grinned, scoffing. "You've got to be shitting me."

"That's enough!" Katie shouted, stomping a foot. "Both of you are so juvenile! Now, stop it!"

Sam never flinched. He stared hard at the man across from

him.

Caleb was suddenly uneasy "This isn't over." He backed away, stomped to the exit, paused, and looked back. "Teacher, I'm sure your bosses would be interested in your visits here. You know...the flowers?"

Sam raised a brow, perplexed. Why hadn't Caleb *already* snitched on him? He was a known collaborator. Sam cataloged the puzzle; he'd dwell on it later.

Caleb turned and stormed out, slamming the door. Bells jingled wildly.

Head hanging, Katie sighed.

"I'm sorry you had to witness small town pettiness," Sam said. "Those Jefferys are just a little high-strung. Too much refined sugar in the diet."

Uncertain, she tossed back her hair. "Are you really a Triad guy? Or was Caleb—"

"He's right," Sam interrupted. "I'm a Directorate member. Even down to the 'doohickey' on the collar."

Katie's eyes instantly went to his bare collar.

"It's at the jewelers getting polished."

"Why are you here?" she asked, eyes narrowing.

"Katie, I have no idea."

"How illuminating." Katie glanced to her grandmother, and the older woman nodded. Katie turned. "Come with me."

Sam followed the girl.

"Too much refined sugar, huh?" she asked, marching down a hall. "And it's out getting polished?"

"Yeah."

He swore he heard a snicker.

The two halted by a door leading to a stockroom.

"Let me," Sam said. But instead of reaching for the door, he reached down, tossed away a throw rug and yanked on a metal ring in the floor. A trap door swung up.

Katie stared, incredulous. "You know about this place?"

He smiled, flipped on a nearby light switch, and calmly disappeared down the steps.

She hurried after him.

The two drew up in the middle of a small basement, both surveying half-filled bookshelves. Katie quickly stepped to a box on the floor that was crammed full of books and swatted at an open flap. "Granny said you might be interested in these."

Sam strolled up and paused by the box. "Your grandmother said you attended university. May I ask where?"

"Syracuse Institute of Technology."

Sam raised a brow.

"My degree is in broadcasting," she said, "but I minored in Farsi."

"What the hell?"

"Foreign language comes natural to me. I was hoping for job security."

Sam looked at her, curious. "So, what kind of work will you be doing? Translating I assume?"

"No—and it's a long story for another time. Instead, in two weeks, I start my job with...with..." She hesitated, clearing her throat. "I'm employed with National-Regional Broadcasting. I'll be working out of NRB's Charleston studios."

Sam could only stare.

"Go ahead—say it." She shoved hands in back pockets. "You have the right."

Tense seconds passed, and he scrutinized the woman in front of him. "I'll let you say it."

Katie brushed her thick, curly hair behind an ear. Two silver studs sparkled. "Even though I work for the Directorate, it doesn't mean I'm part of it, or condone what they do."

Sam smiled subtly. "You take their money, don't you?"

"But I haven't sold my soul."

"Are you referring to me?"

"You are one of *them*, aren't you?"

"Depends."

Hands on hips, Katie shook her head. "I can't believe my grandparents would befriend a Directorate member."

"How do you know it wasn't the other way around...that I befriended them?"

"Directorate members don't have friends," Katie said with biting sarcasm, "only accomplices."

Struggling to remain cool, Sam winced inside. He fiddled with the open box flap and glanced to her. "Last time I checked, NRB was the Directorate's media arm. Darlin', you and I are all part and parcel of the same wind."

"You are so wrong."

"How so?" Sam asked. "The only difference between us is that I perform in front of a live audience."

"You mean a *captive* audience," she replied. "No offense, but there's a big world out there that you—cooped up here in Perchance—know little about."

"I'm kept up to date," Sam replied defensively. *How ignorant could this girl be*? "I have codes, access to the Party-only news link and what's going on throughout the Domain and why."

"Oh, yeah?" Katie stepped from around the box, eyeing Sam. "Tell me, Mr. Directorate man, about the relocations that are happening in Boston?"

Sam blinked, stunned. *That* was supposed to be a clandestine affair. With his eyes on a crack in the cement floor, he cleared his throat. "It's classified."

"'It's classified,'" she sneered, pacing the floor. "How do you hide the forced removal of over one hundred thousand people to another part of the country?"

"What *exactly* is your job?" Sam asked, now thoroughly annoyed.

Katie halted. "Don't change the subject."

"As a Directorate member, I have the right to know."

"I wondered when you'd play that card." Katie walked away, and then she paused with her back to him. "Typical Directorate attitude. And here I thought that maybe, with my grandparents taking you into their confidence, you might be different." She began pacing again.

Sam's eyes followed her. A freshly trapped lioness in a cage—dangerous, yet one who understood her captors. She waited for their miscue. Was *he* a captor? He cleared his throat. "You never answered my question."

Katie turned, with her arms tightly folded. "I'm a producer of *The Scope and Sequence News Hour.*"

"Well now..." Sam's eyes widened. "You're the Party's extension into living rooms." He hesitated as a thought took seed. *What if Katie were a spy sent here to test his loyalty? Worse, what if the Spencers were spies?* His hand was now square in the cookie jar. He swallowed; Directorate paranoia was contagious. He decided to chance it. "What do *you* know about Boston?"

"I tell and you'll have me arrested."

"Well, there it is..." He plopped down onto the packed, cardboard box. It was firm, holding his weight. "Suspicion has come full circle."

"Isn't that what you guys want?" Katie interrupted. She strolled up with her arms still locked.

Sam sighed. The girl's media position may be useful in the future. And, he hated admitting, she was strangely fascinating. He tapped the box he sat on, and then he gestured around. "Consider this as...as neutral territory." He half-smiled, eyeing her. "Yes, this store, this room, it's neutral—off limits to the outside world." He paused. "Let us, you and I, call a truce and this place be neutral turf, deal?"

Sam could see the indecision in Katie's face, a very beautiful face... He flushed and quickly looked away.

"I can't believe I'm hearing what I'm hearing," Katie said. "You being a Directorate man, and in here with me, and both of us connoisseurs of the forbidden...it does make you an entertaining collaborator."

"I couldn't have said it better."

"How do we know we can trust one another?" Katie asked, scrutinizing him.

"We're both still here, aren't we?" An awkward silence descended. Katie's measuring gaze penetrated him.

"It's a deal," she said, hinting a smile, "a truce."

Strangely shy, Sam hesitantly glanced at her. She grinned, revealing perfect, white teeth. *Oh, crap...* He struggled with an alien feeling of euphoria and crossed a leg, forcing seriousness. "Please, tell me about Boston? What did *you* hear about the reason for population removal?"

Katie's smile vanished. She tossed her head; her hair a dark sea waving around a delicate neck. "I have a friend in Boston covering the story. The official spin given is that the people are being evacuated for their own safety. The Directorate expects a Persian attack along the Domain's northeast coast." She paused. "Is that what you heard?"

Sam hesitated, head hanging.

"If you know something different—"

"I heard the same thing," he said. "That's the official word in Directorate bulletins: *for their own safety.*"

"I understand the evacuees were sent to temporary camps in the Heartland, not far from Dayton?" Katie queried.

Sam nodded.

"The evacuees never arrived."

Sam looked up. "Huh?"

"There are no, and never have been, evacuee camps outside of Dayton," Katie replied, "or anywhere else."

"What! That can't be? How do you know this?"

"I have my sources."

Sam rose, aiming a finger. "That's exactly the reason for Directorate blackouts. One province is never to know the detailed affairs of another; it keeps down the rumors."

"Sam, this is much more than a rumor. The Directorate deliberately keeps us all in the dark...it's one of their joys."

"They have their reasons," he sneered. "It's because of people like you, spreading discontent."

Katie straightened her sweater, ignored the comment, and eyed Sam. "The past few weeks, trains and busses loaded with evacuees from Boston entered the Catskill Mountains from the east. The trains and busses never emerged out the west side."

"There you go, spreading rumors."

"These aren't rumors," Katie murmured, stepping closer. "Trusted locals whispered to me, hoping I would go public with it. They say the busses and trains go into the Catskills full of people, heading west on their way to the evac camps." She paused. "But the trains and busses, they...they're never seen coming out the west side of the mountains. Instead, after a few hours, the trains and busses are seen returning east...empty."

"Locals," Sam said, chuckling. "Rural people are ignorant and nothing but trouble, forever a thorn in the Directorate's side. They're always hatching plots, lying, and trying their damnedest to discredit us. That's the reason why we're shipping urbanites to the country—we need compliant citizenry. Citizenry we can trust."

"Tell me how you really feel," Katie said with more than a hint of sarcasm.

Tense stillness crept over them. Katie shifted, and Sam shoved hands in jean pockets. He chewed a lip, and then he took a deep breath. "Katie, why are you telling me this? You're taking a great risk."

"Because *you* can make a difference."

"You don't know that. You don't know me." He picked at the box flap. "We just met."

"Granny and Papa believe in you," Katie said. "They wouldn't have you here if your mind and heart weren't in the right place." Katie reached into the cardboard box, worked out a leather-bound book and handed it to Sam. "Besides, anyone who likes this can't be all bad."

Moore squeezed the book reverently, enjoying its suppleness. His fingers played over words on the front cover:

To Kill a Mockingbird
Harper Lee

Moore blinked, unsure, then grinned from ear to ear.

"Check these out," Katie said, handing the teacher one book after another.

With the angst from their previous conversation temporarily on hold, Sam reached for first one book then another. He was a kid in a candy store.

Within minutes, books were stacked on a nearby bench as Sam perused the titles. "I'll take this one," he said, tapping Melville's *Moby Dick.* "I've often wondered about Ahab's turmoil." His eyes shifted to another nearby stack. *Fahrenheit 451* by Ray

Bradbury, *The Norton Anthology of World Masterpieces Volume II*, and *The Complete Pelican Shakespeare* were about to find a new home, as were biographies of Abraham Lincoln, Franklin Roosevelt, and Martin Luther King, Jr. On top of those, he placed a well-worn paperback copy of John Wayne's biography and anthology.

Katie stood to one side, nodding at the John Wayne dog-eared works. "I wonder what the fascination is with that man. He was just an actor."

"I'm not sure," Sam said. "Even my father, a commissar-colonel, liked John Wayne movies. He told me it was a window into innocence, back before the decadence set in."

"Have you ever seen a John Wayne movie?" Katie asked.

"Yeah. Have you?"

"No."

"Well, they are simple themes, easy to grasp." Sam paused in thought. "Perhaps that was it. Good and evil were clearly defined back then. In John Wayne movies, you *always* knew who the good guys were, and who the bad were. And, even though good suffered, in the end, they always won." Sam chuckled. "Of course, in the real world, bad is often camouflaged as good and allowed to enter through the front door. And when you discover the mistake, well, it's too late."

"Truer words were never spoken," Katie said.

Sam glanced to her; irony biting, hitting home. Ignoring her remark, he nodded into the nearly-empty box. "No Tolkien?"

"Do you know how hard his work is to come by?" Katie replied. "I was lucky to have found—" She halted in mid-sentence and looked away.

Sam stepped up to her and pointed back to the box. "*You!* You brought the books?"

A long pause later, Katie nodded meekly.

"Do you know the risk?"

She nodded again, remaining silent.

When it came to the Spencers selling banned reading material, it was always *don't ask; don't tell*, and for a good reason. He sighed. "Girl, you could've brought a world of hurt onto your house."

She eyed him. Her gaze was shrewd, almost calculating.

Sam turned back to his purchases, knowing she was judging him. *To hell with her.* He needed to get his ass out of the basement and away from the store before he was straddled with something he couldn't deal with. He was already stretching his luck by coming here.

"There's one more thing," Katie said, stepping to the cardboard container.

He cringed—it was too late.

Reaching back into the cardboard carton, Katie lifted out a small, silver and black box.

"What the hell is that?" Sam asked. Curiosity overcame caution, and he moved next to her. He halted, afraid. No way...

"This is for you," she said, handing it to him. "Keep it secret, and keep it safe."

Hesitating, Sam reached for it, knowing that even by touching it, he committed blasphemy. "Geesus..." Wide-eyed, he examined the device and rubbed fingers over archaic analog dials and gauges. Plastic dial covers were yellowed with age, but the numbers underneath were legible. If the Directorate found this, the whole neighborhood would be burned to the ground and then bulldozed over. Those who survived would be executed. In his hand, he held a death warrant.

A shortwave radio.

He shoved it back to her. "You trying to get us killed! Caught with banned books is one thing, but the radio..." He waved the device in front of her. "Possessing an instrument such as this is considered treasonous. For *me*, a Directorate member, it would be death by hanging—and that's a fact."

Katie jerked the small radio from him, easing it onto a book stack. "It's a chance you have to take."

"Why me?"

She paused, sighed, pulled out a coiled power cord from the cardboard box, and aimed it at Sam. "*You* need to know what the other side is saying."

"Again, why *me*?"

Katie only stared, silent.

Sam stormed away, waving hands. "This is insane. There is no 'other side.' Those who oppose the Directorate are only jealous. They're just a tiny minority of rabies-infected scum trying their utmost to bring down law and order. May a scourge hit their houses."

"You just cursed my grandparents' home."

"I don't want to hear it!" he shouted, jamming palms to ears.

Katie tossed the cord on a bench and stepped after him. "Listen to me..."

"No!" He spun around, raising a hand. "You listen to me. Both of us would be best served if you let me take a hammer to that...that device. I promise, I didn't see it."

"Granny and Papa trust you. They told me you could be the

catalyst for something new."

"Sister, you are crazy."

Katie halted in front of him. Her gaze meet his. "I've never known them to be wrong about character."

"And I know some poor, dead bastards who were just brimming with character."

"With my media contacts, and your Directorate pull—"

"What pull?" Sam said, snorting. "I've only been a member for a year. I have squat for influence." He paused, thoughts full of suspicion...and dread. "Influence for what, pray tell?"

Katie looked away, swallowing. "Those urban 'evacuations' are rolling down the East Coast. New York and Philly are next then Baltimore."

Sam shook his head, stomping back to the cardboard box.

Katie marched after him. "Followed by Norfolk, and then—"

He began angrily stacking books back into the box. "I'll pay for these upstairs."

She paused behind him. "And then Charleston."

He slammed a book into the box. The bench shook. His back to Katie, Sam stared straight ahead, feeling just as vacant as the bookshelf in front of him. *Why didn't she just shut the hell up?*

"'They came for the Jews,'" Katie began, "'and I didn't stop them, because I wasn't Jewish. And then they came for the Christians, and I said nothing, because I wasn't Christian. And then they came for the Muslims, and I shrugged, because I wasn't Muslim. And then...'" She halted, allowing her words to soak in. "'And then they came for me, and there was no one left to stop them.'"

"You can't be serious."

"The Directorate's committing genocide," Katie pronounced. "We have to stop them before it's too late."

Sam stood in stunned silence. He wanted to move but was frozen in place. A creeping dread stole up his spine, and he shivered. He faced her. The girl's skin seemed paler. His throat tightened, and he forced a swallow. "Genocide? That's insane. The Directorate may be a lot of things, but they're not mass-murderers. You have no proof. Only hearsay...rumors."

"Rumors have a nasty habit of becoming reality."

"Katie, with you spouting off, and without proof—"

"If I can get proof," she pleaded, "would you help me?"

"Katie, you're making some serious accusations. The kind that will get you hauled away—or worse." *Damn! What did I just walk into? It started out as just a quiet Saturday.* He bit a lip.

Indecision ate at him. "Even if what you say is true, which it's not, I'm only one man."

She reached out, laying fingers on his hand. "Please, you must."

He jerked at her touch, and his gaze moved to her fingers. They were smooth, almost dainty. From her slender wrist hung some kind of leather bracelet. He had to force his eyes away. "There's nothing I can do."

Katie dropped her arms to her side. Her shoulders sagged. "If I get you proof...?"

Sam sighed and resumed packing books. Katie stood nearby, a silent waif, watching, waiting. He tried ignoring her, but that was like ignoring one's own demise. Within seconds, he cradled the half-full box in his arms and headed for the door. "Bye, Katie. Glad to have met you. Thanks for the books." He nodded to the shortwave radio on the bench. "Get rid of that *thing*."

She stared.

Her penetrating gaze made him uncomfortable. He couldn't leave fast enough. He was almost to the steps when she grabbed his arm, spinning him around.

"You forgot this." She lifted a box flap and dropped the radio inside.

"Hey!"

Katie stuffed in the power cord and closed the flap. "There's no microphone, but I'll locate one, later."

"If you think I'm taking that radio," he said, protesting, "you're wrong." Sam tried to set down the box, but Katie pushed him to the steps.

"Go!" she yelled, shoving him forward. "You and your precious Directorate can't be dishonored. But you know what? You're going to get proof. I'll get you freaking proof!"

Sam worked his way up the staircase, dazed. Damn. For such a small woman, there was surprising strength and intensity. He paused and turned. Katie stood at the bottom of the stairs gazing at him; the girl scared him. He realized that she knew she had uncovered something in him, something he struggled to keep hidden: passion...the hunger for truth. Geesus...He sighed, knowing he couldn't let things end this way. "Katie, it's just that...that I—"

"Don't say another word." Katie's gaze never wavered. "I trust you'll do the right thing."

Sam hurried away. He decided he wouldn't return to the store until the girl was gone. And as for the radio, he'd toss it in the river on his way home. "Genocide," he scoffed, hustling to the front of the store. "Whose side is she on?"

* * *

Sam tossed and turned, fighting his pillow all night. Now wide-awake, he glanced to the clock on the nightstand: 1:58 A.M. He rolled over and tapped a nearby lamp. The room brightened. He rose. Head hanging, he sat on the bed's edge. Near the lamp base, a tiny golden triangle gleamed in soft light. He plucked it from the stand and scrutinized it. One of his young life's highest moments was when he was accepted into the Directorate Party. He was always proud to wear the Triad of Life. It displayed his dedication to a philosophy that brought discipline, equality, and unity to all.

Or did it?

Before the Directorate, the country was in total anarchy. Cities were battlegrounds, and the citizens were living in gut-wrenching poverty. The Directorate changed that. They restored order, and within a few short years, eliminated extreme poverty. Sam couldn't recall the last time he saw a street person. Even the homeless that had lived in cars had disappeared; images of past failures had been swept away. Sam held up the small triangle and ran his fingers over the tiny star in each corner. A thought occurred, and he forced it away.

"No...no..." he murmured, trying to ignore a strange seed of doubt. "Damn her!" He had almost allowed his loyalty to the Directorate to be hijacked by that, that no-nothing girl, Katie Spencer. And what was worse, he couldn't get her out of his thoughts.

Placing the metal triangle on the nightstand, his gaze fell to a black box on the desk across the room. The shortwave radio. Its aged, yellowed dials stared back.

Yesterday, on his way home from the garage, he'd stopped the cart over the Santee River. He climbed out and hustled to the bridge rail, the radio hidden inside his heavy coat. He glanced around; no traffic in sight. Working out the radio, he stretched over the rail and poised to toss the abominable thing into the swirling waters below. Yet, something inside him stayed his hand. Try as he might, he couldn't make his arm go forward. It was as if an invisible force held his arm. He swore. Cradling the radio, he hurried back to the cart. He'd take a hammer to it once he got home.

Yeah, right. Now, there it sat. Not only had he failed to destroy it, he'd gleefully plugged it in. Sam admitted there was something thrilling about committing outlawed acts behind closed doors. Earlier in the century, it would've been partaking in illicit sex, using illegal drugs, or plotting terrorist acts. All would've brought the wrath of friends, family, or government. And yet, part of him was enraptured with the idea of resisting authority.

Now, the latter act was the only one surviving from previous generations. Illicit sex was no longer illicit, and even encouraged among the intelligentsia, and drugs that were once illegal were now legalized but well-regulated. However, the very act of reading unauthorized works, or watching or listening to non-Directorate broadcasts, were jail felonies. The radio was a different animal; it was a communicator to the world outside Directorate control. If caught with the shortwave, he would be the headliner on a Sunday afternoon public execution.

He rubbed the back of his neck. He didn't know what had come over him earlier in the evening. Hooking up the radio was like an addiction—and then the damn thing didn't even work. Part of him was disappointed, part of him relieved. He had marched off to bed, deciding fate had interceded, saving him from himself.

Sam's focus returned to the shortwave. He promised himself that in the morning, he'd destroy the radio, ridding himself of the temptation for good.

From across the room, he thought he heard a faint crackle. What the hell? Since it would soon be gone, what harm was there in trying one more time?

He stepped to the desk and fiddled with a coax antenna cable hanging from its rear. The cable was attached to an outside analog TV antenna. He touched the scratched faceplate. What would he hear? An unknown message enticed him like the forbidden fruit of Judeo-Christian lore. He pushed a button. The faceplate glowed, and he slowly twisted a dial. Nothing, only static, then silence. "Thank you," Sam whispered in relief. He pushed one of several buttons, and the dial and faceplate darkened.

He shivered, noticing the cold. Wearing only boxers and a T-shirt, he darted back to bed and tapped a nearby lamp. Darkness enveloped the room. Tomorrow, he'd dig out that mallet, smash the confounded thing, and bury the pieces. His lids grew heavy, and he drifted off. If only he hadn't met Katie. Katie...

The shortwave radio crackled to life. *Dong-ding-dong.* A low, high, and then low tone echoed throughout the room.

Sam blinked. What was that? Only darkness...his lids again

lowered, and he turned on his side, settling under blankets.

This is Radio Free America—the voice of freedom!

Sam shot out of bed.

We're broadcasting live from somewhere west of the Mississippi, came the feminine voice. *To our brothers and sisters back east, take heart. You are not forgotten. We're doing everything in our power to free you from bondage. You are in our prayers. Now, listen closely. We've received word that the fascist regime known as the Directorate has decided on a Final Solution for its social and political failures. Listeners, beware! The trains to Auschwitz and Dachau are coming for you!*

Sam staggered back as if stung. His mind reeled.

You hearing this broadcast must make quick plans to escape. We welcome you with open arms into the United States of America's Western Alliance.

Sam stared at the faded dial, too shocked to move.

The Directorate is a cancer that must be carved out before our nation can reunite. You brave souls who choose to stay and fight from within, do not despair. God is with you, and we here in the United States will help all we can. Now, we have messages for you brave partisans on the other side:

The cat food is on the counter. The cat food is on the counter. The deck is square. The deck is square. Do not enter the barn. Do not enter the—buzz...

Sam stood, hypnotized. He was dreaming. He had to be. That was the only explanation his mind could grasp. He would wake from this nightmare, and everything would be fine. The old and familiar would return, and he'd be okay. *I will be okay, won't I?*

Buzz...

Sam blinked, snapping from the trance. The Directorate must have jammed the signal. He clicked off the radio and sighed, running fingers through his hair.

What the hell had he just heard! What he had done was so out of character for his strong Directorate upbringing that it sent shock waves through him. Wasn't character about doing the right thing when no one was looking? After hearing that message, right and wrong were hopelessly intertwined. How would he ever sort it out?

In the dim light, Sam paced the floor. He recalled the former Christmas holidays, the ones he'd enjoyed as a child. Now, he felt like a five year old that had just been told there was no Santa Claus. Sam paused. The *United States of America*. Even those words held an innate fear. It was drilled into children at an early age that even uttering the words were blasphemy to Directorate ideals. Only in high school and college had they been allowed to speak of the United States but using only the initials, U.S., and then solely in derogatory terms. He resumed pacing. The broadcast had backed up what Katie had said about genocide. Sam shook his head, unable to comprehend that the Directorate could commit such a heinous act. Maybe Katie wasn't a Directorate spy. Instead, maybe she was a U.S. agent trying to recruit him. He could be used as a propaganda tool for her cause. Sam nodded. Yes, yes, that was it. Katie was a foreign spy. And what better place to be employed than in the enemy's media.

Satisfied with his conclusions, Sam climbed back into bed. He tapped the light, and the room darkened. The way out of his predicament was to never contact Katie Spencer again. Yes, that was it; he'd never see her again. Everything, including his disturbed thoughts, would mend. The craziness would all go away.

He settled under a quilt. A minute passed. He flipped onto his back, hands behind his head, and stared into darkness.

What a crappy day. One of the worst ice storms in recent memory hit the southeast Carolina Province, practically paralyzing it. Yet the teachers began dutifully arriving at the school. Several trudged the half-block from the light-rail station to the school, boots crunching on ice. They were bent low into blowing snow, coats pulled tight, following one another like cattle heading for that lone hay bale in a cold, open pasture.

On the high school's opposite side, ever-obedient students poured from campus dorms. Bundled in dark-blue jackets, they leaned into the wind. No one hurried, no one slowed. They marched mechanically, little robots, one after another.

A cart rolled through frozen slush, ZZ behind the wheel. The school rose just ahead. Sam sat straight in the passenger seat, silently staring out the windshield to the sad procession, watching both teachers and students converge from opposite directions. The two groups had something very much in common: *We're all resigned to our misery. And it's not only from the weather...*

The cart idled into a parking spot, halting. The chemistry teacher killed the engine and scrambled out. Sam touched a button, a gull-wing door lifted, and he climbed out. He reached up, pulled on a handle, and the door lowered on its own, clicking shut. ZZ was already in front of the cart, knocking off ice while tugging on a spring-loaded power cord attached to the front bumper. Gripping one end of the cord in a gloved hand, he bent down and plugged it into the guardrail. A free battery charge, courtesy of the school. Sam watched. *No, not free, he* mused. In the Directorate, *everything* had a freaking price.

Both men turned and plodded silently for the school. Warmth awaited them inside. At least as much warmth as the teachers were allowed to bring.

The day wore on, the school's daily routine adding to Sam's growing unrest. What was eating at him? He couldn't quite put a finger on it, and it tore at him.

In the humanities, a routine lecture, or a routine PowerPoint given by a student from his or her laptop, was the norm. Most students at least feigned attention, and when called upon, gave the expected reply. Administration's data was collected from the ever-present ceiling camera, the never-ending classroom monitors, and a mountain of teacher paperwork that was located on tectonic plates, because the mountain grew every day. Little was left to teacher creativity; most teachers were scared to even try. Then came the routine learning evaluations, all assignments geared toward glorifying Directorate ideals and achievements. The dog chased its tail, and all the while, administration patted itself on the back for a job well done. And the students? Well, the students learned everything that was taught to them, Sam supposed, except how to think. Thinking was *verboten*. The Directorate thought for everyone; no others need apply. The Party was slowly accomplishing its goal: a mindless society that was totally dependent on its Caregiver.

Sam had loved the Directorate. *Had*? Since when did he question his devotion to the Directorate? The Directorate had been good to his parents, and the Party gave him a sense of belonging; he was being groomed as a commissar. What more could he want? The Party also nurtured his appreciation for the finer things in life, yet not the way they had scripted it. His jaw tightened. Something was flawed. When all was said and done, all you actually had in life was your own free will. And the Directorate, in its cold, methodical efficiency, was even gutting that, one wearisome day at a time. Hell, he was even taking part in it. Was *he* flawed?

By the beginning of second period, it hit him that he wasn't a teacher. None of his colleagues were teachers. They were only facilitators. Sam struggled with a simmering resentment and anger. Why did he feel as though the students, his colleagues, and he were stabbed in the back? During third period, while writing an essay prompt on the board, a voice told him to ignore the man behind the curtain pulling levers.

With his back to his students, arm stretched across the board, he paused in mid-sentence. *What was the damn point? You breathe in, you breathe out, and then you die, all for what? The Directorate? I'm not even a freaking asterisk to them.* And here he was pissing away his life just to satisfy some shit-for-nothing bureaucrat's ego. And what about the people? Their children sat right behind him. My God, what was happening to him! He sighed and resumed writing. *Just once, just once, I wish I had the guts to do something meaningful...something right.* His jaw tightened. *What do I know about **right**?*

* * *

It was the middle of fourth period; the day was almost over. Sam strolled up and down the classroom aisle, pausing here and there, making sure the students were on task. They were writing, or rather struggling, with an essay about dedication to the Directorate, and what dedication meant in their personal lives. There wasn't much of the latter these days, he had thought while earlier writing the topic on the board. *Can dedication lead to fanaticism?* he had scribbled under the topic. *Fanaticism— good or evil?* he had added underneath.

Sam paused, glanced back to the board, and smiled smugly. The last two prompts were exactly the kind of crap that got him into trouble. He thought of walking over and erasing them. If classroom monitors came in and saw those two prompts, his butt would be parked in front of Tipton—again. Sam chuckled out loud and resumed strolling. Today, he wasn't worried about classroom monitors, cameras, or Tipton. Screw them. He would *teach.* As for the prompts on the board, they were written in *light green* dry erase marker—the camera couldn't detect light green.

It was by accident a couple of months back that something constructive came from an ass chewing in the commissar's office. Sam had sat across from Tipton as the commissar reamed him good. He couldn't remember why. Totally frustrated, he could only stare past the commissar's red, bloated face and the older man's arms waving in anger. Sam had spotted his empty classroom in the video screen on the wall. His dry erase board was clean. *So, classroom monitors had already gotten to the board,* he thought. Once dismissed, he hustled back to his classroom. He burst into the room, wanting to strike out to someone, to something. Yet everything was still on the board, written in *light green,* just as he'd left it. Anger evaporated. Son-of-a-bitch...he'd had the last laugh. So, light green on white was invisible to the new, high-tech school cameras. It was his little, private discovery. He had given the commissar the finger, in light green marker.

Sam stepped around an aisle and casually moved up another. Now, the commissar was gone for the next month. Tipton would be making life miserable for some other poor bastards in another district. And as for the school principal, Terri Woodriff, he had an unholy alliance. Last year, he began supplying her with contraband cigarettes—Marlboros. After Tipton left, Terri and the classroom monitors had better things to do than visit his classroom, like taking numerous outside smoke breaks.

Sam glanced down, did a double-take, and paused. The new student, Mark Thurmont, wasn't writing. Instead, he was drawing. Sam stared, eyes narrowing. The boy had sketched a flag. It was an old *American* flag...the Stars and Stripes. And it was upside down. "Never seen an essay like that," Sam murmured, reaching for the drawing. "And in color."

The kid looked up. "That's what I'm dedicated to."

Pens stopped moving. The whole class gazed first to the boy then tentatively to their teacher. Not a word was spoken, but dread hung in the air so thick it could be cut with a knife. A teacher's attitude toward respecting—or disrespecting—the Directorate was contagious. If it were the latter, the teacher wouldn't be around long. That was an unwavering fact. He must act quickly, before their young minds could grasp who, or *what,* was actually in front of them now. And he wasn't referring to Thurmont.

"Do you know you can get dorm detention for this?" Sam said, gazing at the paper in his hand. "Or worse?"

"They arrested my uncle for flying that flag in his own front yard," a dark-haired girl a row over said. "That was two years ago, and he just got out of prison last month."

"Aw, Lisa," a boy piped, "you're Uncle Roddy's always doing crazy stuff. He was warned about flying that flag."

"Justin," Lisa said, "why don't you just shut up!"

"Zip it—all of you." Sam folded the paper. "It's over, now get back to work." He stuffed the folded paper into a shirt pocket and eyed the teenage boy staring up questioningly. Normally, he would've taken the student out into the hall to discuss the matter, but this transgression required a swift public reprisal. Sam must let those watching the camera know that disrespecting the Directorate could not or would not be tolerated in his classroom. Suddenly, he cared in the worst way what Directorate administration thought, but for other reasons. His *act* must continue—for now. Stunned at his own inner revelation, Sam cleared his throat. "Mark, you're new here, so I'm going to cut you some slack. You're not following instructions. I said 'write,' not 'draw.'" Sam paused. "Besides, what you drew was inappropriate. You'll serve an afternoon detention in here, today."

Mark gave a hurt, confused look. His blond, crew-cut hair stood straight up. "Yes, sir."

"Now, take out some paper and start over."

The kid fumbled in a backpack and tugged out a spiral notebook. He looked around.

A few students stared at the boy with scorn, but most looked at him with pity. Sam noticed the students' gazes. They were the kind given to an unruly puppy that had just been admonished by its master. The boy hesitated, and then he began writing. Sam walked away.

Minutes later, the bell rang. The room emptied of students, with the exception of Mark Thurmont. Pen in hand, he gazed back to Sam, who stood leaning against a desk in the back.

Sam slid into a nearby student desk in the part of the room where sound carried the least. "You can 'put away,' Mark. And step over here, please."

Mark quickly complied. Grabbing a dark coat and swinging a backpack over a shoulder, he stepped closer to Sam.

Sam pointed to a desk across from him. Mark dropped the backpack, and it hit the floor with a dull thud. Clutching the coat, the student scooted into the desk across from Sam. Apprehension covered the kid's brow. "Didn't mean to cause a stir, Mr. Moore."

"It's okay." The boy had a distinct accent, different from the Carolina twang still heard in these parts. Sam cleared his throat and lowered his voice. "How old are you?"

"Seventeen."

"What part of the Western Provinces are you from?"

"Texas."

"You know that 'Texas' doesn't officially exist, don't you?"

"That's what I've been told," Mark said. He looked Sam in the eye. "But Texas was still there when dad and I left last summer. I reckon it's still there, waitin' for me."

"I reckon so," Sam murmured, hinting a smile.

Mark picked at the hooded coat in his arms. "Things are better there than here, Mr. Moore, no matter what they say."

"Then why are you here?"

"Dad and I came to the Commonwealth looking for Mom. She went to Birmingham to help grandma and grandpa get out. They had their home taken, stolen by the Directorate, because the Directorate said my grandparents were too old and didn't need it anymore."

Sam grimaced inside. "So, your father just let your mother travel alone?"

"No, sir," Mark began, "my uncle went with her. But we didn't know things had gotten so bad here, or we wouldn't have let mom or Uncle Johnny go."

It was that bad here? Sam held his confusion in check. "When was the last time you heard from your mother?"

"Last April. She sent a vidmail. She and Uncle Johnny were in Atlanta and on their way back home. She said grandma and grandpa were taken to Atlanta and put in some kind of homeless people's camp or something." The boy sighed, shaking his head. "She said she'd meet us at this old truckstop just west of Birmingham. Dad and I loaded up the old diesel pickup, bolted up a pair of Georgia plates given to us, and headed this way. Mr. Moore, we didn't get ten miles inside Mississippi when we came up to a roadblock. But instead of cops, it was soldiers. And they were carrying some wicked looking hardware. Dad said to be cool, and it'd be okay, but I could tell he was worried."

"What happened?"

"They asked for our traveling papers."

Sam lifted a brow. "And?"

"We didn't have any papers. We didn't think we'd need any. We were American citizens, in America, and yet they arrested us. They said we were spies and took us to Jackson then to Birmingham. Later, they dropped the spy charges and declared us 'vagrant.' They moved us into one of those homeless camps outside of Atlanta. It was awful. I'd rather be dead than go back." The boy paused, swallowing hard. "It was there that dad and I found out that Mom and Uncle Johnny had been in camp. And that...that," he sniffed, wiping an eye, "and that they were taken away with thousands of others." He glanced at Sam. "Mr. Moore, no one ever heard from them again. It was like, like those that were taken never existed."

Sam blinked, recalling Katie's "pseudo" homeless camps, the ones no one had ever heard of. Now they'd moved south, as she'd predicted. Something inside him was screaming. He flashed back to his early childhood—the tanks, the soldiers— his mother's torn body. Sam forced calm, and reached over, squeezing the kid's shoulder. It was as if someone were squeezing his own. "It's okay, you don't have to—"

"She died, Mr. Moore," Mark blurted. "So did Uncle Johnny. Camp bosses said they both died from typhoid, and that they had to quickly bury the bodies before an epidemic spread." He reached up and brushed away a tear with the back of his hand. "And no one ever heard of my grandparents." The kid looked up with wet eyes. "My dad cursed the Directorate, called it a police state. He called this Directorate man that was questioning us a Nazi and a jack-booted murderer. Before the guards could grab Dad, he jumped up and punched that Directorate dude right in the mouth. They hauled away my old man. I never saw him again." The boy sniffed, clearing his throat. "That was last May."

Sam rose, handing Mark a roll of toilet paper. "How did you end up here in Perchance?"

The young man reached for the roll. "Thanks." After tearing off tissue, he dabbed an eye and blew his nose. "They said that since I was under eighteen, I could go to a rehabilitation home—a halfway house. And that if I did good, they'd allow me to become a Commonwealth citizen." He shrugged, glancing to the teacher. "I didn't know what 'good' meant, but I didn't have much choice, Mr. Moore. It beat that concentration camp I was in."

Sam nodded silently. He should've been stunned at Mark Thurmont's revelations and his choice of words. It bothered him that he wasn't. He sighed, empathizing with the boy's loss.

Mark set the toilet paper on a nearby table. "Mr. Moore, I want to go back home to Texas."

"I'm afraid that's impossible, Mark." Sam rose, stepped to his desk, and turned. "Carolina Province will be your new home." He paused. "I'm sorry." And he truly was.

"But," Mark protested, "I still have family in Texas. Younger brothers and sisters...cousins. They're waiting for Dad and me to bring the rest of our family home. And now," the boy stammered, "and now I'm it. I'm all they have. Mr. Moore, this is America. They can't just keep me here for no reason."

Yesterday, Sam would've winced at the word *America*. Now, he didn't even flinch. Instead, he hesitated, glanced to the tiny black bubble on the ceiling, then back to the boy. The admonishment must look real. Good grief, what was happening to him! He cleared his throat. "'America' was a failed experiment. Thankfully, it no longer exists. Never use that word again, okay?"

"I'm sorry," Mark said, with his head hanging. Quiet seconds ticked off, only punctuated by the boy's sniffs. He looked up. "Mr. Moore, when I'm eighteen, why can't I go where I want?"

Sam knew where the conversation was heading. He must choose his words carefully. "With your excellent grades and high test scores, you can graduate this coming June. I'm sure the Directorate will allow you to attend university. Once you have a degree, you can apply for Directorate membership." Sam paused, forcing a smile. "As a Directorate member, you can pick your assignment." *Bullshit. The Directorate sent you where they wanted you—unless you had friends in high places.*

"Mr. Moore, I see that triangle on your collar, but you can't be part of what Dad called, 'this catastrophe.'"

"I don't know what you're talking about."

"The Directorate is what I'm talking about," the boy said, lowering his voice. "You're not like the other teachers, except, maybe...maybe, Mr. Zhimmer. But he's afraid to do anything."

Sam wrinkled his brow, feigning confusion. *Do anything? What the hell was there to do? Speak out and die a traitor's death?* ZZ wasn't afraid; he had a family to think of. And Sam? He was only one man. What could he do? What could anyone do? They all got the government they deserved. No, he pondered, *his* generation didn't deserve this nightmare; they only had to live in it. Yet, when good men sat back and did nothing... He swallowed. Trying to change the Directorate was like trying to force toothpaste back into the freaking tube.

Mark spoke, breaking Sam's thoughts. "Mr. Moore, sir, you're part of the Directorate. Can't you say something to your bosses about those camps? Maybe tell them that if they don't shut them down, you'll go public?"

Sam looked at the kid, incredulous. "Son, that might work where you come from, but here I might as well put a bullet in my brain." He paused, eyeing the student. "You still have a lot to learn about our ways. Don't let your naiveté jump up and bite you in the ass."

"But—"

Sam shook his head and shifted in his seat. The conversation was as uncomfortable as the desk he sat in. Things were clearly taking a turn for the surreal. "Mark, my inquiry into these camps you speak of would never make it out of an office door—and neither would I."

"Then, sir, you need to help me get back to Texas, so I can warn folks what's happening over here...make sure the same thing doesn't happen at home."

"They already know." As soon as Sam said it, he regretted it.

Mark Thurmont stared and his brow furrowed.

"I mean," Sam stammered, clearing his throat, "if what you say is true, surely word of these camps has reached the Western Provinces." Oh, shit—what did he just say! He knew the kid's next question and dreaded it.

"Mr. Moore, did you know about them...about these concentration camps?"

Sam chewed a lip. "I knew about the relocation centers, but heard nothing about concentration camps." He paused, scrutinizing the student sitting across from him. The young man's head drooped. Sam knew what it felt like to not be taken seriously. "Mark, I'm sorry about your parents and grandparents." Sam reached over and squeezed the kid's shoulder. "But, sometimes, rumors and reality become clouded. Know what I mean?"

"Yes, sir," Mark replied to the carpeted floor.

Rising, Sam released Mark's shoulder. "I'll check into these camps."

Head down, the kid nodded. "Thank you, Mr. Moore."

"You may go," Sam said.

Mark rose and shouldered his backpack.

"So, you really want to go back to Texas, huh?" Sam asked.

"Yes, sir," Mark replied. His face brightened. "It's so much better there, Mr. Moore. It really is."

"How so?"

Lowering his voice, the boy stepped closer. "People are happier there. They smile. They enjoy life. In Texas, we *live* life—not just exist, like here. Back across the Mississippi, we still have hope for a reunited country." He paused. "I mean, back home, you can go wherever you want and you don't need traveling papers. You can do whatever you want, without worrying about breaking a bunch of damn rules."

Sam canted his head. "I understand there's extreme poverty across The River."

Mark cinched a strap. "Sure, we have poor folks. Who doesn't? But, we don't kill ours."

Sam swallowed, wrenching inside, unsure how to react.

Mark stepped past Sam and turned. "Back home, if something is wrong, you can speak out against it without worrying about getting locked up." His brow wrinkled in thought. "Mr. Moore, I guess the main difference between folks back home and folks here is that we still love God, and we love our country. You can feel it there on our side of the U.S., that love..." The kid closed his hand as if gripping his words. "That sense of family and patriotism hangs in the air." He looked Sam in the eye. "You'd do good there, Mr. Moore. You'd fit right in."

"Thanks, Mark, but my home is here."

"No, it isn't, sir. I can tell you hate it here." His arms swept the empty classroom. "The kids, they hate it, too...hate living like this. Can't you see it?"

Sam was caught off guard at the young man's insight—and balls. He cleared his throat, forcing calm and changed the subject. "Don't forget your reading assignment."

Yet the boy wouldn't let go. "Mr. Moore, us kids look up to you and know you'll tell us the *real* truth. And I'll bet most parents feel the same as their kids. There's a lot of folks here who'd back you if you came out and told what was really happening in their country."

Were these people insane! First Katie and now this kid. Did they think he had some kind of special power and could wave his hand and their world would right itself?

Clarity's iron hammer hit Sam so hard that it made him dizzy. He could feel the color leaving his face. He wanted to vomit.

"You okay, Mr. Moore?"

Sam caught his breath. The truth, the *truth*, was a bitter pill to swallow. He blinked and nodded. "Yeah, I'm fine."

Liar. Why don't you tell the young man how you really feel? Tell him how you just woke up to a dystopic nightmare. Tell him how you helped perpetuate that nightmare, how you helped the Directorate kill his parents. You helped them because you, Directorate man, did nothing. You knew the Directorate's stranglehold on freedoms had morphed into a Final Solution, and yet, you do NOTHING! You freaking coward.

"Sir, you don't look well."

Sam looked away. "I think this conversation has reached its conclusion. See you tomorrow, Mark."

The young man gave a rare grin and turned, heading for the door. "This is the best I've felt since I've been here." He glanced back, waving. "Tomorrow, Mr. Moore."

Sam watched the young man disappear out the door. Stunned, he rose, stepped to his own desk, and grabbed his coat. He paused, his psyche scorched, wrecked. *What in the hell just happened?* Damn, he needed a drink. He shrugged into his coat and hurried out the classroom. The door closed and locked behind him.

Late afternoon sun reflected off melting ice as the cart halted in ZZ's driveway. Gull wing doors popped open on opposite sides, and two men climbed out.

ZZ reached behind the driver's seat for a laptop. "Why are you in such a hurry?"

Sam yanked a backpack from ZZ's cart and tossed it into his own nearby cart's open door. "Who said I was in a hurry?"

"You've been acting weird lately."

"Weirder than usual?" Sam offered, climbing behind the wheel.

"You okay?"

"Just freaking peachy," Sam replied, gripping a cold steering wheel.

Concern shadowed the chemistry teacher's brow as he gazed at Sam. "Why don't you stay tomorrow night, have a home-cooked meal, and we can talk."

"Thanks for the offer man, but I'll pass." Sam turned a key, and the cart hummed to life. "Give Haleana my best."

"Sammy, don't do something stupid."

"Hell, ZZ, I'm stuck on stupid." And Sam knew truer words were never spoken.

ZZ was about to reply but instead sighed and shrugged. "See you tomorrow."

Sam nodded, pushed a button on the dash, and the door lowered. The cart backed out, and within seconds, disappeared around a corner.

* * *

At six P.M., right on cue, the North American Commonwealth's Unity Anthem popped on the TV. Four times a day, at six A.M., noon, six P.M., and at midnight, the anthem rolled from televisions throughout the NAC. And you couldn't turn the damn thing off. It didn't matter if you unplugged the television, the Commonwealth's theme continued on its own. All TVs manufactured in the past thirty years had mandatory software installed enabling a TVs control from a central location. You could change the channel all you wanted, or even have the electricity off, but it wouldn't matter: there was that damn anthem. You could freeze in the dark, yet there was the freaking

53

anthem, disturbing your misery, telling you that you weren't freezing but sacrificing for the betterment of the whole. The music would die away and the screen would darken, leaving one feeling even colder.

A pseudo-patriotic, up and down cadence now drifted from the living room. Standing in the kitchen, Sam downed a whiskey. The fiery liquid burned his throat, and he sighed in satisfaction from the liquor's warmth. He poured another. Today's conversation with the Thurmont kid weighed heavy in the back of his mind. Screwing on the cap, he eased the black-labeled, bootlegged bottle onto the kitchen counter, then turned, glass in hand, and headed for the living room. As he stepped through the door, the kitchen automatically darkened and the living room brightened. It was his day for electricity.

The Unity Anthem blared from a TV hanging on a wall. Sam glanced to the TV as he stepped past. A waving, blue flag with a gold triangle in the upper left filled the screen. It was always same old, same old. Never any variance, no creativity. The flag rippled in the background while gleaming city skylines moved across the screen. The skylines faded as tanks lumbered down a wide boulevard, with soldiers marching behind. Then came the jet fighters streaking across the sky in formation, followed by the routine young children innocently at play, laughing and swinging in a playground while their parents watched with approving smiles.

Sam paused, eyeing the screen. "You've got to be shitting me." He took a quick swig.

What was happening to him? A few months back, he wouldn't have dreamt of the disrespect he just displayed. Yet, he could no longer pretend. Under the Directorate, life was vacuous, a pantomime. Sam was only going through life's motions, with no meaning or intent behind it. Something was missing. Surely others felt the same? If he only knew how to tap into that loathing for the Directorate, get the people to overcome their fear of the regime. Sam shivered; even the thought of overthrowing the government sent him reeling. Now he knew why the Directorate banned books about the American Revolution, or anything critical of Nazi Germany or the USSR. He took another swig. Besides, what the hell could *he* do? If he openly objected to Directorate edict, well, one thing he could bank on—he would disappear from the scene.

Sam shook his head in disgust and stepped across the room to an antique, oak desk with a small video monitor on top. He eased into a matching oak chair, careful not to spill his drink. The desk and chair were given to his father years ago as a gift for recommending a well-heeled Directorate member for promotion to the rank of Commissar. The elder Moore bragged that the desk was looted from a U.S. federal building in what had once been Washington D.C., the city now renamed Central City. Chuckling with irony, Sam tilted his glass. He was sitting where some pompous American bureaucrat had parked his fat ass, while unwittingly plotting the demise of his own country. Sam leaned back, and the chair creaked. Hell, the desk and chair might've belonged to a woman for all he knew. Greed and idiocy were not gender specific.

"Messages," he said out loud. The monitor on the desk flashed on, and the screen instantly filled with line after line of updated school proclamations and Party dictum. He touched the screen, nonchalantly scrolling down, ignoring school and Party communiqué. He shook his head and spoke. "Encrypted mail." If he wanted to deal with the Spencers, it must be in secret. Michelle had recently installed bootleg logarithm encryptions in his home computer that changed codes every two hours. The Directorate hadn't caught on, partly because of degrading satellite links, and partly because of the device's next generation technology smuggled over from the West. He could, at least for now, communicate in secret from home. The screen darkened for a long moment, and then two messages popped up. One was from Michelle Spencer; she was due in a fresh flower shipment. His gaze fell to the last message. It was from her granddaughter, Katie.

"Oh, shit," he murmured. "Michelle, why did you do this?"

Rubbing his chin, Sam paused. He hadn't seen nor heard from Katie since that dysfunctional day in the store's basement last month. In spite of their perturbed parting, he often found himself thinking of her. More than once he had set out to contact her but was too stubborn and scared to go through with it. He chewed a lip, afraid to open Katie's message. Her words would probably throw another shovel full of dirt onto his once beloved Directorate. Sam sipped good whiskey, not wanting to ruin a well-deserved buzz. An index finger aimed at Katie's message, but he chickened out and tapped Michelle's vid icon instead. "Open."

An elderly woman's face filled the screen. Sam's breath left him. The woman was so frail and thin that it seemed the slightest wind would dissolve her. He almost didn't recognize her.

Sam, flowers arrived today, she rasped, her voice barely above a whisper. *Leo and I haven't seen or heard from you in awhile. Is everything okay?*

The woman was half-dead, and yet, she worried about him.

Oh, and one other thing. I gave Katie your codes. Hope you don't mind. The woman gave a weak smile. *It would please Leo and me if you'd contact her.* Michelle took a deep breath then had a coughing fit. The coughs were deep and chest-rattling. Pneumonia. After a moment, she calmed and glanced into the camera, managing a few more words. *See you in a day or two.*

The screen darkened. He shook his head. The woman desperately needed medical attention. His jaw tightened. Sam eyed Katie's message icon flashing at the bottom of the screen. Her message would have to wait.

He rose, and within seconds, stood in a spare bedroom. In a corner, draped in cobwebs, sat his father's small telescope. He stepped to it, knocking away webs. Sam unscrewed the front lens, reached inside the hollow tube, and worked out a faded, unsealed envelope. Tossing the lens on a nearby bed, he lifted the envelope's flap. It was stuffed with blue-green dollar bills—U.S. $100s. Sam peered inside the telescope; it was tightly packed with over 300 envelopes from front to back, each envelope holding 200 one-hundred-dollar bills. The hollow, aluminum tube perched on a tripod was the summation of every under-the-table, back-stabbing deal his commissar father ever cut. In the North American Commonwealth, graft and politics were bedfellows. To Sam, knowing the money was ill-gotten, it had become a creeping dread.

His jaw tightened. He wouldn't dwell on where the cash came from. Where it was going is what mattered. He stared at the salvation in the envelope. No, it wasn't *his* salvation; hell, who knew if or when that would happen? He chuckled inside, because what he was about to do wouldn't even ease his sleepless nights. It would take that which no money could ever buy to quiet the scream inside. He reached inside the telescope for two more envelopes, tossed them on a nearby bed and screwed on the telescope's lens. He'd give the envelopes to Leo. The old man would know what to do with them.

Gathering up the money envelopes, Sam headed for the living room. He dropped the envelopes on his desk and worked down sweatshirt sleeves. The ancient farmhouse was cold and drafty. The 130-year-old brick home had developed a quirky— at times, annoying—personality. During the summer, if you stepped hard onto the wooden front porch, the open living room windows would slam shut. And when you turned on the kitchen sink, the toilet tanks began filling. Recently, the roof started leaking—again. The last thunderstorm had sent him scrambling for pans. The minute he laid out the pans, the leaking stopped. And now, the last few days, the front door required almost Herculean strength to open. It was as if someone were next to him, pushing against the door, forbidding him to leave. Yet, once open, the confounded door closed and opened with ease. Go figure. He reasoned that the neglected house and he were kindred spirits who knew, for better or worse, their time had come.

He paused near a radiator heater, adjusted the thermostat, and stepped back to the desk and vidphone monitor. Katie's message icon flashed. He tensed up. "Open."

Feminine features materialized on the screen. Her short dark hair was gathered into a stiff ponytail. *I hope this finds you well,* she said. *And, I apologize for the way we parted last month.*

Her eyes held a strange light Sam wasn't sure about, but sincerity shone through. Feeling foolish, he swallowed. Why hadn't he manned up, contacted her, and apologized first? Yet, he knew why. Katie made him nervous in a way he wouldn't admit.

I can't say much, Katie continued, *except that, Sam, we need to talk. I'll be in Perchance this weekend. If you can, come by Granny and Papa's.* Concern shadowed her face, and her voice lowered. *Don't reply to this.* She paused, and her gaze softened. *Hope to see you this weekend...bye.*

The screen switched to the message home page. Sam stared at the monitor, unsure of how to react. He sipped whiskey, contemplating. Did Katie have some kind of proof that those homeless camps were really extermination camps? If she had actual proof, it also meant she had signed her death warrant. And maybe his.

Welcome to The Scope and Sequence News Hour, came the audio from the wall screen behind him.

Sam rose and glanced to the computer monitor. "Standby." The monitor went black as the computer slipped into sleep mode. Drink in hand, he stepped in front of the TV.

The Commonwealth's shore defenses were once again successful in repelling Persian landing forces. Our glorious navy has intercepted and surrounded a Persian fleet fifty kilometers off the coast of Upper New England Province. An order of unconditional surrender has been issued to the Persian fleet commander. As to date, there has been no reply from the Persians.

"Those pseudo-Persians will die of old age first," Sam murmured, watching video of artillery firing. The scene changed to Commonwealth aircraft launching missiles, and then what appeared to be an enemy naval vessel exploding. He took a sip, scoffing. For the past six months, the same ship had exploded at least two dozen times. The scene shifted to a dramatic tank duel in a desert. "Finally, something new."

Out west, Commonwealth armor rules the day. Rebellious western provinces are teetering on collapse as the Commonwealth pounds the rebel forces into submission. Yet, the Directorate, in its compassion, has issued new orders, stating that if rebel forces immediately lay down arms, a peaceful means will be sought to bring our rebellious brothers and sisters back into the Commonwealth's humane fold. Critics have decried the Commonwealth's alleged harsh treatment of the western provinces as barbaric. This morning, President Henshaw responded to the accusations, releasing a statement, saying that the "Commonwealth is only responding to the civil strife out west as a caring parent would respond to a defiant child."

"'Defiant child?'" Sam sneered. "'Critics?' The token critic *you* manufactured." Sam knew the "critics" were only a facade. No one would dare openly criticize the Directorate. And, even if one could pull off the unthinkable such as publicly condemning the Party, it would never be reported. The Directorate controlled the media; the Directorate *is* the media.

Sam turned away in disgust. What sickened him even more was that he had bought into Directorate ideals, believing the Party's doctrine of fairness was sound. He thought he was part of an elite, knowledgeable assemblage that brought order and unity. Instead, stagnation fell as acid rain, slowly—but most surely—poisoning society. And creativity? Nowadays, *creativity* was only found in a dictionary somewhere between *crayon* and *crowbar*. The freedom to speak out, to worship, even to travel, were only distant memories. Sam ran fingers through his short hair. How could he have been so naive? So wrong? He wanted to shoot himself. No. He wanted to shoot *them*. The Directorate's ideals and values were nothing but maggot fodder. The Party wanted *unity*. Unity against what—its own citizens? Directorate concepts of an organized, compliant society made him want to vomit.

Sam turned away while the news program droned on wearily in the background. *Remember, citizens, ballet week will kick off the first week of Culture Month. After this newscast, you can follow your favorite ballet performers' rise from humble beginnings to stardom. Just a reminder, next month is Paper Month, emphasizing the importance of recycling... Celebration parades will be held each Saturday. Attendance is mandatory. Flags will be distributed at the parade site...*

Sam stiffly set the whiskey on an end table and cupped his face. What kind of world did his father and he help create? *My God.* Confusion wracked him, and he stifled a choke. *I'm only one man, yet I have to do something.* He still had that damn shortwave radio and the nightly messages were an addiction. However, certain addictions can lead to suicide, and not necessarily by one's own hands. He stared, unsure. Pandora's Box wasn't opened; it was kicked over and smashed, but its contents had escaped earlier. If Western Alliance messages were to be believed, a shaky, underground movement was forming in the NAC. Sam was already privy to that info; recent Directorate memos told members to be on the lookout for any reference to a hate group called The Patriots. The Patriots were on the terrorist watch list and, according to the Party, the group was behind several unnamed violent acts.

He downed the whiskey and paused, his jaw flexing with resolve. The hopeless, forlorn looks on his students' faces haunted him. He was their teacher; he should give those kids hope. He couldn't undo the totalitarian stain of his father's generation. But he could be the architect of a Second *American* Revolution. Those thoughts were treasonous to the Party. He swallowed with anticipation. *Yes! Yes! Wonderful, beautiful treason!* Yet, he'd sworn allegiance to the Directorate. Now, he must make amends for that mistake. He had to sleep at night...

Giddy, Sam marched into the kitchen. He rinsed his glass, set it in the sink, and leaned against the counter top. For the first time in his life, he would follow his gut instinct, and that instinct told him that *freedom* and *democracy* were more than mere words. Finally, he would *do* something. He may never live to breathe liberty's air, but by God, those kids in his classroom would know it, breathe it. He gripped the counter and goose bumps rose on his arms. There *are* things worth dying for. He recalled his biological father, whom he vaguely remembered had disappeared during the war. He was sure the man died a soldier, fighting against this way of life. Was his death in vain? Sam wondered if that father would now be proud of him. He recalled the softness of his biological mother and an inexplicable strength foreign to him. And it wasn't the whiskey speaking to him.

That night, Sam slept better than he had in years.

Lunch duty sucked. Forty wasted minutes of watching teenagers eat. Thankfully, it rotated weekly among the faculty. This was Sam's week. The cafeteria was actually a cafetorium—combo cafeteria and auditorium. However, no actors had performed on the cafeteria stage in over twenty years. It was now an observation post. Seated alone on the stage, Sam gazed out to the sea of blue and khaki and chuckled...the irony. Only fitting that teachers were posted on the stage.

In the middle of the cafeteria, something caught his eye: the Thurmont boy. A month had passed since their after-school conversation. The kid had made a lot of friends since then. He watched Mark place a food tray onto the bench-style table and a green 42 lit on a huge screen full of numbers, the "bingo board," hanging from a wall on the cafeteria's far end. Forty-two was his assigned cafeteria seat number. He seated himself next to a cute, blond-haired girl named Regan Hampton. She smiled and grabbed his arm. Two other boys sat across the table. They nodded and leaned toward Mark. One boy, Jason Myer, patted Mark's arm. The other kid, Phillip Benivades, nodded and glanced around as if searching for the lunch monitor. Obviously, the Latino was a lookout.

A monitor headed their way. Phillip elbowed Jason. As if on cue, all four at the table began eating. The monitor, a middle-aged woman, strolled past, casting a suspicious eye on the kids. Her gaze lingered on Mark. After she was out of earshot, the four became animated. Mark gripped a fork, aiming it at Phillip. Regan grabbed Mark's arm, pushing it down.

What the hell? Sam had all four in his fourth period class and knew them well. The past two weeks, the four had been hanging together, doing a lot of whispering. He eyed them. "Some kind secret shit going on." Scanning the cafeteria once, he rose, gradually eased down the stage steps, and ambled their way.

Sam paused, spotting a gray-clad, thick woman hurrying to his students' table. It was that busybody bigmouth, Ms. Devon. The kids tagged her as "the lunch monitor from hell." Sam knew she earned that title and was proud to wear it. She squeezed her hulk through the throng of tables so fast that she reminded him of a jelly donut he'd dropped and watched roll on the floor. He picked up the pace, dodging tables, but the monitor would reach Mark's table first. Her harsh, smoker's voice drifted his way.

"I'm hearing a strange conversation at this table," Ms. Devon rasped. "And take your hand off him, young lady!" She heaved her thick body around to Regan, placing hands on wide hips. "You know the rules on PDA."

Regan jerked back. "Yes, ma'am. I'm sorry."

The monitor's gray hair was pulled back into a tight bun, giving her round face a stretched look. "I heard a forbidden word over here," she continued. "Now, someone can tell me what you were talking about or you can tell Ms. Woodriff." She paused, eyeing each individual student. "What's it going to be? Me or the principal?"

A hush fell over the lunchroom as necks craned. Sam halted a table away, watching. All four students sat with their heads hanging. In their own minds, they were already condemned... Directorate training. In the Directorate's eyes, you were always guilty. Always. However, to show its "compassion," occasionally the Directorate would allow you to prove your innocence. Of course, it was always a show trial. In the end, the most you could hope for was a guilty verdict and a "pardon," which meant you would be punished another day.

"I was doing the talking," Mark said, breaking the silence.

The monitor folded her arms. "And they were doing the listening, right?"

She tapped a foot, staring hard at Mark. *If looks could kill,* Sam mused, *the boy would be carried out in a stretcher.*

The monitor glared at Mark. "You're that Thurmont kid, aren't you?"

"Yes, ma'am."

"Yes, we know about you...always whispering about how good things are where you came from, filling these kids' heads with all sorts of crazy ideas." She sneered, nodding. "Believe me, we've got our eyes on you."

"I was only telling them that winters aren't as cold where I come from as they are here," Mark said innocently.

Regan shifted and looked up. "Ma'am, I was the one that asked him about the weather."

Sam saw Mark shove his leg against Regan's.

The woman aimed a crooked finger a Regan. "I'm not addressing you, little missy." She turned back to Mark. "I think you need to come with me."

"No one's going anywhere," Sam said, strolling up, "at least not until the bell rings, and then they're all going straight to class."

"Mr. Moore," four relieved voices shouted.

Sam turned to the lunch monitor. "Ms. Devon, I'll take it from here."

"But, but..." she sputtered, "they were talking about—"

"I said, I'll handle it," Sam repeated firmly, eyeing the woman. "Goodbye, Ms. Devon."

Out of the corner of his eye, he caught Mark trying to suppress a smile. It was too late for the other kids, who were grinning from ear to ear. He knew the monitor wanted to say something. Oh, she wanted to reply in the worst way. But to counter a teacher and a *Directorate member*, was she that stupid? Sam decided she was.

The woman contemplated him, and then she finally worked up the nerve to speak on her own behalf. "Ms. Woodriff would be interested in knowing what was said today, and by whom."

"Is that a threat, Ms. Devon?"

"No, sir. I don't threaten."

"Well," Sam said, never taking his eyes off the woman, "if you want to complain about something *I* said or did, there's a 'Mr. Samuel Moore complaint box' that's just been installed outside the principal's door. It's emptied twice a day—by a custodian."

Snickers came from several nearby tables.

"Or," Sam continued, "you can tell Ms. Woodriff what you *think* you heard when you people are on one of your numerous smoke breaks."

Several students laughed out loud. The wind left her sails. The woman turned pale, and her heavy shoulders sagged.

"Did I say something wrong, Ms. Devon?" Sam asked, smiling innocently.

"This isn't over." She turned and left.

"I wish I had a dollar for every time I've heard that," Sam replied after her.

"Way to go, Mr. Moore!" Mark said.

"You showed her," Jason added, chuckling.

Regan stared with concern at the teacher. "I think you just made another enemy, Mr. Moore."

"I'm an enemy magnet," Sam replied. "No matter where I go, I seem to draw enemies like filings to a magnet."

The bell rang, and everyone rose. Sam glanced to the standing kids. "If you four clowns have any after-school plans, cancel them. We're going to have a little after-school pow-wow about what just happened. That is, if I'm not in front of Ms. Woodriff."

"Yes, sir," came a chorus of voices.

The four teenagers exchanged glances before following the others to the cafeteria exit. Sam stood silent, staring after them. *Definitely something going on.* Seconds later, he headed in the opposite direction. Just before Sam stepped into the academic wing, he spotted Caleb Jeffery's nephew, Cory Jeffery, heading for the front office. The kid had been sitting at the lunch table next to Mark. Sam's brow wrinkled as he watched Cory disappear into the office.

The bell rang, the school day ending. Everyone in class rose with the exception of four students. The four sat dutifully straight in their seats, watching the teacher erase the whiteboard in front.

Sam felt their gazes on his back. He was eager to learn what he'd walked in on at lunch, but he was careful not to show it. He tossed an eraser on the rail and turned. The students cast nervous glances at him then to each other. Sam cleared his throat. "Okay, you guys..."

All four rose and hustled to the room's "quiet corner" in the back. Sam followed. So, something was up, or they wouldn't have moved. He grabbed a plastic chair, set it in the corner near the flower vase, and plopped down. The kids settled into desks, scooting them around in a semi-circle to face him.

Sam cleared his throat. "Now, tell me what you all did to piss off Ms. Devon. No BS—only the truth." Several moments of strained silence followed. Sam noticed all eyes kept returning to Mark. "And...?" Sam said, eyeing Mark.

Mark sighed in resignation. "I was talking about Texas... again."

"Haven't I warned you about that?" Sam replied harshly. "You're setting yourself up, son." He glanced to the girl across from him. "Regan, what's your part in this? What are you doing running around with these rebels?"

"Everything is my fault," Jason blurted. The husky boy shook his head. "I'm the reason Mark was talking about Texas, the reason Regan and Phillip are here."

"You?" Sam said, raising a brow. "Jason, you hardly say two words in class. And now you're in charge of the 'intrigue' department?"

"They say it's the quiet ones you have to worry about," Phillip said.

Sam tapped the table. He gazed silently at each and every one. To his surprise, the kids' gazes never wavered. There was apprehension in their eyes for sure, but it wasn't about the lunch incident. There was something else going on. "Out with it."

Regan glanced to the boys. "We have to tell him...trust him."

"Tell me what?" Sam asked.

"Mr. Moore," Jason said, gesturing, "we—"

Mark quickly reached over, stilling Jason's hands. He held up a finger, quieting him, then patted his shoulder. Jason nodded, and Mark settled back into his desk, facing Sam. "Mr. Moore, we're leaving."

Sam's tapping stopped, and the room went eerily still. "What do you mean, 'we're leaving?' Leaving to where?"

Mark gestured to himself and his classmates. "All of us, and their families, are leaving the NAC. We're going to Texas."

Sam normally would have laughed. Instead, he straightened in his seat and methodically loosened his tie. "Mark, I can understand you wanting to go back." Tie loosened, he paused, gesturing to the others. "But, you can't be dragging these kids into your homesickness."

"Mr. Moore, Mark didn't have anything to do with it," Jason said. "Maybe he helped with the location, but our families were planning to leave long before Mark got here."

Sam shook his head. "You can't be serious!" Yet, he knew they were. The somber gazes told him all he needed to know. "You won't get fifty miles before you're nabbed."

"Not if you're with us, Mr. Moore," Mark said.

"Now I know you're crazy," Sam replied. He ran fingers through his short hair. "I should report all of you. It would save your lives."

"But you won't," Regan said, eyeing the teacher. "You did your job well, Mr. Moore. You opened our eyes. You, of all people, know the NAC is nothing but a lie. And...and we can't live that lie anymore."

Sam stared. They had guts, he'd give them that.

"'We hold these truths to be self-evident,'" Mark began, 'that all men are created equal, that they are endowed by their Creator with certain unalienable rights'—"

"'That among these...'" Sam murmured, talking to himself as much as to the students, "'that among these are Life, Liberty and the pursuit of Happiness.'"

Sam and Mark exchanged glances. Sam shivered from openly uttering those forbidden words. The other students gazed in bewilderment.

Jason gawked at the boy from Texas. "Wow! Where did you come up with that stuff?"

"It's not mine," Mark said flatly. "It's from America's Declaration of Independence. Where I come from, it's required study."

"Thomas Jefferson is its author," Sam said. "Those words

also belong to all of us in this room...all of us in the NAC." Silence enveloped them, and Sam scrutinized each student. "You guys need to remain in Carolina. Don't forsake your homeland. It's your generation that will spread those words, set things right. It has to come from within."

"Mr. Moore," Phillip said, "we didn't forsake our country. Our country forsook us."

"It picked up and moved west of the Mississippi," Jason added. "And we intend to follow it."

Sam shook his head, flustered. Part of him wanted to go with them. Hell yes, he wanted to go! He fantasized about the day he would tell the Directorate to kiss his ass. The thought of starting fresh out west, in the new United States, had haunted him many a night lately. Now, he faced a crossroad. One thing was as sure as the heart beating in his chest: Life, as he knew it, was over. He glanced to them. "When are you guys leaving?"

"Two weeks from today, at the nine-week break," Jason answered.

Sam nodded. "Are there other adult that feel this way?"

Regan, who had remained quiet the last few minutes, finally spoke. "Hundreds...thousands...maybe millions. There's something just below the surface, Mr. Moore. I can feel it but can't describe it, except maybe, maybe it's like boiling water. I think our parents know what's happening, but they don't want to scare us." She paused, lowering her gaze. "All I know is, I think a lot of people are going to die, and soon. And our parents know this, too."

"That's why we have to leave as soon as possible," Phillip added, "before we get caught in whatever's going to happen." The boy paused. "My parents also say there's going to be a war, and it won't be from the Persians."

"A Second American Revolution," Sam murmured. "It's about time."

The students whispered nervously among themselves, all except Mark Thurmont, who studied the teacher. "Mr. Moore, if you stay, you'll be the first one they come after."

"I know." Sam stared past them. "And I'll have a little surprise for them."

"You can't," Mark whispered, "they'll get you, like they did my father."

"Your father was a brave, devoted man," Sam said, gazing at Mark, "but he didn't know our system. I do. I'm part of it."

"What's he talking about?" Jason asked, leaning toward Mark.

"Mr. Moore," Mark pleaded, ignoring Jason, "you can't stay."

"I have to," Sam said, gazing first to Mark, then to the others. "I have unfinished business here, but you guys probably don't understand that...at least not yet."

"Sounds like 'payback time,'" Mark said.

Sam eyed the young Texan. "Perhaps *you* do understand."

Mark nodded subtly. "My daddy always said, 'Son, there's two things you need to know before you seek revenge. One: make sure the wrong was intentional. And two: make sure you don't end up on the wrong side of right.'"

"I would like to have known your father," Sam said. "We have a lot in common." He suddenly felt a pat on his arm. It was Regan. Her eyes were wide as saucers.

"Mr. Moore, what are you going to do if you stay?" she said.

Now that was a helluva question, Sam thought. He'd been wondering that himself and would give all the money in that old telescope for an answer. Sam gazed into her young, gray eyes, reading concern and confusion. "Don't worry about me," he said. "You guys just focus on getting to Texas. Two weeks isn't much time." He glanced around. "You said the decision to leave—to escape—isn't a sudden idea though?"

"My family has been planning this for the past year," Jason said.

"So has mine," Phillip added.

"The way we figure it," Jason continued, "by the time we're missed, we'll already be in Texas."

Regan cleared her throat. "All of our families have worked together in secret for months. It's all set. Except for you, Mr. Moore. You're the final piece that'll help us make it." She paused, gazing at the teacher. "Don't stay. We need you."

"You mean you need my Directorate position."

"That, too," Regan said, "but we need *you*."

Mark nodded. "She's right, Mr. Moore. You gotta come with us."

"That discussion is now closed," Sam said and then grew quiet. It wasn't their words as much as the pleading in their eyes that got to him. Sam eased up and turned away. Arm out, he leaned on a wall, fighting with the lump in his throat. *Not in front of the kids, you idiot!* Quiet seconds passed. He composed himself and turned to Jason. "Pray tell, how are you getting to Texas? You know carts are out of the question. They're too small, and the battery charge wouldn't even get you halfway." Sam glanced to the students. "And traveling papers? What about those? You know you must have papers to leave the county."

"The paperwork's been taken care of," Jason said. "And we've got several old diesel pickups."

"Where have you been hiding them?" Sam asked. The last civilian pickups rolled off the assembly line twenty years ago. Today, only those in agriculture were allowed to own and drive trucks, and those trucks were bought at government surplus auctions. Most farms were being taken over by the government anyway and turned into collectives. The former owners became reluctant renters, modern sharecroppers, or in some cases, outright evicted from their own private property. Those who knew little about farming now operated most commercial farms in the NAC, and they used cheaply-built, Chinese-made equipment. Reliable, American-made, civilian-built pickup trucks were now relics of the past.

Jason hesitated and glanced to his classmates.

"Go ahead, Jason," Phillip said, nodding. "It's too late now."

Jason eyed the teacher. "We've got four good pickup trucks stored at my granny's old farm."

Sam raised a brow. "*Inside* a barn, I assume? Otherwise, satellites—"

"Yeah, in a barn, along with extra fuel and supplies."

"Geesus," Sam murmured, pacing around the tiny semicircle of desks. All eyes were on him.

"Mr. Moore, we're serious." Jason said.

"I'll say," Sam replied.

"The past few months, our parents have been secreting a few things out to Jason's granny's," Regan began. "Friday after next, we'll all meet out there after dark, and then it's 'goodbye Perchance, goodbye North American Commonwealth.'"

"*Adios amigos,*" Phillip said, grinning.

"And 'hello America,'" Jason added.

Sam paused, rubbing the back of his neck, trying like hell to digest everything. "You're just going to abandon your homes?"

All heads nodded. Sam looked away. Yet, what were they really leaving? The three students from Perchance came from what had been upper-middle class families, families of substance. Take Regan Hampton's family. At one time, they were considered wealthy. Her father had owned several auto, and then cart, dealerships. With the economy moving from free-market to command, a burgeoning government gobbled up most large corporations. The Office of People's Cooperatives—OPC—bought her father's last dealership five years ago, for pennies on the dollar, and then they closed it. Everyone knew the OPC was the lipstick version of the Directorate. True to its word, the

Directorate had accomplished its goal—a classless society. Now, there was only one class: poor.

"There's a four-door truck per family," Jason said, breaking Sam's thoughts. "And one truck to carry extra fuel and supplies. As you can see, Mr. Moore, we're traveling light, but there's still room for you, if you change your mind."

Sam thought of that day when he was a boy on horseback, and how he came upon that sad family walking next to that horse-drawn old car. He quickly forced thoughts elsewhere. "Thanks, Jason. I'm not saying I won't follow you guys, but now's not the time."

Mr. Moore, are you in there? came a voice from the ceiling.

"It's Ms. Woodriff!" Regan exclaimed. "Oh, God—"

"Shh!" Sam whispered, glancing at four frightened faces. He stepped into view of the overhead camera. "What do you need, Ms. Woodriff?"

I'd like you to come to my office, please.

"I'm on my way." Sam stepped back to the students. "You all get out of here."

The students turned their desks around and scrambled up.

"Mr. Moore," Mark said, cinching up a backpack, "we didn't mean to get you in trouble."

"Don't worry about it. I stay in trouble."

"Mr. Moore," Jason began, "what do we do?"

Sam eyed the worried students. He had to calm them, but what about himself? "Come here," he said, signaling for them to gather round. "Do nothing. Keep your plans. I'll handle it, understand?"

Four nervous faces moved up and down.

"In case they ask," Mark said, "I told Ms. Devon we were talking about the weather in Texas. But, Mr. Moore, I don't know what she heard."

"Got it," Sam said. "Now, all of you get outta here. Go."

"I'll pray for you, Mr. Moore," Regan said, looking back as she hurried to the door.

"Don't forget about yourself," Sam replied.

Backpacks bouncing, the four teenagers scrambled out the classroom door. Sam hoped Terri Woodriff was following her regular routine. If so, the kids wouldn't be spotted leaving his room. The commissar was still gone. That meant the cameras in her office were probably off, as she called the cameras a distraction.

Sam hurried to his desk. Grabbing his coat from a nearby closet, he slung it over an arm. Then he reached for the backpack on a chair behind his desk. He lifted the flap, making sure the red carton of Marlboros was there. He swallowed. It may take more than cigarettes this time. Hoisting the backpack, he slung it over a shoulder and stepped to the door.

"**C**ome on in, Sam, and close the door."

"How's it going, Terri?" Sam said, pushing the door shut. He glanced around the sparsely furnished room. The walls were bare, except for the usual Directorate posters. On a cluttered desk was a picture of her husband, teenage daughter, and young son. The daughter, Jamie, was a junior at the high school. Sam also knew that Jamie was Regan's close friend.

"Have a seat," Terri said, nodding to a wooden chair in front of her metal desk.

Sam dropped his coat and backpack into a nearby chair. He glanced to the wall behind him. Only one of four cameras were on. Oh, no. His classroom's corridor filled the screen. He swallowed, seating himself. He was about to speak, but the serious expression on the older woman caught him. There were bags under her eyes, and for the first time, he noticed wisps of gray hair.

"I'm sure you know why I called you in."

He thought of playing dumb, but Terri wasn't stupid. The act would piss her off. "The little incident at lunch today?"

The principal brushed dark hair behind an ear. "That 'incident' is only a sidebar." She paused to glance at a sheet of paper in front of her. "Mark Thurmont, Jason Myers, Phillip Benivades, and Regan Hampton are students of yours, right?"

"Yes, ma'am."

She picked up the paper, eyed it, and dropped it back on her desk. Her gaze returned to Sam. "A piece of disturbing news recently crossed my desk, and it concerns those four. I was wondering if you know anything about it?"

"I have to know what it is you heard first?" he said, shrugging.

"Were they just in your room?"

"Well, yeah," Sam said casually. "All four are in my fourth period class."

"Did they talk to you after school?"

Sam hooked a thumb to the video screen behind him. "Come off it, Terri. You just saw them leave."

"Do you remember me telling you back in November that your behavior was going to cost you?"

"Playing with fire,' I believe was the quote."

The principal leaned back in a padded chair.

Sam stared past her to a poster of smiling children in front of a school, all superimposed over a silver triangle. The caption read: **Their Future Demands Your Compliance.** He wanted to puke. He glanced to the principal. She was shaking her head at him. That's what Terri Woodriff did when she was confused. Sam swallowed. There was still an opening.

Terri leaned forward, grabbed a pen, and began clicking it. "I would ask you if those four have been acting weird, but I don't think you'd recognize 'weird' if it stomped in front of you and dropped its pants."

"Thank you," Sam said, hinting a smile.

"Have those four mentioned anything about running away?" she asked.

"No," Sam replied. Plausible deniability. *The kids never mentioned running away. They said they were leaving, not running away. There is a difference.* "Regan is your daughter's friend. You probably know the girl better than me. Do you see anything in her that's different? I don't."

"Neither do I." Terri dropped the pen. "Sam, if I'd only heard this from one source, well," she shrugged, "but two different people? And both saying the same thing?"

"I haven't heard anything about them running away." Sam crossed a leg and rested his hands on a knee. "I mean, who would want to leave paradise?"

"Give me a break." She leaned forward, clasping her hands. "If you hear anything, let me know, okay?"

Sam nodded.

She waved her hand. "Go."

He rose.

Terri looked up. "Sam, you've always been truthful with me, at least I'd like to think so."

Sam cringed inside. *Here it comes.*

"What were those four doing in your room after school?"

And there it was. His character was cornered. His guts twisted. Lives, hopes, dreams other than his own, depended on what he now said, or did. He stepped silently to the chair holding his coat and backpack. Donning the heavy coat, he grabbed the backpack, allowing a flap to open, exposing the cigarette carton to Terri but not to the cameras. "I was tutoring them."

She glanced to the carton and swallowed. Then she turned blue eyes on him. "All four? What a coincidence?"

He closed the flap and worked the backpack over a shoulder. "Yeah, just a freaking coincidence."

"Thanks for your cooperation, Mr. Moore," Terri said in a loud voice. "Have a good weekend."

"You, too." Sam turned and left.

* * *

A street light at the end of the ally glowed a silver orb through the rare falling snow. The fluffy flakes landing on his idling cart seemed like tiny, elfin kisses, pure and innocent. The falling snow was like the flowers he would buy tomorrow. The snow and flowers came from different worlds, yet to Sam, they both had so much in common, and it wasn't just their beauty.

A cart loomed up in front of him. Headlights out, it idled up and halted, with the driver's window opposite his. One night in the future, this might be a setup, but not tonight—he hoped.

Sam mashed a button, lowering his window. The window opposite him lowered, framing a feminine face.

"I got here as quick as I could," Terri Woodriff said.

"No problem," Sam said. "Catch." He tossed a carton of Marlboros to her.

"Got anything extra tonight?" she said, cradling the carton.

"Like...?"

"Pills. I need pills."

"No *micadon*," Sam said. "Especially not for you, not tonight."

"Sam..."

"Terri," he murmured, hesitating. "You okay?"

"Things aren't good at home."

Even in the shadows, he could make out her strained features. "I'm sorry."

"Johnny and I are separating. It's been a long time coming..." She paused, swallowing a sob. "I can't take it anymore."

Sam sighed, bowing his head. "No pills."

"Sam, I need something other than smokes."

"Or you'll tell Tipton about today?"

"You know me better than that. I hate that bastard." Terri halted. "I would never betray—"

"Betray whom? Those kids? Me? Or yourself?"

Unstable seconds passed between the two. Silent snow continued falling, blanketing everything with forgotten innocence.

Sam felt sick. What was he even doing here? He had to get away. Without thinking, he reached back between bucket seats, coming up with a one-liter bottle. "Here," and he shoved the bottle to her, "say hello to Jack Daniels."

The principal grabbed the bottle. Then she fumbled in her purse. "What do I owe you?"

"The usual."

Terri eased down her purse. "Don't worry about Ms. Devon. I'll take care of her."

"Thanks."

She set her purse and the bottle on the passenger seat and faced Sam. "Tell the Thurmont boy to notice who's around him before he spouts off, especially at lunch."

Sam nodded, raising a brow.

Terri put the cart in gear and glanced back out the open window. "One last thing. Don't be seen alone again with those four students. Tipton's coming in tomorrow afternoon to review reports and video. You know he'll officially be back at school on Monday."

Sam gave a disgusted groan. "Yeah, I know."

"Today's reports will be buried so far down, it'll take over *two weeks* for him to find them."

Sam stared.

"Merry Christmas, Sam."

"Merry Christmas, Terri."

Her window rose, and the cart disappeared into the snowy night.

Sam stared after her. "Geesus…"

Oh *little town of Bethlehem*... The words drifted from the shortwave radio perched on a desk in his bedroom. The carol ended. Sam scooted the chair closer and turned up the volume.

To our fellow Americans east of the Mississippi, may this Christmas Eve find you safe and with hope. Do not despair. We, here in the United States of America, have not forgotten you. You are in our thoughts and prayers. Partisans in Northern Pennsylvania were successful this week in destroying a major rail line leading to a death camp located in the western part of the state. And in Nashville, an explosion occurred at Directorate Headquarters, killing at least two high-ranking government officials.

Sam wanted to applaud but couldn't find it in himself to celebrate death. Yet, suppose he was called on to commit acts of violence in order to free others? He shuddered. Wanting freedom was one thing, achieving it quite another.

Videos secreted to the West show massive roundups of political prisoners, the poor, and the elderly in several major eastern cities. One video shows a rare glimpse inside a death camp. The scene is appalling and will not be described on this holy night. Suffice is to say, the photographer put him or herself at great risk to video and then smuggle the truth out. We know there is a news blackout in the East, therefore most of you know little of what is happening around you. Flee if you can! For those of you brave patriots who choose to stay and fight—and violent it will be—as usual, we will help all we can. Now, for tonight's announcements: The shovel is in the shed. The shovel is in the shed. She likes purple. She likes purple. The hotdog needs mustard...

Sam clicked off the radio. His earlier shudder had turned into a nonstop shiver. He rose and rubbed his arms. Dressed in heavy sweats, he was still freezing. Yet, it wasn't from the cold draft. What was he getting himself into?

Maybe he should go with those kids and their families. He certainly had enough money to buy their way across the South, and for all of them to start over. Yes, that would be the logical, *safe* thing to do.

Sam stepped to his bed and turned back the blankets. He

had always taken the safe, logical path through life. He paused, pillow in hand, and chuckled. There was only one choice, really.

He crawled into bed, clicked off the light, pulled up the blankets, and stared into darkness. Funny, he had never thought of himself as a patriot.

* * *

That week he had Saturday school duty, which ended at noon. The rare snowfall from the night before was now only a memory. Sam returned home, changed, and headed for the Spencer's. It was a sunny, late afternoon when his cart pulled into the two-*car* driveway and parked behind a late-model, blue cart. Sam climbed from behind the wheel.

Sam glanced around before stepping to the house. The temperature was quite pleasant for late December. Wearing a sweatshirt, jeans and tennis shoes, he made his way up to the old frame house. He was careful not to trip over cracks in the fifty-year-old cement driveway. He paused at the screened front door, feeling strangely giddy and shy at the same time. Katie was supposed to be inside. He hated admitting that he wanted to see her. And it wasn't just about the camps. In fact, even after what he had heard on the shortwave, he still found it hard to swallow that something so heinous as death camps existed.

Sam raised a hand to knock when the door suddenly opened, and he stared into the bearded face of Leo Spencer.

The older man opened the door and stepped aside. "Come on in, stranger, and Merry Christmas."

"Merry Christmas," Sam replied, still not exactly sure what it meant. He stepped past the large man and into a shadowy living room. A double window with curtains pulled back was the single source of light. A hint of cigar smoke and kerosene, followed by the pleasing aroma of roasting turkey, drifted in the air.

The two shook hands. "Good to see you again, son," Leo said, grinning. "Excuse the lack of light. They turned off all the electricity in town. They do it every Thanksgiving and Christmas, trying to stick a fork in the eyes of everyone who still celebrate it...the sorry bastards."

"I hope I can help you do something about it," Sam said, looking the older man up and down. "Leo, I swear you look younger and meaner."

"Just meaner," came a soft voice behind him.

Sam turned at the words. It was Michelle Spencer, or what was left of her. He tried not to stare. The poor woman was nothing but a walking skeleton, yet, she was still hanging in there. Leo was up to the task of taking care of her. He had no choice. Sam was sure that by now both believed that "assisted living" meant assisted death in one of the camps.

"Come here," she said.

Sam stepped to her, and she wrapped a thin arm around his neck and patted his back. "Merry Christmas. You've been away too long. Leo and I worry about you, worry that something may happen to you."

"Merry Christmas, flower girl," Sam said, returning the hug. He stepped back, casting a curious eye. "What do you mean 'something may happen to you?'"

"There's whispers around town that you're filling those kids' heads with crazy notions." Michelle paused. Her eyes twinkled. "Notions like the need to return to freedom and democracy...that your bosses are lying to its citizens. You know, stuff like that."

Sam's breath left him, and he could only stare. If the town knew about his disgust with the system, most certainly the Directorate knew. Maybe they left him to teach, so he could hang himself.

"Surely you knew?" Leo asked, walking up. He placed a hand on Sam's shoulder. "Son, there's a lot of folks who are behind you. Why, you've become some kinda' underground hero."

"Geesus..." he murmured, "me?" It hit Sam that his days of teaching were numbered. Hell, maybe even his days... For the first time, he knew his future lay in another direction, another path. And it scared the living hell out of him.

The old man gave Sam a shrewd look. "We'll talk more of this later."

Michelle smiled, changing the subject. "I see you got my vidmail this morning about Christmas dinner."

"Yes, ma'am," Sam said. He forced down the Spencers' revelation and tried to act as normal as possible. "As a boy of three, I vaguely recall Christmas but never a Christmas dinner."

"And that's a shame," Michelle said. "Well, if you'll excuse me, I need to get back into the kitchen."

Sam glanced around, trying not to appear too obvious that he was looking for Katie. He'd only been in the Spencer's home once before. Nothing had changed that he could recall. The living room was just that—a living room. The worn furniture gave the place a homey feel. A large American flag hung above the fireplace.

Leo caught Sam staring at the flag. "Only take it out on special occasions."

Sam silently nodded. While moving closer to the fireplace, his gaze never left the Stars and Stripes. It was the largest American flag he'd ever seen, and to have it so brazenly displayed...

So, this is the flag Leo fought for...?

Leo Spencer had been a U.S. Marine earlier in the century and had fought in Iraq, Afghanistan, Iran, and in the Korean War II in 2026. Leo's opinion of the Directorate was well known, and he didn't mind sharing it. He also had a lot of friends who could cause trouble, as in social unrest, as in a mob riot. And the Directorate ignored a dying object. Giving attention to a relic would only give it meaning. Sam reasoned the Directorate decided to let the Leo Spencers of the world die a natural death. Again, a major flaw with the Directorate. Never underestimate your enemies—even one old man. And the Spencers fought the Directorate in their own way. Flowers, outlawed literature, black market cigarettes, bootlegged liquor, and other sundry items that identified man as human could be had from the Spencer's. And Sam suspected Leo had more dangerous ways of getting even.

"Sam."

He turned. Standing in a doorway was Katie Spencer. Her dark, curly hair fell about her shoulders. Wearing a green pullover sweater with red trim and faded jeans, she stepped toward him, and he swallowed.

"Hey, Katie," was all he could manage. *Damn, she was even cuter than he remembered. Quick, say something witty.* "Good to see you." *That's witty? You imbecile...how freaking lame.*

"I think I'll help Granny," Leo said before disappearing into the kitchen.

"Glad you could make it for dinner." Katie stepped closer, pausing in front of him. "I'm going to have a cup of tea. Would you like a cup?"

He preferred a beer, but what the hell. "Sure," he said, looking her up and down. His six-foot frame towered over her. He never realized how small Katie was. In tennis shoes, she might have been scratching five-feet—maybe. And her perfume, or body lotion or whatever it was...he'd never smelled anything so divine. The fragrance made his racing heart thump even faster.

"Have a seat, and I'll be right back," she said.

Sam nodded, trying to look away. He caved and eyed her retreating figure. *She did justice to those jeans.*

Katie turned. "You and I have something important to discuss."

Oh crap! She saw me gawking! Or was I leering? You idiot! He chided himself as Katie walked away. Sam surveyed the room.

A decorated Christmas tree sat in a corner with a single present underneath. It was the first Christmas tree he could recall seeing up close. Not wanting to feel like a tourist, he decided he'd check it out later. His gaze continued around. One side of the room held a sofa with a coffee table in front. On the other side of the room were two stuffed chairs, side by side, separated by a large end table. *Umm...if I took the sofa, and she sat in a chair, that'll tell me all I need to know. Wait, stupid, if she took a chair, and I was on the couch, we'd have to shout to each other, unless I took a chair and she sat in the other—*

"Here we go," Katie said, carrying a tray with two cups and condiments. She headed for the sofa and set the tray down on the coffee table in front.

Sam eased to the sofa, unsure. He watched as she set two coasters on the table and placed two saucers with steaming cups on them.

Katie nodded to the couch. "Over here." She seated herself near the sofa's center.

He hesitated. *What the hell are you thinking, guy? Are you crazy! You're here for life-saving reasons. Not to hit up on—*

"I brought honey," Katie said, dipping a spoon into an open jar. "Do you like honey?"

"Very much so." Sam eased down a half-cushion away. "It's been years since I've tasted it, though. Do you know how hard it is to find a simple jar of honey?"

Katie stirred her tea, suppressing a smile. "You're forgetting who my grandparents are."

Sam smiled and stirred the tea bag around, feeling a little more comfortable now that she had made that momentous decision on seating arrangements. He glanced to her. "How long will you grace Perchance?"

"I have to be back at work on Monday."

Nodding, he reached for the spoon sticking up from the honey jar. Moving his cup to the jar, he pulled out a glob and let the sticky mass fall into his cup. If he were alone, he'd shove the spoon of honey into his mouth. Sam replaced the spoon in the jar and stirred his tea. He sensed a subtle tension building. If it wasn't broken...

He swallowed.

They spoke each other's names simultaneously.

Katie gazed at him. "I—you go first."

"No, ladies first."

"No," Katie said, holding up her cup, "I insist."

Several seconds ticked off. Sam picked at the teabag string.

"I want to apologize for the way we parted."

"Good. I'll let you," Katie said. Her brown eyes scrutinized him. She took a sip and replaced her cup. Her face lit up. "*I am happy that you're here, though.*"

Staring at the worn, carpeted floor, he blushed. *The way she looked at me...* "Thank you." He glanced to her. "And I'm glad I'm here, having tea with you." *If that's all you can say, you need to shut the hell up while you're still ahead.*

"You're from Virginia," she said.

"Huh?"

She scooted around, facing him. "You're from Virginia. I can tell by the accent."

"I was born in Virginia."

Katie gave him a strange look.

Sam continued stirring. "I wasn't aware I had an accent."

"You do. You try hiding it, but it comes through now and then."

Sam's brow wrinkled. "Why would I hide it?"

"You tell me." She took a sip, eyeing him over her cup. "Maybe an accent gives one a distinct place of belonging, and that distinctness goes against Directorate dogma. An accent makes one stand out, become an individual."

"Here we go again," Sam murmured.

"Don't take it wrong, Sam." Katie replaced her cup. "I love the smoothness of a Virginia accent. You need to let it flow."

"Why, Katie, whateva do you mean?" Sam shot back in an exaggerated Virginia drawl.

Both laughed, the ice breaking. Sam cast a quick glance at her, and Katie looked away shyly. He knew their world was about to implode, but at the moment, Katie Spencer was the center of his world. He blinked, as if coming out of a trance. "And I've never heard a New York accent like yours," he said.

She stirred her tea. "I was born in Binghamton, raised in Buffalo."

Sam tilted his cup. "I sense a story here."

"No big story. Mom and Dad met over in Charleston, where they married. Dad was a chemical engineer. Mom was a city librarian. After they got married, she didn't have to work. Dad was transferred to Pittsburgh, then to Binghamton where I came along, then on to Buffalo."

"Your parents still live in Buffalo?"

"No." Katie replaced her cup. A shadow moved over her face. "The flu pandemic took Dad back in thirty-three."

"I'm sorry."

She cocked her head. "I understand you lost your mother last month?"

Sam nodded.

"It's my turn to say 'I'm sorry.'"

"Thanks," Sam murmured. He fiddled with the little tag at the end of the teabag string. "Any siblings?"

"Mom remarried. I have a ten-year-old half-brother named James. Mom, James, and my stepfather, who's a pharmacist, live in Albany." She paused, eyeing him. "Granny told me you were adopted."

He was hoping Katie wouldn't ask about his family, but she had every right after he asked about hers. Sam reached for the teacup. "Yeah, I'm adopted. Dad died four years ago. Mom last month. I'm pretty much it." He sipped tea. An expectant silence hung over them. Katie picked at her sweater, as if waiting. She knew a commissar colonel had raised him, yet it didn't seem to faze her. He cleared his throat, deciding to steer the conversation in another direction. "I could have siblings, but I guess I'll never know."

She gave him that strange look again. "It must be hard not knowing...always wondering about who you *really* are...whose blood you really have?"

Sam sighed, focusing on a napkin in the tray. "My adoptive parents loved me, as much as any parent could love a child. I mean, my adoptive parents are the only parents I know, although..." Sam hesitated. "Although, I've been having strange dreams lately...dreams about my real parents. I sense love, tenderness." He glanced to Katie. "I remember this shadowy figure, a man, picking me up, carrying me on his shoulders. And I recall my real mother tucking me in at night, telling me bedtime stories." He paused. "Katie, it's like having two distinct childhood memories. I'm haunted."

"You were probably just at that age where memory was forming," Katie said. "How cruel. It would've been easier on you if you were younger, or even a few years older. Either you would have no memory or one you could comprehend."

"And put behind me," Sam said. "It's so freaking frustrating."

"Sam."

Reaching for his teacup, he halted. The way she said his name, the tone.

Katie squeezed her brow, eying him. "I'm not supposed to tell you this—Papa and Granny are going to do it later."

"You've already started...out with it."

She picked at a sofa cushion. "Papa and Granny knew your

real parents, your biological mother and father."

"What!" Sam came off the sofa. He stared at Katie, stunned. "These dreams are getting crueler."

"No, Sam, it's real." Katie looked up, eyes glistening. "Granny used to babysit you...change your diapers."

"I don't believe it!" Sam said, pacing the floor. Yet, it all made sense in a convoluted sort of way. No wonder the older couple was so eager to befriend him and treat him like a grandson. He'd always felt a strange connection to the Spencers. "They've known all this time and never said a word...why?"

"Maybe my grandparents wanted to see which way the wind was blowing," Katie said, "which way you were headed? You can understand that, can't you?"

Sam stepped around the coffee table and eased down next to her. "It's so unbelievable," he murmured. "Your grandparents knowing my real parents. If that's true..."

"It's true, Sam, it's true."

"Then I've got a thousand questions."

"Hope you're ready for the answers," Katie replied. "Sam, please don't tell them I told you. I've already said too much."

He eyed her. "How long have you known?"

"I just learned this morning." She twisted a paper napkin corner. "Granny and Papa were going to tell you about your real parents this evening, sorta like a Christmas present."

Quiet seconds passed as Sam played with a frayed jean cuff.

"Sam," Katie said, breaking the silence, "on another subject...do you still have the radio I gave you?"

He had wondered when she would get to that. "Yeah."

She dipped her tea bag and then set it in the saucer. "You've been listening to it, haven't you?"

Sam tilted his cup, eyeing her through rising steam. "Why?"

"Anyone who'd read biographies of George Washington, Abraham Lincoln, and John Wayne couldn't possibly accept Directorate ideology."

Sam grinned, nodding. "I didn't know you thought that highly of Washington and Lincoln to include them in the same sentence with John Wayne."

Katie chuckled. "Seriously, though, why would you keep something as dangerous a shortwave radio if you weren't listening to it?"

"Did I say I was listening to it?"

"Who are you trying to shit?"

Myself, maybe? Of course, when they came for him, he could explain that he was only using the radio to gather information on the enemy. The irony; that was *exactly* what he was doing. "Yeah," he said, toying with his cup, "I've heard a few broadcasts."

Katie leaned back. Her gaze never left him. "What do you think?"

"About...?"

"Let's not joust. Granny and Papa told me about what's going on here in Perchance. Sam, I think what you're doing with these kids is right on and gutsy. And your beliefs are held by many others whether you see it or not." She paused. "Those ideals of personal responsibility, freedom of speech, freedom of assembly, those rights given to us by God and written in the American Constitution—*our* Constitution—those natural human rights can't exist as long as the Directorate exists. The doctrine of free speech is catastrophic to the Party. They'll do anything to crush even whispers of insurrection. Their Sanctuary Facilities are only the beginning."

And there it was. Katie voiced what he already knew but was afraid to admit. Sam sipped tea, gazing over his cup to the young woman. Sighing, he replaced the cup. China clinked. He had just climbed off commitment's fence. "Those camps are to make sure that freedom's seeds are never sown. Katie, I'm not sure what to do. I'm only one man."

Katie leaned forward. "Join us, Sam." She touched his arm. "Join us!"

The eagerness in her eyes set him back, and the feeling of her fingers on his arm caused a shiver. "Us?"

"*The American Underground Movement,*" she whispered. Her brown eyes searched his blue ones.

Sam was laid bare. Katie was reading his freaking mind. "I...I—"

"Sam, you must!" Her hold on his arm tightened. "Think of the world your students are going to inherit?"

He'd been thinking a lot about his generation's legacy; it kept him awake nights. Now, a chance to do something, to act on his newfound ideals and back up his talk with action, well, that chance just fell into his lap. The Directorate would soon come for him. They had to. And then he would pray for death. If he didn't act now—

Sam hesitated, swallowing. "Katie, what can I do?"

She gave his arm a quick squeeze and smiled. "Sam, we're going to try to put our country back together, the way the Founding Fathers intended." Katie paused. "Call me a radical if you want, but be prepared for violence."

Sam studied her. Katie's seriousness jumped out, and yet

she held it in check, just another facet of an extremely complex woman. Complexity...passion...were the two intertwined? Feeling flushed, he coughed and looked away, forcing thoughts to the present. "It always comes down to violence," he said. "John Fitzgerald Kennedy once said, 'Those who make peaceful revolution impossible will make violent revolution inevitable.'"

"Bloodshed is inescapable, Sam. I wish it weren't so." Katie paused. "Can you picture the Directorate willingly giving up power and holding free elections? Because I can't."

"That will never happen," he admitted. "I hope we're making the right move, because there's no going back. We can't say, 'Oops, we're sorry, we didn't mean to assassinate a Directorate chairman.'"

Katie reached for her cup. "Just remember, Sam, we all have choices, and we all have consequences."

Leo came rushing in from the kitchen. "Mardoc Keptner up the street just called." He glanced to the couple. "He said there's a man in a gray cart parked behind the Dumpster at the end of the block, and he's trained binoculars on this house. He thinks it's an OIS agent."

"Oh, no," Sam breathed. The Office of Internal Security was the Directorate's version of the FBI, Gestapo, and KGB all rolled into one. Once you've been arrested by the OIS, you were never the same. That is, if you were ever seen again. "It's this," Sam said, shoving up a sleeve. A tiny scar glared just above his wrist. "I'm chipped. They're tracking me."

"Papa," Katie said, "it could be me they're after. I saw some suspicious men hanging around the studio yesterday. It could've been OIS. They know my engineer, and I have the goods on them."

"No, kids, I think I rank even higher," Leo said, drawing the drapes. "The government's been watching me off and on for decades. I'm in their training manuals."

"In the chapters on Dissidents?" Sam asked.

Leo nodded, winking.

The room grew even dimmer. The only light came from kerosene lamps in the kitchen. To Sam, the gloominess fit the moment. "Paranoia," he murmured. "To live someplace where there's no paranoia. What a dream."

Katie nodded in agreement and rose, stepping behind her grandfather. "See anything?"

Leo's fingers cracked the drapes. "Here comes that gray cart."

Sam darted to the two near the curtains. "Anything I can

do?"

"No," the old man said, eyeing the moving cart. "If they were going to hit us, they wouldn't warn us like this."

Sam peeked out a curtain.

"Get back!" Leo shouted.

Sam dropped back, glancing to an approaching Michelle.

"Leo!" she shouted. "Don't let whoever's out there see you!"

"There he goes," Leo murmured, ignoring her. "Just cruising on by, pretty as you please."

All three crowded behind Leo, sharing worried glances.

"Damn, he's slowing," Leo continued. He focused through a narrow curtain slit. "What? That son-of-a-bitch is scanning the plates of the carts in the driveway!" He released the curtain. "I'm going out there." He turned and headed for the door.

"No!" Katie and Michelle yelled in unison. They grabbed his arm, tugging him back.

"Sam, help us!" Katie shouted.

Sam stepped in front of the door, blocking Leo's path. The larger man drew up, eyeing him.

"He's driving away," Michelle said, peeking out.

Katie released her grandfather's arm. "Papa, sometimes I don't know whether you're brave or just plain stupid."

The old man gave all of them a hard look. "I'm not going down without a fight. And I'll take out as many of those squirrelly-ass bastards as I can before I go."

"Leo," Michelle said, stepping to him and gently patting his arm. "Watch your language. It's Christmas Day."

"Yeah, yeah..." he grumbled, glancing to Katie, who was lighting an oil lamp at the end of the coffee table. "Have you talked to him?"

"Yes," Katie replied, with her eyes on Sam. She blew out the match, tossed it in an ashtray, and returned to the couch. "Sam's with us."

Sam felt their scrutinizing gazes and knew that from this moment on, his life was interwoven with all in the room. Survival meant trust, unwavering trust. He wasn't sure what he had gotten himself into, but he did know that five minutes ago, he had become a different man.

"Sam," Katie said, breaking his thought. "Your tea's getting cold."

Confused, Sam returned to the sofa and took a seat next to her.

"That turkey's ready to come out," Michelle said, heading back to the kitchen.

Leo followed. Then he sidestepped to the coffee table, and glanced down at Sam. "When you get back home, you might want to pack a couple of 'ready bags.' Keep one on hand at the house and one in your cart, 'cause the day is surely coming when you'll have to bug-out and not look back."

"Yes, sir," Sam replied. He was perplexed; they all seemed so nonchalant about what just happened. Was this the other side of hell? Right now, the Spencers were the hunted, and *he* was now part of that group.

Leo held Sam's gaze. "Later, you, me, and Granny need to talk."

Sam nodded.

"Leo!" came a shout from the kitchen.

"Guess I've got a turkey to carve."

Katie faced Sam. "You asked what you could do?"

"Yeah," Sam said, sipping lukewarm tea, "they now know my cart is here, so I'm already guilty in the Directorate's mind. I might as well do something to earn that guilt."

"Good," she said, holding his gaze. "I need Directorate communication codes."

Sam choked. Tea dribbled down his chin and onto his sweatshirt. He hurriedly set down the teacup and reached for a napkin, but Katie came to his rescue. She began wiping his chin and shirtfront.

"I'm sorry," she said, as her fingers dabbed. "I didn't mean to..."

Sam reached for her hand. It was so soft. Her hand slowed. A slender finger intertwined with his, and he shivered. "Don't worry about it," he said, trying to act normal. "Did I get any on you?"

Her gaze met his. "No."

He tried breaking her gaze but was mesmerized by the brownness of her eyes and the life teeming therein. His heart seemed to stop. *You fool. You can't afford this!* Sam cleared his throat, looking away. "You want Directorate Com codes? Why?"

Smoothing her sweater, Katie glanced away. "Remember the camps I told you about?"

He nodded. "I heard about them from elsewhere, too." He related the shortwave messages and told her about his student, Mark Thurmont, having been held in a similar camp.

"That kid's not exaggerating, Sam." Katie fiddled with her teacup. "As you recall, I'm an assistant producer of the regional edition of the *Scope and Sequence News Hour*."

"And?"

"My engineer and I were called in and told to report on the camps but only for Directorate eyes. We were told it was our patriotic duty and a way to help improve camp conditions. Of course, the Directorate will doctor the footage for that inevitable day of accountability when history finally snares them." She hesitated. "What I saw were whole neighborhoods being rounded up. People from all ethnic groups were herded onto trains and buses and shipped away. I walked a camp..." Katie paused, shading her eyes. "I'll always carry those scenes of inhumanity, and I wasn't allowed to see, much less film, the worst—thank God. The Directorate added a new twist."

"Which is?"

"President Henshaw has ordered forced sterilization for both males and females." She paused, composing herself. "At fifteen, and if you're from a certain social class..."

"Can we say, 'homeless?'"

Katie nodded. "Sam, the government starts with fourteen-year-old girls, telling them they're only being x-rayed for their own health. Then, without the girls' or parents' knowledge, the monsters eradiate the girls' ovaries. A technician bragged about their efficiency. It's awful!"

"A bunch of sick bastards," Sam murmured. He knew the sterilization program was being considered, and it had repulsed him. He had no idea it had already been implemented. "I recently came across a Party memo that stated 'passive sterilization,' as they call it, is only another tool to 'reshape society for the betterment of all.'" He shook his head. "Just another form of subjugation, of total control."

Katie's chin tightened. "And just another form of terror. If we don't do something now, we're looking at our future."

Sam placed a hand on her shoulder. It was slender and fit nicely in his palm. "Do you have a copy of your camp visit?"

"Government officials confiscated our equipment before we left, and they made it clear what would happen if we blabbed." She paused. "I don't know why they didn't simply film it themselves?"

"'Plausible Deniability,'" Sam said. "In the Directorate's twisted way, they think that by bringing in the pseudo-autonomous press, they're showing their openness. They believe by allowing you to visit and video the camp, it gives their regime, and the camps, legitimacy."

Katie eyed him. "You're part of the Directorate. Do you think we really have a chance to change anything?"

Sam shrugged and remained silent. What could he say that

wasn't discouraging? "This 'American Underground Movement' must think of itself as the 'sleeping giant.'"

"So, you'll get me communications codes and passwords?"

"Katie, I'm on the bottom rung of a long ladder full of ass-kissers. I have very little in the way of codes or passwords. Most of what I have deals with the Education Ministry." He wrinkled a brow. "Why do you need Directorate codes?"

Katie rose and stepped around the end table. It was her turn to pace. Cradling an elbow, she tapped her shoulder. "What if I could get that video that was shot at the death camp to be broadcast at the exact same time nation-wide? Even the Western Alliance monitors our broadcasts."

Sam stepped toward her. "So, you do have a copy of your visit?"

"I risked pulling the flashdrive." She fluffed the hair around her neck. "I finally put these curly locks to good use."

Oh, how he wanted to run his fingers through that luxurious hair! He cleared his throat, collecting himself. Several seconds passed as he soaked in the crucial, dangerous step the woman across from him had taken to expose a corrupt regime. Could *he* do the same? His admiration for Katie Spencer increased tenfold. "If you had been caught with that flashdrive..."

She canted her head. "But you're going to make it worth that risk, right?"

"I can't promise anything."

Katie stepped closer, with her eyes on Sam. "All I need is a way to shut down or jam the Directorate's override signal. My engineer could write the book on hacking, and he's one of us." She paused. "There's one more thing."

"There's always 'one more thing.'"

"We got word from the Western Alliance that if we pull this off, they'll help out."

"What?"

"You know those Persian ships that are allegedly just off the coast?"

"Yeah. And 'allegedly' is the correct word, right?"

"Oh, there are ships out there, all right," Katie said. "But they're not Persian. They're *American.*"

Sam stared. "You're shitting me."

"They've already sent in Navy SEALs and Green Berets to work with Movement organizers," Katie said. "They're just waiting for a word, a sign that we're still alive inside," she tapped his chest, "that we're still *American,* and that we'll stand up to the Directorate."

Sam blinked, stunned. "Unbelievable," he said, shaking his head. "Is this going to be a full-scale invasion or a diversion?"

"I don't know." Katie shrugged. "I pray it's an invasion. The People's Army will be concentrated in coastal cities. If the Americans invade, the East Coast will carry the brunt of the fighting, leaving *us* to control the rural regions. If the citizens see that the Movement can hold its own, the citizens will risk backing us."

"We'll control the countryside," Sam said, "and the people's hearts. It'll become guerrilla warfare, the last thing the Directorate wants. They know the rural areas are already seething with discontent. All this area needs is a spark."

Katie eased closer. "We'll give them that spark."

"What you're planning..." Sam murmured while gazing past her to the American flag hanging above the fireplace. "If you're successful, all of us will be on the run. If we live that long."

"I know." Concern shadowed her brow. "We'll truly be 'underground,' living the life of partisan fighters."

Sam nodded silently, hoping his courage could match Katie's. "I'll do what I can. When do you plan on doing this?"

"In a week or two, after I receive those codes." She stepped even closer. "You'll have plenty of warning, don't worry."

"It's not myself I'm concerned about."

Katie reached out, touched his sweatshirt. "Sam..."

He stopped her hand, and her slender fingers curled around his.

"Okay, you two," Michelle shouted from the small dining room, "dinner's ready!"

Sam didn't remember much about the meal except that he had never tasted turkey so tender. His adoptive parents had never celebrated Christmas. In his family, Christmas was just another day. What he did recall about the meal, and with great vividness, was Katie seated across from him. He never knew a woman who could smile with her eyes, and it scared the hell out of him.

After the meal, Granny and Katie cleared the table. Leo headed for the living room, with a hurricane lamp in hand. Sam stood near the kitchen table. "Can I help?"

"No," Michelle said, holding stacked plates. "Go visit with Leo. Katie and I will be out there shortly."

"Sam," Leo said from the doorway, "come on out here."

Sam followed the man. There was something eating at the old guy. Was it about the couple knowing his biological parents and not telling him? Undoubtedly, but Sam sensed there was more. Hell, Leo's wife was dying, how was the guy supposed to act? Sam felt for two money envelopes stashed in his back pockets; he also had something to discuss with Leo.

"Have a seat," Leo said, nodding to the sofa.

Leo set the oil lamp on an end table and settled into a nearby padded chair. Their shadows played large in surrounding murkiness. He glanced to Leo lounging in his home and wondered if he would ever reach Leo's age and do the same.

The old mechanic rolled up flannel shirt sleeves, reached into a chest pocket, and worked out a half-smoked cigar. He shoved the stogie into his mouth, thumbed a propane lighter, and took a long puff. Thick smoke curled around the man's bearded face, and he sighed.

Sam cringed inside as he breathed in cigar smoke. Those patriots before him wouldn't have given the smoke a second thought.

"The ol' lady and I will be celebrating our fiftieth wedding anniversary come March," Leo said through a cloud of smoke.

"Congratulations," Sam replied. "I hope I get an invite to the celebration."

Settling deeper into the chair, Leo groaned. "Consider yourself invited...if you're still here."

Sam ignored the remark. Sitting cross-legged, he examined a shoelace.

"I met Michelle while I was stationed in the Philippines, back in nineteen-ninety-eight," Leo began.

"Was she in the military?" Sam asked.

"No, no, not her," he said, chuckling. "She was the stuck-up daughter of a North Carolina preacher."

"What was she doing in the Philippines?"

"Aw, she'd just graduated from college," Leo said. "Had her head full of all this idealistic bullshit." He glanced to Sam. "She was a Baptist missionary who was going to save the locals."

"Most Filipinos were Catholic, weren't they?"

"Yep," Leo said, nodding. "Chelle never does things the boring, easy way, though. No, sir, she never does. She headed to the southern islands, down in Muslim country...gonna show 'em Jesus."

"Not a wise move."

"You know what she did?"

"What'd she do?"

"That girl went and got herself kidnapped."

"You're kidding."

"Nope. And they were gonna chop off her head."

"What happened?"

Leo took another puff. Smoke swirled. "That's when I got involved. They sent a squad of us jarheads into the jungle to get those damn missionaries out. There was a lot of shootin', but we came out on the winning end."

"It's not every day you meet your future bride in the middle of a firefight."

"Yep," Leo said. "Rescued three girls and one guy who couldn't find his ass with a road map." He paused, nodding, remembering. "She was skinny, had torn clothes, and wore one of those headscarves...Chelle was all raggedy-looking, but it didn't matter to me none. To me, it was love at first sight. Here it was, pourin' down rain, me charging in, holding an M-16 on her, and her standing there shivering." He glanced to Sam. "I knew right then and there I was gonna marry that girl."

"Good thing she said 'yes.'"

"Took me two friggin' years of camping out on her porch for her to say 'yes.'"

He flicked an ash into a large, nearby ashtray. "And we never looked back."

"Unbelievable, sometimes, how people meet...and their fate."

"Things were different back then," Leo said. He took a slow draw. The cigar tip turned a bright red. "Back then, folks had enough time to kinda get to know one another. Not like now. Right now, you blink, and someone's gone, poof, disappeared."

Sam glanced to him, silent. He felt the man scrutinizing him. His bright blue eyes missed nothing. It was as if Leo were reading his thoughts.

The old man took another draw, letting his vignette soak in. He squinted through the smoke to Sam. "Chelle and I see the way you and Katie look at each other." He paused, chuckling. "The ol' lady told me about that day back in November when she introduced you to Katie girl. She said you shied up like one of those teenage boys you teach. Yes, sir, she said you were speechless. And she'd never known you to be lacking for words."

Sam looked around, trying to find a place to hide. "I, uh, I'd be lying if I told you I wasn't attracted to Katie."

Leo wasn't finished. "You know what Chelle told me?"

"Guess I'm going to find out."

"She said, 'Leo, that boy looked at Katie the same way you looked at me that rainy night in the jungle.'"

Sam sighed. He dearly wanted to ask of Katie's expression but didn't want to ruin the fantasy.

"I asked her, 'What kinda look did Katie have?'"

Oh, shit. Sam swallowed. "I really don't want to know."

Leo flicked an ash and laughed. "Chelle said that when Katie saw you, 'that gal's face just lit up like the Fourth of July'...if you know what that is."

"You've got to be kidding."

"Son, you have a lot to learn about women, and you're running out of time."

Sam blinked, wondering how he missed that and wondered what else he had missed.

The room brightened as Michelle ambled toward them holding another kerosene lamp. Katie followed behind. "You bending Sam's ears with your war stories again?" Michelle said, placing the lamp on an end table across the room. She stepped to the other padded chair next to Leo while Katie took a seat on the sofa next to Sam.

Leo reached over and patted Michelle on the knee. "I only told him about the one that matters."

She playfully slapped his arm. "You're one crazy old man."

"Tell me, Granny, how you really feel," he said, chuckling.

Sam glanced at Katie, who smiled at her grandparents. It was obvious that age and sickness had not lessened the couple's love for one another.

"I think it's time, Papa," Michelle said.

"I was thinking the same thing," Leo said, rising.

"I'll get it," Katie said, standing up.

"Thank you, little darlin," Leo said. "But I think I'm the one that needs to give it to him."

Sam glanced to both. What the hell?

Katie eased back next to Sam. Was she sitting closer than before? Her scent filled his nostrils. Most definitely closer.

Leo worked over to the Christmas tree sitting forlornly in a dim corner. He reached down, and with a groan, came back carrying the single gift. Halting in front of the coffee table, he handed the gift to Sam. "This is for you, Sam. Merry Christmas."

Sam rose, reaching for it. "What is this?"

"Duh, it's a Christmas present, silly." Katie said, grinning.

"It's from Chelle and me," Leo said. He headed back to his seat.

"Sam," Michelle said, "it's something we should have given you a long time ago." She paused. "It rightfully belongs to you. We've only been its caretakers."

"Thank you," Sam said, glancing to the older couple, "thank you. Sorry, I didn't bring anything." Oh, but he did. He just couldn't let them know yet. He eased back down, examining the outside of the present. The wrapping paper was covered with the Star of Bethlehem and Christian Crosses. To Sam, it felt like a book of some kind. Bless them. They knew his love for books.

"Well, aren't you going to open it?" Katie asked.

He nodded, pensively tearing at wrapping paper.

Katie slapped his arm. "Slowpoke!"

He tore a little faster, exposing a book corner. His heart thumped, wondering what piece of forbidden text they had acquired. One final rip, and the wrapper fell free. The cover was blue felt, and the pages were heavy cardboard. He paused, feeling all eyes on him. Sam swallowed, staring at what was in his hand. It wasn't a book at all.

It was a photo album.

"You can stop wondering about your 'real' family," Michelle said, dabbing an eye. "They're right inside."

He held up the album. "How...how did you come by...by..."

"It's a long story," Michelle said.

Katie's arm encircled Sam's, and she gazed at him. "If you'd rather not open it here, we understand."

"No," Sam replied, looking first to Katie then to the elderly couple sitting across from him, "I want to share this moment with all of you. You guys are the only family I have. You're my guidebook to another world."

The old couple smiled and hurried to the couch. Another lamp was placed on the coffee table, lighting up that part of the room. Katie gently shoved out the coffee table and sat down on it, facing Sam. She looked eagerly at him as Leo and Michelle surrounded Sam on the couch.

"I know you'll want to look at some of this alone," Michelle said, "so we'll just hit the high spots."

Sam blinked, incredulous. Shadows danced eerily on the wall as those that cared surrounded him. A strange warmth, one he'd never known, blanketed him, and he swallowed hard. He glanced first to Michelle then to Leo. "I want to know who you guys *really* are?"

"Sam," Leo began, "your daddy's name was Jacob Wainright. He was a United States Marine Captain. He and I were stationed up the coast in Camp Lejeune when the war broke out. Your daddy was my commanding officer."

"We all lived on the base together," Michelle added. "I knew Molly—that's your mother—before you were born. I used to babysit you," Michelle grabbed Sam's arm, laughing. "I even changed your diapers."

Sam glanced to Katie. She winked subtly.

"Here," Michelle said, flipping over the front cover, "let's take a look."

Sam glanced down. Goose bumps rose. He was staring at a family portrait. A man Sam's age, wearing Marine dress blues, sat in a chair. Next to him was a pretty woman with long, dark hair. She wore a white dress and white heels. Seated in her lap was a child of, perhaps, two. The little boy had dark hair and large eyes. Sam's breath left him. He'd never seen any photos of himself as a toddler.

"That's Captain Wainright," Leo said, tapping the plastic-encased photo. "That's your daddy, son." His finger moved to the woman. "Molly, your momma," his finger dropped to the boy, "and there you are."

Katie moved in closer, examining the portrait. Then she looked up, scrutinizing Sam. "You favor your mother."

"Yeah, he does," Michelle said, "but he's got his daddy's blue eyes."

"And his temperament," Leo growled good-naturedly. "Sam, I swear I've never met anyone so hard-headed as your father until I met his kid."

"Then," Sam murmured, hesitating, "then I was an only

child?"

Michelle and Leo exchanged glances, and Leo nodded. The older woman gently held Sam's hand. "Your momma was up in Jacksonville when that damn People's Army rolled in. She was six-months pregnant with a little girl when...when..." Michelle's chin quivered, and she fell silent.

"Sam," Leo said, "you have to understand. It was a time of hellish chaos, war. Millions simply disappeared...presumed dead. If it hadn't been for your adoptive mother, Elizabeth Moore, we would never had known what happened to your real mother."

Michelle rested frail fingers on his arm. "We thank the Good Lord every day that young people have little or no memory of the Takeover. Those were the days of horror. The first thing that happened was the wealthy had their property seized and 'redistributed.' If you complained, you were summarily executed. Then the Directorate came after what was left of the middle class. You were lucky to be saved. War orphans were everywhere. Some say there were maybe a half-million. The kids wandered the streets, some lived under bridges, stealing food, eating dead animals, or just starving. It was appalling."

"What finally happened to them...the kids?" Sam asked.

Leo glanced first to his granddaughter then to Sam. "The Directorate gathered them up and placed them in special 'kid camps.' The new government fed and clothed them but never allowed them access to the outside world. Those children never learned love, compassion. Those orphans who survived became nothing but human misery machines groomed as tools of terror and used against those who were brave enough to stand up."

"Perfect Party loyalists," Sam said. "Little Hitlers, Stalins, Pol Pots..."

"You got it," Leo said, nodding. "Those orphans, now adults, are the ones running these death-camps."

Sam sighed in disgust. "Sounds like the Bolsheviks during the Russian Civil War."

All grew quiet.

Sam focused on the oil lamp's flickering flame. "I remember mostly just shadowy figures, like a nightmare that you can't recall but you're still shaking from. I do remember the tanks rolling in and the machinegun fire...my mother falling down." He whispered as if to himself. "The screams, and then this woman grabbing me, saving me." He deliberately left out seeing the pools of blood.

Katie stared silently at Sam.

Michelle touched his arm. "Elizabeth was a good woman.

She loved you as her own son."

Sam noticed nothing was said about his adoptive father, and he knew why. The moment needn't be spoiled. But, what of his real father? He blinked, afraid to know more, but he had to ask. "And Jacob, my father?"

The older couple again exchanged glances. Leo reached over and flipped to the back of the album.

Wedged inside the plastic-covered page was a set of bent dog tags. Sam traced the lettering. His finger moved around the dog tags' rubber edges. He flipped back a page, and two sealed envelopes were stuffed into the page. Though faded, he could still make out the writing in the dim light of oil lamps. One envelope was addressed to *Molly Wainright*, the second to *Samuel Wainright*. He would read them in private, with a stiff whiskey on the side.

"Sam," Leo said, "your father was killed trying to hold a Shenandoah River crossing." Leo glanced to his wife, shaking his head. "Chelle, I've always dreaded this moment."

"I know, and it's okay." She nodded. Seconds passed. "Sam."

He looked up.

"Leo was with your daddy when he was killed."

"We lost a lot of Marines that day," Leo began, "including your father. He gave his life while saving not only other Marines but dozens of civilians. He died a hero."

Sam flipped back to the album front. He mechanically turned the page, too overwhelmed to think straight. He glanced down, doing a double-take, and his breath left him. "I remember when this picture was taken." It was a photo of a man in camouflage holding a small child on his shoulders. The man's camouflage cap hung like a lampshade over the little boy's head, almost hiding his face. Both father and son grinned widely.

Katie twisted her head, examining the photo. "You're so cute!"

Sam flushed. He paused, glancing to all the smiling, eager faces around him. The people in the photo album weren't his only family. Sighing, he closed the album. "I've seen enough to keep me awake for a month."

Leo rose and sauntered back toward his chair, but Michelle remained seated next to Sam. Katie eased to the floor, kicked off tennis shoes, and sat cross-legged at Sam's feet. Quiet seconds ticked off. Sam was still unnerved at discovering his *other* family. He worked a finger over the soft album cover. Then he set it on the coffee table. "Thank you," he said. "I don't know what to say, except, why are you just now giving me this?" He glanced first to Michelle then to Leo. "And how did you guys come by the pictures?"

Michelle glanced to her husband. "You want to tell him, Papa?"

Leo nodded. "His best friend, Captain Charles, found 'em while going through his gear. You know that formal portrait in the front of you with your mother and father?"

Sam nodded. "Yeah, and?"

"Your father kept that picture on him at all times. I'm the one that found that photo. I kept it, hoping to give it to your momma—or you."

Sam glanced down, unfocused, feeling Katie's soft touch on his wrist. The kerosene lamps flickered. Light and shadow fused, surrealistic. "How did you guys end up with all the other photos?"

"Captain Charles was killed two weeks after your daddy, before he could send your daddy's things back home." Leo paused, glancing into space. "Funny thing was, we *were* home."

No one said a word. Sam glanced to Katie. There was a strange resolve in her eyes, as if she were saying, *now you know why we must do what we must do.*

"Anyway," the old man continued, "I ended up with your father's belongings, what little there was. With your momma gone, and most of Camp Lejeune with her, Granny and I stored his things. We hoped one day his son would come sniffin' around, and by some miracle, here you are."

Sam nodded, hesitating. "Where's my father buried?"

Leo's jaw tightened. "It was kinda like the First Civil War. We buried them close to where they fell. Your father's remains, along with several other Marines, are buried on a high bluff overlooking the Shenandoah River. We tried to go back for them after the war, but the place is off limits." Leo snorted, leaning back in the chair. "Hell, we can't even leave the county now without some damn traveling papers, which one never gets."

"Do you know where my mother, Molly, is buried?" It was bizarre to have two sets of parents.

"It's your turn, Granny," Leo said.

Michelle gave Sam a sympathetic glance. "We're not sure. There were mass graves dug just outside of Wilmington."

"And the Appalachians are full of graves," Leo added.

"There are mass graves outside all major cities east of the Mississippi River," Michelle said. "And they're all off limits."

"I know," Sam said. He paused, feeling as though his brain was about to explode. "I've been here for three years, and neither of you ever spoke a word. Why?"

"Elizabeth made us promise not to say anything until she was gone," Michelle said. "If she knew that you knew, it would've broken her heart."

Sam glanced to the older couple. "How did Elizabeth learn you two knew my real parents?"

Michelle eyed Sam. "You know the clout your adoptive father had. They knew who you were, who your mother and father were. And after Frank died, Elizabeth only wanted you to be happy." Michelle stared at the carpet and spoke as if to herself, "I think Elizabeth wanted to make amends in her own way...a way of saying I'm sorry for everything that happened." Michelle gazed at Sam. "She moved here to Perchance and looked Leo and me up. You know the rest."

"Finally, it makes sense why she moved to Perchance. You two were here, and she knew that with her being in poor health, I'd follow her and meet you guys."

The older couple nodded.

Katie, who had remained mostly silent, spoke up. "The day of reckoning for those who dug those mass graves is almost upon them." Her eyes met Sam's. "Our generation will be the one that sets things right."

Sam shivered inside from her gaze, her words. Katie had an uncanny sense of history.

"Katie girl," Leo said, "in a couple of weeks, there are a few families from around here who are heading to Texas. It'd suit your granny and me just fine if you and Sam would go with them."

Sam eyed the old man. "How do you know about the 'heading to Texas?'"

"Not much goes on around here that I don't know about," Leo said, puffing his cigar. "Where do you think they got their fuel?"

Michelle rejoined her husband in the chairs across the living room. After seating herself, she glanced to the young couple across from her. "Papa's right. As much as we love you two, we'd give you up knowing you were living free."

Sitting on the floor, Katie glanced to her grandparents. "I can't speak for Sam, but *I can't* leave the *NAC*—at least not yet."

Michelle gave an annoyed sigh. "Katie, honey, listen to me and Papa."

"I have unfinished business here," Katie said. "You know about the camps. They have to be exposed for what they are."

"Let someone else do it," Michelle said.

Sam eyed Michelle. "We are the 'someone else.'"

The older couple grew silent. Michelle fidgeted with worry, yet Leo gave a subtle, approving nod. He ran gnarled fingers through the gray hair on his temples. "I always knew it would come to this...the grandchildren..." His words held sorrow. "I was hoping our kids' generation would've put a stop to this insanity. But with the war, the flu epidemic, and then so many of them hightailing it across the river, that generation lacked the numbers. Hate to say it, but some even lacked the will. Just go along to get along, let their children—my grandchildren—deal with it."

"Granny, Papa," Katie began, "Sam and I have a plan."

Michelle held up a hand. "We don't want to know."

"She means," Leo said, "we don't need to know the details."

Sam glanced to the older couple. "The details, well, we're not sure about ourselves. But, Leo, you said that there are others who are willing to shake things up?"

The older man nodded, and his brow raised in curiosity.

"Then they need to be ready," Katie said.

"Ready?" Leo asked.

Sam and Katie glanced to one another. Sam cleared his throat. "You said you didn't need to know details."

Leo nodded in resignation. "Okay, what the hell are you two planning?"

Katie highlighted her plan.

Michelle shook her head, and Leo tapped the chair arm.

"When that broadcast hits the airwaves," Sam said, "there's going to be rioting in the streets."

"And bloodshed," Michelle murmured.

"We have to make sure it's not our blood that's shed," Sam replied. "Leo, that's where you come in."

"You want me to organize a protest?"

"No, I want you to organize an army."

"You're crazy," Leo snorted. "The American Underground Movement is just that—a movement, not an army. Oh, we can do a little sabotage now and then, but, but," he sputtered, "we can't come close to standing up to the People's Army. We'll be crushed."

Katie explained about U.S. Special Forces working with the underground and U.S. warships plying East Coast waters, preparing for a possible invasion.

"Knew about the Special Forces," Leo said. He eyed his granddaughter who sat innocently on the floor. "Didn't know about our Navy out there." He rubbed whiskers. "This might change things." He glanced to his wife, who shook her head, rolling her eyes. "Chelle, we've been waiting for this for over twenty-five years."

"I don't know, Leo," Michelle murmured. "We're getting too old for this."

Sam got to his feet. "I've got to go."

Katie lifted a hand, and Sam pulled her up next to him. She straightened her sweater. "You can't stay any longer?"

Was it his imagination, or did he detect disappointment? *Wishful thinking.* "I need to catch *Radio Free America* tonight. It's my duty, for all of us."

"I understand," Katie said. Her chin tightened, and she tugged on her shoes.

His heart raced; the disappointment was genuine.

"Keep that radio safe," Leo said. "Our lives may depend on it."

Sam nodded, reached for the photo album on the coffee table, and headed for the door.

Katie was right behind. "I'll walk you out."

"I'd like that." *Hell yes, I'd like that!*

"Come here, Sam," Michelle said, stepping toward him, with Leo at her side. She moved up and squeezed his neck. "We so enjoyed this evening. You need to come by more often."

"We'll be seeing more of him," Leo said, hinting a smile, "a lot more."

Sam returned the hug. God, she is skin and bones. He remembered the envelopes in his back pockets. Openly giving the money to them was out of the question; the old couple was too proud. And, even in private, Sam knew Leo would vehemently refuse the money. What to do? A plan in mind, he released Michelle.

Leo thrust out a scarred hand. "Take care, son. We'll be in touch."

The two shook hands. "This was the best evening of my life." And Sam meant it. He held up the photo album. "Thank you two so much. I can hardly wait to pick your brains about, about..."

Leo winked. "I look forward to that talk over a few beers. One thing your daddy could do was really put the beer away."

"Leo!" Michelle cried.

The old man shrugged, chuckling. "Man, do I ever have some stories."

Sam smiled, gave the couple one final nod, and headed out the door, with a silent Katie at his side. A chill hit him, and he shivered.

"Merry Christmas, and goodnight!" both shouted, waving.

"Goodnight," Sam said, "Merry Christmas, and thanks again."

Album under his arm, Sam slowly walked to his cart, feeling Katie's closeness. *Should I? Should I? They were almost to his cart. It was now or never. What the hell*—he reached for her hand. Katie's slender fingers closed around his, squeezing tightly.

"I haven't enjoyed myself or worried myself sick this much since I don't know when," Katie said. She paused, gazing at him. "Sam, I'm honored that you would allow me to sit in on something so private as discovering your biological parents."

Sam drew up next to her. Geesus, she was so tiny, and yet, he'd never met such a dynamo of life. "I'm glad you were here, Katie, and that I could share something personal with someone I care about." *Shit—there I go again! I'm as subtle as a freight train.*

She grinned, and he melted. Heart in his throat, he swallowed, forcing calm, and stepped toward his cart. They walked the rest of the way in silence, hand-in-hand.

The carts loomed up in still darkness. With no electricity in town, the blackness closed in, but it was soft and comforting. Sam stepped up next to his cart, set the photo album on a fender, and released Katie's hand. She slid into his arms, molding against him. Her scent enveloped him, forever seared into his synapses. The woman who held so much strength now felt so vulnerable. She quivered against him, and he cradled her.

Sam ran fingers through her silky, curly hair. "Katie—"

"Shh," she whispered against his chest, "just hold me."

Butterflies rose as Sam felt the beat of Katie's heart against his. Absorbing her heat and passion, he leaned down.

Katie gently pushed away. "Sam, we're moving too quickly."

Sam stared at the broken sidewalk, thankful the darkness hid what he knew was his crimson face. "Yeah, you're probably right." *I just blew it...what an amateur.* Embarrassing seconds passed, and he glanced up. "Can you come over tomorrow?"

"I don't think that would be wise."

She just rejected me. No way will she be alone with me at my home. Man, I'm such a moron!

"Besides," Katie continued, "I promised the grandparents I'd attend worship services over at the Hampton's tomorrow morning. Then I'm leaving for Charleston afterwards."

Sam nodded, silent.

"Why don't you come with us tomorrow? Church services are at the home of one of your students...Regan, I think is her name. You'd fit right in."

"Thanks, but no thanks." Quiet seconds passed. He knew she wasn't finished.

"Sam..." Katie said, hesitating.

Here comes the coup-de-tat. Well, it serves my ass right.

She stepped closer, brushing her fingers against his. "I'm sorry."

He shrugged, cursing himself for assuming she felt the same as he did. Would he *ever* get it right when it came to women? He felt the gentle squeeze of Katie's fingers on his own. *What the...?*

She gazed up at him. "Sam, pushing away is my instinct when I...when I get close to someone...when I care for someone."

Sam stared. "Katie..."

She released his hand and touched a finger to his lips. "Let me finish. One way or another, our world's flying apart. In the end, I...I want to be with someone who cares."

"Just another loved one to lose."

She ignored the comment. "Will you look for me? Because I'll look for you."

"You will?"

"Yes."

"Be on the run together?"

"Yes."

"Katie..."

"In the end, all we will have is each other."

Outwardly, Sam remained stoic. Inside, an avalanche of craving, doubt, and confusion cascaded from his soul. "If you pull it off, you get away fast. I'll find you, I promise."

Katie reached for his hand again. "Promise?"

"Promise." Her face was silhouetted in darkness, but Sam swore her eyes glistened. Withdrawing his hand, he worked out an envelope full of cash from each back pocket and handed both to her. "Give these to your grandfather."

Katie reached for the folded paper. One envelope was open, and she lifted the flap. "What is this?" she murmured. Her voice trailed off. She glanced up. "Oh, my God, Sam, what is this!"

"Tell Leo it's to help treat Granny."

Katie waved her arms. "He won't take this money."

"You tell Papa to take another look at his bride, and then get back to me."

Katie circled, staring in disbelief at the envelopes. "How did you...?"

"Don't ask." Sam pushed a button on the cart's side, and the driver's gull wing door lifted. Grabbing the photo album from the fender, he paused by the open cart door.

She bolted to him and wrapped her arms around him. "Granny was right about you. Sam, you *are* a good *man*."

He crushed her lithe form to him. "Don't know about the 'good,' baby, but I do know I am a lucky man...a damn lucky man to have met you."

He released her, and she stepped back, dabbing an eye. "I'll call after services tomorrow," she said, "before I leave for Charleston."

Sam nodded and climbed in behind the wheel. "I'll never forget tonight, Katie."

"Do you remember your promise?"

"Yeah."

"I'm holding you to it, mister."

Sam grinned. "I know."

"Goodnight, Sam" She held up the envelopes. "May God bless you."

What God? Sam turned a key, and the electric motor hummed to life. "Goodnight, Katie." He punched a button, the door lowered, and he backed out. Katie stood in the dark driveway, waving. He shoved the gearstick into forward, waved back, and sped away.

An hour after Sam left, Katie said goodnight to her grandparent's and retired to the guest room. Now she stood in front of a dresser, tapping the stacks of $100 bills, each stack holding $1,000. "Eighteen, nineteen, twenty," she counted out loud, touching the last stack. "Whew...unbelievable..." She shook her head in both alarm and awe. How in the world did Sam come by this amount of cash—and in U.S. currency? He certainly didn't earn it on a pitiful teaching salary. Yet, Sam's Directorate membership did come with more pay and certain perks. Should she be concerned? Katie recalled Sam's background. Granny told her that his late adoptive father, once a Directorate Commissar Colonel, had advanced into the upper echelons of the Party. So, Sam was raised in wealth, and knowing the Directorate as she did, some, if not most of that wealth, was probably ill-gotten. *Sam probably inherited the cash.* Katie shook her head, reached for the money stacks, and stuffed them back in the envelopes. It didn't matter. What did matter was that it was definitely going for her grandmother's treatment.

Envelopes in hand, she stepped to her backpack on the bed. Tomorrow she'd find a way to slip the money to her grandfather. And if Papa argued, well, as Sam said, all he had to do was look at Granny.

Katie paused and touched her lips. Sam—the way she fit into his arms... For the first time in her life she glowed inside. The feeling was foreign to her, yet exhilarating, and she smiled. Suddenly her smile disappeared.

"No," she said, "not yet. I can't get sidetracked. We still have work to do." She unsnapped a flap and shoved the thick envelopes into a side pocket. From another side pocket, she retrieved an old vidphone. The GPS card had long since been removed, and the old vid could no longer communicate or be tracked, or even detected. As a matter of fact, it now served only one purpose...

Katie dug out her keychain from a jean pocket and sat on the edge of the bed, with the old vidphone in her hand. She set the vid on the bed, flipped over the key fob in her other hand, mashed a small compartment, and a tiny door popped open. She turned the fob upside down and a fingernail-sized, wafer-

104

thin silver disk fell into her palm. It was a copy of the flash drive she had removed, scanned, and carefully replaced back in the government video camera provided that day she and her engineer were allowed to visit a Directorate relocation camp. Of course, they had to leave the camera. Her engineer, also a patriot, had kept their guide distracted while she discreetly copied the entire visit from the government camera.

Katie reached for the vidphone, tapped the scan button, and moved it over the tiny disk in her palm. She quickly but gently replaced the flash drive in her fob, lest she lose it. Turning to the vid, she hesitated. This was Christmas night, a holy night, and she didn't want to ruin it. She paused. *Ruin it? How dare I be so condescending!* Katie's chin tightened, and she tapped the small screen.

The screen filled with the images of half-starved people dressed in rags, warming themselves over sooty burn-barrels. Their ages were hard to tell, but their lost dignity was clear. The image sucked one in, because one knew this was your horror, too. The ghost-like images moved silently here and there in the dim light, like forgotten wraiths in a sea of savagery. Their eyes were hollow sockets long stripped of humanity's light. An infant's ceaseless wail echoed, and there was a constant murmur, a mournful whisper that seemed to come from all around. *What you're witnessing,* came Katie's voice from the vidphone, *is Dante's Seventh Level of Hell. This is a Directorate "relocation camp." This is where the poor, the elderly, and the destitute breathe their final, painful breath.* Katie held the phone in her hand. Her gaze focused on the screen, knowing but still dreading what followed. The scene switched to a medical room. People of all ages lay in stretchers dozens deep. They appeared anesthetized. Around their necks hung large ID cards. A medical attendant using a laser scalpel carved ID numbers into bare, protruding forearms. *It is here,* Katie's tiny voice narrated, *where innocent people are permanently tagged just as cattle at an auction. And we all know what eventually happens to that cattle.*

The picture went black.

"Now the coup de grace," she murmured.

A ghastly image filled the screen. It was a pit filled with bodies twisted together. Katie winced, recalling the sight and stench. The camera panned the pit's edge, catching a bulldozer shoving dirt over the slaughter. The time and date at the bottom read 1423 10 June 2049. *This is not Auschwitz from one hundred years ago,* came her voice from the phone. *What you see was taken last summer. This mass grave is located outside of Blue Ridge, Virginia, twenty miles north of Roanoke.*

The horrific scene faded to black Waving stars and stripes filled the screen. *Arise, Americans!* a male voice boomed out. *Arise! Arise! You Americans held hostage by the Directorate— today freedom is upon you! Today is the day you cast off your chains and take back your country!*

Katie tapped the lower left corner of the screen, and it went black. With Sam's help, along with the Underground and one of her TV engineers, she hoped to hijack a satellite link and get this video broadcast coast-to-coast in a few weeks. She placed the phone next to her on the bed, paused, and prayed silently. After a moment, Katie covered her face.

For the first time, she noticed her hands shaking.

Sam stood in front of the classroom, pointing to the essay prompt written in black dry-erase marker on the whiteboard: *In the North American Commonwealth, compliance leads to harmony.* "In a two-page essay," he said, "explain what that statement means to you." Written in green was another prompt: ***"If there's a worse place than Hell, I'm in it." Abraham Lincoln, 1861.***

A few groans were followed by several chuckles as students read the second prompt.

"Mr. Moore, which one do we write about?" a boy in the third row asked.

The student behind him kicked his desk and shot him a mean look.

"There's only one sentence on the board," Regan Hampton said casually.

Sam cleared his throat, forced a straight face, and strolled down an aisle. Glancing down to students' papers, he smiled inside: *Lack of free speech is worse than hell... Living in the Commonwealth is worse than Hell... Worse than Hell is having a teacher like you.* He halted, glancing to the student who wrote the latter. The sentence belonged to Cory Jeffery. Sam had not seen nor heard from the kid's uncle, Caleb, since that morning in Michelle's store, back in November. Cory wasn't boisterous like his loser uncle but quiet, more introverted. Academically, the kid was average. Yet, even though his family had been in the county forever, the boy just didn't seem to fit. He came up through the grades with most of the other students in the high school but still had few friends. He wasn't a "bad" kid, per se, but Sam sensed some kind of internal defect. Being a Jeffery, that wasn't surprising. Maybe the other kids sensed it, too. Last week, Terri hinted that someone is waiting for an opening to nail Mark Thurmont as a traitor. He recalled the cafeteria scene earlier that day and the Jeffery boy sitting nearby, taking it all in.

Cory looked up, with a strange defiance in his eyes.

Sam tapped the paper. "Great thesis statement, Cory. Please continue. I look forward to reading your essay." Sam wasn't mad or hurt. But he did wonder why the normally passive boy was now trying to goad him. If Sam showed anger, the kid would win. Having elephant hide was a necessity for teaching high school. Hands behind his back, Sam wandered away, feeling the kid's eyes on him. He found himself standing over a flower bouquet in the corner, admiring white chrysanthemums. White mums symbolized truth. Their purity radiated throughout the classroom, countering the lies, the evil, outside classroom walls.

Sam had another epiphany: he would miss teaching. He'd miss the kids, this fourth period class for sure. To these young adults, he was a rare drop of sanity in a sea of lunacy. They needed him as much as he needed them. Very soon, he'd be forced to abandon both.

Day after tomorrow was Friday and the end of the nine-weeks. The kids would be released for the weekend. Four would not return. The act of *moving* without authorization is a felony. If caught, all would face stiff punishment, and the kids could forget college; they'd be blacklisted. Those families weren't moving, they were fleeing, in which case they would be considered traitors to the state and shot on sight. Sam forced his thoughts elsewhere, sauntered to a window, and gazed out to a chilly, rainy afternoon. A charcoal sky loosened a soft but steady drizzle. Sam wished he were out there, with his arms outstretched as the light rain washed away past sins.

He glanced back. Pens were moving, and the students were diligently writing. He turned back to the window, thinking of Katie. Last Friday, he sent her the Directorate communication codes and a way to retrieve Directorate passwords. All was sent through antique email, which, these days, was seldom monitored. She acknowledged receipt through a text. By the time the Directorate, in its bureaucrat morass, discovered who did what, well, there may be no Directorate by then. Either way, Sam knew he'd be long gone.

Knock, knock, knock.

Startled from his thoughts, Sam turned. Pens stopped, the whole class stared at the door. No one knocked anymore; they just barged in. He hurried to the door and pulled it open. It was Ms. Hagler, a teacher's aide.

The young woman stepped inside. "Mr. Moore, Mr. Tipton wants to see you," she said. "I'm here to watch your class."

"Oh, no," Sam heard Regan whisper to a nearby Jason Myers. "What do you think it is?"

The boy swallowed, eyeing her nervously. "Start praying."

Sam turned to the class. "Keep writing. I'll be right back." He paused just inside the door. "Make sure the board is cleaned if I don't get back before class is over." Several students jumped up, and Sam shook his head, eyes narrowing. All but Mark Thurmont returned to their seats. The blond-haired boy from Texas made his way up front, grabbed an eraser, and went to work. Sam caught his eye and winked. The boy gave a subtle nod, erasing everything in wide sweeps.

Sam glanced to the aide. She was standing in the corner, admiring the mums. He didn't know if she would report the flowers or not, nor did he care. Sam was sure the flowers were the least of his worries. He stepped into the hall, and the door automatically closed behind him. Why didn't they just call him on the phone? That gave him pause. The commissar had been back a week-and-half and hadn't yet stuck his freaking pointy nose into local faculty affairs. There was some behind-the-scenes shit happening that Sam couldn't put a finger on but knew was out there. Were *they* onto the Underground in Perchance? Sam made his way down the hall. One ugly scenario after another played in his mind, and he grew more nervous with each step. So damn much could go wrong the next week or so. Reaching the bottom of the stairs, he turned left, heading to the main offices. He made another left into a narrow hall, passing Terri's office. Her door was closed. Sam swallowed. Five steps and he turned right and halted. He stared at the nameplate on the closed door.

North American Commonwealth Office of Commissar Jonathan Tipton Colonel 10th District

Sam swallowed again, composed himself, and then he reached up and knocked.

"Enter," came the squeaky voice from the other side.

Twisting the knob, Sam pushed and stepped inside Tipton's office. Familiar wall monitors greeted him. Terri Woodriff sat in front of the commissar's teakwood desk. Next to her was an empty chair. "You asked to see me, sir?"

The older man eyed Sam over wire-rim glasses before pointing to the empty wooden chair. Terri glanced up, with a blank expression on her face.

Sam made his way over and eased into the chair.

Tipton glanced to a small video monitor on his desk, and then he turned those dead-fish eyes on Sam. "It recently came to my attention that four of your students are planning a little vacation—as in a permanent one."

Sitting upright, Sam cleared his throat. "No disrespect, Mr. Tipton, but my students also have three other teachers."

"The students I'm referring to consider *you* a friend," Tipton said.

"I told him about our conversation last week, Mr. Moore," Terri said, "and my concern for some 'certain students.'"

Tipton quickly held up a hand to the principal. "Thank you, Ms. Woodriff, but I'll handle this."

Oh, shit! How much did Terri spill to the bastard? He felt her shift uncomfortably in her chair. Surely, she wouldn't have sold him out...

"Mr. Moore."

"Sir."

"I understand Mark Thurmont is one of the students in question."

Sam nodded.

"Thurmont has made it no secret that he wishes to return to Texas.'" Tipton's narrow face twisted as he sneered the last word. "Could he have convinced others to attempt something so foolish as to desert a nation which has given them so much?"

You've got to be shitting me! "No one would be that foolish, Mr. Tipton," Sam said. "Most of the students believe the Thurmont boy is a nut job."

"That 'nut job' seems to have made a multitude of friends." The commissar paused, straightening a stack of papers on his desk. "Mr. Moore, do you recall our last conversation about the boy?"

"Yes, sir."

"Have you detected any kind of rebellious attitude in the young man?"

"No more than what's normal for a seventeen-year-old kid."

Tipton glanced to the principal. "How about you, Ms. Woodriff? Have you seen anything unusual in the boy's demeanor, or perhaps, a difference in his interaction with his peers?"

"No, Mr. Tipton," Terri replied, "I haven't seen anything unusual in his behavior. If anything, I believe the Thurmont boy has accepted his life here and looks forward to becoming a citizen in this great nation."

Sam rolled his eyes and immediately regretted it.

Tipton caught Sam's reaction. "What was that all about?"

"What was what about, sir?"

The commissar stared coldly at Sam. "Ms. Woodriff," he said, though his eyes never left Sam, "you may leave. I need to visit with Mr. Moore a while longer."

The principal rose, pushed back the chair, and smoothed a khaki skirt.

The commissar's glassy eyes returned to Terri, who stood

in front of his desk. "Cancel weekend leave for all the students in question."

"But, Mr. Tipton," Terri protested, "the parents will lodge a formal complaint."

The commissar waved a hand. "Let them complain, for all the good it will do."

Sam knew that to the Commissar, losing a student, much less four, was like a warden having a prison break. Runaways would reflect on his record, especially at promotion time.

"But..." Terri sputtered.

"Are you questioning my authority?"

Her shoulders sagged. "No, sir, never. I was only thinking as a parent."

Tipton shoved up his glasses with a forefinger. "Your parental concern is noted, Ms. Woodriff. You may leave now."

Terri turned, shooting Sam a quick glance. She stepped behind his chair and left the room. To Sam, it seemed she was looking at one condemned. The door clicked ominously, and he swallowed, eyeing a seam on the carpeted floor.

"Mr. Moore, do you like being a Directorate member? It is a privilege, you know?"

He looked up, caught off-guard at the question. *Oh, how I would love to tell the truth.* "Yes, sir. I consider it an honor to be a member of such a patriotic party."

The commissar opened a top drawer and pulled out a remote. "I'm glad you said that, because I'm sure you have an explanation for this." He swiveled around, aiming the remote to a monitor. The corridor scene disappeared, and there was his classroom. He was standing in front, giving a lecture. Tipton turned back to Sam. Overhead lights reflected off the commissar's thick glasses, giving him an even more pallid look. He wore a sick grin. "Here comes the good part. Shall I turn up the volume?"

Sam's stomach knotted.

...the Constitution of the North American Commonwealth is not just deeply flawed, but fundamentally flawed...

Sam forced down vomit.

...and anyone who would honestly consider defending such a document is not only amoral, but also depraved...

The commissar watched the video, thoroughly enjoying Sam's situation. "'Depraved,'" he said, chuckling. "I'll say, you do have a way with words, Mr. Moore."

Sam looked away. His gaze landed everywhere but on the video. He knew it word for word, as he had said those things last week while Tipton was gone. Sam had figured that by the time the asshole saw it, if ever, he would be long gone.

The commissar clicked off the monitor and faced Sam. The silence was sickening and a favorite weapon of Tipton's. With his elbows resting on his desk, the older man clasped his hands and stared hard at Sam. "I'm waiting."

He must think clearly. Lives—including his—depended on it. "I was only paraphrasing what I came across in a Directorate bulletin about what the western provinces were saying about the NAC."

"Do you recall the bulletin number?"

"No, sir."

Tipton unclasped his hands, reaching for a pen. "I would've remembered *that* bulletin." He began clicking the pen. "Even if there were such a bulletin, pray tell, why would you repeat confidential information in a public classroom? Those students are very impressionable. They might go home and give their parents ideas. Besides, you know Directorate communiqué are for our eyes only."

Sam shifted in the chair. "These are seniors I deal with, soon to be citizens. I think they need to know the lies and propaganda the other side is spreading about our great land."

The commissar flew out of his chair, aiming an accusing finger at Sam. "You, sir, are a liar!"

Sam swallowed. "I'm not lying," he said calmly, "I read it in a Party bulletin." He wanted to break off the bastard's finger and force-feed it to him. Instead, he deliberately hung his head, hoping his sheepish act was convincing. "Mr. Tipton, I may be guilty of poor judgment, but that's all." He looked up. "I'm completely loyal to the Directorate."

Tipton stepped from around his desk, arms folded, and paced the floor. "You know I can have you arrested?"

Sam eyed the chubby, little man. He hated Tipton. "I wasn't aware I did anything that serious."

The commissar paused, pointing over his shoulder to the blank monitor. "If I were on a Party review board, I'd say the man in that video committed treason."

Sam stared, blinking innocently.

"You know what's done to traitors?"

"They're executed."

Tipton's pudgy face screwed itself up into a sadistic grin. "That's right. And ex-Directorate members are not just hung. They're strung up and slowly strangled."

Sam shivered inside. He'd been forced to watch a video of a

Directorate execution as part of his indoctrination. The scene of a kicking man, dangling from a gallows, pissing and shitting all over himself, had haunted him for weeks.

Tipton's demeanor changed. He calmly brushed a sleeve of his dark-blue dress shirt and straightened his tie. "Of course, this video doesn't have to leave this room."

Oh shit. Here it comes.

The commissar slowly moved behind Sam. "I know you know the Spencers. You bring their contraband flowers to school all the time."

Sam jerked around. "Sir?" Forget the flowers. He was alarmed at the Spencers being brought into such a lethal conversation.

Tipton let out a nauseating laugh. "Oh, you didn't think I knew about them, did you? The flowers? Or the Spencers? You have flowers in your room right now, even after you were warned not to bring that degenerative contraband to this place of learning."

To hell with you, you weasely bastard. "Yes, sir, I am guilty about the flowers."

Tipton marched back to his desk and eased into the padded chair behind it. He leaned back. "Mr. Moore, Leonard Spencer is a known dissident. You were seen with him. Several times, I may add."

Sam wanted to march over to Tipton and vomit in his face. He'd never hated a person so much in his life. "I've done business with the Spencers," Sam replied casually. "Most of the town has. Mr. Tipton, Leonard Spencer owns one of the few garages in town, and his wife, a dry-goods store. Spencer replaced my cart's battery pack back in November." Sam shrugged. "We're casual acquaintances, no more."

Tipton nodded, pursing his lips. He leaned forward, examining an official-looking document. "On December twenty-fifth, you spent the afternoon and most of the evening at his personal residence." Tipton eyed Sam. "'Casual acquaintances?' Ha! While you were there, I'm sure you celebrated 'Christmas' with them." Tipton sneered at the word *Christmas*.

"I was invited over for a home-cooked meal." Sam forced a smile. "I get tired of my own cooking."

The commissar removed his glasses, reached for a tissue, and began rubbing the lens. "Just 'casual acquaintances,' huh?"

Sam glanced to Tipton. The man's eyes were mean gray spheres, void of compassion. "Like I said, I hardly know Mr. Spencer." He almost slipped, about to call him *Leo*.

"Was there anyone else in his house other than his wife?"

Oh, God. He'd been fearing this question. If he lied and was caught, the whole gig was up. He sensed there was a way out of this entire predicament, and it all hinged on what he said now. If he said Katie wasn't there, and they had a photo of the two outside... It was obvious the commissar had her cart's license number. Sam wasn't sure how to pray, but now, he gave it his best shot. *Oh, Dear God, please.* He cleared his throat. "The Spencers had a granddaughter visiting, and yes, Mr. Tipton, you were right, they were celebrating Christmas." Sam must call the commissar's hand. "The granddaughter wasn't there when I was there. I believe they said she was visiting a close friend."

"A Christian family not being together on one of their most treasured holidays? I find that strange, don't you?"

"Well, sir, I couldn't comment on that. I know very little about Christmas or Christians."

"I see," Tipton murmured. Holding his glasses, he picked up the document. His index finger skirted the page.

Sam swallowed, continuing to pray. If the commissar had a hand, he'd play it now.

Tipton dropped the paper and shoved on his glasses. "Mr. Moore, I'm giving you another chance to prove your loyalty to the Party."

Inside, Sam breathed a sigh of relief. *Thank you, Lord.*

"I want you to get yourself invited back over within the next two weeks."

Sam's brow wrinkled. "Sir?"

"Did you bring them a Christmas gift?"

Sam thought of the money. It wasn't a Christmas gift. "No. No, sir. I don't believe in that stuff."

"Well, you had a change of heart. You feel guilty, Mr. Moore, for not giving them a present. So guilty, in fact, that you decided to buy a gift, and you're going to give it to them within the next two weeks."

Sam's heart stopped. *No way.*

Tipton's lips curled in what passed for a smile. "Those old houses are always having gas leaks, and well..."

"Mr. Tipton, please don't ask me to do this. The Spencer's trust me."

"Exactly." He glanced over his glasses. "Remember, Party loyalty?"

Sam gazed at him. "But..."

"Now, Mr. Moore, it would be a shame if that video we just watched found its way out of this room." His lips twisted back, and he gave an irritating click. "We'd hate to lose such a dedicated teacher, but we'd get over it. We always get over it. Life must go on, you know."

Sam visibly shook, as hatred and loathing gripped him. For the first time in his life, Sam wanted to kill another human being. The revulsion was so strong, he was sure it would keep him awake at night until he killed Tipton. He didn't just want Tipton dead. Sam wanted to run a dagger into the commissar's heart at midnight. Unlike Dostoevsky's Raskolnikov in *Crime and Punishment*, remorse would be a no-show. Indeed, he would throw a wild party after Tipton's death. Sam glanced in scorn and disgust to the evil across from him.

The commissar must've mistaken Sam's gaze for fear, as he forced a soothing voice. "It will be okay, my boy. You won't be nearby or even implicated. And maybe, maybe your gift will get you back into Party good graces."

The teacher regained control, and a strange coldness enveloped him.

"Welcome to the Directorate, Mr. Moore."

Sam stared at the commissar. "Why?"

"It's not your place to ask 'why.' But..." Tipton glanced to his nails. "Spencer's a dinosaur, an anachronism from another era. We once saw him as only an irritant, but now something has come to light." He paused then continued. "We suspect he's supplying weapons to terrorists. To admit there were terrorists among us, in our peaceful realm, well...you understand."

Sam's heart raced. Yet outwardly, he remained poised. "Why not just arrest him?"

Tipton looked up. "Mr. Moore, I'm surprised *you* would ask that? He'd be a martyr, of course. And then again, there's that publicity... However, now that I have *you*, arresting him won't be necessary." He paused. "This will enhance both our careers, don't you think?"

Sam's jaw tightened. He stared, unfocused.

"We'll work out the details in the coming days."

Sam nodded, numb. Of course, he wouldn't do it. Hopefully, Katie's mass-murder documentary would've hit the airwaves by then. And he'd be gone within a couple of weeks, one way or another. Sam's departure would most definitely serve Tipton; if he stayed, he'd put a bullet in the commissar's brain.

"That will be all, Mr. Moore. You may leave."

Sam moved slowly, feeling as if he were in a nightmare.

"Leave the door open on your way out."

Try as he may to hurry, Sam's feet were lead blocks. "Yes, sir."

"Oh, and Mr. Moore?"

Sam mechanically turned.

Tipton focused on a desktop video monitor. "You may keep the flowers. I don't understand their significance, nor do I care to." He glanced over his glasses to the teacher. "In a couple of weeks, whatever you see in them will soon be forgotten."

Sam wanted to lunge across the desk and strangle Tipton until his lifeless face turned purple. The Commissar stood for the hollow, the trite, and a lie Moore despised. Instead, he swallowed his anger and trudged from the room. The offices were empty. Apparently, the bell had long since rung, ending the school day. To reduce distractions, bells were kept off in the offices. He almost collided with Terri hurrying out of her office. A long coat hung from her shoulders, and she carried an umbrella.

"Sam," she whispered, "I'm sorry."

Glancing back to the commissar's open door, he gave her a questioning shrug.

"Cory Jeffery was in Tipton's office this morning," she whispered.

He nodded dumbly. At least a shred of what just passed now made sense.

"Sam, I tried."

"I know," he whispered, squeezing her shoulder.

"I've got to go."

Sam stepped past her into the dimly lit, deserted hall.

A dreary, wet mid-January afternoon, and an electric car worked through town, with ZZ behind the wheel. "What's wrong with you, man? You've hardly said a word since we left school."

Gazing straight ahead, Sam blinked, torn from his thoughts. "Can you get the wife to bring home a scalpel by tomorrow?"

ZZ swung the wheel, and the cart made a left at a green light. "A scalpel? Sam, what in blazes do you need a scalpel for?"

"Because I don't have anything at home sharp enough to do a quick job on myself."

ZZ's eyes widened, and he struggled to keep the cart in its lane. "Sam, buddy, I don't know what's going on, but it can't be bad enough to take your life!"

Sam chuckled and held up a forearm. "The transponder. It's coming out."

"What the...? You can't do that."

"Yes, I can. The freaking transponder is coming out."

ZZ gave an exasperated sigh. "You're a member of the Directorate. It's against the law to remove the chip. A felony. You want to commit a damn felony?"

Glancing to the chemistry teacher, Sam lowered his arm. "Unless you want to hear my real answer, ask someone who gives a shit."

"Sammy, what's gotten into you?" ZZ asked, gesturing. "You haven't been yourself since your mother died."

"It started long before then. I just didn't recognize it until now."

"I don't know, Sam. I just don't know."

"Call Haleana, ZZ. Ask her to bring a scalpel home tonight or tomorrow."

"You're really serious?"

"Yep."

"Do you want to talk about it?"

"Nope."

The two rode in silence. Within minutes, the cart approached the Windward Community guardhouse. Seconds later, with the guardhouse behind them, the cart hummed down a narrow avenue, heading for ZZ's duplex.

Sam stared out a side window to the bleak, drizzly landscape.

He was supposed to move back to the Community in two weeks, yet he knew that would never happen. The coldness that seized him in the commissar's office had now evolved into reckless, steel resolve. A train called Fate was blowing down the tracks, and he couldn't stop it—as if he wanted to.

The cart idled into a driveway, halting next to Sam's cart. Sam punched a fob button on a keychain, climbed out, and tossed a backpack into his cart's now open driver's door.

ZZ scrambled out from behind the wheel. He stood, staring around the open gull-wing door to his friend. "Sam, I'll call Haleana, ask her about a scalpel, okay?"

Facing ZZ, Sam leaned on his raised cart door. "Thanks."

"But one thing. You gotta talk to me, man...say something."

"ZZ, you need to find another cart-pool partner."

The older man slowly stepped from around his cart. "Geesus, Sammy..."

Sam ducked under his cart's gull-wing door and climbed in behind the wheel. He looked at the approaching teacher. "Next week is my week to drive," Sam said. "Plan on taking your cart the latter half of the week. Sorry, but if things go as planned, I'll be gone."

"As in leaving?"

"Yeah."

ZZ halted by Sam's open door, concern shadowing his brow. "What's going on, Sam?"

"You'll find out soon enough." Sam turned the key, and the cart hummed to life. "For now, ZZ, the less you know, the better." He paused. "Let me know about the scalpel."

"Sure."

Sam nodded, pushed a button, and the door lowered, clicking shut. He backed out, leaving the stunned chemistry teacher standing in the driveway.

* * *

The next evening, Thursday, Sam sat in a chair behind his home computer. A program on upcoming water rationing droned on in the background. He rolled up his left arm sleeve, scrutinizing the butterfly tape. ZZ's wife, Haleana, not only brought home a scalpel, but also performed the illegal, minor surgery in the couple's kitchen. Due to a nationwide shortage of medicines, he had to forgo the anesthesia. However, before he could even think about the pain, Haleana, a skilled RN, made a flick of her wrist, and using a tiny pair of tweezers, plucked out the device. In less than a minute, she had the incision cleaned, taped, and ZZ, Haleana, and Sam were felons.

Tilting a beer bottle, he examined the red and white label—*Budweiser*. When he got home this evening, two cases of beer—one Budweiser, one Coors—were on the front porch. It had been years since Sam had seen those brands. Like everything else reminding people of the old days, the brands were banned. Leave it to Leo to give an appropriate "thank you." He took another swallow, relishing the brew, and held up what looked like a chrome sliver between thumb and forefinger. Hardly larger than a rice grain, the innocent-looking device was the epitome of technology's sinister use. Not only could it track you anywhere on the globe by satellite, but the transponder also allowed real-time body temperature, blood pressure, and heart rate to be monitored; a de facto lie detector. Tipton had a bio-monitor in his office, but it was out of service thanks to a software parts shortage.

Sam titled the bottle. Come to think of it, there seemed to be an epidemic of software parts shortages…shortages of everything, for that matter. The United States Western Alliance's recent blockade was part of it. The NAC was heavily import dependent. New, updated computer software from India and China had slowed to a trickle. American factories were shuttered decades ago, with labor being outsourced. Even before the breakup, America had written its own epitaph. Not only had it outsourced its industrial base—to nations that would do her harm—it had also out-sourced its culture to those very regimes who would wipe their shitty boots on America's face if given the chance.

He gently placed the transponder on the desk and rose. It haunted him that his students, and their families, were forced to remain in hell, this place with no future, because of a single bureaucrat…a single, freaking bureaucrat. Those kids trusted him. He had to do something. Sam paced the floor. If he ever took up smoking, now would be the time. He took another swallow of beer, mulling over a thought. All the software shortages and system failures… Hell, the metal detectors at the school's entrances hadn't worked all year. A video in Tipton's office showed a lit corridor when in fact, the corridor was pitch black most of the time because of bulb shortages. He knew about the camera failures in the dorms, and it went on and on… And of course, human failures were a given.

Come on, moron, think of something. He slammed the empty beer bottle onto the desk, chiding himself. That well of ideas, of schemes was going dry. He sighed, rolled down flannel sleeves, and stepped out the back door. Dead potted plants crowded one side of the cement patio, just where his mother had left them.

His adoptive mother had loved those plants. It was a disgrace to her memory to allow the poor things to be seen in that condition. Once lush and green, the ferns, peace lilies, dracaenas, a ficus, and other plants he couldn't identify, were now brown and shriveled from winter's frozen breath. He should've brought them inside with the first freeze last November. Yeah, well, he should've done a lot of things, but didn't.

He eased down the three steps and gazed up; a glowing swath of the Milky Way streaked a moonless sky. The stars were the only constant in life. The air was chilly but not cold. All was dark and eerily quiet...the calm before the storm. Then he heard it. The unmistakable hum of a cart. It was coming from in front of the house. He sprinted around the side, crouched, and peeked around shrubbery to the road in front.

A cart with its lights out idled slowly by and then parked on the shoulder, maybe twenty yards past his house. So, he was being watched.

Sam plopped down on damp grass and made himself comfortable, eyeing the cart's silhouette just beyond his property. He lived on thirty acres out in the country, and nowadays, there was little traffic on the country lane out front. After what he guessed may have been twenty minutes or so, he began to shiver as the night air took its toll. Crickets began their nightly serenade. Not a sound came from the cart. The more time that passed, the more pissed he got, not that it did any good. He didn't have Leo's guts to confront whoever was in the cart. To hell with it. This was his home. The intimidation factor sucked. At least he'd let them know he wasn't scared and that he saw them. Sam rose, brushed grass from jeans, and stepped into the front yard. Instead of heading to the front door, he stepped in the direction of the strange cart out in the road. Sam had full intentions of stopping in the middle of the yard, when the cart started up and drove away.

He dashed after it, pumping a fist. "That's right! Run you chicken-shit bastards!" Shaking, he halted, adrenaline pounding. *What if someone had climbed from the cart and confronted me? What then, huh?*

"You, stupid..." Sam murmured, cursing himself for such a foolish act. If this was what he expected from himself, those four kids at school, not to mention Katie, were in big trouble.

Stepping into the house, Sam began packing a spare backpack, taking Leo's advice about preparing for the worst.

Beep-beep-beep. Beep-beep-beep.

He had a text. Sam darted from the bedroom and into the

living room and stopped in front of the computer. It was from Katie. His eyes followed the words as they scrolled from bottom to top:

*Sunday evening. **Will have unexpected help. Listen to my gift to you on Saturday. If it's a definite go, do not forget the scrapbook. Do not forget the scrapbook...Do not forget the scrapbook.***

And do not forget your promise. CU soon.

The message ended. Sam stared at the blank screen, heart racing, part from fear, part from excitement. So, Sunday evening was when the Directorate's jackboot would be wrested from society's neck. Thankfully, it wasn't Friday. Yes, the distraction would've helped him free the kids from the school, but security forces would be swarming over the roads, making it almost impossible to travel.

Now that he had a timetable, a plan materialized, and it was so easy. As a Directorate member, Sam was authorized to sign out the kids, and that's exactly what he would do. He'd drive up, sign them out, and drop them off at that barn where their trucks were located. But what if he was followed?

Sam again paced the floor. It didn't matter. Those children must be reunited with their families regardless of what may happen. He reached for the vidphone. Leo knew those families; he could contact them, let them know what was going down. He paused. What if his calls were monitored? Screw it. He better get used to taking chances. Sam mashed a button on the tiny communicator in his palm and headed for his bedroom.

Standing over the nightstand, he yanked on the drawer and worked out his commissar father's favorite weapon: a 1911 .45 Colt Commander. Sam hadn't shot the old-style automatic since he was a teenager. He twisted the pistol from side to side. The weapon looked wicked, intimidating. He was an excellent shot and had been told he was a natural, but he hadn't practiced in years; he didn't believe in guns. As a matter of fact, he hated guns. Besides, firearms had been outlawed for decades, except for law enforcement, the military, and Directorate members. He was scheduled to take his first firearms class in March and didn't relish the idea. Yet, Sam could've taught the instructor. He chuckled, ejected the full magazine, and worked the action. The pistol's balance was superb. It was like riding a bicycle; you never forget.

Friday, 1: 49 P.M. Beginning of fourth period.

"**M**r. Moore, sir, you gotta do something," Mark Thurmont pleaded, standing just inside the door.

Regan Hampton stepped next to Sam, dodging students entering the classroom. "Mr. Moore," she whispered, chin quivering, "they can't do this to us!"

Sam pulled both students away from the door as more teenagers poured in. "Listen, guys," Sam murmured, "I'll get you four out, don't worry. Have *one* bag packed." He moved closer to the door and away from the camera. "I'll be at the dorm at six this evening to pick you up, take you out to those trucks. Be ready to go, understand?"

"But what if they won't let us out?" Mark said.

"Oh, they'll let you out." Sam patted the boy's shoulder. "They won't have a choice."

Jason Myers and Phillip Benivades shuffled past, both eyeing the teacher, worry shadowing their young faces. Sam glanced to them, giving a reassuring nod. He turned back to the two teenagers in front of him. "Pass the word to the other two, understand?"

Both nodded.

"They're going to watch me hard this period," Sam continued. "I can't be seen casually talking to you four." He glanced first to one then the other. "Six O'clock—be ready."

"Okay."

"We will."

They didn't sound encouraged. Sam entered the classroom. Mark and Regan followed behind.

The ninety-minute class dragged, seeming to last forever. Sam wasn't the only one watching the clock. Glancing out the window, he noticed carts lining up outside the dorms, waiting to take away the children, parents knowing they had only two days to de-program young minds.

The bell rang. Sam swallowed, a lump rising. This would be the last time he'd stand in this classroom...see these kids. He wanted so much to say goodbye but dared not. He wretched inside. Part of him was pouring out the classroom doors now.

Would they remember him, he wondered. Is that the best we could hope for...to be remembered?

There was crying in the hall. Apparently, others knew the four wouldn't be back. A girl wailed, and Sam fought with himself not to go out there; he'd break down. A teenage boy's sobs drifted. The distressed voices soon faded down the corridor, a passing storm sweeping all before it, leaving nothing but tears and recollections in its wake.

Sam shrugged into a light coat, heaved a backpack over a shoulder, and stepped from his classroom for the last time. The classroom darkened, and the door closed behind him.

* * *

The only thing missing was the barbed wire, Sam mused, as he made his way up the cement walkway to a two-story, red brick building. The windows were barred, and an eight-foot-tall chain link fence surrounded the student dormitories. A small, treeless, cheerless courtyard separated the girls' and boys' dorms. He stepped through the open gate. The gate closed and locked at 6 p.m. every day, including weekends, except on *nine-week Fridays*, where it remained open until eight. He glanced around; the place appeared deserted, and only one dorm overseer should be present. Tall posts topped with cameras were everywhere. Half the cameras were dummies, another quarter were broken. He glanced back; his cart was the only vehicle parked in the circle drive in front.

The sun had fallen below the horizon. Her orange shafts highlighted in a cobalt winter sky. **Girls' Dormitory** in black, block letters hung over the double-door entrance. Underneath the dorm sign was the ever-present silver triangle—**Awareness, Compliance, Unity**. Sam pushed through, and another set of double doors greeted him. A list of visitor rules was posted on both doors. Prominent and in bold were the words, **Parent or Guardian must produce National Identification**. He snorted and shoved, stepping inside.

A middle-aged woman seated behind a counter looked up from a monitor. "Hello, Mr. Moore. We've been expecting you."

It was Ms. Devon, the bitch from the cafeteria. A man stepped from a dim corridor. Caleb Jeffery. He wore sweats. In his hand was an ampstick, which he slapped against the other hand. One touch from the stick, and a person was down and out. "Just have a seat, Moore," he said. "You're going nowhere until the commissar gets here."

The woman held a vidphone. She was calling Tipton. Why did the commissar need to be notified by phone? All he had to do was look out his office window to Sam's cart in front of the dorms. Jeffery pointed with the ampstick to several empty chairs against a wall. "I said, sit down!" He was two inches taller than Sam, and maybe twenty pounds heavier. "I hate teachers. You teachers think you're so privileged, living in your own, sheltered little world, looking down on us common folk like we're scum."

Sam sighed; time was wasting. "Caleb, not now. Just bring me Regan Hampton."

"I'm not one of your teenagers you can bully around. The girl ain't goin' nowhere and neither are you. So, how do you like that?" The big man pointed with the stick and spat in front of Sam. "I heard about the lies you're telling those kids in that classroom...that the NAC is worse than hell. Buddy, you don't know what hell is, but you're about to find out."

Sam rubbed his eyes. "I'm so freaking tired of useful idiots."

Jeffery took a threatening step. "I said, sit down!"

Sam whipped out a .45 from the small of his back.

Jeffery froze, staring down a cavernous barrel.

Sam waved the pistol at the woman behind the counter. "Toss me the vid."

Ms. Devon couldn't throw the device fast enough. It sailed over Sam's head and hit the tile, shattering into three separate pieces.

"That'll do," Sam said. "Now, grab the master key and get over here." His aim shifted back to Jeffery as the woman, key in hand, scrambled from around the counter.

A twisted grin spread across Jeffery's face. "You really think you can pull this off?"

"I'm giving it a helluva try." Sam gestured with the pistol to the two in front. "Let's get Ms. Hampton."

Ms. Devon nervously shuffled forward, but Jeffery hung back. "Moore, I don't think you've got the balls to pull that trigger." He stepped toward Sam.

Boom! The .45 jumped in Sam's hand. Rolling thunder reverberated. A spent casing sailed.

"You shot him!" Ms. Devon screamed.

Jeffery jerked back, slapping a hand to his right ear. Blood oozed between his fingers and trickled down his neck, coating his collar and spotting the floor. "I'm shot! The bastard shot me in the ear!"

"I was aiming for your forehead, moron." And he was. "The next one won't miss." Sam gestured to the dorms behind.

Jeffery dropped the ampstick and scrambled back toward the rooms, the woman behind him. He had both hands mashed against what was left of an ear. Blood dripped. Crimson spots splattered white tile. "I'm gonna bleed to death!"

Sam followed behind, with the pistol covering them. "Caleb, shut the hell up."

Within seconds they halted in front of a door at the end of the corridor. Keys jingled, and the door swung in. Regan sat on a bunk with her face buried in her hands. A backpack was propped against her.

The girl looked up and glimpsed Sam. "Mr. Moore, what was that noise? A gunshot?" She jumped up, frightened at the sight of a bloody Caleb Jeffery. "Is he going to die?"

Sam hustled the two adults into the dorm room. "Unfortunately, no. He's just nicked."

"You just gonna leave me?" Jeffery asked.

"Yep," Sam replied. He glanced to Regan. "Grab your backpack and let's go."

Regan yanked the rucksack from the bed, slung it over a shoulder, and hurried behind Sam. She nervously peeked around him to her former guards. The girl shot them the finger.

Jeffery, dripping blood, and Ms. Devon glared.

Ms. Devon pulled her gaze from the girl. "But you just can't leave him like this! The man needs medical attention."

"Then give him attention." Sam reached back, gently shoving the girl. "Let's go, Regan."

The girl disappeared out the door, and Sam backed out into the corridor. He pulled the door closed, locked it with a key and shoved the pistol into his waistband.

"You'll pay for this!" Jeffery screamed from the other side.

Regan and Sam, side by side, hustled down the dark hall.

"Mr. Moore, I can't believe you shot that man. I mean, not *you!*"

"Regan, you're going to see a lot of stuff that you can't believe."

"Have you gotten the boys yet?"

His jaw tightened. "No, but I'm about to. And if this is what I'm to expect..."

The two entered the lobby just as the double doors opposite them swung open. Sam reached for the pistol then stayed his hand. Three teenage boys wearing backpacks burst into the lobby, followed by a man rolling up a ski-cap. It was Leo Spencer. In his hand was a 12-gauge, pump shotgun.

"Got here as quick as I could," he said. Leo eyed the blood-spattered tile and the shattered vidphone and gave an approving nod.

"Are you okay, Mr. Moore?" Jason asked, stepping up. Jason, Mark, Regan, and Phillip gathered around their teacher, all exchanging nervous glances.

"Yeah. Let's get the hell outta here."

The kids rushed from the building, backpacks jostling, heading for two carts. Sam and Leo, the latter with ski-cap pulled back down, were right behind. Security lights peppered the darkening sky; their harshness enhanced the surreal episode. Sam paused and threw the dorm keys as far as he could. All six halted at the carts to unsling gear.

"Hey, that's my dad's cart!" Jason shouted.

"How about that," Leo said.

Sam shook his head. "Leo, if you hadn't come along..." Commonwealth carts were designed for two adults and two preteen children, not five adults with bulging gear.

"You would've been drawing straws for who gets the inside," Leo said, "and who gets the hood and roof."

Gull wing doors lifted on both vehicles, and they tossed in backpacks.

Sam eyed the old Marine. "Okay, Leo, it's your game."

Leo stood by his cart's open door. "We're heading straight to the rendezvous point. Their folks should be there by the time we arrive."

"Do you know how to get to my granny's farm?" Jason asked.

"Hell, boy, I used to date your granny."

All chuckled. Sam nodded, glad Leo was there. He needed to share the unspoken insanity with another adult. He and Leo must keep these kids believing in themselves, believing in the impossible. The adults knew they were already in an unmarked grave, but they couldn't let it show. And this was the easy part. Sam climbed in behind the wheel. Mark was already in the passenger seat, and Regan's slim form was scrunched between backpacks in the back.

"We have real cars in Texas," Mark said, glancing back to Regan. "Not these itty-bitty golf carts. You'll see."

"What's a 'golf' cart?" she asked.

Both carts pulled away from the curb, with Leo leading. Sam expected the commissar to come flying out of the school, arms waving, eyes bulging, or to see a police perimeter set up, but surprisingly, neither showed. Except for the electric motor's hum, all was quiet, and no one spoke. On *nine-week Fridays*, traffic was usually heavy, but only an occasional cart passed by. In the dim light, he spotted black smoke rising in the east from the direction of the Communities, blanketing a third of the sky. Sam swallowed, trying not to dwell on the smoke and its meaning; he focused on what lay ahead.

Forty minutes passed. They'd been out of town for quite awhile. Would the battery charge hold in the overloaded carts?

"Mr. Moore," Regan said, breaking the silence.

He glanced back. "Yes?"

"How can we ever thank you?"

Sam turned back to driving. "By holding on to your dreams, Regan."

"What are *you* going to do?"

"I'm not sure..."

"You can't go back to school."

"I know."

"And...and you couldn't even say goodbye. That must've hurt."

Steering the cart, Sam nodded, silent.

"Come with us."

"Regan, we've already had this discussion."

"But what you did today, even though it was right, is going to make them come after you."

"Yeah, but not only for today."

Quiet seconds passed. Sam felt warmth on the back of his neck, then dampness, as Regan lay her head against his shoulder. Mark sat upright, staring out a window, silent.

With the lights out to conserve juice and avoid detection, the carts' silhouettes slipped eerily through the South Carolina night. The countryside was haunted; Sam could feel it. Blood was spilled on this land; the soil absorbing the angst of American generations. As antiquity's saturation point neared, history slowly divulged its ghosts, and American phantoms now roamed her tidewaters, pine slashes, and hills, seeking not revenge but purpose. There could be no revenge without purpose.

Sam strained to see Leo's cart ahead. Brake lights flashed, and the cart turned a hard right. Sam swung the wheel, following. They bounced along a twisting, gravel road. A minute later, they made another right onto an asphalt driveway. A man cradling a rifle materialized out of darkness and trotted alongside Leo's cart.

"That's Phillip's father," Mark said.

A two-story house loomed up on the left. It was dark and lifeless. Seconds later, the carts halted outside a huge, old barn. A strange sound, like an idling dynamo, came from within. Sam was about to climb out when the barn door swung open and bright light streamed out. The man carrying the rifle signaled for the carts to enter. The carts moved forward, disappearing inside the barn, and the door quickly closed.

Sam's jaw dropped as he stopped the cart next to Leo's. Four beautifully restored pickup trucks sat idling. The behemoths—two Fords, a Chevrolet, and a Dodge—were four-door and dwarfed the electric cars. The trucks had to be at least twenty years old but looked as if they had just rolled off the showroom floor. The diesel engines clattered. People scrambled around, opening doors, while others inside the trucks quickly stored gear. It was organized chaos. Not a movement was wasted, though. Even young children labored at assigned tasks. It reminded Sam of videos he'd seen of a moon rocket launch pad moments before liftoff. And, in a way, it was.

Leo clambered from a cart as Sam stepped out from his. "Mom! Dad!" the teenagers shouted, pouring from the carts. Mothers and fathers grabbed their children, crushing them. Mark Thurmont hung back before following his classmates.

Within seconds the kids' parents mobbed Leo and Sam, and there was backslapping and handshaking. Shouts of "we owe you" and "we'll always be in your debt" were heard.

A clean-cut man in his forties worked through the crowd and thrust out a hand to Sam. "Casey Myers, Jason's father. You must be Sam Moore."

Sam shook his hand. "Yes, sir."

"What you did today was a brave thing, Mr. Moore. None of us will ever forget it."

Sam hooked a thumb to Leo. "I couldn't have pulled it off without him."

Myers nodded. "Leo, as usual, we owe you."

"I'll send you a bill."

Another man stepped up to Sam, with a woman at his side. "Mr. Moore, I'm Regan's stepfather, John Banner, and this is my wife, Regan's mother, Audra."

Sam shook Banner's hands. Then he extended his hand to Regan's mother, but she shoved it away and gave him a quick hug.

"Regan just told me what happened," she said, releasing him. "God bless you for bringing back my baby." She pushed blonde hair aside. "Regan thinks the world of you."

"As I do of her." Sam looked past the couple. Myers and another man were talking, both looking his way. Oh, no. Before he knew it, all the parents were in front of him.

Myers, the apparent leader, stepped up. "Mr. Moore, the kids told us how you and Leo rescued them." He paused, scrutinizing the teacher. "I'm not worried about Leo here, but you...you have to come with us."

Well, there it was. His resolve would not only impact *his* future, but that of *American* generations. Sam knew he was part of a deadly play. Today, after school, he'd returned home and packed. A backpack, the shortwave, and a gym bag stuffed with nearly two million U.S. dollars were loaded into the cart. What happened at the dorm would determine if he could return to his old life or would need to head to Texas with the families, or... "I, I don't think..."

"You have no future, here, man," Myers insisted. "You no longer have a career. There's nothing here for you."

"Mr. Moore," Banner said, "after today, you're a wanted man. You being part of the Directorate, I don't have to tell you what'll happen if they catch you."

"I..."

"Mr. Moore, please?" Mark Thurmont said. He grabbed Sam's shoulder, shaking him. "You gotta, sir. You can live with one of my uncles, or with my cousins and me. We got a big house just outside of Corpus Christi. You can walk to the Gulf. There's no winter there. T-shirts and shorts year-round, and folks are nice and friendly. You, being a rebel teacher from the Nac, schools would line up to hire you. Mr. Moore, *you* know the *real* meaning of what's happening, what we stand to lose."

Oh, it was tempting! It would be so easy to throw in with these good, solid people, the salt of the earth. His stomach knotted, and he chewed a lip. To start over, be free...

"Mr. Moore," Jason said, "you know everyone's right. You can't stay here."

His former students crowded around him. The pleading in their eyes tore at him, ripping him to shreds. He didn't know what to do, so he glanced past them to Leo for help. The old man shook his head and looked away. Sam swallowed. "Kids..."

Regan, who had remained quiet, stepped up and gave him a shy glance. "Mr. Moore, forgive me, but..."

Sam eyed her. "Regan, what?"

"I'll be eighteen in three months. You can live with my parents and me, and then when I'm eighteen, maybe—"

"Regan—no. It won't work."

"Then I'll stay here with you. Whatever you decide to do, I'll be with you."

What was happening? Regan was just a kid. Besides, he'd made a promise to another. And she was counting on him to stick by that promise. The cloudy future suddenly cleared. If he left now, it couldn't be more wrong. He could feel it in his soul—if there was such a thing—that leaving now was not in the cards.

"He's staying..." Myers murmured. "I've seen that look before, that look when a man knows his destiny."

Sam eyed each teenager. "Jason's dad is right. It's not that I don't want to go. I can't. As I said, I still have unfinished business here. I'm not yet sure what that business is, but my gut tells me to stay."

Someone shouted at Myers, and he nodded.

"Kids, you need to finish up here," Myers said, "it's time to go."

Sam sighed, eyeing his now former students. "Come here."

The teenagers grabbed their teacher, clinging to what part of him they could, building poignant but cherished memories. Sam hugged each and every one as tears flowed. He released Mark, and the boy wiped his eyes on a coat sleeve. "You suffered more," Sam said, "and have experienced more than the others. And you've seen more than most adults. It made you strong, Mark. You're a man now. Everyone in this group will be looking to you for leadership. I know you won't let them down."

"Yes, sir."

"But don't let it go to your head."

Mark chuckled. "Do you remember those essays I used to write?"

"How could I forget?"

"I knew you felt the same. You just didn't know it yet, so I had to point it out to you."

Sam laughed, dabbing an eye.

"I understand why you can't leave," Mark said. "Mr. Moore, I hope one day I can be like you."

"God help us." Sam reached out and ruffled his hair. "Get outta here."

The boy nodded and took off to a pickup. The other boys followed, scattering to their families. Mark looked back once and waved.

Sam waved back while Regan hovered nearby, hesitating. She was the last one, and the one that worried him.

"Mr. Moore..."

"Regan..."

Regan fell into his arms. Her fingers clung to his coat collar. "You won't change your mind?"

He held her close. "No."

"Regan, let's go!" a man shouted.

"I'll never forget you, Sam."

"And I'll never forget you, Regan."

Sniffling, she pulled away. "Goodbye, Sam."

"Goodbye, Regan."

The girl darted to a truck.

Engines gunned anxiously as Myers ran up to Sam. "If you need a place to lay low, you can stay in the house as long as you want. There's no food, but there is electricity and heat."

"You're just abandoning your home?"

"I received a notice of government seizure a few months back. It takes effect February first."

"Those sons-of-bitches."

"Tell me about it," Myers said. "They said my home, a home that'd been in our family for over a century and a half, was too large for a single family. The government was acquisitioning it along with all the land. And get this: they said my wife and I and our three kids could still live here but only in two rooms. The rest of my home, two thousand square feet, would house six to eight other families."

"Now you know why I'm staying. This *must* stop."

Myers nodded. "I'd stay to fight the cocksuckers, but I have a family to think of."

"Yeah, you do."

Myers gripped Sam's hand. "It's always the politicians who start these things, and it's always young men like you who have to end it, right the wrongs, clean up their shit."

Sam squeezed his hand. "Take care, Mr. Myers. I wish I could go with you."

"I know." He released Sam's hand. "Again, thank you for risking your neck for our children...for everyone's children. God bless you, Mr. Moore."

Sam reached into a coat pocket and pulled out four envelopes. All were sealed. Three of them had a family name on each envelope, and the fourth was addressed to Mark Thurmont. "Take these, please."

The older man reached for the envelopes, examining them. "Is this...?"

"Yeah, it's a stake, and I don't want to hear a word from you."

Myers looked at him in disbelief. His chin quivered. He patted Sam on the arm then hustled to a truck. Leo jogged to the barn door and pushed it open. Truck doors slammed. Running lights in the bumper of Myers' Ford pickup snapped on, and the truck rumbled out of the barn, followed by the others, one by one, with their headlights out and truck beds bulging and tarped.

The last truck was loaded with dozens of jerry cans bungeed to the back of the cab. Sam and Leo waved as the trucks passed by. Tinted windows gave up nothing within, and the convoy dissolved into murky ether. After several seconds, the rattle of diesel engines faded, blending into the stillness. A time stream washed over Sam, leaving him internally drenched but still on life's shore, well aware that destiny's next wave would crash over him, sweeping him into eternity.

The whole episode, from the moment they rolled in with the students until now, had lasted perhaps ten minutes. Tree frogs began screeching. A major chapter in Sam's life had just closed, and today—Friday, January 14th, 2050—would loop over and over in his thoughts for as long as he lived. Sam stared into darkness, wondering if he'd ever see the kids again. Part of him had just driven away with those trucks.

"Get Myers' cart," Leo said, shaking Sam's thoughts. "Leave yours inside. At least for a while. It might make 'em think you went with the families."

Sam headed inside and climbed inside his cart. Once jammed full, the vehicle now seemed as empty as his life. His was the only gear inside. He grabbed the pistol, yanked out the backpack and gym bag, and started for the other cart. After tossing gear inside, he went back for the shortwave.

Leo shut off barn lights, leaving Sam's cart inside the dark, forlorn structure. The ancient barn and land now belonged to history. The barn was just another tragic story, another ghost added to a growing, haunted procession of phantoms that flitted over the countryside as dried autumn leaves before winter's first gale.

Sam glanced back to the cavernous building as Leo pushed the door shut on yet another of history's forgotten vignettes. Sam fantasized that the nation was once again united under the Stars and Stripes, and he was a college professor, leading a class on a tour of the old barn, a local historical monument...

"Where were you, Dr. Moore?"

"This is my old cart." He'd pat the rusting relic and point next to it. "Leo's cart, with old Leo behind the wheel, was parked right there. And there were these huge pickup trucks, over there, packed with bare essentials, families scrambling, quickly loading gear, hoping to escape tyranny and start a new life."

"What was passing through your mind at that very moment, Dr. Moore?"

"Desperation." He'd turn to the students grouped around him. "It was a time of deep sorrow, desperation, and destiny."

He'd pace in front of the group. "I was a young high school teacher back in those days, full of life and promise. I saw that same life and promise in my students. Yet the old regime, the Directorate, obliterated originality, all but exterminating the future. The Directorate strangled life itself."

"Professor Moore, you risked your life to save some of those students, one of them, Governor Regan Hampton-Smith. The Governor said that you were the bravest man she ever knew."

"Brave? No, I wasn't brave. That night, when Leo and I rolled in here with Mark, Jason, Phillip, and Regan, I was scared shitless, but I couldn't show it."

Chuckles would move through the group. "You still remember all their names!"

"Of course. That day, those kids turned me into a **man.***"*

Leo shoved a bar across the barn door. The clang broke Sam's thoughts. A heavy padlock clicked. With his shotgun slung over a shoulder, the old man headed for Myers' cart.

Sam sighed. Within a few weeks, the barn would probably be razed and used for firewood.

Leo reached inside the open passenger door and eased the shotgun onto the backseat. He caught sight of Sam's .45 wedged inside the center console. "Nice hand cannon you have there." With a groan, he climbed in. The door lowered, and he turned to Sam. "Remember what I said about not looking back?"

Sam nodded. "Yeah."

"Suck it up, son. Your job's done with those kids. You taught them well. Now, you're needed here."

"I don't know what to think or believe anymore, Leo. I can't go back home, at least not for a while."

"There is no 'not for a while.' Forget home. You have no home. *But* you do have a future. After today, you start a new life. You can forget your parents' house and property. As of now, your old life is over. What you do from now on will be recorded in history."

Sam stared through the windshield. "I know."

Thoughtful seconds passed, and Leo sighed. "It would've been easy for you to go with that bunch, to start over. The natural thing to do. Would've tempted the hell outta me. Don't know if I could've resisted it...resisted *her.*"

"Believe me, Leo, those kids were getting to me. I wanted to go with them so damn bad. And then Regan..."

"I could see. When I saw that little lady cryin' in your arms, I said, 'well, he's gone.'"

Sam gripped the steering wheel. "I've got commitments

here."

"You did the right thing, Sam. Maybe not the smart thing, but the *right* thing."

Sam glanced around. "I need to hang around the area, see what happens Sunday evening. I'm sure you know about Katie's plan."

Leo nodded.

"How about I drop you off," Sam said, "and I come back here?"

"How about you drop me off in town and you stay."

"Leo, that's too dangerous for both of us."

"Now you tell me," Leo said, snorting. "Well, are we just going to sit here all friggin' night? I need a beer and a smoke."

Sam clicked on headlights and eased the cart away. The vehicle followed the long driveway to the gravel road, which ended at a main highway. He swung left, pointing the cart to town. The electric motor hummed, and a quiet trepidation settled over the two men. Neither spoke, each lost in his own thoughts.

Sam was first to break the silence. "Something's been bugging the hell out of me ever since we left the school."

Leo glanced to him.

"Where was the commissar and the cops? Leo, I've never seen that school, or the community, so devoid of law enforcement."

"Guess you didn't hear."

"Hear what?"

"There was an explosion over in Leeward Community this evening."

Sam grinned. A certain, high-ranking *Silver-Triad* commissar colonel lived in Leeward. "No shit?"

"No shit."

"But wouldn't Tipton know that it might be only a diversion and double up on guards at the school?"

"Not if it was his house that blew up."

Sam glanced wide-eyed to Leo. "No way!"

Leo nodded, giving a wry grin.

Sam chuckled, focusing on the road. "On the way back to school this evening, I thought I heard something like a sonic boom. We've been hearing a lot of those the past few months. But then I saw all that smoke on the horizon..."

"What you heard this evening was no sonic boom. And all that smoke you saw was Tipton's house going up."

Sam stared straight ahead, not knowing whether to laugh or cry. "You know who's going to get blamed for it, don't you?"

"Yes, sir, I do."

"Me, Leo. They'll charge me with it."

"I'm sure they will."

"They're going to say I planted it just like...like..."

"Like what, Sam? You have something to tell ol' Leo?"

Sam related his visit with Tipton and the commissar's plans.

Leo glanced nonchalantly out a window. "Well, you know what they say: you get what you pay for. No, sir, you just can't find good bomb-makers these days. Everyone and their sister wanting to be a bomb-maker have watered down a once-honorable profession. And one of those amateurs had the gall to show up at the garage last week, sniffing around, thinking *I* had supplies. Imagine that! That's like being hung with your own rope." He glanced to Sam. "I was down-right offended."

"Leo, you already knew about Tipton's plans, didn't you?"

"Some folks are just naturally blabby, I guess. Get a few drops of good Tennessee shine in them, and they never shut up."

Sam laughed. "So, did you give him defective parts or something? And there he was, assembling a bomb in Tipton's house and—"

"I didn't sell him a damn thing."

Sam squeezed the wheel, digesting what the older man was saying. "Leo, you didn't..."

The older man yanked off the rolled-up ski cap and scratched his head. "I'm not saying a word."

"Was anyone killed?"

"Don't know, except the commissar wasn't there. He and the law were sitting at school, waiting on you, when the call came in that his house went up in a mini-mushroom cloud."

"One of these days, they're coming for you, Leo," Sam said, gazing into passing darkness.

"Yeah, maybe, but it won't be for this one." He worked the cap back over his head. "You're right, Sam. They'll pin this bombing on you. By tomorrow, the Provincial Guard will be combing the countryside, looking for a certain humanities teacher charged with numerous crimes against the Compassionate Commonwealth. And I'm sure there'll be a fat reward out on your head, Mr. Enemy of the State."

Sam's jaw tightened. That knot in his stomach twisted itself into a pretzel. He forced calm. "We're coming into town. Think the cops will be thick? I'd hate to have blown up a commissar colonel's home, rescued four kids from oppression, and then get busted because a taillight's out."

"Nah, just keep going. I'll tell you where to turn. I know

where most of the local constabulary hangs out." Leo glanced to Sam. "Besides, a lot of the local law are with us. Most folks in town did a high-five when Tipton's house went up in an orange fireball."

"What's a 'high-five?'"

Leo chuckled, shaking his head. "Damn, do we have to teach you kids everything?"

"Forget it."

"Here, hold out your hand."

Sam took a hand from the wheel, holding it out to Leo.

"Not like that, like this." Leo raised his hand, palm out, and slapped it against the younger man's.

Sam's brow furrowed. He withdrew his hand, with a quizzical look on his face.

"That'll do for now," Leo said.

"What's it mean?"

"It means 'atta boy,' 'way to go,' or 'job well done.'"

Sam nodded, focusing on driving. Quiet seconds passed. "Leo?"

"Yeah."

"Thanks for showing up. I couldn't have gotten those kids out of there without you."

"Hell, that's the least I could do. And I wasn't doing anything anyway. There was nothing on TV but those damn game shows, ballet, and symphony programs...public service documentaries... you know, the usual propaganda shit." He paused. "Besides, you'd do it for me."

Sam swallowed, nodding.

The cart passed outlying buildings, and then it eased through an empty intersection. Perchance seemed deserted. Sam glanced to the dash clock—9:23. "Nine-week Friday curfew isn't until ten," Sam said. "You thinking what I'm thinking?"

"Shit..." Leo breathed. "A dusk to dawn curfew. We need to get off the street."

"We're only a couple of blocks from your house, Leo."

"We ain't going to the house." Leo pointed to an opening on the left. "Quick, in there."

Sam swung left onto a narrow lane, barely missing a light pole. The cart bounced through a pothole, jostling the two inside. Sam hit the brakes and clicked off the lights. The cart sat idling in an alley. The streetlight behind them cast an eerie shadow.

Leo surveyed the surroundings. "We weren't going to the house anyway. We're heading to the garage. We'll spend the night there. By tomorrow afternoon, this cart will be scrap metal."

Sam nodded. "Can we get there taking only alleyways?"

"Yeah, except for one major intersection we'll have to cross." He pointed straight ahead. "Let's go."

The cart, with its lights out, silently rolled forward in the dark. They paused at streets, making sure they were clear, and then Sam nailed it. The cart shot across into the alley on the other side. Finally, two blocks from Leo's garage, the alley ended near a major intersection. Its traffic light flashed red on all sides. The cart came to a stop just inside the alley. Both men studied the empty intersection.

"This is the one that worries me," Leo said. "There's always a cop hangin' around here, one of the suck-asses always nabbing people for curfew violations."

Sam twisted around, eyeing the large Dumpster they'd just passed. "Maybe we should park behind that Dumpster, sit it out until dawn."

The old man nodded, contemplating. "It's safe there, but someone might spot this cart going into the garage in the morning. Nothing may happen, but knowing human nature as I do..." He stroked a short, gray beard. "We can't chance it. Darkness is our friend."

Sam stared out a window. "I guess that's my life's script now, huh?"

"Yep, get used to it. The moment you left that school dorm with those four youngsters, you officially went underground."

"Do you think they suspect you?"

He tapped the ski cap on his head. "I was Casey Myers, coming to get my boy."

"Always a plan."

"That's why I'm still here." Leo glanced to the .45 sticking from the console then to Sam. "I see you had a plan."

Sam nodded.

The old man's gaze again fell to the pistol. "A literature teacher packing heat. Helluva note."

The two sat quietly for several minutes. No vehicle was seen or person spotted. Leo pointed straight ahead. "Let's do it."

Instead of stepping on it, Sam eased the cart into the road, swung left, and rolled up to the light. "It's clear over here."

"All's clear here. Hit it!"

The cart leapt forward, zooming down a deserted avenue.

"Screw the alley," Leo said. "Stay on the street. The garage is right around the corner."

Sam nodded, now in familiar territory. At the second street, he turned a hard right and eased off the throttle. The cart silently moved through a dark neighborhood street near the town square. After several long seconds, the cart slowed, and Sam swung it against a curb, halting a few yards from a stop sign. Leo's garage rose on the right, but the garage entrance was around the corner.

Leo hit the door-opener button, climbed out, and turned back. "Stay here. I'll come get you."

The passenger door lowered as Leo disappeared around the corner. Sam's heart thumped. So, this was what it was like to be on the run. It really sucked. And it had only just begun.

What seemed like forever, but was really seconds, Leo limped toward him, signaling. Sam stepped on it, whipping the cart through the stop sign and around the corner. The garage entrance yawned on the right. The cart swerved a hard right and disappeared inside. Before the cart stopped, the garage door lowered.

Saturday night, one minute before eleven, a single overhead lamp bathed the room in soft light. Sam, Leo, and Michelle sat in the basement of the Spencer's home. Their attentions were focused on a nearby shortwave radio. The radio wasn't Sam's but Leo's.

"Sam, do you know what to listen for?" Michelle asked.

"Yes, and you guys will probably recognize it, too." Sam studied the elderly woman. She'd already seen a cancer specialist. The cancer had spread, and there was little they could do; she was too weak for surgery anyway. Michelle had begun chemical treatment in the form of pills to keep it contained in her cervix, but the prognosis was grim. With proper medical care, she may have a year, perhaps more. Yet, a little color had already returned to her cheeks.

A three-pitch tone yanked him from his thoughts.

This is Radio Free America, came the female's words, *the voice of freedom! Greetings, patriots! Now for tonight's news: NAC forays into Western Alliance territories have increased, and all have met with disaster. We believe the NAC is acting in desperation. Commonwealth military is poorly armed, and its morale has decayed to the point of internal collapse. Commonwealth POW counts have increased five-fold since last fall. Some enemy units surrender without firing a shot. We, here, west of the Mississippi, pray that this continues. American pitted against American, brother against brother, is what the evil Directorate regime dreams for.*

The roundup of the poor and elderly in the NAC has not only increased but has also taken a heinous turn. Reports are coming to us that forced sterilization is now occurring. And Directorate political prisoner count has increased to the point that there are separate "gulags" operating in remote parts of the Appalachians. These political prisoners—those who dare to speak out against the Directorate—are used as slave labor. Oh, what evil has befallen on our brothers and sisters east of The River! You cannot sit idly by while your fellow Americans are abused and butchered. Americans, arise! Arise! Arise before it's too late! You have the might of the United States of America's Western Alliance behind you! Throw off the yoke of tyranny!

All three glanced silently to one another.

Now it's time for tonight's announcements: The bricks are in the alley, the bricks are in the alley.

Sam rose, stepping to the radio on the shelf. The couple's eyes followed him.

The wheelbarrow has a flat. The wheelbarrow has a flat. When the big hand hits six. When the big hand hits six.

"Come on." And Sam held his breath.

Do not forget the scrapbook. Do not forget the scrapbook.

"Yes!" Sam burst, pumping a fist.

Leo stood up, grinning from ear to ear, and Michelle struggled to her feet, shaking her hands like a cheerleader whose team had just scored.

The underground messages continued for another minute, and then the American National Anthem played, signifying the broadcast's end. Michelle turned to Sam. "You did pack the scrapbook, didn't you?"

"Of course. The photo album was the first thing in the backpack." Sam paced in front of the standing couple. Euphoria of the moment passed. He swallowed as realization crept in. He glanced to the others and shrugged. "Anyone have a clue as to what's going to happen tomorrow after Katie's broadcast?"

Leo stroked a neatly trimmed beard. "Your guess is as good as mine, son. Here in Perchance, we're not as affected by the population removals as, let's say, over in Charleston. American patriotism runs strong through this community."

"Charleston's just over an hour away," Michelle said. "Folks around here have relatives that live in Charleston."

"Yeah, like us," Leo said, pausing. "I guess around here, there may be a street protest in front of the Directorate sub-courthouse on Monday. Maybe a few American flags flown."

"I hope like hell parents keep their kids home from school— for good," Sam said. "Children need to be in school, but there are no *schools* in the Commonwealth, only indoctrination centers. For now, home-schooling is the only way to go."

Leo chuckled. "We tried home-schooling a few years back, remember? The government seized the kids and threw the parents in jail."

Michelle wrung her hands, giving the others a nervous glance. "I'm worried about dear Katie."

"So am I," Sam said.

Ring-ring-ring.

Leo worked out a vidphone and held it to an ear. "Yeah." A strained look shadowed his face. "Okay. Thanks." Leo clicked off the phone. "That was Will. He says the law is making roundups here in town, hauling away people."

Michelle gave a worried sigh. "Not again..."

Sam looked on, unsure of what to do. "They're looking for me."

"They're looking for revenge," Leo said.

Whop. Whop. Whop.

Michelle glanced to the stairway. "Oh, my God. They're already here!"

Whop. Whop. Whop.

Sam hustled up the steps. "Maybe if I surrender, they'll leave."

Leo darted after him. "Sam. No!"

Sam was almost to the door when Leo grabbed him, but Sam shrugged him off.

"Son, you don't know what you're doing," Leo said. "We'll hide you in the cellar."

"There'll be a time and a place to hide," Sam said. "Now isn't it."

"But if you turn yourself in, you may never get another chance to—"

"What choice do I have, Leo?" Sam glanced hard to the older man. "Huh? What choice?"

Michelle stepped next to her husband. Dread swept over her face. "Sam..."

"This has Tipton all over it," Sam continued. "He won't quit until I'm in custody."

"Or dead," Leo said.

Sam's jaw tightened.

Leo quickly reached into an overall pocket and mashed a button on the vidphone, frying the insides. Then he stuffed the device back into a pocket. Pausing, he glanced first to his wife and then to Sam. Pushing past both, he headed to the front door.

Whop. Whop. Whop.

Leo pulled back the deadbolt and grabbed the doorknob.

The door burst open. Several helmeted men wearing black fatigues and aiming automatic weapons rushed into the room. Ski caps hid their faces. Two men trained weapons on the couple while three more fanned out throughout the house.

Another black-uniformed man in his early thirties, with a holstered pistol on his side, casually stepped through the door. Instead of a helmet and ski-cap, he wore a black baseball cap with a red eagle patch and the initials **O.I.S.** sewn underneath—

Office of Internal Security. Captain's bars were pinned to a collar. He paused in front of Sam. His gaze was that of a carnivore. "I'm looking for Samuel Moore."

"That's me."

The captain snapped his fingers, and two men bounded over to Sam. One trained a rifle on him while the other jerked Sam's hands behind him, snapping on handcuffs. "We have a warrant for your arrest, Moore," the captain said. "You're charged with terrorist acts, sabotage, subversiveness, possession of a firearm, attempted murder of three government officials, and aiding and abetting others in the commission of felonies." His eyes never left Sam. "And that's only the beginning." He nodded to the soldiers and pointed at Sam then to a bare wall. The soldiers yanked the teacher to the wall and shoved him against it. One soldier pinned Sam against the wall with his rifle while the other held him at gunpoint. The captain strolled over to Sam and grinned. "You get a ringside seat to the game, see what happens to those who think they're untouchable. Enjoy."

"Sam, oh, Sam!" Michelle shouted, wringing her hands.

"Don't worry, son," Leo called to Sam, "we'll have you back in no time."

"I wouldn't bet on that," the captain said. He turned from Sam and stepped over to Leo. "And to you, Spencer, I'm to deliver a message."

"A message? What the hell are you talking about? A message from whom?"

"This." The captain viciously punched Leo in the gut. "And I think you can figure out from whom."

Leo doubled over with the wind knocked from him.

"Don't hurt him!" Michelle yelled, reaching for her husband.

"Shut up old woman or you're next."

A guard grabbed her and shoved her back. She tripped over the coffee table and banged her head hard on the edge. Her still form lay crumpled on the floor.

Sam struggled with the guard pinning him but the other guard wacked him hard in the shoulder with a rifle butt. Sam went limp, grimacing in pain and anger.

The two guards laughed.

The captain snapped his fingers again. "Let the games begin."

More soldiers charged through the house. Crashing sounds filled the air as the soldiers ransacked the place.

Sucking air, Leo tried lunging for the captain, but a guard hit the older man behind the knee with a rifle butt. Leo collapsed, grabbing his leg, wincing. "Chelle—Chelle, you okay!" he gasped.

She didn't answer. Leo crawled over to her and cradled her head. "Chelle, girl. Talk to me."

"You've already got me," Sam shouted, still pinned against the wall, "let them go! They had nothing to do with what happened!"

The captain ignored him as black-clad men marched into the living room and tossed bulging sacks into the middle of the floor. The captain nodded approvingly before striding over to the fireplace. Gloved hands on hips, he gazed up to the American Flag. "Well, what is this filthy thing?"

"More contraband, sir," one of the guards replied.

The captain yanked the flag from the wall and held it at arm's length. "My, my, it's been a while since I've seen this symbol of hatred so blatantly displayed." Pulling a dagger, the captain held out the American flag and began slashing it. After several seconds of animal-like thrusts, he tossed the shredded red, white, and blue cloth on the floor and urinated on it. Sneering, he glanced to Leo and nodded to the remains on the floor. "I gave it the burial it deserved, don't you think?"

Holding his wife's limp form, Leo spat on the man's boot. The captain savagely kicked the old man in the face. Leo turned his head, taking the blow to the jaw. Blood trickled from Leo's mouth, splattering his beard.

A heavy crash came from the kitchen, and glass shattered as Michelle let out a slow moan. "Leo," she whispered, "what are they doing?"

"Hush," Leo replied, working bloody fingers through her hair. "Lie still. You've got a nasty concussion." A tumultuous crash blasted from the kitchen, shaking the whole house. Breaking glass, snapping wood, and twisting metal created a horrific, cacophony of destruction. The elderly couple's home was being torn apart from the inside out.

"You punks are just so freaking brave," Sam said from across the room, "picking on an old couple, someone who can't fight back...and that's just like the losers you punks are."

Whack. Sam doubled over from a rifle butt to the gut.

The captain marched over to the dining room entrance, wearing a cruel grin. "There's something to be said for job satisfaction."

"Go to hell." Leo's hard gaze bore into the man. "This isn't over."

"You're right, Spencer, it isn't. But round one goes to *us.*" The captain kicked a ripped sofa cushion, sending it sailing.

"Let's go, men!"

The two men guarding Sam jerked him to the door. "Leo, Michelle, don't give up!" Sam shouted as he was shoved toward the door.

Three black-uniformed men hurried from the dining room. Slung over their shoulders were black bags stuffed full of canned goods, assorted food, and other loot. Other soldiers hauled away the rest of the plunder, leaving the captain alone with the couple. "Next time I pay a visit—and there will be a next time—I won't be so civil."

A woman in civilian dress appeared, holding a tiny videocam in her hand. She aimed it at the captain. He turned to the couple on the floor and tilted his cap. "Sorry to have disturbed you, ma'am, sir. Have a good evening." The woman clicked off the camera and disappeared. The captain strode out into the winter night, leaving the door swinging wide open.

The large van jostled through dark streets, hit a pothole, and the overhead light flickered and went out, throwing the prisoners into darkness. Sam gazed to the other five men around him. The shadows couldn't hide the hard, grim expressions. All sat upright on metal benches. Their hands, now handcuffed in front of them, were shackled to eyelets in the seats. A lone, unarmed guard stood in the aisle. One of his hands held a Maglite, and the other hand gripped an overhead rail. He glanced nonchalantly out a barred window.

Sam recognized a prisoner across from him. The man, forty-ish and with slight of build, wore a faded, camouflage American Army ABU shirt. He wiped a bloody nose on a shirtsleeve. "You're Sam Moore, one of my son's teachers."

"Shut up, you," the guard growled, shining the flashlight in the man's face.

Sam nodded to the man in acknowledgement; he was James Dixon, Perchance's mayor. Dixon's son, John, had been a student in his first period class. Sam stared at the diamond-plated floor. *Had been?* Teaching already seemed a lifetime ago.

Ten minutes later, the van backed into a dock in the rear of the local police station. Shackled together, all six men were herded to a small processing center.

A huge wrecker parked under a nearby street light caught Sam's attention. A large Ford pickup truck was chained to the bed. He choked in horror—it was a truck from the students' convoy. The tires were flat, and the cab was bullet-riddled. On the driver's side, a gaping hole in the windshield was dark, fathomless, an epitaph. "Oh, God, no. No..." he murmured. He recalled the lives, the desperation, and the unspoken hope. Sam hung his head as despair darkened his heart even more.

The guards shoved the shackled men inside the door and told them to halt. One of their guards sauntered up to a counter, nodding to a tan-uniformed man standing behind bulletproof glass. "I've got Federal prisoners for morning transfer to Charleston," he said to the jailer.

The jailer slid an electronic notepad through a slot under the window. The guard signed it and slipped it back. The jailer punched a button. A loud buzz sounded, and the door to the cellblock opened.

The group was hustled down a corridor and to a dimly lit 20x20-foot jail cell. Benches hanging from chains were bolted to cell walls. In a corner, a single toilet jutted from the floor. Rolls of toilet paper sat on the tank. A guard punched the keypad outside the cell, and the cell door creaked sideways.

Two black-uniformed men armed with old Mark-10s stood guard. One guard stepped up and unshackled the men, one by one. "Inside, now!" he shouted to each one as they shed their cuffs. With all six prisoners inside the cell, the door clang shut. "And I don't want to hear a peep from anyone."

Sam sat hunched over in the back of the cell with two other men. He rubbed his wrists, watching a guard hang the shackles on outside wall pegs before striding away. Hatred welled from deep within, burning away fear. "I hope you guys made peace with your maker," Sam said in a low voice, "because once we're in Charleston, we're not even statistics."

A thin man of perhaps fifty looked up from a bench. A ragged coat drooped from his sloped shoulders. "Sounds like you know something we don't."

"He *was* one of *them*," Dixon said. He glanced to Sam. "I'd hate to be in your shoes."

The men turned wary eyes on Sam. "What did you do?" asked a black man sitting across from him.

"It's not what I did," Sam said. "It's what I thought."

A couple of men nodded silently in agreement. The black man rose and crossed the cell. Worn boots thumped on the cement floor. He stopped in front of Sam. "Know why they nabbed me?"

Sam scrutinized him. Maybe in his forties, he wore a neatly trimmed goatee flecked with gray. His countenance was what struck Sam: solemn, as if one who knew his destiny. Faded jeans and dark flannel shirt peeked from under a black overcoat.

"He was preaching the Gospel," Dixon said, "and in his own home."

The man standing in front of Sam thrust out his hand. "Turner Wells."

"Sam Moore," Sam said, shaking the preacher's hand.

"I've heard of you," Wells said. "The whole town's heard about you bucking the system...and your generosity."

Sam glanced away. "You see where it got me."

"The Lord has his reasons, ones we're not privy to. You'll be rewarded in ways yet unknown." Wells' voice lowered. "And there are those who will soon reap what they have sown."

Sam gave a start. Did Wells know something about tomorrow evening's broadcast? It sure sounded like it. He wished he had the preacher's faith. *Faith?* He didn't know a damned thing about faith.

The preacher clomped back to his corner where, like a canine, he turned several times before easing down to the floor. With his long legs drawn up, the man covered his head with his coat and remained still.

Sam glanced around. The other men had also settled in, some on benches, others curled on the floor; their coats and their fates enveloped them. How could they sleep at a time like this? Didn't these men know what awaited them? They weren't in here for breaking some local ordinance. They were political prisoners, enemies of the state. After coerced to confess to whatever they were charged with, if they were lucky, they may find themselves in a Labor Camp for several years. If they were unlucky, as he was sure to be, the men's families should start planning funerals with bodies *in absentia*. Sam's jaw tightened. He felt helpless. Snoring startled him from his thoughts.

"What the hell," he murmured in resignation.

He rose from the bench and found a spot on the floor against a wall. He eased down, and the cold cement chilled him, reinforcing the bleakness he felt inside. Wrapping his coat tightly around him, Sam stretched out. His thoughts went to the students he had helped escape. If he hadn't helped them, would they still be alive today? Yet, there was only one truck outside. Maybe some or all had escaped. At any rate, those kids and their families were out of his reach. But there was someone who wasn't: Katie. He recalled the warmth of her skin, the depth of her eyes, and how she seemed to read something in him that lay dormant. Somehow, someway, he had to get out and start searching. He had to find Katie. He'd made her a promise; she would need him. Need him for what, he wondered? Sam's eyelids lowered. Those kids had trusted him, and look where that got them.

* * *

"Moore—Samuel Moore!" came a shout from the corridor.

Sam yawned, rolling over. Several men lay scattered throughout the cell.

"Would you shut the hell up," came a muffled cry from a corner.

"Who said that?" the guard growled. "No breakfast for anyone until I get a name."

Silence.

"Yeah, you're quiet now. Just wait until you get to Charleston. You'll be offering up your own mother so you can keep talking." He stuck his face to the cell bars. "Where's Moore?"

Sam rose, groaning, feeling as cold and stiff as a mannequin.

"Front and center, Moore!" the guard ordered, keys jingling. "Were you the one who told me to 'shut the hell up?'"

"Say what?" Sam asked, running fingers through short, unkempt hair.

"What are you...deaf and dumb?" The guard, a bloated man in his forties, stood in the cell's open doorway. "Later, I'll deal with you personally. Now get your ass over here."

The cell door opened, and Sam stepped through it. After closing the cell door, the guard loosely shackled Sam's wrists to his waist, and led him down a corridor to a door at the far end. "Hold it," the guard said, grabbing his chains. The guard opened the door, shoved him through, and pulled the door shut.

Sam staggered. A black-uniformed guard stood just inside the door. Sam surveyed his surroundings. An iron table with two wooden chairs across from one another sat in the room's middle. He did a double-take. A man in a black leather coat— with a gray turtleneck underneath—sat stiffly in one of the chairs. It was Commissar Tipton.

"My boy, you should've gone with those kids." He yanked off his glasses and rubbed the thick lenses with a handkerchief. "Although, in the end, it wouldn't have made a difference, except perhaps you and I would've had more sport." He glanced up, replacing the glasses on his nose. "Have a seat, Moore."

Before Sam could speak, he was pushed roughly to the table and shoved into the chair across from Tipton. He gazed at the older man, silent. The commissar's walleyed stare made the man even more revolting than usual.

"After all the Directorate has given you—what *I* have given you—this is how you repay me?"

"You wouldn't know anything about 'giving,'" Sam said. "Only about *taking.*"

"Yes, yes, 'taking' is a word you may use." Tipton's waxy features morphed into a stiff glaze. "You took an oath to preserve the North American Commonwealth. And now, you have violated that oath."

Sam glanced to his manacled wrists; he was a trapped animal.

Tipton rose, walked around the table, and slowly paced the room. "And what shall we do with you, I wonder?"

Sam's eyes followed him.

The commissar paused, with his back to Sam. "Normally, an example is made of what happens to traitors. However, these aren't normal times."

Sam blinked at Tipton's last words. Did the bastard know something, or was he just fishing? Either way, the Party had ways of extracting what it wanted. Sam shuddered.

"You repay my kindness by destroying my home?" Tipton faced Moore. "But we'll get to that later. Two days ago, the National Regional Broadcasting's satellite linked was hacked."

A wave of nausea hit him, and yet he showed no emotion. "So? Why are telling me?"

"The hacking was down in the Charleston area." Tipton stepped closer to the table. He glanced to the black-uniformed guard, standing at parade rest in front of the door, then back to Sam. "A Directorate administrative password was used to override the link," he said in a low voice.

Sam shrugged innocently, but his gut was churning. "I don't know what you're getting at."

Tipton leaned on the table. His face was only inches away from Sam's. "No one knows that password but me. And that password was downloaded from a server here in Perchance."

The commissar's breath reeked from stale coffee. "Kinda narrows the field, doesn't it?" Sam said, forcing a smile. "So, Commissar, are you going to arrest yourself?"

Tipton straightened. *Whack.* He backhanded Sam across the mouth.

The sting worked up to his face, but Sam remained silent. His gaze was cold and steady. Blood trickled from the corner of his mouth, streaking his unshaven jaw. He wiped the blood on his arm.

"There are only three in Perchance with access to sensitive Directorate codes."

Sam froze, holding his breath as dread took hold.

The commissar shook his head as if disappointed. "Ms. Woodriff was a good principal. She had an instinct for handling kids." He paused, using silence as another weapon. "Alas, she knows nothing. A pity she won't be back, though. We will miss her, but only for a little while."

Hatred was a millstone wedged in the pit of Sam's gut. He must clear his thoughts. "What did you do to her?"

"*Me?*" Tipton said, chuckling. "*I* never laid a finger on the dear woman." He paused. "I will say she wasn't a shrinking violet. No, indeed. A strong-willed woman she was. But in the end, the truth, like sweet cream, *always* rises to the top."

149

"You son-of-bitch."

Tipton picked flint from his leather coat. "That only leaves you, Mr. Moore." He again leaned on the table, staring harshly at Sam. "I want to know what you were planning to do? And who are your conspirators?"

"I don't know a freaking thing."

Tipton casually strolled behind Sam, who was seated and shackled.

Sam twisted around, straining to follow the commissar. Out of the corner of his eyes, he caught Tipton reaching into a coat pocket. *Here it comes,* he thought, tensing up.

Thud. But instead of a blow, a clear plastic bag full of what looked like chicken hit the table in front of him.

"Pick it up," Tipton said, stepping to one side.

Sam tentatively reached for it then recoiled. Inside were human body parts.

Tipton nodded to the guard, who strode over. With gloved hands, the guard grabbed the bag and shook the contents onto the table.

An ear, a hand severed at the wrist, and several fingers slid from the bag. Sam froze in horror. The body parts appeared to belong to a young male. He heaved, leaned over, and vomited.

"If you cooperate with me, I'll make sure there are no *fresh* appendages for your viewing pleasure. Those in Charleston won't make such a generous offer."

"You son-of-a-bitch!" Sam shouted.

"You want to see a bitch for your next order?" The commissar gave a sick grin. "I believe that can be arranged."

Sam lunged, flipping over the table. Body parts went sailing. Tipton was knocked to the floor. His eye glasses crunched under him. The guard whipped out an ampstick, and Sam knocked it away with the chains. The unarmed guard dove at Sam, and Sam kicked a chair into him. The guard dropped as the wind was knocked from him. A whistle shrieked from outside. Sam bounded over to the dazed commissar, wrapped his manacles around his neck, and yanked him up from the floor. "You're mine now, you freak-of-nature." He jerked, tightening the chains around Tipton's neck. Tipton struggled but was no match for Sam. Sam twisted the chains. Tipton gurgled, and his struggles weakened. He turned blue. "This is for those kids... and Terri." Sam strained, and the chains bit into flesh. A clear voice screamed in his head. *No! Don't do this!* Sam paused, loosening the chains in his shaking hands. The commissar's gasps throbbed in his ears, bringing a moment of clarity. Sam dropped the chains as if it they burned. Tipton hit the floor, writhing, gulping for air.

The door burst open, and guards poured in, with MAC-10s raised.

"Don't kill him!" someone shouted. "Charleston wants him alive!"

Sam circled the room like a trapped tiger. Six men, holding ampsticks low, charged. Sam struggled, slashing one across the face with his chains. Crimson sprayed, coating everything. Ampsticks jabbed into him and his brain seemed to explode. Every nerve burst with pain, and he knew no more.

The late-winter sun had long since dropped behind the eight-story building. Electric cars hummed quietly up and down Charleston's 200-year-old avenues. Katie tossed a small backpack into the cart's back storage area and climbed in behind the wheel. She glanced to the man fastening a seatbelt on the passenger side. "Sergio, are you sure you can do it from out here?"

"Would you rather be back in the studio?" he replied. "Sister, at least out here in the parking lot we have a running chance."

She sighed, unsnapped her coat, and scrutinized the man, admiring how his fingers played over the small touchscreen in his lap. At thirty, Sergio Cotter was beyond genius when it came to manipulating software.

Katie turned the key, and the cart hummed to life. "Did you notice the looks security gave us as we were leaving the building?"

The man continued tapping the interface. "Told you we shouldn't have left together."

"It's too late now." Katie glanced to her studio camera engineer next to her then to the clock in the dash. "We have three minutes until the broadcast."

"The guards will be out here before then."

"Gee, thanks." Tense seconds passed. Katie glanced up to a tiny, metallic bubble mounted on a nearby overhead light. She swore under her breath. Everywhere one turned there was a camera. *Soon,* she thought, *if everything worked as planned, the Directorate would have those cameras shoved up their—*

"Got a lock on the satellite link!" Sergio looked sidelong to her. "We're about to find out if those codes your Directorate friend sent you will work."

Katie shuddered inside, trying not to think of Sam. She had received word this morning that he'd been arrested the night before. And it was her fault. This day, she felt the weight of the whole world on her shoulders. Today, more than a country was at stake. Hijacking their TV station's satellite signal was a *must,* a crucial first step. Replacing the news programming with her prerecorded death-camp documentary was step two, a trick that the electronic magician across from her was also in charge of.

The final step depended on something no amount of money or computer expertise could foster: will power. Would the people finally rise up against their totalitarian masters? Her grandfather believed so, as did Sam. If she were successful, so many more would perish when called upon to give that final sacrifice. Yet, victory meant America would reunite once again...a *free* society. Her only solace was her grandfather promising her he'd try to rescue Sam during the mass confusion that was sure to follow her unauthorized broadcast.

"Here goes," Sergio said, breaking her thoughts. "Three— two—one." *Welcome to the Scope and Sequence News Hour.* He touched the flat screen in his lap, turning up the volume. *We begin this evening with news from the war fronts—buzz—*

Both in the cart held their breaths.

Sergio grinned, shoving the screen in front of her. "Look!"

The grimness of a death camp met her gaze. She'd never, ever forget the horror she'd beheld first hand. She shoved the flat screen away. *What you are witnessing,* came her tiny voice, *is Dante's Seventh Level of Hell...*

She stared at her camera engineer and caught movement just past him. Three armed security guards along with the station manager bolted from the building, hurrying their way. "Oh, shit. Sergio, we've got to get outta here!"

The man's fingers danced over the screen. "Just five more seconds—"

The guards drew pistols.

Katie shoved the gearstick forward. "We don't have five seconds!"

"The virus is almost downloaded—"

The guards broke into a sprint. Katie gripped the wheel and mashed the throttle. Tires chirped, and the cart shot forward.

Sergio was thrown back in his seat. "Hey!"

Katie twisted the wheel, and the cart slid around a corner, speeding to the parking lot exit. A guardhouse loomed up. Cross arms were down on both sides, blocking their path. A guard stepped out with his pistol drawn.

Sergio eased the flat screen to the floor, staring straight ahead. "I wasn't counting on this."

Katie shook her head, easing off the throttle pedal. "We should've left earlier."

"And we never would've downloaded that virus into the station's computers," Sergio shot back. He glanced to her. "We did our part. Gave it our best shot."

"Like hell we did." Katie glanced around, frantic. Without

warning, she twisted the wheel and stepped on the throttle.

"What the hell? Katie give it up. We're trapped!"

Ignoring the man's pleas, she aimed the cart at the guardhouse. A second guard jumped from a side door. Both guards trained their pistols on the speeding cart.

"Katie, are you crazy! We can't make it!"

"Just shut up and hold on."

The guardhouse rushed up. The guards scattered. Katie jammed on the brakes. The two were thrown against their seatbelts, and the cart skated sideways. The cart's tail slammed into a cement barricade and bounced off. She tromped on the throttle, steering the cart around the left side of the guardhouse to the cement barricade surrounding the building.

Pow! Pow! Pow!

Sergio twisted around, looking back. "Jesus Christ! If they don't kill us, you will. Stop the freakin' cart!"

"I saw something this morning—" Katie slowed the cart, pointing to the barricade. "There it is!"

One of the guards was dashing up from behind. The other was outside the guardhouse, speaking into a mike on his collar.

Sergio's gaze followed Katie's, and he grinned. "I'd forgotten about that."

"So did the guards." In front of them, orange construction tape stretched across a narrow gap in the cement barricade. Earlier in the week, a road crew's tractor had accidentally knocked a hole in the barrier. The damaged section was removed. A new cement block sat nearby, waiting to be installed. Only plastic tape lay between the cart and the outside world. The cart rolled forward, snapping the tape.

"Halt!" came a shout from behind. "Halt or I'll shoot!"

"Make it quick, Katie." Sergio glanced back. "That crazy bastard's almost on us."

The cart crept through the opening. Cement scraped the sides. The sickening tear of fiberglass filled the cab. The cart suddenly jerked to a stop, wedged tight. Katie gunned the motor. Nothing.

Sergio pressed window buttons—nothing. "Damnit! We can't even make a run for it!"

The overweight guard jogged up, puffing hard. "Okay, you in there," he shouted, waving a semiautomatic pistol. "Driver, hands on the steering wheel. Passenger, hands on the dash." He wiped a sweaty face on a sleeve. "I want to see those hands!"

Katie shoved the gearstick into reverse and gunned the motor. "And I wanna see you flattened!" The cart shook, budged, and then shot backward.

The guard jumped aside but was too late. The thousand-pound cart rolled over the man's ankle, crushing it. The cart continued backing several yards before stopping.

Katie glanced out the window to the writhing guard on the ground and shot him the finger. She slammed the gearstick forward and tromped the throttle. Tires squealed, and the cart leaped forward, taking aim at the hole in the barrier.

Sergio gripped a handhold. "Katie, if you're off by an inch, they'll be scraping us off the wall."

The cart shot into the opening, cement gouged into fiberglass, and doors buckled. The cart slowed, and Katie buried the pedal. The cart popped free, weaving down an empty side street.

The guard, grimacing in pain, aimed his pistol. *Pow!*

"Whew! Too much excitement for one day." She glanced to Sergio. "I'll drop you off at your cart around the corner and—"

Slumped against his shoulder harness, the man's head lolled to one side.

"Sergio!" Katie jammed a fist into her mouth, stifling a scream. "Oh, dear, God, no!" She sobbed, shaking, as tears streaked her cheeks.

Five minutes later, Katie's cart rolled to a stop behind a black cart parked against a curb. Several other carts were parked nearby. She gripped the wheel, trying to calm herself, and glanced up to the decrepit apartment that Sergio called home. Sergio was divorced, with a five-year-old daughter. He lived alone. Katie wondered about loved ones and if she should try to find them. "No," she said aloud. That would be stupid, all for naught. He would want her to get away, live to tell others what happened after it was all over. Katie turned the ignition key, and the humming faded to nothing. Unstrapping herself, she reached across the console, struggling to release the dead man's harness. "Got it." Sergio slumped forward as if he were pushed. His head banged against the dash, and he rolled sideways, crumpling over the console. She gasped. In the gathering dusk, she saw a pool of blood on the seat and floor. Blood coated everything. She wretched, knowing what she had to do. "I'm sorry, Sergio, but I gotta borrow your cart." Katie rifled through his pockets and tugged out a key chain. Again, she thought of taking his wallet and other personal effects in hopes of returning them to family, and again, she thought better of it. She didn't have the time or the stomach for such a task.

With the keys in her blood-coated hand, Katie climbed back to the driver's side and pushed the exit button that operated both doors. Her door lifted a couple of inches then stopped. The passenger door never budged. Swearing, she put a shoulder to the door and shoved up. Nothing. She tried again, but it wouldn't give. Shoving keys in a coat pocket, she swiveled around, wedged her booted feet against the door, and pushed with all she had. The door moved maybe another inch before snapping back. "Shit!" She kicked at the door, fighting down panic. Still nothing. She mashed the window button. Nothing. "Damnit!" To have come this far, only to be trapped in her own cart like a caged animal. *Think,* she told herself, *think!* Her heart pounded in her ears. *Of course!* She climbed into the back, rummaged around, and climbed back into the front seat with a tire iron and shop towel in her hand. About to swing at the window glass, she paused, hesitating. The breaking glass would draw attention. Yet what choice did she have? Sit calmly in the cart and wait for the police to extract her, which they would do with glee.

Katie's arm came down. *Whack. Whack. Whack.* In less than thirty seconds, the window glass lay in chunks on the pavement. A backpack followed by another bag sailed out the window, landing on broken glass. Hand wrapped in a shop towel, she gingerly picked glass shards from the window frame. Seconds later, Katie squeezed through the window opening, hopped down, gathered up her gear, and dashed to Sergio's cart. Somewhere in the distance sirens wailed. "Oh, God, oh, God..." She cast a quick glance back to her battered cart. "I'm sorry, Sergio, but I know you'd understand." Keys jingled as the cart's door swung out and up. Katie tossed her gear in back next to Sergio's. Within seconds, she was behind the wheel and the cart was humming. She glanced around, expecting to see flashing red and blue lights coming up the block, but all seemed eerily calm. Perhaps everyone was still glued to a TV screen. The documentary was only 21 minutes long, but Sergio had programmed it for a continuous replay.

Katie shoved the gearstick forward, fighting instinct to step on it. Easing the cart away from the curb, she struggled to remain calm. *No hurry,* she thought, *do nothing to attract attention, act like you belong.* She drove casually a few city blocks and still no cops—so far, so good. Another block and she was on the freeway. Adrenaline began wearing off, and her heart rate returned to what seemed the new norm; a drumbeat in the chest.

Katie exited to another freeway, heading northwest, out of town. She reflected on her after-broadcast plan, discovering, to her chagrin, that there really wasn't one. Sergio's and her life the past two months was consumed with getting her documentary over the national airwaves. That done, now what? After she was to drop Sergio off at his cart, they were to part company. For obvious reasons, neither was to know the other's plan after the broadcast. They only knew their old lives would be over. She glanced in the mirror. Traffic was thinning, and still, no law. Something wasn't right; she always saw local and provincial authorities on this stretch of road. Her thoughts moved to what had just happened. Her line of work sometimes led her into gruesome reality. She had seen things that had kept her awake at night, but she had never seen anyone killed right in front of her. The image of her co-conspirator's lifeless body slumped in his seatbelt, and his pooling blood, were forever seared into her synapses.

Katie's grip on the wheel tightened, and her booted foot stepped down on the throttle. Of course, she was heading to Perchance. Sam. She had to find Sam. She reflected on the last time she was in his arms; she'd never felt so secure. And now, she felt ashamed that she had never told him how she...if she'd have kissed him, it would've been all over for her. Katie swallowed. She didn't need a man in her life, yet she had told Sam she wanted to be with him through the turmoil her broadcast was sure to launch. Why? She had even made him promise to look for her. And now *she* would search for him. Katie shook her head. She was a stupid girl. The local Underground was ready to whisk her away, but she had turned them down so she could be with Sam. She'd had boyfriends here and there, but Sam was the first *man* she had ever—

A siren's wail snapped her thoughts, and she glanced into the mirror. Flashing red and blue lights reflected back, stabbing her soul. "Oh, God. Oh, God..." Fear gripped her, and she shook, barely able to steer the cart to the shoulder. She halted, shutting off the motor. The police cruiser followed in behind her.

Step out of the cart came the command from a loudspeaker behind.

It was fight or flight. Katie climbed from the cart. Her knees knocked, and she felt faint. So, the gig was up. She glanced past the cruiser to an unmarked white cart pulling up behind the cop. They had her dead-to-rights.

A stocky, black-uniformed policeman stood outside his diesel-powered cruiser, talking into a mike hanging from his black helmet. He paused to address her. "Step back here to the rear, hands in sight."

Something inside of Katie snapped. Orders, orders, always orders! Fear morphed into anger. To hell with them—to hell with everything! She had accomplished her goal. *Ha! Let them try to undo the broadcast!* Escaping was only dessert anyway. Hidden inner strength welded up in her, and she strolled confidently to the cart's rear.

Standing at the cruiser's front fender, the policeman pointed to the cart's small trunk. "Up against there."

Katie shot the cop a hard glance before obliging.

The cop unsnapped a hand-held scanner from a utility belt and aimed the pistol-shaped device at Katie's eyes. "Eyes straight ahead while I ID you."

She stared straight ahead as anger seethed. They knew who she was. Why go through this bullshit? Just take her in, get it over with. A tiny red beam flashed over Katie's eyes then vanished.

"Okay," the cop said, examining a small monitor on top the scanner, "seems you're Katie Ann Spencer, DOB one, twelve, twenty-five. Five-foot-one, one-o-five pounds, brown hair, brown eyes. Blood type, 'O-positive'...Charleston address..." He looked up from the screen. "Doesn't say that you're wanted for murder, though."

"What?"

"But since it just happened, that info wouldn't yet be in the database."

Another man, taller than the cop but slenderer, strode up. Dressed in professional civilian clothes, he halted and turned to the cop. "Who do we have?"

"It's the woman Channel Five accused of sabotaging the evening news. They said she forced a co-worker to help her, and then she shot and killed him."

She should've known that would be the government's spin. Yet, it still infuriated her. "You're right about my coworker and me hijacking their lies, replacing them with a few minutes of truth!" She raised a fist. "But I didn't kill him."

"You're in a vehicle belonging to Sergio Cotter," the cop said, "the coworker who was found dead in your cart in front of his apartment building a few minutes ago."

"Have to admit," the other man said, "it doesn't look good for you."

"*They* shot him!" Katie shouted, pointing in the direction of downtown. "As we were trying to leave, security pulled guns and started firing. There's a freaking bullet hole in the back window and the seatback. A blind cat could see it!"

The policeman pointed to Katie's hands. "You've even got his blood on your hands."

"I didn't shoot him! He was my friend!" Katie stared defiantly to the two men. "*They* murdered him, just as *they* murdered those thousands you saw in that broadcast."

The men scrutinized her. After several tense seconds, the civilian-dressed man, who apparently held some kind of higher authority, stepped away and nodded for the policeman to follow. "Don't move," the cop said before stepping with the other man. The two halted just out of earshot.

Katie fumed, more disgusted than scared. Standing in the cruiser's headlights, she folded then unfolded her arms, not liking the feel of dried bloodied hands against her coat. What were they discussing? Were they going to rough her up before hauling her away? It seemed the more she talked about *lies*, the harder they looked at her. *Oh, God, here they come to pronounce a roadside verdict.* Katie swallowed. Her heart raced.

"Okay," the plain-clothed man said, "do you have any belongings?"

"Yes," Katie replied, uncertain, "a few bags."

"Get them and place them in that white cart behind this car."

Katie furrowed a brow, hesitating.

The cop looked down at her. "Well, don't just stand there. Do what he said."

Katie stammered. Then she hurried to Sergio's cart and climbed in the open gull-wing driver's door. Within seconds, the passenger door opened, and a backpack followed by a gym bag were tossed onto the ground. She'd leave Sergio's gear where she had found it. Katie climbed back out, slung both bags over her shoulders, and hustled to the white cart idling behind the cop car. "What's going on?" Katie asked as she passed the two men who stood in the dark just outside headlight beams.

"Just get your stuff inside the cart," the plain-clothes man said, "then come back here."

Katie hurried to the white cart and stuffed her gear inside. Hands shaking, she closed the passenger door. Something wasn't right. They should've arrested her by now. Moments later, she stood before the two lawmen.

The plain-clothes man eyed her. "There's a roadblock up ahead where the highway narrows to two-lanes. You'd never get past it in that black cart."

Katie stared, confused. "What do you mean?"

"There's an APB out for a young woman in a stolen black cart," the cop said. "It says she's armed and violent."

"Well, I'm neither," Katie said, eyeing them suspiciously.

159

"You guys are just going to let me go?"

They nodded. The civilian-dressed man scribbled in a note pad. He tore off the sheet of paper and handed it to her.

She reached for it and held it up to the headlights. **1776** was all that was written, followed by a scribbled signature. She folded it, stuffed it in a coat pocket, and looked up, staring at the men. "I don't understand."

"We can slap the cuffs on you if you want."

"No! I mean—"

The plain-clothes man hooked a thumb behind him. "Those men up there at that checkpoint are city cops. They answer to me. You get further down the road, you're on your own."

The uniformed cop nodded. "The city cops at the checkpoint are *with us.*"

"Won't they recognize the cart?" Katie asked

"Probably," the plain-clothes man said. "It belonged to a smuggler, but it doesn't really matter anymore. Your little TV special was a game-changer. After tonight, things will be different."

"But, but," Katie sputtered, "you're letting me go?"

The man eyed her. "What you did this evening was a brave thing. Thank God there are still people like you in the government media. You've done your part. Now, Scott and I are doing ours. We're *American*, like you."

"Demonstrations are already breaking out all over the city," the cop said. "It will get violent and nasty before it's all settled."

Katie blinked in disbelief.

They stared at her. "Girl, you need to haul ass before the *Guard* arrives."

"Thank you! Thank you!" Katie sprinted to the white cart. "I won't forget this!" She clambered in behind the steering wheel. In a quick second, she had the cart backed up and pulled out onto the freeway. As she passed the cops, she waved, and they waved back.

Three different carts in less than an hour, she mused, as her hands gripped the steering wheel. And she was still free.

Traffic was lighter than normal. A sign? The calm before the storm? How was Sam faring? She prayed his luck was as good as hers. But what if they nabbed her at the checkpoint? She felt for the sheet of paper in her pocket and wasn't reassured.

Fifteen minutes later, she came to stop in a line of traffic. A quarter-mile ahead was the Charleston city limits where the freeway narrowed into a two-lane highway. The cart crept forward before halting again. Katie's heart shifted into high gear.

So much could go wrong. Her life depended on a single sheet of paper with four numbers and a signature. A stinking piece of paper! However, she knew that throughout history, momentous fates often rested on the mundane and simple such as a clerical error, a message not sent or misinterpreted, or merely being at the right place at the right time. She let off the brake, and the cart inched forward and stopped. She slammed a hand on the wheel. This was maddening. She strained to see ahead. *Oh, Christ!* Deputy cruisers were everywhere. Where were those Charleston cops that man back there had promised?

She was within a few cart lengths of the well-lit roadblock before finally spotting a Charleston police cruiser, but no cop. Only tan fatigue-clad deputies were manning the checkpoint. "Oh, no, no..." she breathed. And some of the deputies were eye-scanning. Again, she fought not to whip the cart around and run for it. Her cart crept forward. Only two remained in front of her. She clutched the paper given to her. Maybe a pass to live another day. She eased the cart forward. Still, no city cop. *Oh, God...* She was up next. Should she give the paper to the deputy? Her government ID lay in her lap. Should she hide it and take her chances? A thousand jumbled thoughts raced through her mind, all leading to hell. She was up next. Her drumming heart was so loud she couldn't think. A deputy stuck his head into the window of the cart in front of her, shining a flashlight around. He straightened, and then he flagged the cart on. His eye-scanner remained hanging from a utility belt.

Katie lowered her window and pulled forward, numb with panic.

The deputy—his garb more like a soldier's—leaned down. "Where are you heading this evening?"

"To my parents' home in Perchance."

"Perchance is off-limits, as in closed." He paused, shining a flashlight around the cart. "What's your name? And I need your traveling papers."

Before Katie could reply, a uniformed man stepped up, shoving the deputy aside. Reaching in, he grabbed her shoulders, hugging her. "Hey, Julie! Heading home to see the folks?" He paused and whispered, "Tom."

The dumbfounded deputy stood aside, staring.

The young Charleston city cop eased out from the window. "This is my sister-in-law, Julie Nicholson."

She eyed the name badge on the cop's uniform—Nicholson.

Katie swallowed. "Yeah, Tom, but this deputy says, 'Perchance is 'closed.'"

"Perchance is off-limits," the cop replied, "except to those who live there, like you." The city cop turned to the deputy. "I'll handle this, Harrison. It's family business."

The deputy stepped away. "Suit yourself. But she's blocking traffic."

The cop pointed to the road's shoulder. "Just pull over there, Julie."

Katie drove through the checkpoint, steering the cart to the shoulder.

Nicholson stepped up to her open window. "You have something for me?"

Sitting behind the wheel, motor idling, Katie thrust a sheet of paper out the window.

Nicholson glanced at the note and handed it back. "Keep it. Never know when that signature will come in handy."

Katie folded the paper, shoved it in a coat pocket, and looked up at the policeman standing by her door. "I can't thank you enough, Officer Nicholson."

"Like I said, it's Tom." He hinted a grin. "Are you one of old man Spencer's kids?"

Katie gave a start, uncertainty furrowing her brow.

"It's okay. I grew up in Perchance."

She gave a relieved chuckle. "Yes, 'old man Spencer' is my grandfather."

Nicholson frowned. "And you don't know the Nicholsons?"

"I didn't grow up there. My father did, though. I was born and raised in New York."

"Should've guessed by the accent." He glanced back to the checkpoint. "Cops were called back into town. The mayor even activated the reserves. Seems there's a little celebrating going on—as in firebombings and such. Two more minutes, and I would've been gone, too."

"And I would be in handcuffs."

Nicholson nodded. "Be careful on your way to Perchance. The *really* bad guys love the turmoil.

"What's going on in Perchance?"

He shrugged. "I'm not sure. Just a sketchy report that the police station was bombed and that a Guard helo was shot down by the *Resistance*."

"Jesus..."

"Anyway," Nicholson continued, "the town's been quarantined. No one in, no one out."

Katie rubbed her forehead. "Well, I have to try. There's someone I have to find."

Nicholson stepped back from the window, spoke into a tiny microphone on his collar, and glanced to Katie. "I have to go."

"So do I." Nodding to the cop, Katie shoved the gearstick into forward. "God bless you and your fellow officers who helped me this evening."

Nicholson nodded and headed back to the checkpoint.

Looking over her shoulder, Katie eased the cart back onto the highway. Traffic had thinned and would get even lighter as she got farther from town. It was an hour to her grandparents' home, but that was driving the speed limit. She stepped on the throttle. The electric motor whirred, and the cart disappeared into the gloom.

Twenty minutes later, the pounding in her ears subsided. Her neck and back felt as if they'd been used as crossties. Only an occasional cart passed in the other direction, and she came upon no one going her way. The lack of traffic, especially law enforcement or government troops, sent a cautious shiver down her spine. The roadblock accounted for only the lack of civilian traffic. She had figured that the roads would be crawling with deputies, provincial police, or the Guard. Were the authorities caught unawares? She glanced to the clock: 7:35. Her documentary only hit the airwaves at six. By this time tomorrow, a rabbit wouldn't cross the road without the government knowing it. She gripped the wheel tighter. But then again, maybe not.

Headlights high off the ground and wide apart, a signature of a government vehicle, approached slowly from the opposite direction. Were they looking for civilian stragglers who made it past the checkpoint? Katie slowed to the speed limit and glanced out the window, scrutinizing the vehicle as it sailed past in the dark. It wasn't government. It was an old pickup truck, the kind a few farmers still used. She glanced into the mirror. "Keep going...keep going." Brake lights flashed. Headlights bounced as the truck made a U-turn. "This is definitely not good."

Although electric carts with their low center of gravity could outmaneuver most of the older generation cars and trucks, there was no way she could outrun that pickup truck. Carts, by national law, were governed at fifty miles per hour. That truck could do well over 100. Her eyes went to the mirror; headlights were growing. She glanced around. This had been a smuggler's cart and probably built to outrun God only knows what. There was a reason that cop back there drove this and gave it to her.

Katie nailed it. The motor whirred to life, and she was thrown back in her seat. "Damn!" She stole a peek at the speedometer. It was stuck at 70—its highest reading—and she was still gaining speed. Headlights receded and held steady. She flew past a mileage sign. **Perchance 16** reflected back. Headlights slowly grew again. Katie gave a disgusted sigh. Her grandfather had showed her several ways in and out of town off the beaten path in case she was ever followed. But those behind her probably knew them, too. And for the umpteenth time that evening, adrenaline surged into every muscle and every neuron. She buried the throttle. The cart leapt forward. Her skin grew flush, tingling from the acceleration. She had to be doing well over 100. Could she pull it off? She glanced into the mirror. Up ahead, she'd have to slow for an S-curve, but that old pickup would *really* have to slow or risk a rollover.

Katie let off the throttle, swept through the first curve, and stepped on it. The cart was slung sideways. Her gear clattered around in back, but the cart seemed glued to the pavement. The cart shot through the curves and raced down a straightaway. She glanced into the mirror—only blackness behind. "Yeah, take that!" she shouted, smiling.

A yellow warning light flashed, and her smile vanished. Only thirty minutes of power remained. She pounded the steering wheel. "Shit! Shit! Shit!"

She frantically searched for a side road, someplace to hide before that old truck emerged from the curves. It was a moonless night and darkness swallowed all. The cart raced past a gray slash in the shadows on the right. Katie slammed on the brakes. Tires screeched, and the cart slid sideways. She spun the wheel, doing a U-turn. "It was right...over...here... There it is!" The cart swung left, bouncing onto a caliche road, just as headlights blinked from the direction she'd just come. Did they see her? The yellow light glowed, bathing the inside with forewarning and imminent peril. Katie switched off the heater. The yellow light didn't flicker. Risking darkness on an unfamiliar road, she clicked off the headlights. The evil, little light still glowed. She had to stop before the battery went completely dead. Katie strained to see, barely able to make out a ghost of a trail. The path curved, and she stopped the cart, twisting around, staring back the way she'd come. Her heart thumped, and she tried to swallow but couldn't. A quarter-mile back, headlights shot past the road she was on. She chewed a lip, unsure. They just might keep going, thinking it wasn't worth it. Then again...

Headlights appeared back where the dirt road met the highway. "Oh, God, no!" Katie swung back around and tromped on the throttle. *Wump.* The right, front fender dropped, and the cart jerked to a stop. She gunned the motor—nothing. The cart was stuck fast, and she didn't have time to free it. Without thinking, she jumped out and reached back in for her gear. Shouldering a backpack, she slung another bag over a shoulder. As an afterthought, she snatched the keys from the ignition. She pushed a button on the key fob. The door lowered and locked. The rattle of a diesel engine echoed behind her, and she shook. *Think!*

She glanced around. Dark forest rose on both sides of the road. She sprinted across the caliche and into the woods, totally blind. After perhaps twenty steps, briars and vines grabbed her, but she tore free. *Whop.* She smacked into a tree and hit the ground, momentarily stunned. Groaning, she worked up to a knee, feeling her forehead. Warm stickiness met her touch. The diesel clatter grew louder. Risking a light, she worked her vidphone out from a coat pocket and clicked on its tiny flashlight. A cobalt beam pierced the darkness. She was totally surrounded by heavy thicket, interspersed with pines. Over her shoulder, she made out bouncing headlights. *Run! Run!* the voice shouted in her head, and yet she stepped cautiously forward, pushing away brush. Distance was what she needed. Whoever was in that truck wouldn't go to this trouble unless they had an agenda. The backpack bounced on her shoulders as she half-trotted through the brambles. Although out of sight, she heard the pickup stop. They must've found her cart. The engine clatter vanished. Except for her tromping through the brush, and her pounding heart, all was silent.

Katie halted, breathing in ragged gasps, and glanced to the vidphone's glowing SOS button. The signal, a homing beacon, went to her grandparents' phone. It also went to Sam's—and he was in custody. She had to take the chance. She mashed the button, clicked off the phone, and stuffed it in a coat pocket. Dropping to the ground, she scooted on her belly behind a knee-high yaupon holly. The smell of decayed leaves, pine needles, and dank earth filled her nostrils. Voices echoed through the clear, night air.

"Still think it's a woman?" a man said.

"Yep," came the reply, "or she wouldn't have gone to this much trouble. Just like females to run from their own shadows and get themselves stuck like this."

Katie blinked in disbelief. She recognized that last voice. It belonged to Caleb Jeffery.

"Doors locked," Jeffery said. "Clint—"

"I'll get a tire iron," the man called Clint said.

Murmurs drifted. The sound of breaking glass tore through the night, followed by several moments of silence.

"You were right, Caleb—checkout the sweet smell."

"Well, now. I've smelled *that* before. And after what I saw on TV this evening, I figured a certain woman would be heading this way."

For a fleeting moment, she had thought of going out to him, but his words carried a sneer that shook her to the bone. Last time she was in Perchance, she had spurned Caleb's advances, instead choosing to see Sam. For Caleb to find her now... She cringed even more.

"It's okay, Katie!" he shouted. "You can come out. It's just me, Caleb!"

She eased the backpack off and burrowed further into pine needles and soft earth.

"You talkin' about old Spencer's granddaughter?" Clint asked.

"Yeah. We dated. She likes me."

"You creepy slime," Katie whispered, "we never 'dated,' and we never will."

"Caleb, if she liked you, why ain't she coming outta the woods?"

"Might not be her," Caleb replied. "But it doesn't really matter. There's a gal out there. Let's look around."

"If she's an old girlfriend, that means you ain't gonna share her. Why should I risk breaking my neck in the dark if I don't get a piece? Besides, if that is Spencer's granddaughter, I don't cater to finding myself on that old man's shit list. I say we get back to doing a little fishing out on the highway while we can."

Caleb spoke in a low voice, and Clint laughed. Katie couldn't catch their words. She didn't need to.

"Come on, Katie!" Caleb shouted. "Don't play games. It's too cold and too dark for that. Let me sneak you into town, take you to your granddaddy's."

Katie shivered and not just from the cold. She saw a flashlight beam flickering through the brush. The sound of snapping twigs grew closer.

"Caleb," Clint shouted near the truck, "we ain't going to find her out here in these woods, not in the dark."

"I know she's out here..."

"Hell, man, she could be anywhere. She might've called someone. Let's get outta here before her granddaddy or the law shows up." Clint paused. "You know the law's gotta be looking for her."

"I can smell her," Caleb replied. "I know I'm close."

In spite of the cold, sweat dripped into Katie's eyes, stinging them. She couldn't stop shaking. If he found her, they would never find her body. Well, she wouldn't go down without a fight. She would kick, bite, scratch, and scream. Oh, yes! Caleb Jeffery would know he had tangled with a she-devil. For sure she would leave her mark on him! Without warning, twigs snapped to the right, not ten feet away. A shadow waved a flashlight.

Reaching for the backpack, Katie ever-so-gently crawled to the left, keeping the holly bush between herself and Caleb. She burrowed deeper into soft pine needles and damp humus.

The flashlight beam lit her former hiding spot and highlighted the bush she hid behind. She prayed silently. *Oh, God, oh, God, help me! Sam, I need you!*

The beam moved away then jerked back. "Katie—or whoever you are—I know you're here. Let us save you, take you into town."

Katie stifled a cry. He wasn't speaking in her direction! She held her breath. The beam flickered around her, past her, and then moved away.

"Damnit, Caleb, let's go!" shouted the voice back at the truck. "I'm getting bad vibes about this!"

Holly twigs scraped her, and she covered her head. *He had found her!* She was a split second from jumping up and rushing him, gouging, all teeth and nails, when the trampling of brush receded. He had passed not two feet from her. She peeked over an arm. The flashlight beam waved in the woods back toward the pickup.

"Jeffery, man, we're wasting time out here."

"Oh, shut up!" Caleb yelled. "Damnit, now my ear's bleeding again." He stomped up to the truck "There's just this gut feeling I have about that little bitch. She's probably watching us and laughing right now."

Watching she was, but laughing she wasn't. Katie lay her head in her arms. Exhaustion set in. Simply breathing in and out was an effort.

Murmurs drifted from the direction of the truck and cart, but she no longer cared. The pounding in her chest lessened, and her eyelids lowered, tense muscles finally giving in, relaxing...

"Katie, it's okay."

She felt warm fingers working through her hair and caressing her face. Her eyes fluttered open. "Sam?"

"Yes, princess, it's me, Sam."

She rose to an elbow, feeling Sam's loving gaze. Her arms

shot out, encircling his neck, and he crushed her to him. "Sam, don't leave me!" she choked, sobbing. "Please don't ever leave me again!"

"I heard you crying and got here as quick as I could." He cradled her, stroking her hair and back. "I'll never leave you, Katie—never, ever—"

"Am I still your doll?"

"Yes."

Katie clung to Sam and wept quietly against his chest. "Sam, I need you..."

Katie's head jerked up, startled. "What was that!" It was so black she wasn't sure her eyes were even open. Something rustled in the brush a few feet away. She was lying in damp leaves and pine needles. Slowly, her eyes adjusted, and strange silhouettes took shape around her. "Sam?" She whispered. "Sam?"

The evening's horror came rushing back, and she choked. She covered her eyes with filthy hands, fighting back tears. Again, something stirred the nearby bushes. Forcing calm, she worked out the vidphone from a coat pocket and risked a light. A pair of yellow eyes, maybe a foot off the ground, reflected back. The eyes vanished, and the faint thumping of padded feet receded into darkness.

Katie switched off the light and glanced to the tiny glowing numbers at the bottom of the device: 0552 47 degrees F. She glanced around. Which way was the cart? Were Caleb and his friend still around? She never heard them leave. She blinked, frightened and confused. *It'll be light in another hour,* she thought with comfort. At dawn, she'd take stock of things. Gripping the phone, she lay back down, shivering in her coat, never noticing the cold until now. And her forehead throbbed something awful.

Yes, perhaps the light of a new day would bring new promise.

Two prisoners sat alone in back of the speeding van. Heavily manacled, Sam leaned against the van's worn walls. Was it four or five days ago he was in his classroom going through the motions? And this is what *action* got him. Dark streaks on the steel floor caught his attention. Rust or bloodstains? It no longer mattered.

"Man, they worked you over pretty good," Turner Wells said. Also shackled, the tall preacher sat hunched over on the bench across the narrow aisle. "You okay?"

Sam shifted and groaned. "Only hurts when I breathe."

"Should have gone ahead and killed him. I would've helped you plead your case to Jesus."

Sam managed a chuckle, and then he grimaced as his battered chest ached. A spasm shot through his right side—cracked ribs. He licked split lips and managed to sit upright, gazing through the swollen slits that were his eyes. "Not even Jesus can help us now."

"He takes that back, Lord," Turner said. "When things seem the darkest is when the Lord really shines." Turner leaned back. "Most of the time."

Sam winced. "Yeah, well this ain't one of those times."

"We don't know that." Turner shifted, and chains rattled. "What seems an end sometimes is a beginning...or an out."

"If you've got a direct line to Jesus, now is the time to use it."

Seconds passed, yet no other words passed between the men. The vehicle creaked. Chains rattled and bleakness, with its iron blanket, descended.

After a moment, Sam glanced to the van's front; a solid wall with a wire-mesh window. On the other side, the driver and a guard were engaged in an animated conversation.

The preacher followed Sam's gaze. "Something's going on."

Sam remained silent, studying the guards.

"Looks to me like they're arguing about something," Turner added.

Sam zeroed in on the guards' words. *War* was repeated over and over. "So, it's happened..."

"Something sure happened," Turner said, eyeing the guards.

"Didn't you notice how everyone was rushing around when they loaded us?"

"I was a little out of it."

"Yeah, guess you were."

Sam glanced to the man across from him. "Where are the others?"

"Took them away around noon, yesterday. Had all of us together, but you were in bad shape, man—and they wanted you alive for sure. So, they took you and me over to the old courthouse jail until today...don't know why they held me over."

"What day is it?"

"Monday." Turner glanced at him. "Good thing they moved us, too. There was a lot of commotion going on last night... somebody even blew up the detention offices."

Sam tried to laugh, but it hurt too much. "Anyone killed?"

"Naw...just a few cuts and bruises. Hardly anyone at home."

Sam nodded...seemed he was on the verge of missing a lot of things. In too much agony to think clearly, he scooted around, trying to ease the throbbing in his chest. Rifle butts to the body was not a way to start a day. He sighed and swallowed. "How is it, when you try to do good, do the right thing, *wrong* always turns and punches you in the mouth?"

"Trial by fire," the preacher said. "Don't ever give up or give in."

BOOM.

"Hot damn. He heard me!" Turner shouted.

The van swerved, careened into a ditch, and came to a crashing stop. Sam and Turner were tossed into the air, colliding violently with the walls and with each other. The guards up front began shouting, struggling to exit the vehicle. Wedged under a bench, Sam lay stunned.

Pop-pop-pop. A staccato blast of automatic weapons' fire ripped through the air. Several rounds tore into the cab with an ugly *smack*. More shouts and screams, and then all was silent. On his side, Sam tried to rotate to see but was stuck under the steel bench, facing the wall. "Preacher man?"

Nothing.

Orders were barked outside, and a voice came from the cab's back window. "Anyone in there!"

"Hell yes!" Sam shouted back. "There're two of us. Get us outta here!"

More voices and the sound of jingling keys came from the backdoor. Within seconds, someone tugged on his shoulders and back.

"You must be some badass for them to chain you like that," a man said.

Another pair of hands grabbed his legs, and he was lifted out from under the bench.

"I've got his ankles," came a second voice. Still face-down, he was half-carried, half-dragged out the back door. Sam glanced to the side and learned why Turner Wells couldn't speak; he would never speak again. Lying against the wall, his head was twisted at an odd angle. Sam's jaw tightened, and he looked away.

Seconds later, with dusk closing in, the men sat Sam upright on the ground. A hooded man knelt nearby, fumbling with keys, trying to get one to fit the shackle lock. Sam glanced up to another man leaning over him.

Wearing dark clothes and a baseball cap, a dark-skinned, clean-shaven man around his own age stared back. "We figured any prisoner the OIS had would be an ally of ours. You have a name?"

"Sam Moore."

Click. "Got it," the hooded man said. He began unwrapping chains from around Sam.

"I'm Rob," the dark-skinned man said. He nodded to the man helping Sam with the shackles. "That man freeing you goes by Buck."

Groaning, Sam heaved himself up. Chains fell away. Bruised, battered, and with what seemed a hot poker stuck in his chest, he nonetheless breathed deeply. His coat was torn, and there was a chill in the air, yet the taste of freedom pushed everything aside. Freedom was exhilarating. He rubbed his arms, trying to get circulation back and wondering what lay next.

Rob nodded to the van where another man dragged out the guards' lifeless bodies from the cab. "The other prisoner didn't make it. Was he a friend?"

"Yes," Sam said, "and he was a man of God."

"Sorry, man," Buck said.

Sam nodded, noting the men's strange accents. The two definitely weren't from the Carolinas. Swallowing, he extended a hand, shaking first one man's hand then another. "I can't thank you enough. Talk about timing."

Rob, who stood as tall as Sam, nodded. "Glad we could help."

Sam glanced to Buck. Shorter and stockier than Sam, he was in his thirties and sported a short, neatly trimmed beard. He moved deliberately. A morose silence hung about him. Both were

171

well-fed, well-clothed, and well-armed. They were shouldering modern assault rifles, a type Sam had never seen. Military web belts wrapped around their waists were filled with ammo. A guard's pump 12-gauge shotgun and two semiautomatic pistols lay on the ground nearby.

Rob reached down for the pistols and tossed one to Buck. They expertly checked the weapons before nonchalantly stuffing them inside their web belts. Two days earlier, Sam would have been disturbed that the men in front of him could behave so casual after killing two men. But that was another life.

Buck reached down for the shotgun, racked the pump action, and shells spilled out onto the ground. He gathered them up, stuffed them in a pocket, and thrust the unloaded gun to Sam. "This is yours if you want it. You can have the shells later."

Sam hesitated before reaching for it. His fingers gripped the action. It felt alive.

Buck released the shotgun to him. "Ever counted coup?"

Unsure of how to react, Sam paused. "No, can't say that I have."

Rob lit a smoke. "First war trophy, huh?"

Sam glanced to the weapon in his hand. "Is that what you guys call this? 'Counting coup?' 'War trophy?'"

Buck shook his head from under his hood. Rob exhaled. Harsh smoke swirled into growing darkness "That's the way it is, man. It's called war."

"In case you aren't aware," Buck said, "as of last night, we're at war. The United States of America declared war on the NAC. They're calling for the destruction of the Directorate." He paused. "Some are calling it *Revolution Two Point O*."

Sam blinked. His heart pounded. Katie must have pulled it off. That was the only explanation. "What did I miss?"

The men exchanged glances. Rob faced Sam. "The Underground hijacked the airwaves last night, finally exposing the Directorate for what we already knew: fascists and mass murderers. The Western Alliance—the United States— announced over the airwaves a call to arms." Rob pinched off the fire from his cigarette and stuffed the remains into a pocket. "We need to get out of here. You can join us if you want. By the looks of you, you must've really pissed off someone high up." He eyed Sam. "The enemy of my enemy..."

Sam bit a lip. "Where am I?"

"You're on a back road," Rob answered, "ten miles east of Saint Stephens. Guess the guards were afraid of an ambush or something."

Buck chuckled.

"There's someone I have to find," Sam said.

"You won't find him out here," Buck said.

"It's not a 'him,' it's a her."

The guerilla fighters exchanged glances. "Wife?" Rob asked.

"No," Sam replied. "She's a close family friend." He swallowed. "That message the other night...was there anything said about death camps?"

They again glanced to one another, and Sam read their uncertainty in the dim light. Rob finally spoke up. "Yeah. A gruesome show, man. It finally lit the match."

Buck glanced from under his hood to Sam. "Which brings us to...what is your point?"

Sam hesitated. It meant giving away that he was once a member of the Party of Terror. In their mood, they might shoot him outright. He touched a sore lip. "I had a hand in getting that message over the air. That's why the OIS arrested me. And I have to find the woman who put that documentary together. We're close friends. I told her that if *we* could pull off the impossible, it could lead to war and—"

Rob gave a start. "What the...this is getting screwier by the minute."

"There was a woman narrator in that story," Buck said, eyeing Sam. "You trying to say that you two are partners in crime?"

Sam nodded. "Something like that."

"Well," Rob began, "whoever you're looking for won't be out here."

Sam held his breath, waiting for them to ask what his part in it was.

"You can tell us later how you two got that video over the air," Rob said. "Right now, we have to haul ass."

Sam breathed in relief. That would give him time to make up a story.

"Kurt!" Rob shouted to a man dragging a lifeless guard from the van. "Let's go!"

Sam glanced to the van for the first time and noticed that it wasn't a man laying out the dead guards. It was a teenage boy. The boy had stripped everything useful, even their boots and bloody coats, and stuffed all into a nearby backpack. So, this was what war was like? Stark brutality. Yet the Directorate, a party he had been proud to call himself a member of, was every bit as brutal.

The boy shouldered the pack and hustled up. "Got it all."

Sam scrutinized him. Unlike the two men, the kid spoke in the familiar Carolina twang. A wicked-looking hunting rifle hung from his other shoulder. Perhaps sixteen or seventeen, the boy had tousled brown hair and a wispy beard. Yet it was his eyes that caught Sam's attention. They held a cold maturity that he had seen only once in one so young. His thoughts went to Mark Thurmont, then to the other kids and their families. Did any escape?

"He coming with us?" the boy said, eyeing Sam suspiciously.

"For now," Rob said, hoisting a rucksack.

The boy glanced to Rob. "You said we weren't bringing back any strangers."

"We need all the help we can get."

"But—"

"Case closed," Rob snapped. "Let's move out." He stepped into the nearby forest.

Buck, with his hood pulled low, followed behind. He passed the gawking boy. "Kurt, don't ever question orders."

"Yes, sir." The kid fell in behind Rob. Buck paused and eyed Sam. "You coming with us?"

Sam hesitated. "Yeah." Shouldering the shotgun, he followed the three into the bush. Tense darkness closed in, swallowing all.

Katie's eyes fluttered open. She rose to an elbow, yawning. Speckled light met her eyes. Still gripping the phone, she glanced to the time: 0815. Groaning, she climbed to her feet, wobbled, and caught herself. "What a nightmare," she said, recalling yesterday's desperation and the night terror.

Dream fragments flashed through her conscience, and she was strangely comforted. It was Sam. He had held her. The images dissolved, and she sighed loudly. She recalled the one time they had held each other, how strong his arms were, and how secure he had made her feel. She longed for that tenderness again.

Katie forced her thoughts to the present and surveyed her surroundings. Centuries-old slash pines—their orange, block bark testifying to their age—towered over the forest. Interspersed here and there were bare sweet gums, hickory, and smaller, naked dogwoods. Clumps of hollies and other evergreen shrubs she couldn't identify dotted the forest floor. Ever-present briars filled in the gaps. Even in late winter, the forest was breathtaking. In another circumstance, in another season, she would love to return and share the magnificence with someone special.

Dropping the vidphone in a coat pocket, she brushed off leaves and pine needles. Something glinted through the forest shadows. She slung the backpack over a shoulder, hung the overnight bag from another shoulder, and crept through the brush toward the object. After a few yards, she halted. It was the cart, alone and stark in the morning sunlight.

Stealthy as a fox, Katie picked her way around thickets, growing ever closer to what she hoped might carry her to safety, but she feared the worst. She paused just inside the woodland shadows, kneeled, and peeked around a pine sapling. The dirt road was ten feet away, but things didn't look promising. Shattered glass was strewn in the road around the cart, and the cart's battery box cover lay off to one side. "Those bastards," she murmured. Her chin tightened as she studied the scene. Five minutes passed as the suspense mounted.

"I can't take it," she said, stepping out in the open.

She paused. Nothing. All seemed quiet. Caleb wouldn't nab her here anyway, where she might escape. He'd wait until she

175

was preoccupied with the cart. Katie took tentative steps toward the vehicle. Still nothing. She crossed what passed for a road. A sick feeling rose with each footfall. The driver's door window was gone, and the windshield was smashed in. Shaking her head, she stepped to the cart's tail, dreading what she'd find. Katie drew up, not wanting to look, but she knew she had to. She gazed down to the batteries, and her worst fear was realized. All the battery cables were cut, and the main electric harness had been ripped out. The cart was dead. She glanced to the tires and chuckled grimly. Leave it to Caleb Jeffery to forget the *coup d'état*—the tires were left untouched.

Katie grabbed the vidphone from a coat pocket and tapped the screen.

All circuits are busy... came the reply. She swore. Her pressing the panic button last night was probably for naught. On second thought, all concerned were probably better off if her call didn't get through. If poor Sam were still in custody, or even if he wasn't, the authorities most certainly had his phone and could use it to locate her. What a stupid thing it was to press that panic button... She swallowed. There was one more thing she dreaded doing, but she knew it was a must. She stepped back to the driver's side and forced herself to glance into the still intact outside mirror.

"Yikes!" She stared in horror at her reflection. Her disheveled hair looked like a bird's nest. Wincing at the inch-long gash that streaked her forehead just above her left brow, she began picking pine needles from her hair. A scab had formed, and even if it were possible, the wound was too late to suture. "I'll carry this for life," she murmured. Dried blood left dark tracks on her forehand and cheeks. Her face was drawn and haggard.

Katie dropped the backpack and let the other bag slide from a shoulder. She glanced around. Nothing, no one. Kneeling, she unsnapped the backpack's top flap. Seconds later, an emergency medical kit lay open on the ground. She tilted a water bottle over grimy, blood-caked fingers and wiped them on a clean cloth. Then, alcohol pad in hand, she stared in the cart's mirror and gingerly dabbed her head wound. Another alcohol pad made a dent in the bloody streaks and filth on her cheeks. She carefully dropped the used pads in a Ziplock bag. The less anyone knew of her condition, the better. After closing the medical kit, she stuffed it and the plastic bag into the backpack and secured the top flap. Keeping a constant watch for the unusual, she quickly pulled a hand purse from the small gym bag. Out came a hairbrush and hairpins. Moving quickly, deftly, she pinned up her hair.

With everything packed away, she unsnapped her coat, rolled it up, and secured it on top of the backpack. **SYRACUSE** was spelled out on her gray sweatshirt. She worked the larger rucksack over her shoulders and slung the smaller bag around her neck where it hung loose at her side. Lastly, she adjusted a faded green baseball cap, careful to keep it away from the laceration. Feeling somewhat fresher in both body and spirit, she placed hands on hips and studied the way back to the highway. What looked like military vehicles rolled past. A second later, the roar of a heavy engine and lug tires reverberated and receded. "Hell, what's ten or twelve miles? At least I'm still breathing... and free." She cast one last glance to the forlorn cart before marching toward the highway.

After watching that seditious broadcast night before last, Commissar Jonathon Tipton knew it had been a wise move to stay in Perchance. Charleston was burning. After a flurry of violence here the last two nights, things had settled into an uneasy stalemate, at least *in town*. Teacup in one hand, he pushed aside a drape corner with the other and peeked out from his temporary quarters in Leeward Community on the north side of town. Bright, mid-morning sun almost murdered his eyes. Two hundred yards to the south, out on the highway, a company of blue-camouflage clad Provincial Guard troops marched amid a convoy of boxy, Chinese-made Humvee knock-offs called All Terrain Troop Movers, or TMs. Some of the vehicles were on their way to Charleston, others were part of a perimeter established yesterday around this shit-for-nothing town. "What a waste of resources," Tipton murmured.

Knock-knock-knock.

Tipton released the drapes. "Yes."

A black-uniformed man entered the room. Removing a black baseball cap, he halted in front of Tipton. "Commissar, I have news of the missing van."

Tipton adjusted the bandage under his dress-shirt's gray collar. He tilted the teacup, sipped, and then he moved to a small coffee table to replace the cup on a saucer. "Let it out, Captain Norton." he said, nodding to the curtains. "I'm sure it will fit into the narrative out there."

The man stepped closer. His heavily-starched fatigues made a rasping sound. "That second van with the two prisoners—"

"Tell me it's arrived in Charleston."

The man swallowed. "The van was found in a ditch this morning, shot full of holes, ten miles south of Andrews. Ambushed, we believe yesterday. The guards were murdered and..."

Tipton stared. "The prisoners?"

Norton hesitated. "One prisoner was found dead inside."

"Please tell me the prisoner inside was—"

"It was that preacher, Wells."

Tipton's small eyes twitched behind thick glass lenses. "And Moore? Where is he?"

"We don't know." Norton cleared his throat. "There was no sign of Moore. His shackles were lying nearby. It's possible he's with whoever ambushed the van."

With his arms behind his back, Tipton began pacing. His loathing for the anarchists, especially Leonard Spencer, was only superseded by his hatred for Samuel Moore. And it wasn't that Moore had come within seconds of choking the life out of him. A cornered animal—even one as timid as Moore—had buttons that, when pushed, forced the unpredictable. He had no idea that the humbled teacher would strike out with such violence. And to think those human body parts he'd tossed in front of Moore didn't even belong to his former students. The morgue had brought the grisly props over at his behest. The ears and fingers had belonged to a young Commonwealth soldier; they were all that remained after a roadside bomb last month. No, it wasn't only that the teacher had physically assaulted him. What ate at Tipton was that Moore had made him, Commissar Jonathan Tipton, laughable. The fox had been out-foxed. *No one* can do that and live to brag about it. "Any idea who's responsible?"

"Militants."

"Obviously," Tipton said with a hint of sarcasm. "Was it the same group of heathens led by Leonard Spencer that are operating around here?"

"No, sir."

"How do you know?"

"The local dissidents here use older, obsolete weapons."

"Which seem adequate enough," Tipton added with a bite.

Norton ignored Tipton's comment and unsnapped a fatigue shirt pocket. He dug out a two-inch metal bullet casing and held it up to the commissar. "Dozens of these were found around the van's ambush sight."

Tipton halted in front of the captain and reached for the spent cartridge. "Something different?"

"It's from an experimental assault rifle, the XM-Eight." Norton nodded to the casing in the commissar's hand. "It's issued to U.S. Special Forces, mostly Green Berets."

Tipton gave a start, examining the spent .30 caliber cartridge between his fingers.

"Commissar, that van's protected with half-inch steel armor, yet it could've been wrapped in foil for all the good it did. Those rounds punched right through. Some even exited out the other side."

Tipton's gaze fell on the young captain. "Green Berets...are you sure?"

Norton nodded. "Two were killed near the Western Front this past year, both carrying XM-Eights."

The commissar tossed the casing back to Norton and resumed pacing. "Are you suggesting that enemy Special Forces are now operating on our soil, and with impunity?"

"Those weapons may have been smuggled in," the captain suggested, "given to the local anarchists."

Tipton stepped back to Norton, studying the younger man for several quiet seconds. OIS officer James Norton was of medium build, athletic, agile, and carried himself as a professional soldier, which he had been. A war orphan, Norton was the product of Directorate Youth Camps. And he was a perfect fit for his current position. Only the most trusted—and ruthless—belonged to the Office of Internal Security. The man's loyalty to the Directorate was unwavering...or was it? Tipton had heard about Norton's grumblings that the Directorate was becoming "bloated and lazy" and "too tolerant of the disloyal." But weren't those words themselves treasonous? Upon hearing about Norton's recent gripes, a seed was planted in the commissar's mind, but what type of plant and what type of fruit it might bear, he did not yet know. The younger man's unhappiness was catalogued—but not forgotten. Tipton cleared his throat. "What's your professional assessment of the situation, Captain Norton? Be frank."

Fiddling with the hat in his hand, Norton shifted. "Mr. Tipton, M-Eights are too rare and too expensive to be in the hands of rebel riffraff. I visited the van's ambush sight twenty miles from here. It was a professional job. And someone among the rebels knew the terrain. The ambush spot was perfect." Norton paused, eyeing the commissar. "The van's front end was blown away with a high powered, yet compact, explosive. The attack was organized and probably over in seconds. Hit, loot, and fade away. Whoever ambushed our van had lots of practice."

Tipton faced the man. He slowly removed his glasses and wiped the thick lens with a handkerchief. "U.S. Special Forces working with locals perhaps?"

The captain nodded. "More than likely."

"And operating in *my* district. No doubt Moore could've led us to the traitors. And now..." Tipton shook his head, giving a disgusted sigh. "President Henshaw has waited too long for action. He was informed last year that enemy agents were among us, recruiting, hoping to create an insurgency. And what did he do?"

"I believe upon hearing the news, he conferred with advisors and then played a round of golf."

"And I suppose he's still 'conferring' and golfing, while civil unrest spreads and explodes into violence." The commissar paused, gauging the younger man. "I sat on the committee that appoints the president."

"I didn't know that."

"I thought the OIS was up on everything?"

For a split second, confusion moved across Norton's face, and he stood, silent.

Tipton resumed pacing. "And I wasn't the only dissenter on that committee, let me tell you." He glanced to Norton, wondering what the security officer *really* thought while watching his once vaunted Directorate metastasize into something unrecognizable. Tipton knew he took a chance of having his own loyalty questioned, but it was his nature to use, to make allies, or flush out enemies when the opportunity arose. The ability to retreat, advance, or *modify* was a trait that had served him well throughout the years. He sighed inside.

Change...the idea had been growing stronger.

No! He forced the latter from his thoughts and concentrated on the here and now. What was needed now was swift, decisive action. Yet, the Party seemed to trudge in cement galoshes. Apparently, Norton saw that, too. The commissar halted and faced Norton. "The Directorate has grown soft, lazy, giving too much power to the Office of the Presidency. We all know the President is only a figurehead, giving the Directorate human form, making Party resolutions more palatable to the masses."

"Or to shake an angry fist at."

"Yes," Tipton nodded, "that, too." He waved an arm. "And now look where Directorate inaction got us?"

The captain rolled the bullet casing between thumb and forefinger. "Commissar, I find it bizarre that anyone with a brain would join a movement to overthrow the government. We're the best thing the people have going."

The commissar swore inside. The captain didn't take the bait, at least not yet. However, Tipton was all about Tipton and no buffoon. There would be another time to test the captain for his usefulness. He decided to go with the younger man's thinking whether it was contrary to his own or not. "To think that some people believe they're better off as *Americans*," he added, sneering the last word. "The United States was flawed at its founding. People *cannot* rule themselves. That's a proven fact. Look where it got them—total chaos." He replaced the glasses on his nose, pushed them up with a forefinger, and stuffed the handkerchief back into a pocket. "The Directorate brought them order and virtually stamped out crime, even exterminated extreme poverty."

The captain gazed at Tipton. "Mr. Tipton, after that broadcast, the word *exterminated* is officially taboo."

The commissar waved off the comment. "I know, I know, but you must admit, those beasts are treated humanely, which is more than they deserve."

Norton nodded, shrugging. "They are animals with no earthly contribution to the betterment of the whole. I don't understand the outrage. The filthy creatures shown in that broadcast were nothing but a drag on society. A tumor. We're only eliminating that which is diseased so the rest of the body can live on, healthy and productive." The captain sighed. "Yes, the citizens should be thanking us for removal of those dregs."

Tipton stared past Norton. "I want that old bastard, Spencer, out of the picture—permanently. One less hoodlum to worry about."

"What about Moore?" Norton's brow wrinkled. "As an ex-Party member, doesn't he pose a bigger threat?"

Tipton chuckled, holding up a tiny black box. "Moore's vidphone. And guess what? It went off the night of the telecast. A certain someone hit the panic button."

Norton grinned, stuffing the empty bullet casing back into his fatigue shirt pocket. "I wondered why you weren't as perturbed with Moore's escape as I thought you would be. So, who was it?"

The commissar examined the device in his hand, smiling, knowing he was once again in the catbird seat. "It was the woman who hijacked the news program—Moore's accomplice. And..."

Norton raised a brow. "And?"

"And her name just happens to be Katie Spencer."

Mouth agape, Norton stared. "We wouldn't have the good fortune of her being related to—"

Tipton nodded. "Yes, we would. She's Spencer's granddaughter. After committing those heinous atrocities, she somehow managed to elude the authorities in Charleston. She *was* heading in this direction."

"Was?"

"Instead of the jailer holding Moore's phone for me, it was stuffed into another prisoner's personal effects envelope. This morning, I stumbled across the phone in the preacher's envelope." Tipton held up the tiny device. "If I would've had this all along, the Spencer girl would now be in custody, and possibly Moore with her." He shook his head, snorting. "Incompetence comes with a price. Those local jailers were imbeciles. No wonder their jail is now a smoking crater."

It was the captain's turn to pace. "When and where did the call originate?"

Tipton gave a subtle frown; he was the one always asking the questions. But making an enemy of an OIS officer was worse than swallowing one's pride; for now, he'd play along with him. "The call originated from inside the old Francis Marion National Forest at twenty-forty-five, the night of the broadcast."

"That's just southeast of here," Norton said. "But that was night before last. She's probably already come and gone. Escaped to the other side."

Tipton dropped the phone into a slack's pocket and faced Norton. "Perhaps not. She may be hanging around town, waiting for Moore."

Norton glanced to the commissar. "How do you know she's going to wait for him?"

Tipton shrugged. "Just a hunch." In his possession was a photo taken last December of the Spencer girl locked in an intimate embrace with Moore. Tipton chuckled inside; the two were more than just comrades.

"One would think," Norton said, breaking the commissar's thoughts, "that Perchance is the last place Moore would head to."

"He has a vested interest here." Tipton stepped to an end table, lifted a cup, and sipped lukewarm tea.

"You believe the girl really means something to him?" Norton said, gazing to the older man.

Tipton took another sip then gripped the cup, contemplating. "Not just her. The whole Spencer family. They're all he has left." Tipton faced the OIS officer. "I want a twenty-four-seven guard on the Spencer home. If old Spencer, his granddaughter, or Moore show, I want them immediately taken into custody." He paused. "Do what you want with the old man. Once he's out of the picture, I want his house—no, the whole damn block—burned to the ground. Let that be a lesson to traitors and collaborators."

Norton nodded, giving a rare grin. "You and I have a lot in common, Commissar Tipton."

"Possibly." Cup and saucer in hand, Tipton headed to the kitchen. "I want to pay a call to whoever is in command of securing the town."

"I'll send over a couple of men for escort."

"That will work," Tipton shouted from the kitchen. Moments later, he stood in the kitchen door, gazing at the younger man. "Is there anything else I need to know about?"

"No, sir." Norton turned and stepped to the door. With his hand gripping the doorknob, he hesitated, gazing down to the carpeted floor.

"What is it, Captain?"

"I should notify the Charleston office of your plan."

Arms folded, Tipton stared innocently at the security officer. "Yes, that is your duty, I suppose."

The captain glanced up. "But you're going to do that, right, Commissar? Report your plan?"

"Most certainly I shall."

"Then my report would only be redundant and unnecessary."

The commissar shifted his feet. "Why add another burden to those who already have their hands full?"

Norton nodded. "Right. And by all reports, Charleston *is* in chaos."

"Rioting, burning..."

After a moment, Norton stepped through the open doorway and glanced back. "I'll send those men right over, Mr. Tipton." He disappeared, and the door clicked softly.

Tipton stood staring at the closed door, tapping a forefinger to his lips. After a moment, he stepped back to the window and a forefinger pushed aside a curtain. He gazed, unfocused. Thanks to rebels years ago, his life was now off-kilter. If he couldn't catch Samuel Moore, he could at least steal from Moore that which was stolen from him.

And then what?

Sam slumped over in a canvas chair. His elbows sat on a worn, folding table as he cradled a steaming mug of potato soup. Raw lacerations on his wrists from the chains shone stark in the dim light of a kerosene lamp hanging from a tent support rod. He tilted the mug and caught a potato chunk. Eyes half-closed, he chewed slowly, mechanically, not really tasting but contemplating. Where was Katie in all this? Was she okay? Was she even alive? Of all the despair and suffering he'd been part of the past few days, it was amazing how clear he could recall her face, the feel of her soft curves as she pressed against him. No, he wouldn't go there...not yet.

Sam forced his thoughts to the present and focused on Buck, who sat on a nearby cot cleaning a high-tech assault rifle. The man wasted no motion, working with deliberate expertise—a professional. Sam glanced to Rob, who lounged in a folding chair across from him, smoking. The man's gaze was as Sam's had been: unfixed. His thoughts perhaps on a fair memory that drove him, kept him going in his bleakest moments. And now, in a rare, quiet moment, recollection had its way. Sam couldn't understand how the two could act so nonchalant after what just happened. Death's casualness, its callousness, lay heavy on the two. Would he become like them, he wondered? A shiver moved down his spine. Uneasy seconds passed, and he cleared his throat. "It's obvious you guys aren't from around here. The way you two handled yourselves this evening, I'd say you're military. And the question begs to be asked—whose?"

Cigarette smoke drifted, and the tense silence increased. Neither would divulge one iota of information, or so he thought.

Buck shoved a cleaning rod through a short barrel. "We're from the Western Alliance."

Sam stared.

Rob puffed thoughtfully, and then he scooted up his chair next to Sam's. "U.S. Special Forces. Our mission is to help organize the Resistance into a viable fighting force."

Buck snapped the black gun barrel into the composite stock. *Clink.* "Chaos and mayhem makes us sleep better at night."

Sam gazed with deadpan, exhausted eyes, but inside, his nerves shook. There was no going back to his old world. To

185

Moore, the Directorate had been like an abusive parent. Yet, even a battered child sometimes harbored affection for the parent, affection born from security. Whipped, punched, and pummeled became the perverted norm. And it—*they*—were *always* there, pounding fist into palm, waiting. Yes, the Directorate was *always* there. Except for the first few years of his life, the Directorate was all Sam knew. In a sick, convoluted way, the constant psychological beatings gave his life that sense of security. One could always count on the beatings. His jaw tightened. Even if he could escape the long arm of the Directorate, what would he do? Yet, isn't this what he had wanted, what he had hoped for—to be free?

Now he was *free*. Sam's breath left him as if he were hit in the gut with an iron club, and he felt dizzy. He was never taught how to think for himself without first checking with the Directorate.

Sam nodded to the kid stretched out on a sleeping bag in the corner, with his back to them. A soft snore drifted. "He your guide?"

Smoke swirled around Rob and lazily floated across the tent. "Yes. Kurt knows the region, the locals, and most importantly, he knows who to trust."

Buck rubbed a clean cloth over the weapon's magazine, glancing up. "What did you do to get chained up like that, man? You kill someone important?"

Sam eyed his cup, feeling both men's gazes. "Worse."

"Worse?" Rob queried.

"Yeah." Sam held the aluminum cup in both hands and examined a dent. "I was a mass murderer."

Rob did a double-take. "A what?"

Buck stopped cleaning. He sat motionless, silent. His cold, black eyes were on Sam.

"I murdered hundreds of young minds, one freaking day at a time." Sam looked into the dim shadows, speaking as though to himself. "I was a Directorate Party member."

The men glanced to one another then back to Moore.

"I was a school teacher," Moore continued. "High school. By the time I got them, though, most of the damage had already occurred. Yet, there at the end, I did what I could to try to undo the brainwashing. There were some I could still reach." He thought of the three families he had helped, wondered if that help had cost them their lives. Well, at least they had acted, had done *something*. Now it was his turn. But hadn't *he* done something, too? Otherwise, why would he be here now? Sam sipped from the mug and gave a subtle nod. It hit him that his task wasn't over—not by any means. But what was his job now? His goal? There must be a goal. Otherwise, life would continue with the absurd. And his death would be meaningless.

A stir came from the sleeping bag in the corner, and the boy rolled over. He trained bleary eyes on Sam. "You that teacher who blew up the Commissar's house over in Perchance?"

Allowing them to believe he was capable of violence could serve him in an uncertain future. And to his alarm, he'd found he was very much capable of violence. Sam remained silent.

"Was he in it?" Buck asked. "Was he in the house?"

Sam eased the metal cup to the table. "We weren't that fortunate."

Buck glanced up from the rifle. "We?"

Sam had learned something from Tipton, after all: he used silence as a tool.

Buck studied him a moment, and then went back to cleaning the rifle.

Rob took one last draw from the cigarette and pinched off the fire. Smoke rolled from his mouth and nostrils as he spoke. "Heard there were three kinds of hell in that town last night. A battalion-sized force now surrounds it. No one in, no one out." He glanced through the smoke to Sam. "You the cause of that?"

"I won't take all the credit," Sam replied calmly and yet alarmed inside at hearing the news about the soldiers. But with Leo and his gang turned loose, he wasn't surprised. Or were the troops deployed in the hopes of catching Katie, or himself? "Like I said earlier, I've been out of action the past few days. Been locked up, had the hell beat outta me."

The men remained silent, measuring his words. The boy, propped up by an arm, eyed him from the sleeping bag on the dirt floor.

Sam rubbed his face in his hands, too tired to decipher their looks. "All I know is that I have to find the woman who put that death camp video together."

"You and about ten thousand others would like to grab her, too," Rob said, chuckling. "Half would give her a medal. The other half would slit her throat."

"And that ain't no lie to the latter," Buck added, inspecting the weapon in his hands.

Sam glanced from man to man. "Her name is Katie. The video was her idea, but we worked together on releasing it. I supplied Directorate communiqué codes. We had promised each other that once the fireworks started, we'd go through this 'revolution' together."

"What she did would've been impossible without other help, too," Rob said. "We may have more allies than we think."

Buck yanked back the weapons action and peeked into the spotless barrel. "Guarantee you one thing, she was long gone from wherever she was at when that video hit the screens."

Sam looked to first one man then the other. "Katie has family in Perchance. They have connections...could stash her somewhere. She would've tried to get there." He sighed inside, wondering if he, alone, would be enough to draw Katie back to Perchance. Did she remember their promise? Did she even think of him? After all, it had been almost two months since they last saw one another. He felt a twinge of doubt and swore inside at the flash of uninvited emotion. Why was he even wasting precious time thinking about what Katie might or might not do? He needed to focus on the here and now if he was to survive. There was a country to piece back together—or what was left of it.

"Like Rob said," Buck began, breaking Sam's thoughts, "that town's locked up, at least for now. Unless you want to get nabbed again, I recommend it off limits. Stick with us. We could use your help, use your expertise on the authority's mentality." He gave Sam a curious look. "We understand that firearms were confiscated in this police state years ago." He placed the futuristic looking weapon next to him on the cot. "Ever shot a pistol or a rifle?"

Before Sam could reply, the boy spoke up. "If he belonged to the Directorate, he carried a gun. Seen one of those Directorate bastards pull a pistol on a friend's dad."

Rob, who had remained quiet, glanced to the teenager on the floor. "What was the dad doing, Kurt?"

Kurt sat up, rubbing a hand through shaggy hair. "He had an American flag in a window."

Sam glanced at the kid. "That's just asking for it."

"It was in a *backyard* window," Kurt continued, hinting a sneer. He glanced to the other two men. "Shows you how sneaky they are. This Directorate dude was riding in a garbage truck in the alley when he spotted the flag."

The two soldiers listened intently.

"Common practice," Sam said, addressing the young man. "The Party was watching someone in your neighborhood, looking for evidence that could lead to charges of subversion." Sam gave a knowing smile, speaking to no one in particular. "But the 'bastards' never really need a reason. If the Party wants you, your ass is theirs."

The boy's temper grew hotter as he waved his arms. "All I know is, this Directorate guy called my friend's dad out into the backyard. Next thing I know, the dude pulls out a pistol and holds the dad until the cops get there. Then they handcuffed him and hauled him away—all for just showing an American flag in a window that's hidden from the public!"

Rob raised his hands. "Easy, Kurt. Don't get so wound up."

"I'll be damned," Buck murmured.

Kurt cast a suspicious eye on Sam.

Sam returned the boy's gaze. "You don't trust me, and that's okay. I don't blame you."

Kurt's jaw tightened. His glare was unfriendly. "You were one of *them.*"

"Which makes him invaluable to us," Rob said, giving the teenager a hard glance. He turned to Sam sitting across the small camping table. "What did you say your first name was?"

"Sam."

Rob rose. He hesitated before extending a hand. "Well, *I* trust you, Sam."

Sam stood, reached for the offered hand, and shook it. "Thanks."

"If you want to do something meaningful, stay with us. We'll work on reuniting our country."

Sam nodded, releasing his hand. The words *our country* didn't escape him. And that Buck had suddenly remained quiet wasn't lost to him, either. There was something odd about Buck.

Buck nodded to Sam and broke his silence. "On the other hand, you're free to go on your way. We'll give you a compass, backpack, and a few MREs, and it's *adios amigo.* You're on your own—and you never saw us."

Sam was about to speak when he felt a tremor beneath him. The ground shook from a loud metallic rumble, causing the tent to sway. It was like chains spun inside a huge drum, and the roar grew louder. The hanging lantern swung crazily, and Rob grabbed it just as it fell off the hook.

Sam's heart pounded and the urge to run gripped him. He fought to remain calm, not show weakness. He'd heard that iron thunder of death before—twenty-five years ago—when his mother and others lying in a pool of blood.

"Tanks," Buck said, "and lots of them."

"And we're over a mile from any road," Rob said, easing the lamp to the ground. Buck bolted from the cot, and all four scrambled outside.

Cold night air slapped Sam on the cheek. He shivered in his coat. At first, the rumbling seemed to come from all around them, piercing the thick forest with its unnatural, alien sound. Any second, Sam expected the tracked, iron beasts to come crashing through the trees. Everyone twisted around nervously, praying not to see the product of that terrifying noise. After tense seconds, the sound slowly retreated, and the party began breathing again.

"They're rolling west," Buck said, "heading to the front lines where we'll blast them into scrap metal."

Rob faced west into the darkness. "And those front lines are moving closer every day."

Sam chewed a lip, unsure. He looked up, glimpsed a wide swath of the Milky Way, and wondered how many men before, on the eve of war, had looked up, seen the same shining specks, and had the same thoughts as he did now? He may never see on this earth the stars' divine perpetuity again. He swallowed and spoke. "By the time the front lines reach here, there won't be anything left to reunite."

Rob turned to him. His dark skin highlighted white teeth. "Think so?"

"I know so. It'll be the Directorate's last directive. Scorched earth...and the people with it."

Buck and Kurt gathered around the two men. The rumble of tank tracks faded into the night. A slight breeze whistled through the tops of tall loblollies, and Sam could feel them swaying. Here and there a lone cricket chirped. He noticed for the first time that he was the only one not holding a weapon. Sam sighed; he would have a lot to learn.

"What are you going to do?" Rob asked. "Still thinking of searching for that woman?"

Sam faced all of them. "I have to."

Kurt pointed his rifle in the direction the tanks had taken. "Perchance is west of here, maybe twenty or so miles. You know it's also a major crossroads for these parts. There's probably more than just military there." The young man paused, studying Sam from darkness. "If you're ex-Directorate like you say, there's gotta be a price on your head. Like these guys said, I'd steer clear of Perchance for a while."

Sam nodded and stared at the dark ground. Of course, the kid was right. Sam wouldn't be just some citizen walking around. He had come within a breath of killing a commissar, and not just any commissar. Jonathan Tipton was a *high*-ranking official who held political clout. And Tipton was infamous for his grudges, which often morphed into blood feuds. Sam knew that one way or another, Tipton would come after him. No matter the outcome of the war, as long as Tipton lived, Sam would have to look over his shoulder. "I don't know. I would only be in the way. If I stayed with you guys, I don't think I'd make a good fighter...a good soldier."

Rob patted his shoulder. "You may surprise yourself." He paused. "If that woman you're looking for is part of the Underground, there's a good chance we'll run across her, or at least learn of her whereabouts."

Sam's jaw tightened. There was a reason he didn't escape with his students when he had the chance. It wasn't in him to forsake an obligation, and not just to Katie, or his country. A future was at stake. "I want my children born free," he said and was amazed at his own words.

Rob nodded. "Then we'll teach you what you need know to make that happen."

Sam's insides chilled, and not from the cold. All of them standing here weren't just part of history; they were *living* it.

Buck cocked his brow at Sam, and then he shook his head and stepped back to the tent. "Hoorah."

PART
II

Two months later. April, 2050

The rhododendrons' fragrance floated sweetly. Bees danced on their soft petals and buzzed around him. Cradling an M-18 battle rifle, Sam sunk deeper into the dense, pink brackets just inside the tree line while keeping a careful eye on the road below. It was a bright mid-morning, and the perfume of a South Carolina spring hung in the air, a lush green softening the countryside. The scent was saintly and brought an innocence that seemed to elude him. He wished he could lie there amid the flowers and meditate, let his mind wander to what he had imagined were happier times. He chuckled inside; *happiness* was alien in the Directorate. Life under Party rule was devoured and vomited back in your face. Directorate aspirations were an anathema that you scraped off your body every night, until one night, you didn't have the will to do even that. And just like that, the Directorate became the pimp, and you, its whore.

He stared straight ahead, awash with a new resolve. He was free. And if he should die today, he would die a free man. Yet, nowadays, it was hard to think of himself as an individual, as one; he was now part of the men and women around him, and they were part of him. What had been a team of four had now swelled to over 200, all united in a great cause: overthrowing the Directorate and reuniting the country under *one* flag, the flag of the United States of America. One's background no longer mattered. They were all brothers and sisters in an immense struggle. *The call for freedom was a clarion call,* he mused, *a summons that breathed life. Freedom* and *Liberty* were living strands in an American's DNA.

A muffled *click-click-click-click* crackled from the small, two-way radio attached to his web belt, breaking his thoughts. The expected four-vehicle enemy convoy had been sighted up the road. Sam tapped the radio key in reply and glanced around to where the twenty men sat ready. Several heads poked through nearby brush. He raised four gloved fingers. Heads nodded, and they spread out. Twenty yards down the line, two other men readied a heavy machine gun. Sam heard the sharp *clink* as its bolt was pulled back. He pictured the .50 caliber's black barrel

193

aimed at the road below, prepared to spew out its hell. One hundred yards on his left, back down the road, a sniper team lay in wait. They were to take out the driver of the lead vehicle. The sniper was Buck, and he *never* missed. Several fighters armed with RPGs were hidden near the sniper team. They would finish off the vehicle, a Humvee-like contraption called an All-Terrain Troop Mover, or TM. The TM gone, the remaining heavy trucks and an APC would take off, escaping what they believed was the ambush site. Except, they would rush headlong into Sam's team. Sam stood up, signaling to someone across the road below. A man rose from tall weeds, gestured, and then he and three others disappeared into the shadowy woods behind.

Sam lowered himself back into the brush and raised binoculars. A half-mile down the road, a TM, along with two three-axle trucks called *five-tons,* and an armored personnel carrier sped around a curve, rolling toward them. The partisans were tipped that the enemy convoy carried rations. Food. The partisans always needed the food.

He shoved the binoculars back into a case and worked his weapons action, chambering a round. A 60-round magazine, holding 7.62 caliber armor-piercing ammo, protruded from beneath the weapon's action. Two more magazines rested in a pouch on his side. Gloved fingers hesitantly touched the two bullet holes on the chest of his blue camo battle uniform. He'd stripped the uniform off a dead NAC soldier last month. His fingers rubbed over the cloth, the stiffness no longer felt. But he knew the stains were still there. They would always be there. And today, he may add his own stains. Sam swallowed and focused on the here and now. His heart thumped as adrenaline pumped. He adjusted his OD green bush hat, scampered to a nearby tree, crouched, and concentrated on the approaching vehicles.

Twenty minutes earlier, NAC engineers had swept the road, searching for IEDs. Of course, none were found because there weren't any. Yet, no sooner had the enemy armored-pickup disappeared around a bend, when several men in Sam party swept down the hill, with a man lugging a .105 howitzer shell. Already prepared for remote detonation, the artillery shell was quickly shoved into a culvert lying under the road. Hopefully, the shell would take out the APC or the partisans were in a world of hurt.

The rumble of diesel engines grew, and Sam's stomach knotted. His stomach always knotted before an attack. Even though he was now a seasoned guerrilla fighter, he still felt the fear. Yet, he turned the fear inward, concentrating on the mission. It had been on-the-job-training: you survived and learned, or you died. He swallowed and forced calmness. The convoy was coming into range. He glanced side-to-side and gave a thumbs up. Others, nodded and returned the gesture. Rifle barrels poked through brush.

Down below, a TM with a top mounted, high-tech machine-gun lead the convoy, followed by the two transport trucks. Several yards behind them, a six-wheel APC brought up the rear. Sam focused on the front TM. The machine gun on top worried him. It was computerized, operated by remote control. It targeted heat sources and was deadly accurate. If Buck and his spotter didn't take it out on the first try...

Pow. Sam flinched at the crack of Buck's sniper rifle. The TM shot forward then swerved into a ditch. *Whoosh. Whoosh.* And the RPGs were away. One grenade stuck into the side door—a dud. The second one slammed into a side window, and the TM exploded. Screams came from the flaming vehicle. One soldier tried climbing out the torn-open back. He was instantly cut down. More shots rang out from the sniper rifle. The lead transport truck halted, jerked forward, and then came to a dead stop. The second truck swerved to avoid the stopped truck in front but clipped its rear end, causing both trucks to spin around. The trucks sat sideways in the road, motionless. The second truck backed up, attempting to go around the first. Automatic weapons fire filled the air. Sam's rifle jumped in his hand as he—and the men around him—peppered the truck cabs with titanium rounds.

The APC gunned it, closing on the trucks. Just as the second axle crossed the culvert—*boom.* The entire vehicle lifted from the road in a fireball. Flaming debris and body parts sailed through the air, raining down 100 yards out. Sam felt the concussion and watched in satisfaction as a black cloud mushroomed up from the wreckage. Orange flames licked the sky. How many soldiers the APC had carried, they would never know. Broken into two large, twisted chunks, secondary explosions boomed from the flaming pile of junk. He refocused on the two transport trucks. A door opened in the first truck, and a bloody soldier rolled out, hitting the pavement hard. He tried to crawl, and several shots splattered the ground around him before he lay still. Sam rose, and the others around him followed suit. None bothered hiding their faces. There would be no prisoners. Sam adjusted his backpack, and with weapon aimed from the hip, he zigzagged down the hill. Another NAC soldier scampered from a truck's open canvas-covered back. Automatic fire rang out.

The soldier stumbled and fell. His weapon clattered, and he lay outstretched on the pavement.

Sam approached the rear of an idling truck, with his rifle poised and ready. From where he stood, he could see that the huge vehicle was packed full of boxed rations. He shouted to the men around him. "Clear the cabs—get these trucks back to camp!" Today, God had given them a gift.

A gray-bearded man wearing a mix-matched combat uniform and a NAC helmet trotted up to him. He halted, nodding to the truck's enclosed cargo bed. "Should we check the back for bad guys?"

"No. We don't have time." He glanced up the hill to where Buck had been. The soldier was long gone, scouting behind the team, leaving Sam in charge. A small kernel of pride swelled in his chest. Now, he was part of something *good*. The Special Forces soldiers began trusting him a month back, placing him in charge of small operations. This hijacking was his idea and his largest mission yet; they knew he'd make the right decisions, decisions that could cost lives but save others. He glanced to the fighter next to him waiting patiently for an order. "If we have any hitchhikers," he said, "we'll deal with them at camp."

The man nodded. "You got it." And he jogged away. Seconds later, a diesel engine gunned. Several fighters climbed into the cramped cargo area. A gear ground, and the truck full of food pulled away, rumbling up the road with a patriot behind the wheel.

"Moore, check this out!"

Sam sprinted to the front of the second cargo truck. The truck's engine cranked, then idled. He glanced to the cab. Dozens of fresh, shiny pockmarks peppered the door. The windshield was blood-spattered and full of bullet holes. Blood oozed from the passenger door's bottom and onto a fuel tank, collecting in a crimson puddle on the pavement. Sam's jaw tightened. Compassion may one day return—but not today. This was war. When near the NAC army, one always saved the last bullet for himself. Capture was worse than death. If captured, torture would occur until names and hideouts were revealed. Then there would be certain decapitation. After that, the NAC army would go after the family. Five thousand real U.S. dollars was now the going price for a guerrilla fighter's head. Sam had already seen enough of his comrades' headless bodies dumped on the roadside to fill a lifetime of nightmares. The decapitations were something recent; he suspected where they came from but kept that thought to himself. No, there was no sympathy here, only good or evil, life or death.

A rifle-toting fighter stood over a dead NAC soldier. "Got an officer here, and he's just like the other NAC officers we've seen lately."

Shaken from his thoughts, Sam stepped to the crumpled form on the ground. Others from his team gathered around. He reached down, turned the dead soldier over, and glanced at the black eagle on each collar. "Wonder what a bird colonel was doing riding with these guys?"

"Kinda risky, ain't it?" someone said.

"Probably just hitching a ride," another replied.

Sam nodded. But that's not what really caught his attention. He focused on the man's name strip. The name was unpronounceable. His eyes went to the NAC soldier's blood-stained face. Maybe in his late thirties, he was dark-skinned... Middle Eastern.

"Another Arab officer," someone said. "Nowadays, seems like the NAC army is full of 'em."

"Come on you guys!" shouted an impatient voice from the bullet-riddled truck cab behind them. An arm hung out an open window, and a hand banged on the door. "Let's go!"

"Just a sec," Sam shouted back. He handed his rifle to a nearby fighter, kneeled, and frisked the dead soldier, working out a small wallet from a back pocket. Flipping it open, he scrutinized the ID. The script under the NAC seal was undecipherable, but he knew it read from right to left.

The gray-bearded fighter, wearing the NAC helmet, looked over Sam's shoulder. "Arabic?"

"No." He rose, glancing to the men. All their eyes were on him. He nodded to the dead soldier. "The man's name is not Arabic. It's Farsi."

"What's that?" several asked, casting confused glances.

Sam swallowed, eyeing the bloodied form on the ground. "He's Iranian."

"What the hell's a damn Persian doing in an NAC officer's uniform?" the gray-bearded man asked. The other men murmured, the gray-bearded man having spoken their thoughts.

"Thought those Iranians were our sworn enemies?" a younger man said. "Hell, this doesn't make any sense, Iranians being NAC soldiers and all?"

A fighter handed Sam back his weapon. He checked the action then glanced around. Several teenage boys were collecting enemy weapons and stripping anything of value from the dead soldiers, stuffing bloody uniforms and boots into plastic bags.

Fifty yards behind them, flames crackled from the twisted, melting metal of what remained of the APC. Thick, black smoke billowed up high, drifting north; a calling card for more enemy army. They had to vacate the area—and fast. Sam glanced once more to the dead NAC officer and, as if reaching a conclusion, nodded. He slung his rifle over a shoulder. "Gentleman, I believe things have taken a turn for the surreal."

* * *

The abandoned mobile home had been a ranger station located deep in the heart of what was once known as Francis Marion National Forest. Three men stood just inside the trailer's open front door, staring at the mountain of stacked, brown boxes. "Over five-thousand cartons of MREs," Rob said, smiling and glancing to Sam. "Nice haul, and nice job."

"Yeah, not bad for a trainee," Buck added, nodding to Sam. "We'll make a soldier out of you yet."

Sam gave a rare smile. There was so little to smile about these days... "Thanks." He glanced to the U.S. Special Forces men, reflecting on what a Godsend they had been. Captain Robert "Rob" Fields was from Stillwater, Oklahoma. He was thirty-two, with a wife and two young children waiting for him back at Fort Sill. And Buck? Sam could get little from the guy other than he was Staff Sergeant Charles "Buck" Buckland, thirty-five, from Twin Falls, Idaho, and that he was divorced, with a daughter. The man rarely spoke and definitely was not given to small talk. Sam sensed there was something dreadful in his past. *Oh well,* he had mused, *we all have a past, things we regret, memories that keep us awake at night and haunt us in our most quiet moment.*

He turned and stepped outside. Not quite noon, the air was already warm and sticky. Sam wiped sweat from his brow with the back of his hand and glanced around. A flurry of activity met him. Both enemy transport trucks were backed in on the far end of camp. Someone had already painted a white USA over the bullet-riddled blue triangle on the door. Just as Sam hopped off the last step, a bright flash lit the sky. It blazed brighter than the sun for several seconds before vanishing.

"What the..." Sam strained to see something through the leafy canopy. It was no use; the vegetation was too thick. Yet, he had his suspicions, recalling that the same type of bright light had flashed in the sky back when he was in college. He also remembered what happened afterward.

Others began gathering together, murmuring. Necks craned and eyes scanned upward for any kind of clue to the strange light.

"Ain't ever seen the like," someone commented.

"What do you suppose that was?" another asked.

"I don't hear any noise, like an explosion or anything," said a third voice.

"You won't hear anything," Sam said, walking up to the crowd. "You have to have air for sound. There's no air in outer space."

Rob came trotting up from the direction of the trailer. "Did anyone see what that was?" he asked, looking around and puffing.

Sam glanced to the soldier. "Check your vid."

Rob wrinkled a brow, reaching into a fatigue pocket. He and Buck were the only ones in camp with operating vidphones. The military vids were next generation communicators. They continuously encrypted, rendering their signals undetectable to NAC tracking equipment.

"Bet it won't work," Sam said.

Rob held the small, black device in his right hand. "The damn thing is on," he said as his thumb tapped the screen. "But there's no signal...nothing." He glanced to Sam. "You don't suppose...?"

"Yeah, I do," Sam replied. "Looks like a U.S. satellite took a hit."

Buck, with vidphone in hand, strode up to the crowd of men. "This is some serious shit," and he tapped his tiny phone. "If we don't have communications with—"

Another brilliant white light flashed, brighter than the last, and this time everyone hit the ground. Buried in pine needles, Sam instinctively covered his head. "What the hell!" came Buck's muffled voice next to him.

Silent, interminable seconds passed. The sky returned to normal, and Sam rose, brushing off pine needles and leaves. Everyone else began rising and talking at once.

Rob brushed himself off, glancing to first Sam and then to Buck. "I wonder if round two went to us?"

Buck tucked away his now useless vid phone. "At this pace, we'll be down to spears and slings before it's all over."

Sam stared past everyone, ignoring the loud murmur in camp. The destruction of technology reminded him of how Katie and he had used that very technology to awaken the country. He sighed and eyed an ant crawling near his boot. Katie. Where in God's name was she? Was she even alive?

The past few months, small bands of partisan fighters had

merged to form the company-sized guerrilla unit to which Sam now belonged. Several of the men and women had drifted in from the north, from the direction of Perchance. He'd asked if anyone had seen or heard about a woman named Katie Spencer, and the answer was always the same: a shrug followed by negative head-shaking. Most, though, had heard about her grandfather. Leo was still raising hell up north, keeping the NAC Guard off balance and pissed off. But there was never any word of Leo's family. Possibly that was intentional; family could be a liability.

Mind wondering, Sam stepped away from the chattering group. He knelt, loosened a stone, and tossed it in his hand. Perhaps Michelle, and maybe Katie, were together and in hiding. That would make sense. He tried picturing Katie's face, but her delicate nose and full lips eluded him. In disgust, Sam flung the rock at a sweet gum, just missing it.

So much had changed. What kind of world awaited the patriots? When the fighting stopped and the NAC was defeated, what then? Sam reached for another rock. Would things return to the pre-Directorate days of the haves and have-nots? He had no memory of those days but had read about them and had interrogated those who had lived in those times. That the Directorate was unabashed depravity and should be crushed, there was no doubt. Yet, history has now shown that the first two decades of the 21st century was *not* a time of freedom, at least not the freedoms Americans earned and enjoyed throughout previous centuries. From what Sam had learned, the early 21st century was an era of distraction. Those Americans had entertained themselves to death. The government provided the distraction in the form of entertainment, while one freedom after another was slyly snatched away from unaware Americans. Decadence and immorality were encouraged among the populace. Pleasure was its own reward.

Sam had once asked his commissar father how the Directorate got their foot in the door without a shot being fired. "We kept them busy," he had replied, "we kept them looking the other way." But, some had sounded the alarm. Those who tried awakening the citizens from their spiritual and political malaise were ridiculed, laughed at. The government would counter dissenters by quickly offering up its latest technological gizmo in which to enthrall and ensnare the masses. The tiny but vocal minority that had cast dubious eyes on technology, that allowed government access into personal lives, were considered outcasts and labeled Luddites and "right-wing extremists." In those days, American society generally shunned the 21st century

Paul Reveres.

Sam examined the rock in his hand. He recalled Leo telling him how the American people had *invited* the Directorate into their homes. Once inside, the Directorate became symbiotic with life itself and pillaged free thought. When society finally woke from its slumber, it was too late. Millions fled west, where the Directorate's grip was not as tight. Part of the military mutinied against its own government and fought back. But they were few in numbers, and the Directorate quickly crushed them or starved them into submission.

Sam had recently voiced these thoughts in the night air over many a campfire. The Resistance must have a plan, a goal, other than just overthrowing the Directorate. Sam's jaw tightened. He took aim at the sweet gum and hurled the rock. It hit the tree square in the trunk.

Late June, 2050

A large, stocky man in green camouflage, with a shotgun slung over a shoulder and cradling a rifle, led a small group emerging from thick forest. He raised his hand and all halted. Behind were two men, a woman, and two children. They were a sad-looking lot, worn and haggard. Their backpacks sagged. Bringing up the rear, an armed man in mix-matched camo stood as a guard.

The man in front turned to the group. "You all sit tight." Leaving the others behind, the big man strode across an open field to a group of men standing around a table in the shade of an oak. "Picked up a few more, boss. As usual, they have younguns with them."

Examining a map on the table, Sam glanced to the middle-aged, burly man standing before him. He handled the weapon as if it were a body extension. The man was known only as Kyser. He'd proven trustworthy and had a knack for repairing things out of nothing. He was a scrounger, coming up with whatever was needed. He had also served in the U.S. Army in the pre-Directorate days and was a topnotch fighter. The Resistance was lucky to have him. Sam's gaze fell to the party behind Kyser, and he gave an annoyed sigh. "Just great...now we're turning into Old Forest Daycare Camp. Before long, the kids will outnumber the adults."

Kyser shifted in front of Sam. "We'll I couldn't just let em' wander all over the woods, maybe give away our location." He tapped the shotgun hanging from his shoulder. "The oldest guy was also totin' this."

Sam ignored the shotgun and nodded in reluctant agreement. "Okay, bring them on in. And I suppose they're hungry. They always are. Feed them, and then have someone lead them to the base camp." He scrutinized the travelers standing in the distance. There seemed a familiarity about them. "Did they give their names?"

"Never asked. They just said they were from up north and had been dodging NAC soldiers the past week and asked for food for the kids."

He looked to his compatriots standing around the map table. "Guys, I'll be right back."

Sam stepped to the forlorn travelers.

Kyser paced Sam. "What is it, boss?"

"I'm not sure." Sam's eyes widened behind worn Raybans, and he picked up the pace. "But I think I'm dreaming."

The tall, older man in the group glanced at an approaching Sam and did a double-take. "Holy shit! Is that Sam Moore?"

Sam tore off his Raybans and broke into a trot. "ZZ! What the f—!"

"Sammy!" The older man broke from the group, running toward Sam. "Sammy! We thought you were dead!"

The two collided, embracing each other as long-lost brothers.

"Sam!" the woman shouted, dashing to the two men. A girl of perhaps thirteen and a boy of ten hurried behind her, trying to keep up. The other member of the group stood with the guard. The guard shrugged, shouldered his weapon, and sauntered across the clearing to a campfire, leaving the lone man from the group standing alone. After a moment, he headed toward the reunion.

Sam backed away, scrutinizing ZZ and Haleana. The chemistry teacher was thin and haggard. His jeans and T-shirt were faded. Haleana's dark hair was tucked under a baseball cap. A few strands blew about her face. Her attractive looks were now drawn and weary.

Haleana stepped aside. "You remember Jenna and Taylor?"

"How could I forget?" Sam replied, grinning from ear to ear. "I've broken bread at your table many an evening." He glanced to the children. "You two have grown like weeds. And you," he eyed Jenna, "you're turning into a young lady, and an almost pretty one."

"Almost...?" Blushing, Jenna swatted his arm. And so the five stood there, chatting excitedly, innocently, as if the world were still normal.

Kyser stood nearby, catching Sam's attention. "Family?"

"Sorta. They're from Perchance, my home." He rested a hand on ZZ's shoulder. "ZZ and I were not just friends but colleagues. We taught together at the same high school. He was a chemistry teacher, with no love lost for the Directorate."

"That a fact," Kyser said, eyeing the former chemistry teacher. He shouldered his weapon. "Know anything about explosives?"

Before ZZ could reply, Sam interrupted. "We'll get ZZ and explosives squared away later." He glanced to the travelers. "Bet you guys are hungry."

All nodded. Just then the other man who had traveled with the Zhimmers stepped up.

Haleana touched the man's arm. "Sam, I don't think you've met my younger brother, Brad Carlisle."

Sam stepped to the twentyish-something man, and the two shook hands. "No, but I've heard about you," Sam said. "You were up in Charlotte, in medical school, weren't you?"

"Yes," he said, releasing Sam's hand. "The government closed the school at the hospital and conscripted all the students into the army medical corps." He adjusted his glasses, giving a wry grin. "Guess you could say I'm a deserter."

Bush hat pulled low, Sam donned the Raybans. His camouflaged fatigues were tucked into combat boots. Around his waist was a web belt; a holstered .45 pistol hung from the right side and a two-way radio hung from the left.

Kyser looked Carlisle up and down. "Now we have a doctor. Damn sure been needing one, too."

"I'm no doctor," Brad said.

Sam ignored Brad's reply and pointed to Haleana. "And we have a nurse."

"The hell, you say." The big man broke into a grin. "Then we made quite a haul today...gained a chemist, a doctor, and a nurse in one fell swoop."

Sam nodded. "When you're on the right side of right, good things often happen."

Kyser glanced to Sam. "Plans still on for early A.M., Boss?"

"Yes, and tell the men I'll be right there."

"Yes, sir," Kyser said, nodding and taking the hint. As an afterthought, he unslung the shotgun, handing it back to ZZ.

"Thanks," ZZ said, shouldering the 12-gauge.

"Also, Kyser, would you take the children and feed them?"

Haleana pushed the kids toward the older man. "It's okay, kiddos. This man is our friend. All these men are our friends now."

The kids hesitated, casting a wary glance to the man who had held a gun on them. ZZ nodded to them. "Taylor, Jenna, it's okay."

Kyser gazed impatiently to the children. "Do you want to stand there, or do you want your stomach to start scratching your backbone?" He turned. "Come with me. Let's get some chow in those young bellies." The children hesitated a moment longer, but their stomachs won out, and they followed after him.

ZZ and Haleana exchanged glances then gazed strangely,

almost in awe, at Sam. "Boy have you changed," ZZ began, "And I mean *changed*. Hell, Sam, I could've passed you on the street and never recognized you. If I hadn't heard your voice...are you a soldier now?"

"A soldier? No, I'm only a patriot."

The couple exchanged glances. ZZ slowly shook his head. "I just can't believe this is you. What happened to you, man?"

Sam shifted, feeling uncomfortable. He had a thousand questions for them, and he was sure the Zhimmers had a thousand more in return. He glanced toward the field stove. The children were already sitting on a stump in the shade with a mess kit in their laps, wolfing down grilled venison. Sam turned back to the exhausted couple and to Halaena's brother, Brad. "Let's get you guys squared away. We'll talk later."

That evening, after gear was stowed, rucksacks packed, and weapons cleaned and loaded, fourteen guerrilla fighters, including Sam, sat in a semicircle, focusing on the Zhimmer couple and Brad. Most of the men sat on small tarps or bedrolls. Sam sat on a worn-smooth tree stump. Light from the tiny campfire reflected off grim faces. The partisans yearned for the latest update from *out there,* hoping and praying for encouraging news. But the growing flood of refugees told them differently. It was always the same story: hunger, despair, cruel government crackdowns, and summary executions. Maybe this time the Zhimmers would bring stories of hope. Yet, Sam knew that the very presence of the Zhimmers was an ill omen.

"The hardest part was getting away—escaping—from Perchance," ZZ began. He glanced first to Sam then to the others. "That shit-for-nothing town is now an army-staging area."

"Staging area for what?" Sam asked. "What kind of operations?"

"Elimination of *rebel terrorists*." ZZ paused, glancing to the men around him. "That's what they're labeling you guys—'rebels' and 'terrorist traitors,' and those are the good tags."

Brad had remained quiet since their arrival. Perched on a backpack, he looked to the fighters' silhouettes. "There were rumors around the university that medical experiments were being conducted on rebel prisoners."

Sam nodded. "Doesn't surprise me. As a Directorate member, I was privy to some pretty fiendish material." He paused, reflecting. "I can't believe I was one of them...that seems so long ago."

A few men murmured, nodding in agreement. By now, it was no secret that Sam had been part of the evil known as the

Directorate. It didn't matter. Former NAC soldiers had crossed sides and were now trusted partisans. There was one thing that drew all of the resistance fighters together: the need to assert their *Americanism.*

Sam fidgeted. He wanted to ask about Katie Spencer and Leo. There were rumors that a group of partisan fighters up north were recently captured. He cleared his throat. "ZZ, how is Leo Spencer doing? Have you heard anything—"

"He's dead, Sam. Leo is dead. Happened about a month ago."

Haleana bowed her head. "It was awful..."

The wind left Sam as if he'd been punched in the gut. Stunned, he could only stare into the darkness beyond. Sooner or later, he knew it would happen. Sam was also a walking dead man...everyone in camp was a walking dead man. He spoke, but his words were flat and seemed without feeling. "How did it happen?"

ZZ hesitated, picking at the flap of his backpack. "He was set up. There was a twenty-thousand-dollar reward on him. One of his own men turned on him."

"See what I mean about spies," Kyser chimed from the edge of camp.

"Sounds more like a traitor to me," someone said from behind Sam.

Sam stared straight ahead. "And traitors are even worse."

ZZ looked away.

Heads nodded, and silence settled over the camp, all waiting for Zhimmer to continue.

ZZ turned back to Sam. "The way I heard it, Leo and a couple of other guys rendezvoused with another group of partisans to talk about joining ranks. Only the others weren't partisans. They were NAC Special Operations soldiers. Leo and the others were seized."

"Was he beheaded?" Sam asked.

ZZ shook his head. "No."

Haleana looked up, glancing fearfully at Sam. "There was a mock trial, and he and the others were hung. It was like the Old West, Sam. They built a gallows in the town square. The army forced everyone from their homes and marched them into the square to witness the execution."

"They made the children watch, too," ZZ said, "including ours."

"The low-life bastards..." someone grumbled.

The Zhimmer children had spoken little since arriving at

the camp. Now Jenna shifted uneasily on her backpack and glanced to her father. "Dad, tell them about the signs that were pinned to their bodies."

ZZ gave a loud sigh, staring at the ground. "The army pinned signs on the bodies that read, 'These insurgents will hang for forty-eight hours. This is what happens to militants and terrorists.'"

Haleana shot her husband a quick glance. "Tell Sam what else was on Leo's sign."

"No."

"Then I'll do it."

"Haleana, no!"

"He needs to know." Ignoring ZZ, she turned to Sam. "On Leo's sign, and in large caps, were also the words, 'SAMUEL MOORE, YOU ARE NEXT!'"

Sam blinked. First Leo murdered, and now this... He swallowed, fighting fear and anger. "This has Tipton written all over it."

"Tipton's running the show from behind the scenes," ZZ said. "He's got a vendetta against you, Sammy. Rescuing those students was one thing, but blowing up his house—he won't let that go."

"I didn't blow up his house," Sam replied. "I'll explain later."

Kyser glanced to Sam. "Tipton...isn't he that commissar you almost strangled?"

Sam nodded. "Yeah. And every day I regret I didn't finish the job."

ZZ shot Sam a quick glance. "You tried to kill Tipton a second time?"

Sam ignored the "second time," only giving a subtle nod.

"It all makes sense now," ZZ said, shaking his head.

Sam glanced to the couple on the ground. "You don't know the half of it."

"Heard about that Tipton guy," someone else added. "Heard even the army is scared of him."

Murmurs moved through camp. Sam stared into darkness. Sighing, he again turned to his friend. "How's Leo's wife, Michelle, taking it?"

"She's gone, too, Sam," ZZ replied. "She had a stroke at the hanging...died the next day."

Sam bowed his head, rubbing fingertips over both temples.

"That's not all," ZZ said.

Sam froze, a wave of nausea hitting him. News of Katie... was she also dead?

"They bulldozed Spencer's house," ZZ continued, "and half the block. Said it was payback for not reporting the old man's suspicious behavior."

Sam visibly shook, partly from relief and partly from dread. Relief that Katie was not mentioned, and dread that she may never had made it back to Perchance. And all this time he was dreaming of and chasing a ghost. Sam couldn't yet face it that he may never see Katie again. And still something else crowded his thoughts. In the Spencers' cellar was a backpack with nearly two million U.S. dollars stuffed into it. Also in the cellar was the photo album the Spencers had given him, along with his biological father's letter to him, which he had never opened. He had thought often, not of the money left behind, but of that letter. Money could be replaced, but his late father's reflections...

His thoughts returning to Katie; he couldn't let her go. Sam glanced to the Zhimmers. "Do either of you have any news about the Spencers' granddaughter? Her name is Katie Spencer. I had hoped that maybe she—"

ZZ shrugged. "Don't know anything about a granddaughter." He turned to his wife. "Do you?"

Haleana shook her head. "No. If the Spencers had any living relatives, they weren't in Perchance. At least none came forth at the couple's funeral." She paused. "Of course, the Directorate would have had spies at the funeral. Any relative of the Spencers would've known that and laid low. If the couple had a granddaughter around, Sam, she wouldn't have been at the funeral."

"Yeah, I suppose you're right."

ZZ frowned, rubbing his forehead. "Wait a minute. Sammy, how old is this granddaughter?"

He stared intently at his friend. "Twenty-five, twenty-six."

"Just a slip of a woman? Dark, curly hair?"

Sam shot up so fast that the men near him reached for their weapons. Seeing that it was only their exuberant leader, their hands eased away. ZZ rose, and Sam grabbed him by the shoulders. "Where did you see her? Where did you see Katie?"

"Whoa—hold on," ZZ said. "It might not be her."

For the first time since the Zhimmers' arrival, Haleana smiled. "Pray tell, what is your interest in this granddaughter, Sam?"

"I'll explain it all later." Releasing ZZ, Sam stepped back, eyeing him. "Where did you see this woman?"

The camp went silent. All eyes were on the two of them.

ZZ cleared his throat. "Leo's wife was really sick. With Leo part of the Resistance, there was no one there to take care of her. And you know how the whole town loved that old couple. Well..."

Sam rolled his eyes, exasperated. "Damnit, ZZ—I don't need a freaking dissertation."

"Back in early May, I stopped by the Spencers' to drop off some medicine. I was met at the door by this young woman with," and ZZ move his hands around his head, "all this curly hair. She said Michelle was napping and that she'd see that she got the medicine."

Sam eyes widened. His heart raced. *Oh, Dear God, please let it be her.* "Did this woman have a northern accent?"

ZZ shoved his hands in his pockets. "Yeah. I was just about to say that the girl that met me at the door sounded like she was from New York."

"Oh, sweet Jesus," Sam murmured, backing away. "It's her. It's Katie...she's alive."

He stumbled away then paused, trying to collect himself. He couldn't allow his feelings to go any further...couldn't allow to get his hopes up and have his heart take over. Especially not in front of the partisan fighters. He was looked upon now as a leader; it had taken hard work and sacrifice to earn the men's trust and respect. That a woman could move him in such a way that he appeared weak was the last thing he needed now. Hearing about Katie threw him into an agitated state that the men around him had never seen. He tried to concentrate on the purpose of their mission tomorrow but couldn't. And his failure to focus could cost lives. Rob and Buck had admired Sam's cool demeanor when under fire. They said those were qualities that made good leaders. Sam didn't know about that. But he was able to keep his sense about him when a clear head was needed most. Now, his psyche was under attack. Emotions bombarded him, and he couldn't fight them off. First, the Spencers' deaths and then news of Katie...despair, and then joy. Absorbing the opposite ends of the spectrum simultaneously was too much too fast. Sam leaned against a tree, overwhelmed.

"Sam?" Haleana called after him. "You okay?"

Sam could feel all eyes on him and hear their whispers. He touched the tiny cross under his T-shirt. He'd recently converted to Christianity, but prayer was still new to him. Most of his prayers had been for strength and wisdom to help his country unite under the Stars and Stripes, and he prayed that suffering be kept to a minimum. Sam was reluctant to pray for anything personal, afraid the Lord would consider it vain and never answer another prayer. Yet, yesterday, while they had hiked to this location, his thoughts wandered to Katie. While working through the forest, he risked it and prayed silently that Katie was well and that he would soon hear something about her. And now, a day later, here it was...

"Sam?"

He turned. Haleana stood in front of him. "We're sorry...we know how close you were to the Spencers."

"They were the only family I had."

"There's us. ZZ, the kids, and I consider you family."

"I didn't mean—"

She touched his arm. "I know what you meant."

ZZ walked up behind his wife. "What is it with you and the granddaughter? Of all the years I've known you, I've never seen you react like that. You two have something going?"

Sam looked away. Did they? He still hoped...but that was so long ago. Katie had probably forgotten about him...forgotten about their promise. Sighing in resignation, he turned back to the couple. "Do you remember the woman who narrated *The Documentary*?" The day Katie's death camp documentary aired became known as Documentary Day, or D-Day II.

Haleana and ZZ stared, intently listening. ZZ finally spoke. "Are you trying to say that the woman who did the voice-over was the Spencers' granddaughter? The same one I met at the door?"

"Exactly. We worked together to get that report over the airwaves."

"Oh my God..." Haleana breathed. "That girl is a celebrity—a heroine—and yet no one knows who she is. And, Sam, if you helped her..."

"You're a celebrity, too," ZZ said, shaking his head in disbelief. "Our Sammy...a hero."

"I don't think Tipton would use 'celebrity' or 'hero' to describe me," Sam said. "'Infamous' and 'notorious' are better words."

"He knows you had a part in D-Day Two?" ZZ asked.

Sam snorted. "Hell, yes, he knows. He had me arrested. I was beaten unconscious the day the documentary hit the air. I never got to see it."

Even in the darkness, Sam noticed how the Zhimmers exchanged concerned, puzzled glances. He briefly filled them in on his arrest, his rescue, and brought them up to the present.

The couple stood amazed, gazing with new respect at Sam.

ZZ cleared his throat and glanced to Haleana. "We might as well tell him while no one's around."

Haleana nodded.

Sam eyed the couple. The flickering campfire behind them magnified the surrealistic shadows. "So, how much is the reward up to?"

ZZ eyes widened. "You know?"

Sam nodded.

ZZ rubbed the back of his neck. "You need to watch your back, Sammy. That reward is up to a half-mil. Everyone wondered why it was so high. Now we know."

"And now you know..." Sam murmured.

All three stood in the edge of darkness. Silence ensued, and only desultory tones rose from the camp behind them. ZZ studied his former colleague for a long moment before speaking. "You made the commissar look like a fool. We worked with him long enough to learn what kind of bastard he is." ZZ stepped closer, standing alongside his wife. "Sammy, Tipton won't stop until you are dead."

"I know."

"There are rumors of what he ordered done to Terri Woodriff," ZZ said. "No one has heard from our old principal since the day you and those students disappeared."

Sam's throat tightened at the memory of those last days... the last days he was a school teacher...poignancy followed by horror...

Gripped with a strange emptiness, he gazed past the couple to the campfire beyond. Had that world really existed? He glanced down to his combat boots. His gaze moved up to battle fatigues and halted on the pistol hanging from his right hip. What was he? Sam no longer recognized his old life, nor did he recognize his current self. Were he and his companions truly on the side of right? Was either side right? He felt like he was in a waking nightmare, a torment with no end in sight. Would his country ever be *normal* again? What in the hell was *normal*?

"Sam," ZZ murmured, sensing his friend's dark mood. "Those kids made it. Everyone, parents and all, are safe in Texas. They couldn't have escaped without you and Leo."

Sam stared at ZZ. "What? That can't be? I saw what was left of one of their trucks. It was shot all to hell. And then the body parts Tipton tossed on the table in front of me."

"Don't know anything about body parts," ZZ said, "but several months back, the Underground received word that all the families made it."

Sam's face lit up as his somber mood passed. "I'll be damned." He glanced at the couple. "Tell me about 'home.' What

211

happened at school when everyone came back?"

"No one ever came back, Sam," ZZ said. "The schools closed after D-Day Two. Nobody let their kids return to school, so the Directorate closed the schools, officially 'for renovation.' And with the schools gone, well, so was my paycheck. The Directorate blacklisted all the educators in Perchance, as if there was work in that town, anyway. A few of us teachers volunteered to home school. We met in various homes, depending on the subject."

Sam's jaw tightened. "I'm sorry you guys had to suffer because of me."

Haleana again touched Sam. "You did the right thing. As dangerous as things are out here, it's still better than living under Directorate rule. ZZ and I didn't want our children brought up in that world."

"No one did," ZZ added. "Yet no one had the guts to do anything about it, except for a few like you, old Leo, and his granddaughter."

Haleana eyed Sam. "God bless all of you, and may God protect you and Katie, wherever she is."

"Thank you," Sam said, "and pray for our children and our country, because it's going to get worse before it gets better."

The Zhimmers nodded solemnly. Quiet seconds passed. After a moment, Sam sighed and stepped back to camp. The Zhimmers followed behind.

Haleana stepped over to the children and settled in next to them. ZZ sat nearby, leaning against a backpack. After fiddling with it for a moment, he glanced to Kyser. "So, what is this 'mission' you guys are talking about?"

Kyser glanced to Sam, who nodded his consent. The big man stuffed a cigarette between his lips and flicked a propane lighter. Taking a casual draw, he glanced to ZZ. "We're going to blow up a train."

24

The small, heavily armed party jogged down the shoulder of a fire road. The eastern sky was just showing gray. Explosions two miles back muffled the slapping of gear.

"We grabbed the trophy on this one, boss," Kyser said, puffing.

In the lead, Sam nodded. "Yeah, we did." He grinned in satisfaction at the eerie orange glow in the western sky that his small party of fighters had caused. Were they saboteurs? Absolutely. Were they rebels? Hell, yes. They rebelled against an oppressive government. Were they killers? Sam mulled over the word in his mind. He recalled a banned book he'd read a couple of years back titled *Killer Angels*. The story recounted the bloodbath and bravery at Gettysburg in the American Civil War. The words *Killer Angel* came from a Shakespeare play he wasn't familiar with. One day, if the killing ever stopped, he'd have to read that play. But now, one thing was certain; the killing wouldn't end until the Directorate was crushed. Not just overthrown but thoroughly smashed. The NAC military was demoralized, now even more so after what their little group of partisans had just done. The train they blew sky-high had been loaded with armor and artillery pieces. *Yeah,* Sam mused, *if it weren't for the Directorate cracking a whip at the generals, the NAC military would've folded long ago.*

"Gonzales should be waiting for us right around the curve," Kyser said, breaking Sam's thoughts.

Sam slowed to a trot then a quick walk. The others followed suit. The party marched around a bend and a large, three-axle transport truck called a "five-ton" loomed up in the gray shadows.

"Don't hear the engine running," someone said.

Kyser swore softly. "Hope that knucklehead didn't fall asleep again."

Sam slowed his gait, straining to make out details. The truck was parked in the middle of the road some twenty yards ahead. Everything seemed quiet and as normal as could be expected.

"Maybe Gonzales was worried that the engine noise would give him away?" someone offered.

Sam halted, raising a hand. The group froze.

Chewing gum, Sam glanced warily around. "Something doesn't feel right."

You're surrounded by the NAC army, boomed a magnified voice on the opposite side of the road. *You are now our prisoners. Drop your weapons, put your hands in the air, and you won't be harmed.*

Sam glanced to the men around him. Their heads shook a negative in the dim light. All knew what capture meant. Sam's jaw tightened, and he nodded.

Drop your weapons! This is your final warning!

Sam's party unslung their weapons, but instead of dropping them, they aimed in the direction of the voice.

Instantly, flashes came from the woods on their left. A staccato *rat-tat-tat-tat* tore through the predawn ether.

"Holy shit!" a voice screamed. Several men hit the ground. Some would never rise again.

"Take cover!" Sam shouted.

What felt like a hot poker stabbed Sam's left thigh, and something punched him in the ribs. He staggered, and then he charged into the nearby brush and slammed straight into a standing NAC soldier, knocking the soldier's rifle to the ground. Both surprised men fell, tangled together. Sam's rifle and pistol were under him and out of reach. The soldier wore body armor, and his movements were awkward, unwieldy. The soldier tried to rise, but Sam hooked an arm around his neck, holding onto the struggling man. Sam reached to his boot, whipped out a dagger, and without thinking, ran it into the man's neck, sinking it to the hilt. Blood spurted, and a gurgling scream tore from the soldier's throat. Sam withdrew the knife and stabbed again. The scream broke off. The man shook once then relaxed. Sam could feel a sticky dampness coating his shirtfront, and he heaved the dead soldier away and rose to a knee, panting, shaking from adrenaline. Now only sporadic fire was heard, coming from the other side of the road, and then silence. It was over as quick as it began. Fog clouded Sam's brain and panic gripped him.

No! Think. I must think!

An unfamiliar voice came from near the road, aimed in his direction. "Wheeler! No thanks to you, we got all of them. You run from a firefight again, and I'll personally shoot you. We ought to just leave your sorry ass here."

Sam shoved the bloody dagger into his boot sheath and rose. A searing pain tore through his left thigh. Every nerve ending was on fire. And his ribs felt as if they were used as a trampoline. He unslung his rifle and using it as a crutch, staggered into the surrounding forest, trying to distance himself from the enemy soldier.

The soldier peered deeper into the gloomy woods. "Wheeler, you in there?"

A creek bank yawned before Sam. He stumbled, trying to catch himself, but was too late and half-fell, half-slid down the steep, sandy bank. The pain in his leg and chest was agonizing, and he stifled a scream. Pressing himself into the soft earth, he tried to become one with the soil. A shout echoed. The soldier behind him had found his dead comrade. After what seemed an eternity, but was probably no more than a minute, other voices began drifting through the woods.

"Wheeler bought it, Sarge. Looks like a neck wound."

Sam shook; half in fear, half in pain. Dawn was creeping through the forest, and shapes were now identifiable. He glanced farther down the bank...shit. In the fall, he'd dropped his rifle, and it lay out of reach but in plain sight from those above. Even though he was somewhat concealed, if the weapon was spotted, those soldiers would be crawling all over the creek. His only hope was that they believed the soldier had been killed in the firefight and that all of their enemies were accounted for. Another thought hit him, and he swore. Blood was slung everywhere back there, and he'd undoubtedly left a trail of blood straight to the creek. He prayed it was still dark enough that the blood trail was missed.

"Man, there's blood everywhere," Sam heard the first soldier say. "Check it out."

"He probably took it in the carotid," another replied. "You know how a guy will spray when hit there. Come on, let's get him outta here."

Sam's heart rate eased, and a great weariness gripped him. It wasn't just from the struggle but blood loss. His head drooped, and he lay quiet, listening and praying. The sound of trampled brush drifted. He heard a few voices then silence. Sam moved his bloody, gloved fingers and dug them into the sandy bank. He grabbed handfuls of soil and rubbed them between his hands. Some of the sand stuck to his fingers, and in revulsion, he quickly rubbed his gloves on his right pant leg. He dropped down, becoming one with the creek bank again.

Diesel engines cranked. A gear ground, and the sound of rolling tires on caliche echoed through the woods. Seconds later, the sound of the small enemy convoy receded in the distance.

Wincing, Sam rolled over. Dappled early morning sunlight lit his face, splashing through a leafy canopy, and yet the night's coolness still lingered. He'd made it. He was alive. Now what? Those words the enemy soldier had spoken swirled in his mind. W*e got all of them.* He shook his head, forcing down panic and grief. Should they have surrendered? Those men had been his responsibility, and now he had screwed up. But second-guessing himself wouldn't bring back lives. Surrender was no option. Thing was, he should've died with his men.

Sam gingerly felt the front of his left thigh and winced. Blood soaked the pant leg, and there was a hole in the cloth six inches above his knee where a bullet had torn through. With his gloved fingers, he felt the material on the backside of his leg—another bloody hole where the round had exited. He glanced down to his chest. The camo shirt was dark and sticky with dried blood. Carefully touching fingers to the darkest spot, he saw the shirt was torn in several places across his ribs. A round must've hit a rib or two and tumbled around just under the skin. Even though it hurt like hell to breathe, the chest wound was probably not as serious as the one in his leg; the leg was still oozing blood. If he stayed, he'd bleed to death before help could arrive, as if help were out there.

Groaning from pain and anguish, Sam crawled to the rifle and, using it for support, pulled himself up. Steadying himself, he took an agonizing step up the creek bank, then another and another. He staggered over the edge and nearly fell. If he fell, he'd be hard pressed to get back up. He glanced down to the M-10 assault rifle and did a double-take. The action had a jagged gouge in it where a bullet had ricocheted off, probably saving his life. Except as a crutch, the weapon was useless.

Sam took a step, tottered, caught himself, then began limping through the woods to the fire road. What should have taken only a minute or so now took ten as he agonizingly worked through the forest to the gravel road. Emerging from brush, he stood on the road's edge, leaned on the rifle, and glanced around. Their five-ton was gone. All twelve bodies of his party were lying in a neat row alongside the road for body count and photo record. They were still clothed, although anything of usefulness was stripped. Several bullet-riddled canteens lay strewn about the road. Well, there went his water. Anguish replaced physical pain as he slowly made his way toward them.

He halted, not wanting to look but knew he had to. There was Kyser, Pendelton, Harding...all wearing varying faces of death. Sam's jaw tightened as he stared at the carnage. These men were not only his comrades-in-arms, but they were his friends. And he had led them straight into an ambush. If he survived, how would he explain to mothers, wives, and children that he had gotten their loved ones massacred, while he had survived? Sam swallowed. He was tempted to drop down and die alongside them—that would be his just reward. Yes, yes, that's what he should do. He would cheat fate no longer. Sam wavered, about to release the rifle on which he was leaning. It would be so easy. He'd already lost too much blood anyway. All he had to do was sit and wait.

"Sam."

Sam jerked around. "What was that? Who's there?"

Only the forlorn, green forest met his gaze.

"Come to me, Sam."

Sam snapped around. "Katie! Katie, is that you?"

Nothing. No human was seen. Sam's heart raced. He had heard Katie's voice. He would swear to it. Was she out there? If so, why was she hiding and not coming to his aid? "Katie!" he shouted, and her name echoed. "Where are you?"

Only the innocent chirping of cardinals drifted from the woods.

Sam rubbed the stubble on his jaw. They say that when one is near death, loved ones who have passed on pay a visit. Was Katie dead? Would he soon join her?

"No, she's still alive," he murmured. "I can feel it. Oh, God, I can feel her..." He clearly recalled Katie's face, her full lips, dainty chin, and the way her skin felt when pressed against his. Her brown eyes haunted him. He must live so he could experience her one more time.

Now, Sam wanted to live in the worst way. He nodded to his fallen comrades lying in the weeds alongside the road. "I'm sorry, but 'sorry' won't bring you back. I've gotta go. I'll send someone back for you. I promise."

Sam ripped off part of his torn short and tied off the bleeding leg. With renewed determination, he limped down the gravel road. Maybe six miles ahead, the road swung to the north, heading back to pavement, civilization, and the enemy. However, where the fire road turned north, a rough-hewn, woodland path headed south, plunging deeper into the forest. That path eventually led to the patriots' base camp. The crossroads was Sam's goal. He had to at least make it to the southward trail if he were ever to be found, or his body recovered. The rebels seldom risked traveling in the open, even on the rural fire roads. This morning was a prime example of why.

The morning wore on as Sam limped, sometimes staggering down the shoulder of the road. Deer flies the size of sparrows buzzed about him, but he was too weak to slap at them. The only things on his mind were making it to the intersection ahead and living long enough to find Katie. He pondered for a moment... everything about himself, who he was, the past that molded him into what he was now, it was all dead. No, there was no past. The past was only collective moments of now. And those moments would collect into what fate? The guilt of those dead partisans hung on him like a rotting carcass.

The pain in his left thigh, and the squishy sound in his boot, broke his thoughts. Sam stumbled as lightheadedness overtook him. He glanced around, searching for something, anything he could rest on or against before he collapsed. He made his way to a large, vine-covered stump at the road's edge and eased down. He leaned the rifle against the stump, tugged off his baseball cap, and wiped his forehead. He slowly worked the cap back on his head. Water...he desperately needed water. He thought of heading back into the woods on the right to see if he could find that creek. No, in his present shape, he'd get lost. He swallowed painfully.

* * *

Sam blinked. There was something scratching his face. Weeds. He was lying on his side in tall weeds near the stump he'd been sitting on. Wait. The sun was in the wrong position. It should be late morning. Groaning, he pushed himself into a sitting position and glanced around. The shadows were all different. It was now late afternoon. "Oh, God..." he murmured, "gotta keep moving, gotta keep moving." His crumpled hat lay nearby, and he straightened it as best he could. After brushing debris from his hair, he worked the cap back on. With the rifle in his hands, he pulled himself to his feet. His left leg was as stiff as a two-by-four, yet at least one good thing had come from the "nap." His camo pant leg was stuck to both sides of the wound. The bleeding had stopped—at least for now.

Sam's lips were swollen and cracked, and a great thirst lay on him, but there was renewed strength in his being. Miraculously, the .45 was still strapped to his right leg. He checked the action, shoved it back in its holster, and secured the top flap. Jaw tightening, he turned and ambled to the fire road, heading east.

Speckled shadows grew. The sun was now hidden in the tree line behind. Sam found that if he kept his left leg stiff, the pain lessened while decreasing the chance of renewed bleeding, but it slowed his gait even more. He glanced to the lowering sun behind him and swore. He'd never make the crossroads before dark.

Shadows lengthened, and here and there a cricket chirped from nearby weeds. One leg after another brought him a step closer to his destination. There he could at least rest...at least there his body could be recovered by friends.

Friends. He once had *real* friends. Old Leo and Michelle Spencer, they were real friends. And like everything else in his wretched life, they were now gone. Except for Katie. And for all he knew, she could be dead now, too. He was alone. And alone he would die. One leg after another, one forlorn step after another.

Sam forced his thoughts elsewhere. He recalled the last few weeks of his previous life—standing in front of his class, explaining to young, anxious faces how freedom wasn't free and that sacrifice must be made in freedom's name. Teaching. He couldn't believe that he was once a teacher. Now, that world seemed so distant, a life that belonged to another. Yet he had experienced compassionate moments—helping those kids escape Perchance, flee tyranny. His thoughts drifted to earlier, to that Christmas dinner at the Spencers, receiving his father's photo album, the way Katie and he held one another's gaze, and then held each other in the dark, the promise they had made to one another, the promise that no matter what, they would find the other. And then their world unraveled.

"Well, Moore, my boy," Sam said, "doesn't look like you'll keep that promise." He chuckled in disgust, again focusing on the task at hand: survival.

An hour passed, and Sam struggled to remain afoot. The wound in his leg began bleeding again, and his left side throbbed, slowing his pace even more. Dusk soon gave way to gloom, and the forest seemed close and foreboding. Coyotes yapped from deep in the woods on his left. The caliche road was now only a gray strip in a sea of darkness. Thirst overrode pain. His mouth was so dry, he could no longer swallow. Sam slipped on a rock and fell face-down in the road. His rifle lay under him, wedged against the wounds in his chest. Pain wracked his body, forcing him to rise. With an almost superhuman effort, he struggled to his feet.

"Oh, God, no..." Sam leaned on the rifle, unsure which way to go. Everything looked the same in the darkness. He swore, trying to identify landmarks. The only thing recognizable was the forest's uniform blackness against the night sky. He should be at that crossroads by now...had he been backtracking all along? He could've passed his fallen comrades in the darkness. Doubt, then panic, crept in. Sam forced down the latter as he squinted into the deeper darkness that was the forest, trying to find something, anything familiar. Clouds skirted a quarter moon; not even the moon would give up her weak light tonight. He bowed his head, said a prayer, and stumbled forward. The rifle butt-turned-cane crunched on packed rock, and he limped along, one foot after another.

Sam felt like he was in a waking nightmare. He hobbled along now only by sheer will.

At times, it seemed as though he wasn't even moving. Other times, it seemed the forest was a maze, spinning around him, twisting the road here and there to keep him trapped in eternity. Around every bend was only more road, darkness, brush, and the ever-present timber. The forest controlled it all. The trees now laughed at him; he was a rat in their maze. The pines would play with him awhile and then—

Sam collapsed. The rifle clattered away into darkness. His breath came in bone-chilling gasps. The smell of earth and rock filled his nostril. Groaning, he tried to rise but fell back. He lay helpless in the middle of the road. So, this was the way they would find his body: face-down in the dirt. He struggled to crawl off the road, but it was useless; he was totally spent.

The yapping of coyotes startled him. They were uncomfortably close. With great effort, Sam rolled over and reached for the .45 strapped to his side. Chambering a round, he glanced fearfully to the woods. Fog was forming, and all was silent. Sam was filled with the human horror of being stalked by beasts. Instinct of survival took hold. He tried once more to rise but collapsed onto his back. If he could just make it through the night... Gripping the .45 for reassurance, he eased his head back down. Quiet minutes ticked off. Crickets chirped, and a whippoorwill's haunting cry echoed, and yet the coyotes were now quiet. Had they left? Sam's eyelids grew heavy. He fought it as long as he could, but exhaustion won, and he nodded off.

Sniff, sniff, sniff.

Sam's eyes flew open. "What the—"

Growl—

Sam's throat was too dry to scream. At his feet were two dark shapes. Both growled, unmoving. He aimed the .45 at the center mass of the nearest dog and squeezed the trigger. *Pow! Pow!* The animal dropped, gave a quick whine, and lay still. The other dog scampered off, yapping into the murkiness.

The thumping in Sam's chest eased, and he wiped sweat mixed with condensation from his face with a forearm. He forced himself up on an elbow and took in the scene. Overhead, a large, quarter-moon shone eerily through a thin, pale haze. The night's blackness had given way to a surreal glow as wet mist swirled, enveloping all. Even the coyote carcass heaped at his feet was barely visible.

Sam licked welcome moisture from cracked lips. The air felt and tasted *different*. Was he dreaming or was he dead? He shifted and winced with pain; wherever he was, his gunshot leg had come with him. He paused, listening...no crickets, no night sounds. Wait—what was that? He strained to hear over his pounding heart.

A horse snorted. It was only a suggestion...maybe what he wanted to hear. Sam hung his head. No, he would die where he lay.

There it was again. Sam glanced around, hope rising. Barely perceptible, but there was no mistaking what it was: the *clip-clop* of a horse drifted through the fog. Inside, a tiny flame of hope flickered. No NAC soldier would be on horseback, especially at night. It could be bandits. But on a night like this?

A twig snapped off to his left, and his head jerked around. Sam squinted, struggling to see through the mist. Several yards away a glowing ball swung back and forth. A few feet off the ground, it grew closer and closer. Sam's fingers tightened around the pistol. He could now make out at least one dark shape near the light.

Sam raised the pistol, forcing out his words. "That's far enough."

The light halted. After a long moment, it slowly continued forward. Sam aimed the pistol and squinted. He could just make out dark shadows around a lantern. "Is that you guys?"

Only the crunching of boots on gravel answered. Thirst overcame caution. "Whoever you are," he croaked and waved the pistol, "I hope you brought water." He began shaking, again feeling faint.

Sam thought he heard a murmur of voices, and then two men loomed over him. One of them held out a lantern, and the other thrust a canteen to him.

Sam eased the pistol to the ground. With shaking hands, he reached for the canteen. The canteen was an old-style round, metal affair but looked surprisingly new. Unscrewing the cap, he tilted the container. Cold liquid trickled down his throat, and he coughed it up, unable to swallow.

The stranger patted his back and pulled back the canteen.

Sam nodded and ever-so-gently tilted the canteen. A tiny stream of water seeped down his throat. This time, he swallowed it. The parchness in his throat eased, and he took another swig.

221

The water was cool but had a peculiar taste to it. No matter, it was water, and the best he'd ever experienced.

The man holding the lantern leaned over Sam. He beckoned him to rise.

About to tilt the canteen again, Sam glanced up to the man and froze. A dark beard hung from the man's weatherworn face and a beat-up cap covered shaggy hair. But that's not what riveted Sam's attention: the man was clothed in a tattered Confederate uniform, the type of uniform worn in the American Civil War. Sergeant stripes were on the sleeves, and a musket hung across his back.

Sam took one last swallow before screwing the cap back on. His wary eyes never left the man. He handed the canteen back to the stranger, who slung it over a shoulder. Even though the soldier might've been in his late thirties, the man's fingers were gnarled and bent as an old man's.

The other man standing in the shadows stepped forward into the light. He also signaled for Sam to get up.

Sam did a double-take. The man, also bearded, wore a faded Union officer's uniform with a pistol hanging from a belt. Sam made out captain's bars on his shoulder straps and the letters **US** on a dark, floppy hat. "I'm definitely dreaming," he murmured, "or this is the hell that I deserve."

The Union soldier shook his head, reached down for Sam's arm, and attempted to help him up.

The Rebel soldier standing nearby eased the lantern to the ground and reached for Sam's other arm.

With a man lifting up each arm, Sam struggled to his feet. The soldiers, or whatever they were, now had their faces in the shadows. A shiver corkscrewed down Sam's spine. Where the strangers' eyes should be were glowing points of light.

The Union officer stooped down for Sam's pistol. The modern .45 caliber semi-automatic should've appeared alien to the man, yet he never gave it a second glance. Instead, he handed the pistol to Sam, butt first.

Sam mechanically reached for it, dropped it in its holster, and snapped the cover. He stared, unsure of how to comprehend the moment. He swallowed painfully, eyeing the two strangers, fearing the answer to the question he was about to ask. "Who are you guys?"

The Union soldier shook his head and pointed in the direction from which they had come.

"Can't you talk?" Sam asked.

With a finger over his lips, the Confederate soldier leaned

toward Sam.

Sam glanced to each bizarre man. "But...but...where do you guys live...stay? I mean, my men and I live out in the forest, and no one has ever seen anyone like you two...not in almost two centuries."

The soldiers remained ghostly quiet, only staring with glowing eyes at Sam. After a moment, the Rebel sergeant retrieved the lantern from the ground and both began half-tugging, half-leading Sam away.

Sam took a couple of steps and faltered. The two soldiers grabbed him, steadying him.

The Confederate wedged an arm under Sam's shoulder. and the Union soldier worked Sam's other arm around his neck. The three men began trudging down the foggy road.

The smells of horse, leather, and sweat permeated. Sam glanced first to the man on his right then to his left. "Where did you guys come from?"

The Union officer gestured to the surrounding forest and then to the ground.

Limping along, with the soldiers assisting him, Sam shook his head in fear and amazement. "I'd say I'm delirious, half-dead and that you two don't really exist, and yet...yet..." Sam squeezed the captain's shoulder. "You can't be ghosts. You're warm, flesh and blood, like me."

And then Sam heard it—a barely audible chuckle. The Confederate sergeant gazed at him with those creepy, glowing eyes and chuckled.

Sam's hair rose on the back of his neck. They continued on, and Sam remained silent.

Horses snorted ahead, and a buckboard loomed up in the fog. A tailgate was dropped, and the two soldiers helped Sam into the back. Groaning, he eased against the wooden side. The wood was worn but far from rotten, as it should've been. The wagon rocked as the soldiers climbed in at the front. A sharp whistle sounded, and the wagon creaked forward. Sam's leg ached, but yet somehow, even with the wagon swaying and jostling, he dozed off.

The wagon stopped, and Sam's eyes opened. The wagon rocked as two men climbed down. The moon had disappeared, and the fog had thickened. Sam could barely make out the shadows standing by the tailgate. Chains rattled, and the tailgate swung down. The soldiers stood by the open tailgate, beckoning.

Sam scooted to the men and they grabbed him, helping him down. Their shining eyes were points of light in the fog as they led him to the buckboards front. He touched the horse as he limped by. It was warm, real. The three continued for several more yards before halting.

The captain handed Sam the canteen and lantern, and then he pointed in front of them.

Sam held up the lantern, straining to see through the fog. Nothing. Only white mist swirled around the light. He slung the canteen over a shoulder and turned to the two men who had rescued him from the road.

The Confederate sergeant extended his hand, followed by the Union captain. Sam shook their hands. Their grips were strong and firm. He stared to the points of light where the soldiers' eyes should be. "I...I don't understand any of this."

The sergeant again gave a low chuckle, and his shadow retreated to the buckboard. The captain came to attention, clicking his heels. He tapped his hat and shooed Sam away. Turning, the captain disappeared toward the wagon.

Sam took a couple of hesitant steps then turned back. Only fog, nothing else. It was as if the whole episode had never happened. Then he heard it; the *clip-clop* of horses' hooves retreating into the night.

Sam was so overwhelmed that he could only stare after the echo of an American tragedy from the past. It was incomprehensible what had just occurred, but here he was, upright, with a 19th century lantern and canteen, which he would always treasure. Had he found them while stumbling along, delirious? No. *Someone* or *something* had given them to him and brought him to this place. Those men were as real as the ground under his feet, weren't they? He had to be delirious— that was the only explanation he could comprehend. The stab of pain in his left leg reminded him he was still in dire danger. Turning, he stumbled and then limped forward.

"Halt!"

Sam froze. He strained to see but was met with a wall of fog. The lantern in his left hand swung back and forth, creating an eerie shadow.

"Don't twitch a muscle," came the voice in front of him.

The voice sounded familiar, and Sam ventured a word. "Tillman, is that you?"

A flashlight clicked on. "Moore?"

"Yeah."

The flashlight beam switched to the ground, and a man's shadow stepped forward. "Geesus, Moore, we've been looking for you guys all night but had to quit because of this damn fog." The light beam flashed around. "Where are the others?"

"There are no others."

The man's flashlight moved around Sam, searching the white ether. "Did you get separated—"

"No. We were ambushed. Everyone's dead but me, and I'm halfway there." Sam faltered, almost collapsing.

The man rushed to Sam's side, catching an arm. "Sorry, buddy. Let's get you back to camp."

The pair had not gone far when several others rushed out of the fog. Flashlights clicked on, and someone lifted the lantern from Sam's hand. "Don't remember those guys taking a lantern," someone commented, "especially an antique like that one."

"It's Sam Moore," Tillman said, "and he's wounded. Says they were ambushed and the others were killed."

Sam was met with a volley of questions but hadn't the strength to answer. "I need rest," was all he could manage. He took another step and collapsed.

Jonathan Tipton stared with satisfaction at the dead rebel fighters in the photos. The bodies were laid out neatly in a row. He reached for a set of individual photos, scrutinizing each and every one. "When were these taken, Captain?"

OIS Captain James Norton glanced to the commissar standing across the desk from him. "Early this morning, Mr. Tipton. The ambush was successful."

Tipton perused the photos once more, sighed, and tossed them on the Captain's desk. "I don't see the insurgent I'm looking for." Wearing a light blue, open collar dress shirt and tan slacks, he gazed harshly to the younger man in the black uniform. "The ambush wasn't a success. The whole point of the ambush was to *capture* rebel fighters. And you just told me that there were no survivors."

"None."

"You are sure no one escaped?"

"I wasn't there, Commissar. I'm going on what Lieutenant Nadel told me. I interrogated several soldiers who took part in the ambush, and they all say the same thing. The ambush was thorough and took the rebels completely by surprise." Norton nodded to the photos strewn about his desk. "That's all of them. Not one rebel escaped."

A pacing Tipton halted. "That's the whole damn point! I gave orders to capture, not kill!"

"With all due respect, Commissar, when you're being shot at, you shoot back. I'm not defending Nadel's men, but—"

Tipton held up a hand, silencing the captain. "I am sick and tired of excuses. Must I take a gun and do it myself? I mean, how hard can it be to capture one of those damn insurgents?" He waved a hand around. "The woods are full of them."

Norton's jaw tightened, and he looked away. "We're dealing with suicidal maniacs, sir. They usually put a bullet in their brain before capture."

A tense silence ensued. Norton stepped from around his desk and leaned on it, examining a crack in the plywood floor.

Tipton scratched the back of his head, calming. "Where were these rebels found?"

"About twenty-five miles southeast of here in the Old Forest.

Our patrol recovered a lot of C-four. The lieutenant's sure it's the same rebels that sabotaged the train earlier and probably the same bunch that's been destroying infrastructure in the region. So, at least something positive came from the ambush." Norton indicated the photos. "Those are some *really* bad guys that we no longer have to worry about."

The commissar remained expressionless. Turning, he casually walked around the captain's makeshift office, hiding his growing frustration. Even with a set of pliers in his hand, which was the military, he still failed to yank the thorn from his side. And the festering increased with each patrol's return, mostly emptied handed and never with Samuel Moore. Tipton strolled to a bare window and surveyed the scene. A busy military camp surrounded them. Five months ago, his residence was moved from civilian housing to military quarters. He wanted to keep a direct eye on operations. Receiving several death threats also helped convince him that this was where he should be. Although he carried no military rank, his Directorate rank as a Commissar Colonel gave him *unofficial* supreme authority over everyone in the camp, or in the region for that matter. No one, not even a general, wanted to buck a Directorate Commissar, especially one who had access to President Henshaw. So, his recommendations were usually followed. His *official* duty was to make sure civilians and military alike followed Directorate edict, towed the political line so to speak. The military could do what it wished as long as they didn't impede on the Directorate goal: the destruction of the rebels, their ideas of revolution, and the capture of Samuel Moore. Well, perhaps the latter was *his* goal, but it didn't matter. The only ones who could possibly thwart his plans or give him any trouble was Office of Internal Security. The OIS captain across from him must be dealt with a little differently. He glanced back at the captain leaning on his desk. "I am sorry, Captain Norton, for the outburst. I hope you will accept my apology for my pig-headedness. You have been a great help in the past. I hope we can continue to work together."

The captain reached for a nearby pen and clicked it. "Apology accepted, Commissar. I understand your frustration."

Tipton took off thick glasses, yanked out a handkerchief from a back pocket, and rubbed the lenses. No, the captain didn't understand. No one did. He shuddered inside.

And just below the surface, he struggled to force down an ever-growing cauldron that was sucking the life from him; his refusal to change his goal. Conversion, change, had always been the one constant in his life until now. Tipton had always accepted a modification in thought in his personal life, in his lifestyle—it was called *survival*. There once had been someone whom had given him even more reason to change, to survive. Tipton was reluctant to admit that a tiny part of him still yearned for those days when there had been exuberance, a zest for living. But now...now a festering wound had replaced the lost compassion.

It hit him that he was *alone*—and he hated it.

There was no longer anyone he could love, chime to, vent his anger or joy to, or say "damn to it all." His wife had been killed three years ago when a rebel bomb blew up at the Directorate Constitution Celebration in Central City.

He had married late in life. Yet forty-six was not too late to learn about love was it? For his wife, Camera, it was her second marriage. They had met when he was assigned to Central City, back in the 30s. Camera was a Directorate logistics officer at the Chief Command Center. At forty-two, she was childless, and to Tipton, that had been a blessing. Neither desired children. Hell, he hated kids.

Tipton worked his glasses back on, and pushed them over his nose with a round forefinger. Sighing, he stepped to the door and stood in the open doorway. "Thank you, Captain. Let me know if anything comes across your desk about you-know-who."

"Yes, sir, we'll keep in touch."

Tipton closed the door and headed for his billet, his office-slash-home, across the dusty parking lot. His mind wandered back to when he was a happy man.

Those eight years of marriage was as close to bliss as he would ever get. He had even laughed with Camera. They had taken long walks, holding hands, while Billy, their schnauzer, yanked on his leash. Then in one horrifying instant, an American rebel terrorist ended it all. Now life held no true contentment. There was only an echo of satisfaction when the rebels and their supporters were beaten down, their lifeless bodies left to putrefy in the sun to show others what happens when they defy rightful authority. Those terrorists took away the only thing he had ever cared for. Yes, he had loved Camera even more than he loved himself. Those terrorists would pay. And Samuel Moore was the epitome of the insurgency. Tipton held Moore personally responsible for his wife's death even though the teacher had nothing whatsoever to do with it. Moore and the rest of those heathens must be smashed. Only after the insurgents were humiliated and obliterated would Tipton finally sleep. Or would he?

What you need to do, Jonathan, is forget about Moore and

move on with your life.

"No, I can't," he murmured, "I must, must..." He forced down rebellious thoughts, thoughts that he knew, deep down, could save him. Misery...some simply live for misery.

The commissar scrambled up the steps without realizing he was already at his quarters.

Buzz... Tipton closed the door and retrieved the vibrating phone from a slacks pocket. He glanced to the number, frowned, and wedged it against an ear. "Yes?" Lips pursed, he listened silently for several moments. "I believe an agreement can be reached." Quiet seconds ticked off as Tipton nodded. "I'll be there." The commissar moved the tiny phone away from his ear, and it clicked off. What passed for a smile moved across his face.

* * *

The small helo hovered over treetops for a moment before descending into a forest clearing. Dust and debris swirled up as the chopper settled onto the ground. The pilot touched an overhead screen. The jet-turbine spooled down, and the whirring of spinning blades settled to a lazy rotation.

A side door popped open, and Tipton climbed from the cabin. Dressed in khaki overalls, he cinched up the web belt, feeling the weight of the holstered .9 millimeter pistol hanging from the right side. It had been years since he had worn a gun on his hip, and it felt strange to be openly armed. Smoothing Velcro straps over his armored vest, he glanced to the black-uniformed man stepping from around the chopper's other side. "He should be alone," he said to him.

"He is," Norton replied. The younger man unsnapped the pistol holster, exposing a .45's black pistol grip. "No one else was detected."

Tipton nodded toward a tall, thin man stepping from the forest shadows. "Good. You, that man coming toward us, and myself are all that need know what this is about."

"Yes, sir."

Tipton glanced to Norton. "Shall we?"

Norton nodded, and they stepped to the approaching stranger. In some places, weeds were knee high, and Tipton carefully picked his way through the brush. He adjusted sunglasses, glancing to the man working toward them.

The man was tall and lanky. He wore a camouflage T-shirt and shabby jeans tucked into lace-up boots. A faded green baseball cap covered his head.

Tipton and Norton halted in the intense, afternoon sun as the man stepped up to them. A slow, wry smile moved over the commissar's face. "Why, if it's not the old chemistry teacher, Zack Zhimmer." Tipton eyed the younger man. "Finding any time to teach in between dodging bullets?"

ZZ glanced first to the black-clad OIS captain then to his old boss. "That's what I want to talk about Mr. Tipton." ZZ hesitated. "I'm tired of this, this life. I just want myself and my family the hell away from here—a long way. I want to start over."

Tipton glanced over sunglasses that had slid down his sweaty nose. "And I may be able to arrange that, but of course, you must offer something in return."

ZZ shifted his feet, kicked at a patch of dirt, and glanced up, looking Tipton in the eye. "I might be able to offer up Sam Moore."

"I see."

"If not him, for a price, I can for sure hand-deliver his girlfriend, Katie Spencer."

The commissar was caught off guard. "Did you say 'Katie Spencer?'"

ZZ nodded. "You know, she's the one that conspired with—"

"I know who she is." To capture and parade around one who was directly responsible for this outbreak of violence. And having the Spencer girl might lead to Moore's capture. What a coup. The commissar exchanged glances with the captain standing next to him. Inside, Tipton salivated. Outwardly he showed no emotion. His gaze landed on the chemistry teacher. "I suppose you'll collect any reward."

ZZ nodded, silent.

Tipton paused. "Tell you what, I'll give you a hundred-thousand for the Spencer girl, a half-mil if you can deliver her and Moore together. But keep it quiet about the girl."

ZZ smiled. "You got it, Mr. Tipton."

Tipton eyed the former chemistry teacher, gauging him. "Collecting a half-million dollars is easy, Mr. Zhimmer. Hanging on to it is another matter. Do you know what you are doing?"

ZZ removed his hat and rubbed a forearm over a sweaty forehead. "Yes, sir, I most certainly do. That's why I also ask for safe passage away from these parts for my family and me."

Silence enveloped all three. The chemistry teacher cleared his throat. "I want safe passage across The River."

Tipton gave a subtle nod. "I think we can deal."

26

Sam ran through the forest in what seemed like slow motion. His feet were lead blocks; they just wouldn't move any faster. Focus. He had to focus. If he focused, he could pick up speed. But he struggled to concentrate while trying not to look back. He couldn't, wouldn't turn to see what horror was chasing him. All he knew was that if what was behind caught him...

"Damn you, Moore!"

There was a rush of something behind, and the voice grew closer.

"You're gonna pay, Moore! Do you hear me? You're gonna pay!"

Malevolence reeked, enveloping him. He instinctively glanced back and froze in place.

He was staring at himself. Only this creature's skin was a pasty white and black. Holes filled the void where his eyes should be. The creature halted, leering. It hissed, and a forked tongue slithered from pallid lips. Without warning, it let out a blood-chilling scream that shook Sam to the bone.

"Sammy—Sammy boy! Quick. Over here!"

Sam tore his gaze away from the creature, searching for the source of the voice.

"Sam, damnit get your ass over here!"

Twenty feet away, a cart sat idling on a dirt road. Behind the wheel was ZZ Zhimmer, signaling to him. "Come on, guy, let's get outta here!"

Suddenly, Sam's feet were free, and he bounded toward the cart. "ZZ!"

A gull-wing door popped opened, and Sam threw himself inside. The door snapped shut just as the doppelganger lunged. The creature hit the window, snarling, and fangs bit at window glass, leaving a green, oozing smear.

ZZ stepped on the throttle, throwing Sam into the seat. The electric motor screamed. The acceleration was tremendous. G-forces pinned Sam down. Barely able to raise his head, he shouted. "Okay, ZZ, that's enough!"

ZZ laughed, backing off the throttle. "I think we left him in the dust back there."

Sam nodded, breathing easier. Clicking the seatbelt, he

gave the older man a curious look. "What are you doing here?"

With both hands on the steering wheel, he glanced to Sam. "I heard my old friend and colleague had got himself into a jam once again and since Leo's not here..."

"Good to see you, friend." Sam grinned, extending a hand. "I'm running out of friends these days."

ZZ gripped Sam's hand. "Last time I checked, you'd passed zero and were in negative territory."

There was an odd tone in ZZ's voice, and Sam's grin faded. ZZ's face began to morph. Glasses appeared on a short, blunt nose. ZZ's prominent jaw vanished, replaced by chubby jowls.

Sam looked into the face of Jonathan Tipton.

Tipton gave a hideous chuckle. "You will never escape me. I will be the last thing you see on this planet."

Sam struggled, unable to move. He was no longer sitting in the cart. He was walking...walking, with his hands tied behind his back. He was being led up a set of steps. He reached a wooden platform surrounded by a crowd of people.

"Sam!"

The voice was a woman's, and it sounded familiar. His eyes roved, searching for its source.

A woman stepped from the crowd. "Sam!"

Sam stared down into the face of Katie Spencer. "Katie!"

Tipton stepped in front of Sam, blocking his view. "I hope you kick and piss your pants," he said with an evil grin. In his hand was a noose. Someone from behind worked a hood over his face, and he was in darkness. The noose was looped over his neck and tightened.

"Samuel Moore," Tipton shouted, "for crimes, including high treason against the North American Commonwealth, you are hereby sentenced to death."

Sam felt the rope bite into his skin. He began praying... There was a creaking sound, and he was falling—

"Sam."

Sam's eyes fluttered open. His heart pounded, and his breath came in ragged gasps. Something soft closed around his left hand.

"Sam, calm down. You're okay."

He felt fingers gently caress his brow, and he blinked, determined to focus. As his right hand went to his neck, something nearby rattled, and a cord tugged on his arm.

"Easy, you have an IV in your right arm."

Sam halted, then gingerly felt where the rope burns should be; only smooth skin met his touch. "Thank you, Lord Jesus," he whispered, "thank you."

Now someone loomed over him. Ever so slowly details emerged. A head, dark hair, feminine features. "Katie?"

Full lips parted into a wide smile, revealing perfect white teeth. "Yes, Sam, it's me, Katie."

"This isn't happening. I've died—again."

"No, Sam, you're alive, although it was touch-and-go for awhile."

"Then I'm dreaming."

The woman shook her head. "You're not dreaming either."

"Katie..."

"Yes..."

Sam eyed her, soaking in her features. He couldn't believe Katie was at his side. Her face was thinner, and her once porcelain skin boasted a healthy tan. But now a pink scar lay above her left eyebrow. Freckles spread over her nose and under her eyes. The deep brown was still in those eyes, but the innocence he remembered was gone, replaced with a disquiet dignity. Her once thick, curly hair was lopped off and hung loose, and barely covering her neck. She was clothed in a khaki uniform shirt and combat fatigues, which somehow seemed to suit her.

Katie leaned over him and kissed him gently on the lips. Before Sam could react, she pulled away.

Sam took in his surroundings for the first time. The room was dim, unfamiliar. The only light came in from two open windows. He was lying in a bed—a real bed—and with clean, mismatched sheets. It had been months since he'd felt a mattress under him. His head rested on another rarity: a pillow. He glanced straight up. Wooden beams crossed a plaster ceiling. Wooden beams, or logs, also made up the walls. Next to him sat a nightstand with a small lamp resting on it. Across the room were two more empty beds. A whirring box fan sat on a table in front of an open window, stirring white curtains. A medicinal smell mingled with cedar and salty sea air filled the room. Where was he?

His chest itched something fierce, and he reached up to scratch. "What the...?" His fingers met a large bandage. He tried to rise, but searing pain tore through his chest and left leg

"No, Sam!" Katie touched his shoulders and eased him back down. "Lie still, or you'll start bleeding again. You had a second surgery on your chest and leg yesterday morning. The doctor says they finally got all the shrapnel out of your chest this time."

"Shrapnel?" Sam's brow furrowed. "What the...a second surgery? I don't even recall a first one." His gaze met hers; Katie's eyes glistened. He had a thousand questions, but at the moment, only one thing was on his mind. "Katie, you...I..." Sam reached for Katie, and her arms wrapped around his neck. The two clung to one another. Katie was careful not to press against his wounds.

"Our promise," he whispered, "was always there in the back of my mind. Sometimes...sometimes it was all I had, all that kept me going."

"And I never once forgot that promise...the promise we made back on that Christmas evening. That day now seems a world away." Katie buried her face in Sam's arms. "When I heard you were still alive, I knew I had to find you."

"I kept my eyes and ears open for you, too, Katie. Then I heard from a close friend who said he saw you at your grandparents."

"ZZ?"

"Yeah...you met him?"

Katie nodded. "Yes. He and his wife, Haleana, checked in on you. Haleana was a great comfort to me."

"They're good people." Sam fiddled with the sheet. "Anyway, I was going to head out, hunt for you after we finished that last mission."

Katie gazed at him. "I've been hiding out in the Perchance area since the war started. Both the NAC army and the Directorate were searching for me. If I had been caught..." Katie glanced away. "They found out about our little scheme that started this mess. Naturally, arrest warrants were issued for both of us. If I were caught, they would've used me for bait, Sam, to lure you in." Her gaze fell back on Sam. "And capturing you would've jeopardized the whole underground operation in the region. Hundreds, potentially thousands, could have died."

"*Me?*" Sam chuckled dryly. "Everyone gives me way too much credit."

Katie touched his hand. "You're a hero, Sam. All of you guys are."

"We're only American militia." Sam rested his head back on the pillow. "The only reason the enemy doesn't laugh at us is because we're damn good at blowing things up."

"Laughing is the last thing they would do, especially the Directorate." Katie eyed the man lying in the bed. "That old boss of yours, Jonathan Tipton, has a million-dollar price on you alive. Half-mil, dead."

"Up to a million, now, huh?"

"It went up a week after that supply train was demolished. Of course, whether you're responsible or not, you and your merry lads got the credit."

At the mention of the doomed patrol, Sam's face darkened. He gave a subtle nod. "Where am I?"

"You're in a field hospital run by the *United States* army."

"The *U.S.* army?"

"Yes. They're in control of this sector, but that could change at any moment." Katie gestured around. "This is a recovery room."

"A cabin?"

"Yes, isn't it nice?"

Sam glanced to Katie. "There was nothing like this back at camp."

"You're not anywhere near camp, Sam." Katie smiled. "You're twenty miles north of Charleston. We're on the coast. It's much safer here."

"I don't remember getting here." Sam's brow furrowed. "As a matter of fact, I...I don't remember much of anything, except nightmares...lots of nightmares. I remember stumbling around in the fog after these two strange men found me and saved my life." He halted, looked away, and swallowed, feeling Katie's eyes on him. "Then I stumbled up on Tillman and...and that's the last thing I remember."

"That was three weeks ago."

"What! No way...what day is it?"

"It's Wednesday, July Twentieth."

Their patrol was hit June 25th. Sam frowned. How could he have been out of it for almost a month and have no memory?

Katie cast a worried glance at Sam. "The infection in your leg had spread. You became delirious then lapsed into a coma. The camp doctor was about to amputate, to save your life, when word came that the route to the coast was clear and that there was a field hospital with medicines to counter the infection. The *Movement* couldn't afford to lose you."

"Geesus..." Sam weakly shook his head. "A hospital on the coast? I don't remember one being here."

"We're in an old state park campground. They just began taking in patients a few days before we arrived." Katie paused. "Sam, Charleston's northern suburbs are now under rebel control. Fighting between rebel forces and the NAC army is heavy. People are pouring out of the city. It was decided that a temporary refugee shelter along with a hospital was needed." Katie gazed at Sam. "The U.S. is slowly gaining control of this part of the coast."

Quiet seconds passed, and he focused on the moving window drapes. They fluttered as if excited by what Katie had said. Still a little groggy, Sam was overwhelmed. His gaze turned to the woman sitting on his bed. "Katie, I...a prayer has been answered."

Katie blushed, caressing his face. "Make that two prayers."

Time passed as Katie summarized the last three weeks and her escape from Charleston. Both agreed a detailed synopsis of the past few months would wait until later. Workers appeared and hung bed sheets from the ceiling, placing them between the beds. Soon, two more patients were brought in.

A tall man of about forty, wearing a white physician's coat over blue jeans, stepped around the sheet dividers an halted at Sam's side. He was a well-groomed but somewhat rugged looking man. Katie rose and stepped aside. With a stethoscope hanging from his neck, and carrying a clipboard full of papers, he extended a hand. "I'm Doctor Steven Meens, the surgeon who operated on you."

Sam weakly clasped his hand, shaking it. "Thanks."

The doctor took Sam's pulse and scribbled something down. Without warning, he quickly flashed a pen light in Sam's eyes.

Sam blinked. "Hey!"

Meens clicked off the light and stuffed it in a coat pocket. "Good, good. That's a one-eighty from when you were brought in day-before-yesterday." He glanced to Katie, standing nearby. "How long has he been awake?"

"Maybe an hour."

Meens nodded, and his gaze moved back to Sam. "Other than your leg and chest smarting, how do you *feel*, Sam?"

"Exhausted. Not tired...exhausted."

The doctor scrutinized him with keen eyes. "Your body has been through hell. Now it needs time off to heal."

"But I've been out of it for three weeks."

"Your body has been fighting infection that whole time." Meens gave a subtle nod. "The few surgical skills I have helped, but it was sheer will power from you that kept you going. Frankly, most would have succumbed." He patted Sam's right foot. "*Rest* is prescribed now."

"How soon can I leave?"

Meens gave an annoyed sigh. "When I say."

Sam shook his head, shifted, and winced. "One more thing? When can I get rid of this damn catheter?"

"Easy answer." The doctor hooked a thumb behind him. "When you can make it to the latrine."

* * *

And the refugees came in droves. Sam could hear the sounds

of heavy trucks and buses unloading their human cargo day and night. Voices drifted from open windows...despair...the sound of despair filled the air. Now and then, a distant rumble drifted up from the south, and occasionally, down from the north. A year ago, Sam would have believed it only thunder or perhaps a far distant train. But now, when that sound was heard, people died. The drums of war reached everywhere. He had experienced war, waged it, and had it waged upon him.

Sam's strength quickly began returning. By the next day, he was able to take light meals. The IV and catheter were soon removed. With Katie standing nearby, he climbed into a wheelchair on his own, and she pushed him to the bathroom. She rolled him into the bathroom and left while he took care of business. He was so pleased with himself that one would've believed he had just conquered Mt. Everest. It was amazing how one takes for granted the little things.

On the fifth day after his waking, he received two visitors, one a friend, the other a stranger, and both were together.

A man dressed in combat fatigues pushed back the sheet of his cubicle and paused. "So, there's that slacker! Sandbagging it again, huh?"

Alone in the room, Sam sat in bed, propped up by a pillow. Perusing through a thirty-year-old *National Geographic* magazine, he looked up. "Rob!"

Captain Rob Fields, followed by another soldier, stepped up to his bed. Rob removed his bush hat and reached for Sam's hand. "Man, what some *soldiers* won't do to get out of duty."

Sam shook hands, raising an eye at the way Rob emphasized the word *soldier*. This was his first meeting with Rob since the ambush that fateful morning. Sam swallowed hard. "Guess you'll want to know how the hell I screwed up that last mission."

Rob eyed him, remaining silent. He cleared his throat and stepped aside, nodding to the man next to him. "Sam, I'd like you to meet Lieutenant Colonel James Hall. He's one of my bosses."

Hall extended a hand. "Nice to meet you."

"Same here, Colonel," Sam replied, eyeing the man. Maybe in his late forties, he was tall, with an athletic physique. His uncovered head was bald and tan.

The colonel shifted a large brown envelope in his hand, while stuffing a bush hat inside his web belt. "Heard a lot about you, Moore," he said in a gruff voice.

Just then, Katie walked in. She glanced at the two soldiers hovering around Sam's bed then turned to leave. "Excuse me. Sam, you're busy. I'll come back later."

Rob spoke before Sam could say a word. "Katie, please stay."

Sam glanced to first Katie then to Rob. "You two know each other?"

They nodded. "We met a few weeks back," Katie said.

Sam gave a sheepish grin—and felt a twinge of jealously. "Of course, you would have...when you came into base camp."

The colonel cleared his throat and turned to Rob. "Are you ready, Captain?"

"Yes, sir."

Sam felt all eyes on him. Suspicion was added to jealously. Something was clearly going on, and it had to do with him. He had led those twelve men into an ambush. *He* was the reason those twelve men were not alive today. Were they going to charge him for their deaths? Would he be prosecuted? They would at least shame him and turn him out...take away his sense of belonging. He'd rather be dead than not belong.

Colonel Hall gazed at Sam. "We can't let someone like you skip out on us on a whim. So, what we need from you, Moore, is for you to become an *official* member of the team."

Sam's jaw tightened, and he stared at the colonel. "So, I can be officially charged for the deaths of my teammates?"

Rob and Hall exchanged perplexed glances. Rob placed a hand on Sam's shoulder. "Man, have you got it wrong! You can't be blamed no more than we can blame you for starting this war. Sam, it's not your fault. You did everything as planned. No way could you have known about the ambush—and that's what it was." Rob paused, stepped back, and gazed at Sam. "We can go over that later. That's not why we're here."

Sam frowned. "Then...what?"

The colonel stared at Sam. "We want you to join us, Moore, become an official part of the United States Army, and enjoy all the rights and privileges of a United States soldier."

"What?" Sam said.

Rob cleared his throat. "We need men like you in uniform, Sam. We...I...would like you to volunteer."

"But," Sam sputtered, "but all the training—"

Rob rolled his eyes, giving a wry smile. "You're kidding me, right? You've had OJT since we found you back in January. And you're the kind of leader we need. You're a professional, Sam. It's time you get recognized, rewarded for it." Rob paused, letting his words soak in. "Surely you've given it some thought...signing up?"

Sam stared, dumbfounded. He had never really given any thought to actually *joining* the U.S. military. Besides, in a way, he was already part of the army, helping to lead a militia, a paramilitary unit. He even wore parts of the same uniform, minus insignia and rank. As for reward, his reward would be to live long enough see the Directorate obliterated along with that pudgy-faced Jonathan Tipton. And as far as pay, Sam only thought of himself as a patriot. Compensation would happen with the downfall of the North American Commonwealth and restoration of the U.S. Constitution as the rightful law of the land. He would prefer civilian life. Sam shook his head, unsure. If the United States were victorious in defeating the NAC, destroying the Directorate and re-uniting the country, he would be needed here to help restore a sense of normalcy. Hell, he didn't even like guns. He was teacher, not a soldier. But could he be both? Was he both?

Colonel Hall cleared his throat, breaking Sam's thoughts. "I've studied Captain Fields' evaluation reports on you, Moore. And I agree with him. You're what this army needs." Hall paused, scrutinizing Sam. "And, perhaps, *you* need the army."

Sam swallowed. He had to admit he felt a sense of pride when trusted with a mission. At last he *belonged*. He loved the camaraderie with those around him. They suffered *together*, and they had a common purpose: to have each other's back so they could restore the United States to its former glory and return to loved ones. He frowned inside. But hadn't he *belonged* to that most evil organization known as the Directorate? And look where that got him...

Rob stepped a little closer. "Listen to the Colonel, Sam."

Sam glanced to Katie, who stood quietly in the corner of the little cubicle. Her fingertips were over her lips, and there was a strange look in her eyes. "Katie," and he nodded to her, "come here."

Katie hesitated then stepped to the side of the bed opposite the two soldiers. She gazed down, silent.

Sam reached for her hand, and his fingers closed around hers. "Did you catch all that?"

She nodded, squeezed his hand, but never said a word.

"What do you think?"

"I can't make that decision for you, Sam. You know that."

Sam studied Katie. *God, she was beautiful,* he thought. Yet, now she appeared forlorn. Her gaze was soft, but now there was a sadness about it he'd never seen. He sensed something bothered her other than what she had just heard. Had she come to discuss something with him only to find the two soldiers disrupting her plans? Later, they would talk.

"I know this is a heck of time to spring this on you," Rob said, breaking Sam's thoughts, "you being wounded, sorta out of action for a while. But conditions are changing. Our old camp and all the guys have broken up. Some here, some there, others drifting away to fight their own private war. Even Buck was transferred. Sam, the army needs to know where *you* stand. I recommended to Colonel Hall that you stay with us. You'll make one helluva a soldier. Our country will be stronger with men like you in uniform."

Sam sighed loudly. "If I sign up, how long must I serve?"

Rob glanced to the Colonel. Colonel Hall's jaw tightened ever-so-slightly. "Four years, minimum."

Sam's eyes widened. "Four years! What if the war ended tomorrow?"

Hall's steely gaze never changed. "Four years. There will be just as much a need for you after that NAC Army is defeated. After the war, you'll receive even more detailed training. You can return back here with the authority of the U.S. government behind you to make sure the transition to peace goes peacefully."

"Four years..." Sam said and whistled.

"Think of it this way," Rob began, "at least you won't be out of work. You'll be drawing a paycheck the whole time—and a good one, too. Helluva lot more than what you made around here as a school teacher." Rob paused, summing up a hesitant Sam. "You know, Sam, you gotta think of *your* future. You're going to be dodging bullets no matter where you are. Might as well be drawing pay and have the best toys to play with."

Sam gave Hall a quizzical look. "Colonel, you said 'return' here. So, I'll be doing some kind of basic training? Rob...Captain Fields...said I already have enough training to serve as a U.S soldier in South Carolina?"

The two soldiers exchanged glances. Hall cleared his throat. "Like the Captain said, you've already received most of your training first hand. I'm sure you've learned more in a month than most soldiers who have never experienced combat would learn in two years. But we need to get you up to speed on modern weapon systems and protocol. And you need to know what's *really* happening to our country. Out here," the colonel waved a hand, "you're too isolated." The colonel paused, eyeing Sam. "Moore, I understand you were a Directorate member?"

Sam nodded. "I was only on the bottom rung...mostly on the outside, looking in."

"I'm sure you know more than you think," the colonel said. "Intel would love a little chat with you."

More like an interrogation, Sam mused. So, there it was. And by him being part of the army, he would have little choice but to become their voluntary prisoner. *Prisoner...*he was a prisoner once, and he would *never* be a prisoner again. Yet, he would be in the Western Alliance component of America. They still lived by the Bill of Rights, didn't they? He fidgeted with a bed sheet, unsure. Maybe he should just blow all this off and remain a civilian. He could give them all the info he knew and then, as a civilian, walk away. He released the sheet, sighing loudly.

"I just don't know about all this. Everything is hitting me too fast and all at once." Sam gave Katie's fingers one last squeeze then released her hand. He gazed at her a moment longer. She seemed so dejected...why? Sam chewed a lip, swallowing hard. He glanced first to Rob, then to the colonel. "I just don't know."

Colonel Hall gazed at Sam with cold eyes and raised the envelope in his hand. "When I walk out that door in a few minutes, this goes with me, and I won't be back. The offer to join us will be rescinded. There will be no second offer."

A serious Rob leaned over Sam. "Come on, man. You gotta join up. I know this is a life-changing decision, but this is war... war. We need you, buddy. Your country needs you."

Sam glanced in Katie's direction; her back was to him. "Katie?"

Still facing away, she ignored him.

Sam gave a disgusted sigh, not needing her opinion; he already knew it.

The two soldiers glanced to Katie. Rob shook his head. His jaw tightened. The colonel turned back to Sam. His expression was flat, unchanged. "We don't have the luxury of time, Moore. I wish I could give you more time to mull things over," and he nodded to the woman behind them, "and discuss this. But time is lacking." He paused. His eyes never left Sam. "One must seize opportunity when it strikes. I'm giving you the chance to start a new career, begin a fresh life." His gaze softened ever so subtly. "Son, in the United States Armed Forces, you can make a real, meaningful difference."

It was the colonel's last words that struck Sam. *Meaningful.* He could wage guerilla warfare until the cows came home, or until he was killed, and there would be few who would remember him. And what about after the fighting stopped? If he survived, what would he do? As a soldier, he would still have a life, have a career. As the colonel had said, immediately after the war, as a soldier, he would stand a better chance at quelling the chaos that was sure to follow. Yes, to do something that had a lasting effect. But didn't teaching also do that, give that lasting effect? There was no guarantee of the latter after the war. As a soldier, he would have something to give Katie...or something to leave her. Sam nodded, swallowing, as his inner turmoil reached a crescendo. He glanced first to Rob, to Colonel Hall, and then his gaze finally rested on Katie. Her back was still to him. Sighing, he turned to the colonel. "Where do I sign up?"

Katie's shoulders sagged, and she dashed away, disappearing behind the privacy sheets. A door slammed, and silence filled the room.

Rob stared after her. After a moment, he turned back to Sam. "Her reaction...don't let it get to you. She'll be back."

"I wouldn't be so sure."

Colonel Hall shook his head, turning to Sam. "Are you certain you want to do this? I mean...you can't go into this half-hearted and carrying guilt."

"Yes, sir, I do want to become part of the U.S. Army. I'm ready to sign up."

"Moore," the colonel said, reaching inside the large envelope, "I believe I can oblige you. You can join right now." He worked out several forms and began passing them to Sam.

Rob punched Sam in the shoulder. "Way to go. You're doing the right thing!"

Hall produced a pen and handed it to Sam. "This is normally not how one enlists," he began, "but these aren't normal times. We're in the middle of a national emergency. We do what must be done." He paused, glancing at the papers in Sam's hand. "If you don't know addresses, just leave that part blank. We'll deal with it later."

Using the *National Geographic* as a table, Sam signed what seemed like a dozen documents. His pay would go into a bank of his choosing safely on the other side of the Mississippi River. He held the pay sheet up to Rob. "I actually know very little about what's on the other side. Rob, help me out here?"

Rob scratched his head. "How about where I bank? Lawton, Oklahoma is a safe distance away from the fighting."

"If you say so."

"Just sign the bottom and leave the rest blank for now," Rob said. "I'll fill in the bank's name and yours later, and Uncle Sam will set up the payroll account."

Sam nodded, signing one document after another. He scanned the papers, mostly searching for the highlighted X, signing and handing them to the colonel, who looked them over. Sam just wanted this part over with before he changed his mind.

Then he came to the last document and paused. After a moment, he shook his head. His jaw tightened.

"What is it, Moore?" Hall asked. "Something you don't understand?"

Sam clicked the pen a few times and looked up. "It says 'list next of kin.'"

Both soldiers stared at Sam.

Sam cleared his throat. "Gentlemen, I have no next of kin. They're all dead."

Rob studied his boot snaps. "I'm sorry, man."

The colonel gave a subtle nod. "Sometimes that happens..." He paused His gruff expression softened. "It doesn't have to be kin, son. Is there anyone you're close to, you trust?"

Sam printed Katie's name. "Katie Spencer, address—same as mine—unknown." He handed the document to Hall. "Am I done, sir?"

"Almost," Hall replied, stuffing papers into the envelope. He handed the envelope to Rob and turned back to Sam. Steel-gray eyes scrutinized the younger man for several long seconds as if Hall were finalizing a decision. "Moore, when Captain Fields came to me with this idea concerning one of his partisan fighters, I must admit I was skeptical. But now I'm sure that what I'm about to do is the right thing."

Sam glanced to Rob. The soldier was grinning.

"Moore," Hall began, "I'm giving you a battlefield commission. Do you know what that is?"

"I...I'm not sure."

"Normally, the President of the United States commissions officers, but in times like these, a field-grade officer is authorized to grant commissions. The Department of the Army has approved my recommendations. Therefore, I, Lieutenant Colonel James Hall, Commander of the Four Hundred Ninety-Ninth Combat Engineer Battalion of the United States Army, hereby appoint you, Samuel Moore, to the rank of First Lieutenant with all the rights, responsibilities, and privileges of that rank, on this day, Twenty-five July, in the year of our Lord, Twenty-Fifty. Now raise your right hand."

Stunned, Sam mechanically raised his right hand.

Colonel Hall's right hand went into the air. "Now repeat after me: *I, Samuel Moore,*"

"I, Samuel Moore..."

"*having been appointed an officer in the Army of the United States, as indicated above in the grade of First Lieutenant, do solemnly swear that I will support and defend the Constitution of* the United States against all enemies, foreign and domestic, that I will bear true faith and allegiance to the same, that I take this obligation freely, without any mental reservations or purpose of evasion; and that I will well and faithfully discharge the duties of the office I am about to enter; So help me God."

Sam's arm quivered, and yet his voice was strong as he solemnly repeated every word. "...so help me God."

Colonel Hall lowered his hand, grinned, and reached for Sam's hand, shaking it. "Congratulations, Lieutenant Moore. You're now a member of the greatest army God ever put on earth." He reached into a fatigue pocket and pulled out a small piece of cloth—a black bar with a hint of silver outline—and pinned it on the front of Sam's hospital gown.

Rob pumped Sam's hand. "Congratulations. The colonel kicked you up a notch above a butter bar. You owe him."

"Thank you, Colonel."

The colonel gave a wink but spoke in a firm, commanding voice. "Don't make me regret today."

"No, sir, you won't." Sam glanced down, reverently touching the small piece of Velcro. He wondered how something so simple looking could mean so much. Yet, it represented the United States government. *He* now *officially* represented that government. And he was now also U.S. government property for the next four years, at least. How things had changed in such a short time. Less than a year ago, he was a member of the enemy party, and he stood in front of his class, spewing epithets at those traitors west of the Mississippi. Now, his life surrounded by hardship, facing death at every turn, he was never so proud. He no longer had to live a lie. He gave silent gratitude that this time, he was on the right side.

"Lieutenant Moore," Hall said, breaking Sam's thoughts, "you'll get your orders within the next two weeks. You'll be assigned to the Twelfth Brigade based out of Marshall JSB, Texas. That's our home unit, and I want you in it. Might want to tell your girl."

Sam gave a cautious look. "I'll be based in Texas? But, you said—"

The colonel raised a finger. "Don't worry, you probably won't see Marshall JSB for a while. The 12th is now deployed in Vicksburg. Once you're healed—and the doctors say you should make a full recovery—you'll be sent on temporary duty to West Vicksburg. The army has an interim Officer Candidate School there. We're kind of doing things backward here, but we need to get you graduated from OCS to insure you keep your commission after the war, providing you don't screw up. After graduation, you will probably be sent back here to continue to work with Special Forces teams in this region." He paused. "Special Forces training is something you should consider in the future if you plan on making this a career." He paused. "I'll try to keep you paired with Captain Fields when you return. He can get you squared away on military code of conduct, chain-of-command, etiquette—"

"'Etiquette,' sir?" Sam asked.

Rob cleared his throat. "Yes, like not interrupting superior officers when they're addressing you."

Sam glanced away, sheepish. "Sorry—sirs."

Colonel Hall shook his head, staring at Sam. Sighing, he patted Sam's good leg. "Just get well, son, but don't push it. We need you whole." He reached for the envelope in Rob's hand and turned back to Sam. "By the time you leave here, you'll have everything you need."

Sam nodded. "Yes, sir."

After a few last instructions, Rob and the colonel turned to leave. Hall had already disappeared around a curtain when Rob turned back to Sam. "Do you want me to talk to Katie, explain to her what to expect?"

"I think she knows what to expect. That's why she's pissed. And besides, how do you know Katie and I are *that* close?"

"Come off it, buddy, you just left everything to her. Besides, you should've seen her when she got into camp." Rob eyed Sam. "We couldn't pry her from your bedside."

Sam focused on a tiny rip in a sheet hanging from the ceiling. "I need a good, stiff drink."

Rob turned to leave. "I think I can oblige you."

Sam ignored the crutches leaning against the folding chair as he limped around the room. Gone were the bed sheets used for privacy, along with the other beds. He was alone in the cabin. In the past three weeks since he was brought in after surgery, a prefab hospital was built nearby, including recovery rooms. Sam was allowed to stay in the cabin until he had recovered enough to report for duty.

Dressed in OD green T-shirt, cargo shorts and tennis shoes, he halted and gently put weight on his left leg. There was no pain, only stiffness. He had begun rehab last week. A week ago, he could barely hobble on crutches, and now he was limping short distances without them. If the doctors knew he wasn't using the crutches, they would blow a gasket. They had warned him not to rush it and that he could re-injure the leg. Sam hobbled to the edge of the bed, sat down, and slowly stretched out his left leg. Just visible on his thigh were ten tiny, black sutures covering what seemed an innocent scratch, but bacteria had eaten the muscle inside. The bone was okay, but the muscle tissue must be rebuilt. Fourteen sutures sewed up the bullet hole in the back of his leg. He gingerly touched around them; all the sutures were coming out tomorrow.

Sam flexed the leg as he had been taught, conditioning what muscles were left to again accept movement. As his leg moved back and forth, his thoughts drifted to Katie. She had never returned. Indeed, he hadn't seen her since she walked out of the room just over two weeks ago. He knew that Katie worked with the U.S. military in establishing communications inside and outside of camp. Sam sighed loudly; his heart ached. Katie had seemed like she genuinely wanted to be with him. Geesus, from what she told him, she went through three kinds of hell to find him. And now? Here he was maybe 100 yards away, but it might as well had been 100 miles. It was like he no longer existed to her. How could Katie's feelings do a 180 so fast, he wondered? Had she plans for the two of them that didn't include the army? Seems now those plans also didn't include him. He recalled Katie telling him she was looking forward to the day when he could leave the infirmary and the two of them could walk along the nearby beach. Sam shook his head, pondering.

What happened? Was him being in the army *that* bad? His new job couldn't be any more dangerous than what he was already doing, could it? At least he would have steady pay while so many did without, and he could provide for her...and maybe even...marriage? Yes, *he* had given it some thought, although neither had mentioned it. If Katie were a military dependent, the army would also see to her needs. Marriage would be a win-win situation for them. But what if Katie didn't love him? Did he love her? Was love even necessary? They did care for the other, at least up until two weeks ago.

He had to get out of this blasted cabin and find Katie. The whirring box fan now got on his nerves, and he eyed the door. No way. He was still too weak to get very far. Sam glanced in disgust at the wound on his leg. "Damn you!" He rose and once more began limping around without the crutch, more determined than ever to gain back his strength.

Sam paused near the metal chair and grabbed the crutches. Holding them in his hand, he hobbled to the door. As he stepped outside, the heavy, salty air enveloped him. A strong sea breeze tugged at his shirt, blowing through his close-cropped hair, tickling his scalp. It was late afternoon and muggy. Sam reached back, closed the cabin door, and glanced around. A couple of tall palms rose nearby. Their fronds stirred peacefully in the breeze. A half-dozen cabins like his were lined up in a neat row. Two cabins over, a man and a woman sat outside—the man was in a wheelchair. They waved, and he waved back. That would've been him two weeks back. Sam recalled how Katie had carefully wheeled him outside, and the two would sit, talking, and even in spite of the war, laughing. Her soft fingers would caress him as she rubbed his neck and shoulders. Sam now murmured under his breath and hobbled around outside to the back of the cabin. He glanced past a weed-choked lawn to the distant hospital up the hill.

The field hospital was built on a rise in an open field. It was supposed to have gone up adjacent the cabins, but there wasn't enough open ground. It had been decided a larger, more permanent structure was needed, hence the open field behind the cabins was utilized. The hospital was a large, camouflage, prefab affair. Several carts and a captured NAC humvee were parked near it. The hospital blocked Sam's view of the growing refugee camp on the other side. He could just make out several captured military vehicles on the hospital's far side, and that was it.

The whole complex was farther than it looked; the uphill

part was the problem. Dare he try? No, that would be stupid. Stupid and foolish. What he really needed to do was stop thinking about Katie. Sam studied the path leading to the hospital. He had to know... With a shake of his head, he wedged the crutches into his armpits and headed up the path to the hospital.

You imbecile—what are you doing! the voice screamed inside of him. *You'll hurt that leg again. Turn around, go back before it's too late!* Sam argued under his breath but kept plodding along. *Can't you get it into that thick skull of yours that Katie doesn't want to see you? She doesn't want you anymore.* "If she didn't want to see me," Sam said out loud, "why did she risk life and limb to find me? I can't believe she'd risk all, and then a week later, abandon me." *Who knows? She's a freakin' woman—they do crazy shit. Sammy boy, you're gonna get hurt—and I don't mean the leg. Now turn your ass around!* Sweat trickled into his eyes, stinging them. He drew up, puffing. He'd lost a lot of weight and was unaccustomed to the exertion. Steadying himself on one crutch and his good leg, he pulled up his T-shirt and wiped it across his sweaty face.

Have you thought that maybe she found another guy? In spite of the sweat, a chill moved through him. "It has crossed my mind, but it doesn't make sense," he said. "Wouldn't she have told me?" Besides, if she had found another, it had to have been in the last few weeks. She was by his bedside before that. His jaw tightened. "No. Shut up!" Sam jabbed the crutches under his arms and focused on the hospital. He was now able to make out details. He was already halfway there, but the path had grown rougher. Cracked, dry soil had replaced gravel. It would be easy to misstep, and then down he'd go. Gripping the crutches firmly, he set out. Sam hobbled along. The steady, dull *clump* of crutches filled his ears. The sound mirrored his feelings.

He glanced up in time to see a golf cart come from around the side of the hospital, heading for the single door facing Sam's direction. The driver was the only one on board and glanced Sam's way. Doing a double-take, he spun the cart around and bounded across the field, heading for Sam.

Sam halted, sweat dripping, wheezing, waiting for the cart to close the distance.

The cart rolled up, stopping at Sam's side. An older, bearded man dressed in jeans, work shirt, and boots gazed at him from behind the wheel. A photo ID badge with the words *United States Department of Defense* was pinned onto a shirt pocket. "My, God, man. You need help?"

Sam nodded, trying to catch his breath.

The man pointed to the cabins. "Your phone not working down there?"

Before Sam could reply, the man stepped out of the cart and helped Sam to the other side. "Get in, and I'll get you to a doctor."

Sam tossed the crutches on the plywood bed in back and gingerly eased into the seat. "I don't need a doctor. I—I'm looking for someone. And it's not a doctor."

The man climbed in behind the wheel and paused, gazing at Sam. "Family?"

"Sorta...a close friend really. At least she used to be." He glanced to the driver; he seemed to have a pleasant demeanor. "I'm looking for a woman. Her name is Katie Spencer. Ever heard of her?"

The man fiddled with the point of his beard. "Can't say that I have. Is she from the city?" He hooked a thumb behind him. "Because if she is, she's probably in with those other thousand poor bastards back up there in the refugee camp. There's a register there. I can—"

"No, she works for the army, the U.S. Army. She told me she's installing communications, or something like that."

"I work for the same army, doing maintenance, helping to get the camp started up." He paused, shaking his head. "Hell, she could be anywhere. What's she look like?"

"She's twenty-six and...and really cute." Sam held a hand out over the ground. "She's short, maybe five-feet or so, dark, curly hair."

The man eyed Sam. "She have a Yankee accent?"

Sam's eyes widened. "Yes."

"Yup, seen her around. Heard her speaking, too. In these parts, it sounds like Martian. Told the guy I was working with, 'that gal's straight outta Brooklyn.'"

"Buffalo," Sam said, nodding. "Do you know where I can find her?"

The bearded man sighed, scrutinizing Sam. "You're in no shape to go traipsin' around. I'll take you back to your cabin, and I'll see if I can round her up, tell her you were looking for her."

Sam recalled Rob's offer to help. "I think there's someone already doing that...doesn't appear it's working." Sam paused. "Thank you for the offer, but *I* need to find her."

"Man, if they find out I took you on a wild goose chase in your shape," he nodded to the hospital, "they're liable to can me, and paying jobs in these times are hard to come by."

Sam sighed. Then he swung his right leg out and reached for the crutches behind him. "Appreciate your help, man. I'll just be on my way."

The man rolled his eyes. "Oh, for Christ's sake—stay put. I'll take you up there."

Sam hinted a smile, easing back in. "Thanks."

The cart swung around, heading for the hospital. But instead of stopping at the door facing the cabins, it swung around the left side of the building. The driver glanced to Sam. "We'll go in the front. I think I know where you might find her, or at least find someone who knows where she is."

When the cart turned the corner, Sam's draw dropped. He couldn't believe his eyes. A line of people stretched out in front of him as far as the eye could see. As they drew closer, he could make out their despair. Some wore backpacks or carried suitcases, a few pushed wheelbarrows, while others pulled wagons, all filled with personal belongings. Within seconds, the golf cart swung around the hospital's front entrance and stopped. Sam stared, trying not to gawk. The line stretched south, disappearing around a curve maybe a half-mile away. The people were of all ages, some white, some black, with a few Latinos here and there. Lone teenagers and mothers with infants were scattered throughout the line. Maybe twenty yards from where he sat and across the road, a huge tent had been erected. Scattered behind the large tent were smaller tents. He caught a flash of blue camouflage—NAC soldiers. In front of the large tent, several NAC soldiers sat behind long tables jammed together to make one continuous counter.

Panic gripped Sam—a trap. He had just been delivered to the enemy. Then he caught sight of their American flag armbands. All the NAC soldiers wore American flag armbands and none appeared armed. The soldiers were collecting names, giving out numbers, and confiscating contraband. A sign attached to the front of the tent read: *No firearms, knives, or alcohol permitted.* A heavily armed American soldier in gray camo sporting an American flag shoulder patch was posted near the tent's entrance, and Sam noticed several other armed American soldiers milling around, apparently overseeing the whole affair. One of the American soldiers spoke into a microphone attached to his helmet.

Sam glanced to the man seated next to him then back to the spectacle in front of them. "What the hell?"

The man nodded to the line. "Been like this the past two weeks, and it's getting worse. There's a couple bigger tents like that one that are on the way."

Sam stared at the line of destitute people. "Are things that bad in Charleston?"

"Yup, but they're not all from Charleston." The man pointed to the line. "Some are coming in from the rural areas. Electricity is out in most of the region, and they think they're better off here."

"I wouldn't think so."

"Neither does the army. U.S. soldiers are driving along the line, telling them through a loudspeaker, that if they have a home, return to it. Only those with nowhere to go are allowed in."

Sam shook his head. "Unbelievable..."

The man pointed south and glanced to Sam. "Down there around that curve the line stretches about another mile or so. Land's been cleared for a parking lot. The folks that have carts leave them there. Only ones around here with any wheels are the U.S. Army and us civilians who work for the army. The U.S. Army set up a checkpoint by the parking lot, and it's there that they're handing out rations to the ones they turn away. The NAC army would've let 'em starve. Yup, those *Western Alliance* boys are pretty good fellows, helping folks out and such." He nodded to the NAC soldiers seated behind the tables. "Better than that bunch of horse dung, although once they surrendered, the asshole in them disappeared."

The evil memory of being held captive in Perchance flashed. "Being a prisoner will do that."

The man stared at Sam, gauging him. "Sounds like that comes from personal experience."

Sam nodded silently.

The man extended a hand. "Aaron Caldwell. Friends call me Buster."

Sam shook the offered hand, hesitating to give his real name. The bounty... His jaw tightened; he refused to cower. "Samuel Moore. I go by Sam."

"Nice to meet you, Sam."

Sam decided he liked the maintenance man. "The same, Buster."

Buster eyed Sam with intelligent blue eyes. "Tell me, you that wounded guerilla leader that's rumored to be here?"

Sam nodded. "Was..."

"You don't know how we appreciate you guys." He patted Sam's shoulder. "Yes, sir, you badass guerillas make the North American Commonwealth army look like school girls. Brave stuff you guys do, and it drives those NAC boys crazy. You have the citizens behind you, that's for sure." He paused, reading Sam's tense look. "Your secret is safe with me."

Sam shifted, and his left leg began to throb. "We're not 'badasses.' Just everyday citizens still loyal to the United States and to the American Constitution."

Buster waved a hand at the slowly passing crowd. "You know, if more folks would've gotten angry back in the day, it may never have come to this."

"Things don't get done just because you're angry. Things get done because you take action."

Buster nodded, and the two men fell silent. After a few contemplative moments, Buster spoke up. "When I asked if you were that guerilla fighter, you said 'was.'" He pointed to Sam's legs. "Is it because of that? It's said you guys are as tough as woodpecker lips."

"Now that is a rumor," Sam gave a wry grin, "and one we like to hear."

Buster gave a faint chuckle, tapped the throttle, and the golf cart lurched forward. Within seconds, it came to a halt in front of the hospital.

Sam swung his good leg out and onto the ground. "Appreciate the lift."

"If you'll wait a second out here," Buster said, climbing out, "I'll go inside and see if I can find her."

The hospital entrance was just across from the refugee camp entrance, and Sam caught several guards, both NAC and U.S. glancing his way. He fought down nervousness. Confronting Katie was enough to send him screaming into the night, and now the camp security team seemed to be giving him the once-over. Why should he worry about the latter? Wasn't he now also a United States soldier? He forced calm. An old habit like running from armed soldiers was hard to break. There was still that reward, and it didn't specify *who* nabbed him. Were there flyers out with his picture on them?

Buster signaled to Sam, breaking his thoughts. "Just sit tight, and I'll be right back."

Was it his imagination, or were the soldiers scrutinizing him? Uncomfortable, he swung his injured leg around, hobbled out of the tiny cart, and reached for the crutches in back. "Think I'll go with you."

Buster shook his head, glancing at Sam. "Need help?"

"Naw." Sam ambled up to Buster, and the two stepped toward the hospital entrance.

A U.S. soldier, with his weapon slung over a shoulder, strode over to them, halting next to Sam. He gave Sam an accusing look. "What happened to you?"

Sam glanced to the two small stripes on the soldier's chest armor then eyed the corporal. He was young, maybe in his early twenties, and he seemed too eager to exert authority. Definitely the wrong kind to be guarding civilians.

Sam cleared his throat, smiling innocently. "Just in the wrong place at the wrong time."

The soldier's gaze hardened. "You trying to get cute?"

Sam glanced to Buster, and both men shrugged. "No," Sam continued, "you asked."

"I don't have time for cute. Buddy, in case you haven't noticed, there's a war going on. You don't just come strolling up here and cut in line for the hospital." The soldier stepped close to Sam, grimaced, and pointed to the line of people across the road. "Now you get your ass back in line like the rest of them."

"He's with me," Buster said.

The soldier eyed Buster's ID pinned on a shirt pocket. "I don't care if he's with Jesus Christ, he's going back in line—all the way back." He turned, facing Sam. "You have any ID?"

"As a matter of fact, I do." Leaning on a crutch, Sam slowly reached into a back pocket and worked out a 2X3 inch piece of plastic. Thank God he had grabbed his new military ID before leaving the cabin. He held it out to the soldier, who snatched it from his hand.

One glimpse at the card, and the young soldier's eyes widened. His jaw gave a slight quiver. He carefully handed the card back to Sam and snapped to attention, saluting smartly. "Forgive me, sir. I wasn't aware we had an injured U.S. officer on the premises."

Sam crisply returned the salute as Rob had taught him. "As you were, Corporal." Sam glanced to the U.S. soldiers across the road. All were suddenly busy doing nothing. The young soldier in front of him relaxed but never moved. Sam addressed him. "I know you guys have a tough job, but in the future, *you* need to show a little more humility. And FYI, you can tell your buddies that I'm not 'cutting in line' to get treated. I'm looking for someone."

"Yes, sir."

"Carry on, Corporal."

The young soldier saluted once more then quickly strode to the hospital door. "Let me get that door for you, Lieutenant."

Sam nodded and, wedging the other crutch under his arm,

clomped along behind Buster.

The two stepped through the door, and Buster glanced back to Sam. "Now aren't you just full of surprises?"

With Buster in the lead, the two made their way down a corridor. A medicinal smell wafted, and Sam's stomach knotted even tighter. He hated that smell, always would. What might have been a doctor passed them, paused, and looked back. Brow wrinkling, he continued on.

Turning left into another corridor, Buster halted, waiting for Sam to catch up. "Communications room is this way."

Sam clomped up to Buster. Removing the crutches from under his arms, he leaned them on the wall and stood as straight as possible. "Last time Katie saw me, I was an invalid."

Buster gave an understanding nod. He started down the corridor, and Sam limped along next to him. They halted at a door with a plate reading, *Authorized Personnel Only*. Buster glanced to Sam. "What's her name again?"

"Katie Spencer."

"Wait here."

Sam nodded and slid to the side of the door.

Buster's keys jingled, and he stepped inside a darkened room. Two women and a man sat behind glowing computer screens. Buster cleared his throat. "I'm looking for Katie Spencer."

A woman wearing a headset and sitting behind a computer glanced up, lifting up an earpiece. A lanyard with a photo ID dangled from her neck. "You're looking for who?"

"Katie Spencer."

The woman spoke into the mike, tapped the video monitor, removed the headset, and looked up. "That would be me."

"May I have a word with you, ma'am?"

Katie rose and stepped to the maintenance man standing in the doorway. "What is it, *Doctor* Caldwell?"

Buster stepped aside. Sam gave Buster—Doctor Caldwell—a double-take, and then he moved into the doorway. "Katie."

Katie froze, staring silently. "Sam..."

Sam swallowed, gazing at her. "So, you are still alive."

Katie turned away, and Sam grabbed her arm, holding her. "I thought there was an 'us,' and then you disappear..."

Katie faced Sam. Her brown gaze meeting his blue one. "I have to get back to work."

Sam released her. "So that's it, huh? Just like that."

Katie's eyes glistened. "Sam...I can't do this. I lost you once, and that was enough. I'll not go through that again. There won't be a second time."

Sam swore under his breath, running a hand through close-cropped hair. "Katie, if you mean me being a soldier—"

Katie's chin trembled. "You don't understand, do you? I can't get close again." Her eyes lowered. "I'll not live your death a second time."

"You keep saying 'a second time.'" He grabbed his wrist. His hand squeezed up and down his arm. "Sweet Jesus I'm still here...had me going there for a while. I thought I was a ghost." Then he recalled the strange soldiers who saved his life. They had been just as warm as he was...

"You're not funny." Katie gazed up silently to Sam. "Those I'm close to...Sam, I shouldn't even be in their vicinity."

Sam's jaw tightened. "Never thought you'd only think about yourself."

Katie's eyes flashed. "And I could say the same about you. I thought we were going to stay together, and then you up and join the army!"

"And...?"

The others in the room began staring at the couple arguing in the doorway. Sam felt self-conscious, as if he didn't belong. Everything was spiraling out of control. No matter what he said or did, Katie was gone. His mind refused to grasp what was happening. He focused on the woman in front of him. "Katie, what you're doing is wrong and you know it. You take your leave for all the wrong reasons."

"Maybe so, but..." Katie's eyes glistened, and she swallowed hard. "Goodbye, Sam."

Katie stepped back to her workstation. Sam let her go. The desperate times he'd gone through with nothing but the memory of her arms to keep him going, and the thought of a future with Katie Spencer was at times his only sustenance, and now... Giving a dejected sigh, Sam turned and limped back down the hall.

Buster closed the door and hurried next to a hobbling Sam. "Couldn't help but overhear. I'm sorry."

Sam stared straight ahead. "Thanks."

Buster twirled his beard. "I don't understand why the girl was upset with you being a U.S. soldier. She should be proud of you. Besides, you'd think soldiering would be a helluva safer job than that of a guerilla fighter."

"I don't know what's got into her." Sam shook his head and grabbed the crutches leaning against the wall. But instead of wedging them under his arm, he held onto them and began quickly limping to the exit. Buster followed a half-pace behind. Neither spoke as they made their way outside to the golf cart. Sam halted at the cart's passenger side and tossed the crutches in the bed in back. "I'm through with those things." He eased into the seat and glanced to Buster, who climbed in behind the wheel. "Damn, I need a drink."

The cart backed up and headed downhill to the cabins below. "For what it's worth," Buster began, "she doesn't seem like your type, anyway."

"Katie was my late best friend's granddaughter. The old man gave his life for what Katie and I started...for what we all believed in." Sam paused, staring at a rusted bolt head on the floor. "He would want Katie and me to be together."

"But he's gone, right?"

Sam nodded.

"Life, along with all its beauties and cruelties, goes on, Sam." Buster paused, easing the cart over a dip. "Maybe you and Katie were brought together for a single purpose, and now, maybe that purpose is complete...and it's time to move on."

Sam caught the strange tone in Buster's voice. It was as if he knew who Katie was, what she had done, what they had done together. A chill moved through him; what else did this man know? Sam knew there was a lot more to "Buster" Caldwell than the man let on. But didn't he also covet his past? Was there a flaw in doing that?

Buster tapped the steering wheel. "I'm sure that before long, Katie will look back and regret today."

Sam glanced to Buster. The older man's jaw was firm. His gray-flecked beard jutted out; he was serious. Sam changed the subject. "Katie addressed you as 'Doctor.' Are you an MD of some kind?"

Buster swung the cart onto the gravel walkway where he had picked up Sam. "No. I was an engineering professor at Charleston University."

Sam gave a wry grin. "And you said *I* was full of surprises?"

"Like you, I now do what tasks God directs."

"How do *you* know God's directing me?"

Buster only glanced at him and returned to steering the cart.

They grew silent. The setting sun shone behind them as the cart worked its way downhill and finally halted at Sam's cabin. Sam climbed out of the passenger side, favoring his left leg. Reaching back for the crutches, he glanced to Buster. "I can't make sense of anything anymore." He turned then paused to look back to the older man. "I have another calling now... something I don't think Katie understands."

"Oh, believe me, she understands. But she's confused on how to deal with it...how to deal with you."

Sam wrinkled a brow.

"This war is not over by a long shot. It's only just begun." Buster looked away, nodding, as if he had reached a frightful conclusion to his own thoughts. "Yep, this nightmare will get worse before it gets better." His gaze shifted to Sam. "It's people like you, Sam, who are game changers."

"Thanks, but you don't even know me."

"Experience has taught me how to size up a person."

Sam chuckled. "Yeah? Well, what you see is one scared man."

"Being scared is a good thing as long as it doesn't freeze you."

"What I wanted was to start a family...with Katie." Sam bowed his head, swallowing hard. "Guess that won't happen now. Besides, starting a family in these times is a stupid idea."

It was Buster's turn to chuckle. "If we looked at things that way, none of us would be here."

Sam looked away.

"I've seen guys go off the deep end over a woman. Promising careers wrecked, lives ruined—all for nothing. Don't let that little gal up there and what 'might be' dictate what *you* do, Sam. There are few things more pathetic than when you're my age and you look in the mirror and think, 'shoulda, woulda, coulda.'"

Sam gazed at the older man. "Advice well-noted."

Buster leaned over, extending a hand. "Take care of yourself, son. Let me know if you need anything."

Sam reached for the man's hand and gripped it warmly. "Thanks, Buster, for *everything*."

Buster released his hand, winked, spun the tiny cart around, and disappeared in the gathering dusk.

Sam stared after the college professor in work clothes, a strange feeling coming over him. He hadn't felt this way in what seemed like ages. Kinship...he felt a kinship to Buster Caldwell. In life, when a door closes, another always opens.

* * *

Knock-knock-knock. Sam rolled over and glanced to the alarm clock near his bed; **0010** glowed red in the darkness. *Knock-knock-knock.* "What the—" Sam mumbled, groggy. He clicked on a nearby reading lamp, tossed back the covers, scrambled out of bed, and hobbled to the door. A fan whirred, and a fresh sea breeze filled the room. "Geesus, just hold on." He reached for the knob and pulled open the door.

A woman faced him in the dim light from the open door, and a cart was parked near the cabin. "Sam."

Sam blinked. "Katie."

"Sam, I...I'm sorry to wake you." She hesitated. "I couldn't let things end as they did this afternoon."

Sam stepped aside. "Come on in." Just then, he realized how he was dressed—he wore nothing but OD boxers. He glanced down, turning red. "Sorry for the attire. Let me throw something on." He turned his back to her and reached for cargo shorts in a nearby chair.

Katie did a double take, trying not to stare. "My, God, Sam, what happened to your back? You're scarred all over."

"Thought you'd seen it."

"No...you were wrapped in bandages."

Sam stepped into the shorts, fastening them. "A little shrapnel, a few months back."

"A 'little?' The left side of your back looks like a moonscape."

"Thanks for the compliment." He faced her. His gaze went up and down. It was his turn to try not to gawk. Katie wore jeans, sneaker-type boots, and a tight-fitting blue, pullover top that highlighted her figure. Her dark, curly hair was gathered into a short ponytail.

Katie's gaze fell to Sam's firm chest. "I see those chest wounds have healed nicely."

"Yeah...and to think my own rifle did this to me." He touched near one of the several pink scars, remembering that fateful morning. "It caught a round and parts of the magazine before the bullet found me."

"Don't you wear some kind of protection like body armor or something?"

Sam snorted, shaking his head. "Darlin' do you know how hard that stuff is to come by? We were guerilla fighters. Mostly, all we had was what we took off dead NAC soldiers." He glanced to his chest. "I wore armor when I could get it, but I usually ended up giving it to the NGs."

"NGs?"

"New Guys."

Katie shook her head. "Always thinking of your students... and now, your men. But as a soldier, *you will* wear body armor all the time, right?"

Sam quickly looked up, catching a strange tone in Katie's question. An odd light shone in her dark eyes, eyes that mesmerized him, and he stepped closer. "Why did you come here tonight?"

Katie eased closer. Her gaze never left him. "I...I have something for you."

Sam raised a brow, cocking his head.

Katie reached into a jean pocket and worked out a fine silver chain with a small gold pendant attached. She held it up to Sam, and the pendant dangled. "This is for you."

"What is it?"

"A Saint Christopher. I want you to wear it, always."

"But isn't that Catholic? I'm not Catholic."

"I am. My late father gave it to me when I was a little girl. I wore it all the time. It brought me great comfort. And I saw that bent, bloody cross in your personal things—forgive my nosiness." The pendant swung in front of Sam. "I assume you've become a Christian, too."

Sam nodded. "I wasn't when we last met at your grandparents."

"I know."

"One tends to find Jesus when in a foxhole."

Katie chuckled, smiling. With the Saint Christopher in one hand, her arms came around Sam's neck.

Sam dipped his head as Katie, on tiptoes, looped the chain around his neck. She patted the pendant on his chest. "Saint Christopher is the Traveler's Saint. May this help protect you and bring you comfort in dark times." Katie inched even closer as her fingers traced the chain around Sam's neck.

Sam shivered at her feminine touch. A subtle hint of perfumed body lotion enveloped him. He reached out and clasped her hand in his. "Thank you." His eyes searched hers, gauging her, judging her sincerity. "I got my orders day-before-yesterday. I'll be leaving week-after-next for Vicksburg for twelve weeks of training. Then, hopefully, back here."

"'Hopefully,'" she murmured. "Rob told me that although the colonel would try, there was no guarantee to your deployment." Katie paused. Her eyes glowed. "I apologize for this evening. It's just that—"

Sam touched a finger to her lips. "Shh...no more." His fingers began tracing her full lips.

Katie's eyes closed, and she sighed deeply. "Sam..."

Sam leaned down. His lips brushed Katie's. Her arms slid around his neck, and she melted against him. Their lips met again, and the two kissed deeply, passionately.

* * *

Sam lay on his back with Katie in his arms. Her heart beat against his. Her bare skin pressed against his as his fingers traced a path down her soft curves. Katie climbed on top of him. "Sam, dare we make another promise?" Katie whispered as she stroked his face.

"That next time, we'll never part?"

Katie's lips touched Sam's. "Yes."

"Katie, I...I'll never *willingly* leave you." Katie's hair hung over his face, tickling his cheeks. "Would you wait for me?"

"Yes, I'll wait." Katie leaned down, and their lips met.

And Sam was enveloped in Katie's warmth, fervor, and passion...

PART

III

November 16, 2050. Camp Ulysses S. Grant, West Vicksburg, Louisiana.

It was the discipline and sense of urgency that almost overwhelmed Sam. Soldiers trained and trained as war gripped the country. The moment he arrived at Camp Grant, the gauntlet was thrown down. When not at the gunnery range learning how to operate the latest weapons systems, or hiking miles upon miles with a loaded backpack, he was in a classroom studying military officer leadership. Training was as much mental as it was physical. Many a night, he would pass out, exhausted, with his head buried in a book or snoring near an open laptop. Yet, he pushed with adrenaline-charged determination. For the first time in Sam's life, he felt real purpose. And, always in the back of his mind, he knew there was Katie and her warm arms waiting for him. When he returned, he would ask her to marry him.

Although several of the men in his unit were cadets in their final weeks of ROTC or OCS, most were young, educated NCOs hoping to become officers. Sam was the only commissioned officer, and that presented a problem. Sam's company commander, Captain Scales, was the only one aware of his battlefield commission. The trainees must learn to work together as equals, and Sam, being an officer, would jeopardize the training company's cohesiveness. Sam asked for and was given permission to conceal any rank from the other trainees. Instructors simply addressed him as Cadet Moore, and there were no identifying rank symbols or badges on his uniform.

At first, Sam's healing left leg hampered him. Yet, his goal was not to set records; his goal was to complete the damn training. On Sam's second and final try, he finished the three-mile obstacle course in full combat gear in the required time, squeezing in by mere seconds.

Other than the instructors, of the 200 men in his training company, only Sam possessed combat experience. The six months he had spent as a guerrilla fighter served him well. Working as a unit and *esprit de corps* were already instilled. As an insurgent, he'd pushed physical endurance to the limit, worked with frazzled nerves, mixed-matched weapons, mixed-matched abilities, and conflicting personalities to complete missions. Officer Candidate School—OCS—now gelled his past experiences into a deadly package he could swiftly apply during crisis mode. His current training was invaluable.

Mail from across The River was spotty at best as the Directorate had confiscated then completely halted all mail addressed to those areas in rebellion. Military correspondences came by military courier, and civilian mail came by the Underground. Yet, by the fourth week of training, Sam had already received three letters from Katie. She seemed upbeat and was anxious to know the exact date of his return. He'd written back, telling her graduation was December 5th. What he didn't tell her was that his deployment to somewhere other than South Carolina was a real possibility.

* * *

Sam sat on the edge of his bunk, cleaning the high-tech, M-8 battle rifle when the screen door slammed, and he looked up. His roommate, Sean Ridgeway, entered. Ridgeway was from Texas, completing his final round of ROTC training before commissioning.

Dressed in camo, Ridgeway yanked off a black service cap and tossed it on his nearby bunk. "Ten more days, man, and we're outta here...newly minted butter-bars."

Using a metal rod, Sam forced a cloth patch through the rifle barrel in his hand. "That's too bad. This place was kinda growing on me."

"You've got to be shitting me," Ridgeway said, chuckling and seating himself on a bunk across from Sam. "Got your deployment orders yet?"

Sam sighed, gazing at the man across from him. Sean Ridgeway was slightly taller and heavier than Sam's 180. His dark hair was military-cut, like everyone's. He had a prominent jaw and bright blue eyes that never missed a thing. Although Ridgeway was twenty-four, he looked barely eighteen. At first, other men in the unit gave him hell about his youthful looks and jokingly called him "the boy." But after besting most of them at every physical and psychological challenge, they took to calling him "the man." Ridgeway also had a dry, twisted sense-of-humor that Sam appreciated, and the two were instantly drawn to one another. Sam hoped to keep in contact with Ridgeway after graduation and, one day, perhaps serve with him.

Sam yanked out the cleaning rod, inspecting the cotton patch. Except for gun-grease, it was spotless. "No definite orders yet. Hoping to go back to Carolina Province—ah, South

Carolina."

"'Carolina Province?'" Ridgeway glanced at Sam. "Is that what you guys called the Carolinas?"

Sam cocked a brow. "'You guys?' Ridgeway, I'm just as American as you."

"Sorry, I wasn't questioning your loyalty."

Sam waved off the comment. "Forget it. It was the NAC government that used the term 'Carolina Province.'" He paused, wondering if he should comment further. Sam rode guilt. At one time, he had promoted The Big Lie. Hell he had even been part of it. His eyes had always been open, but it wasn't until last November that he began to *see*. And now a full year had circled. He also missed his students and wondered how they were faring in this time of great crisis.

Ridgeway tapped Sam's knee. "Sammy...you okay?"

Sam nodded, broken from his thoughts. "I just wish things could return to normal," and he held up the black, composite weapon, "so I could put down this freaking rifle and return to the classroom."

"So, you're finishing up college too, huh?"

"Already have...I hold a graduate degree."

Ridgeway did a double-take. "What?"

Even though the officer trainees had been together for three months, there was never time for frivolous talk. What little idle time that was scrounged was always spent studying or getting shut-eye. Sam swallowed, unsure how much of his past to reveal. "I'm a high school teacher."

Ridgeway paused, scrutinizing Sam. "I'll be damned. School-marm-turned-guerilla fighter-turned-army officer." He eyed Sam for several quiet seconds. "It's amazing the paths we chose...and then where life leads us."

Sam polished the weapon's magazine with a clean cloth. "A year ago, I was sitting in a commissar's office getting reamed for not adhering to the political line—the political lie."

Ridgeway raised a brow. "How so?"

"I was defending a new student." Sam glanced to the younger man across from him. "He was from Texas and had lost both his parents. Witnessed his father handcuffed and carted away for speaking out against the authorities. He never saw his father again."

"What did the kid do to get in trouble?"

"He wrote a few lines about freedom."

"That's all?"

"You have to understand, *Freedom* is the F-word in the

Commonwealth," Sam said, recalling that day in Tipton's office. "I should've destroyed that paper, but I held onto it and said nothing to the kid. Then the commissar found it, and..." Sam shrugged, wiping down the gun barrel. "Guess I should've thanked that young man for opening my eyes."

Ridgeway leaned over, earnestness in his gaze. "What happened to the Texas boy?"

"I helped him and three other students, along with their families, escape. The kid, Mark Thurmont was his name, returned to Texas, and those families went with him."

Ridgeway studied Sam. "Bet there was hell to pay for that."

"There was...some of it paid in blood." He glanced to Ridgeway. "But that's only a small part of how I ended up here."

"Geesus...man, you've got one helluva backstory."

Sam nodded silently, working the weapon's action.

Ridgeway glanced down, shaking his head. "I've never done anything that exciting or dangerous."

Sam glanced to Ridgeway. "What about you, Sean? How did you end up here?"

Ridgeway looked up. "Military service is in my family—on both sides. My father's great-grandfather was a Marine, fought in the Pacific in World War Two. My mom's great-grandfather flew Thunderbolts over Normandy. Dad retired from the Marines five years ago, and my older brother, Michael, graduated last year from the new Naval Academy in San Diego. He's finishing up Navy flight school as I speak." Ridgeway paused, thoughtful. "Just seemed natural that I'd follow family tradition."

Sam scrutinized Ridgeway. "What does *Sean Ridgeway* want to do?"

Ridgeway turned red. "This past August, I finished up my college course work. Next month, I'll graduate from the University of Texas with a BA in English...a real soldier's degree, huh?"

Sam hinted a smile, gazing at Ridgeway. "I also have a BA in English and a Master's in humanities...about the same thing."

"No shit?"

"No shit."

"Well," Ridgeway shook his head, "I would never have guessed you had an English degree, you once being a guerilla fighter and all."

"I take that as a complement." Sam worked the M-8's action. "Your English degree tells me that maybe you had alternate plans...plans that didn't include the military."

"Yeah," Ridgeway said, gazing past Sam, "there were. My Father and I went round-and-round about it. But now, all is on hold until we can reunite the country, or die trying."

Quiet seconds passed, with both men wrapped in thought. Sam broke the silence. "Our degrees weren't wasted. Sean, you and I were taught to *think*." Sam hooked a thumb to the east. "And out there, that critical thinking skill separates you from the other warm bodies...and the cold ones. That thinking skill will keep you and your men alive, which gives *all* American's hope. Don't ever forget that. You will be tested out there, and I don't mean in just dodging bullets. You must constantly draw on that concept of *good* versus *evil*." Sam's voice lowered, yet he spoke with intensity. "At times, good and evil will seem to merge, and that blending will trap you...the Sirens' Song. Never forget, evil has no rules. There may come a time that you, as a leader, must become both judge *and* juror in order to protect good. Because, if *good* is not vigilant, *evil* will *always* prevail."

Ridgeway nodded, soaking in Sam's words.

Sam lay the weapon next to him on the bunk. "Sorry. Didn't mean to go off like that."

"You sound like one of my history professors."

"Oh, yeah?"

"Yeah...he got himself fired."

"I know how that feels. Are you trying to tell me something?"

"Actually, they told him to stop telling the truth about good and evil. He gave administration the finger and slammed the door on the way out."

Sam's eyes narrowed. "That's creepy. Sounds like the Directorate."

"We know all about the Directorate...twenty-first century American Nazis."

"You know only a fraction." Sam's jaw tightened, recalling what happened to Principal Terri Woodruff. "The Directorate would never have let him out the door. That professor would have been escorted to the front office, and then he would've simply disappeared. And no one, not even the students, would've dared questioned it."

"Well," Ridgeway leaned back, "we have our assholes on this side of the river, too. Anyway, that professor's got himself a better gig. He's teaching at the Army War College at the new federal capital in Denver. One day, when things calm, I'm going after my Master's. I hope to sit in his class again."

"Sounds like a guy I want to meet."

Ridgeway nodded and rose. "I've got to pull the night shift with the OD this evening."

"Lucky you," Sam said, chuckling. "Officer of the Day...how

rewarding. Something we all will have to suffer through, I guess."

Ridgeway turned and heading for the latrine. "Enjoyed the talk."

"Me, too." Thoughtful seconds passed. Sam rose, shouldered the weapon, and stepped outside. Autumn sun dipped behind tall pines. A chilly, late-afternoon breeze tugged at his collar and service cap. He pulled the cap down tighter and shuddered, wondering if Ridgeway and he would ever make a damn difference.

Katie leaned over the toilet, ID dangling from a lanyard. She tossed the ID behind her neck. Her stomach knotted, and she threw-up. Stomach churning, she leaned against the sink as the wave of nausea gradually passed. She flushed the toilet and quivered, resting momentarily against the sink. After splashing water on her face, she tore off several paper towels, and dabbed her face and neck. Tossing the wadded-up towels into a nearby trash can, Katie glanced at her watch; 7:40. She'd only been at work for 40 minutes before it hit her. And this was the second time this morning; it was going to be a long day. She glanced in the mirror, tucked loose strands into her pinned-up hair, and stepped back into the communication room.

An older, blonde-haired woman glanced up from her computer console, gazing sympathetically at an approaching Katie. "Feeling any better, sweetie?"

Katie plopped down into a padded, folding chair behind a nearby computer. "Not really, but guess I'll survive. Thanks for asking."

The woman, Julie Frisk, turned in her chair and faced Katie. "Have you seen a doctor yet?"

Katie fiddled with headphones. Giving a loud sigh, she dropped them on the desk. "No...I'm afraid, Julie."

"This is your first, isn't it?"

Katie glanced to the woman seated across from her. The woman was perhaps in her early forties and attractive. Like Katie, she wore the khaki uniform top and OD green fatigue work pants that identified her as a U.S. army civilian employee. Katie swallowed and looked away. "It could just be that bug that swept through here last month. I was the only one that didn't get sick."

"But you're afraid it isn't." Julie suppressed a smile. "Come on, Katie, we both know what it is. You said last month's period was a no-show. You've got all the classic signs. You need to get your butt to a doctor."

Katie buried her face in her hands. "Oh, God, I can't be pregnant. I just can't..."

Julie rose, stepped to Katie, and caressed her shoulders and back. "Girl, it's not the end of the world. Having a child is a blessing. You've got to see it that way."

"But not in these times," came Katie's muffled voice.

"Believe me, kids almost always come at the 'wrong' time. Just when you think your plans have worked out, *bam*! Here comes the kid. And then you're back to square one."

Katie glanced up with wet eyes. "That's just it. I no longer have 'plans.' At least, not personal ones. My short-lived career was devoted to exposing the Directorate for what it was. Now that that's done..." Katie shrugged. "I feel as if I'm drifting. I used to feel that way once, feel like my life was wasting away, having no meaning. I hated that frame of mind...I hated it. Then I met Sam, and I don't know anymore."

"What about Sam?"

"He doesn't deserve me or what I now bring to the table. I don't want Sam to worry about me," Katie glanced to her belly, "or us."

Julie was about to speak when red lights flashed on Katie's console.

Katie spun around in her seat, working in an earpiece. Her eyes widened. "Oh, my God. It's another encrypted message from Philadelphia to Central City."

Julie quickly reseated herself behind her own computer. Her fingers danced over a multicolored interface. "I'm patching it in to Denver."

Two months back, Julie Frisk and Katie Spencer were moved to a private com-center next door to the hospital. The room they were assigned was built to accommodate their computer skills and another unique skill; both women were linguists. Julie had grown up in Hong Kong; her father had been an American diplomat to China. She was fluent in several Chinese dialects. In college, Katie had minored in Farsi and had a working knowledge of Arabic. With the North American Commonwealth in an endless war with Iran, Katie had hope to capitalize on her language skills; however, she was refused a Directorate security clearance and ended up in the government propaganda arm instead. The Western Alliance had recently learned that the Directorate was opening secret negotiations with Iran. And down south, it was no secret that China had courted Mexico for decades. Indeed, China had just established a large, military complex in Northern Mexico. The United States Western Alliance was now surrounded by enemies on three sides.

With satellite communications extremely limited, both women were priceless. They were now human eavesdroppers. The clandestine listening post was disguised as a storage room located next to the hospital. Underground cables ran from the room to a well-hidden, 80-foot tower located amid tall pines on a forested hill two miles away.

Katie touched her computer interface, and several tiny indicators flashed. "That didn't take long. Central City is already replying." She glanced to Julie. "It's an Iranian code."

"Been a lot of Iranian activity lately." Julie, with an earpiece dangling from her left ear, swiped a finger over an interface, and a U.S. government seal appeared. She tapped the seal, and the word **SECRET** appeared. She typed in a code, swiped to another screen, and began typing on a keyboard. "Denver broke the code a while back," Julie said with an ironic smirk. "And yet, with all this spy-stuff at our fingertips, you and I will never know what's being said."

Katie's fingers raced over a second keyboard. She paused, pushed a button, and glanced over her shoulder to Julie. "Check your left monitor."

Julie looked down and to the left. Her eyes widened. "Mother of Christ! How did you do that?"

Katie gave an innocent shrug. "I haven't a clue what you're talking about."

"Right..." Julie said, smiling. "Do the good guys know you're a hacker?"

Katie only raised a brow, grinning.

Julie glanced at Katie and did a double-take. "Unbelievable..."

They scrutinized a small, secondary monitor located on the left side of their consoles. The words were stark and plain:

Have thoroughly considered your last message. My cabinet and I have discussed at length your offer of allying our forces. We believe, as you, the greater threat to world peace are the renegade Commonwealth provinces known as the Western Alliance. NAC and Iranian combining forces on land, air, and sea would overwhelm our common enemy. However, I must admit, like you, I have reservations on how our forces can align and who might lead them. We can discuss these things and more in our next meeting. Due to circumstance here, I am unable to meet with you in Tehran this time. I suggest we meet in international waters. Post-haste in your reply.

Robert C. Henshaw, President
North American Commonwealth

"Whew!" Julie sighed. "Can you believe this?"

"Unfortunately, yes." Katie's fingers again danced over the keyboard. "Check out the reply."

RE: allying

Greetings. Mr. President, your assessment of the Western Alliance is correct. They are a cancer that must be removed as soon as possible for the betterment of humanity. Joining in this "grand alliance" between East and West is not only historical but a necessity. I will shortly send the detailed location of our proposed meeting.

Khuda Hafiz—May God Be Your Guardian
Al Rhabhani, Grand Ayatollah
Democratic Republic of Iran

Both women looked up, staring in shocked silence. Katie tapped a button, and a tiny flashdrive popped up from the console.

Julie stared at Katie, incredulous. "What are you doing?"

"What do you think?" Katie reached for the tiny, plastic stick, shoved it into a chest pocket, and snapped shut the pocket cover. "Old habits are hard to break." She patted the pocket. "Never know when this might come in handy."

"Katie," Julie sputtered, "you can't do that! We swore an oath of secrecy! Nothing can leave this room."

"Julie, you worry too much. And I'm not giving away any secrets."

"Then why did you record? You know—"

Katie held up a hand, cutting her off. "It's over with."

"But, Katie, we're trusted with information"

"You'll find *trust* in the dictionary between *take* and *tyrant*."

Julie only stared.

Tentative seconds passed, and Katie tapped another button. The message vanished. "Julie," Katie said, her voice warmer, "believe me, I know what I'm doing. We never saw a thing. We don't know a thing, okay?"

Julie nodded in resignation. "Okay." She gave Katie a nervous glance. "You worked for the Directorate. Would they dare carry out those crazy plans?"

"Absolutely." Katie's chin tightened. "The Directorate will do what's necessary to survive. The Death Camps proved that. The Directorate controls the government. President Henshaw is only a puppet."

"But aren't the Iranians our, ah, I mean, the NAC's enemy?"

Katie turned back to the console and touched an interface. "You know the old saying, 'the enemy of my enemy...' Well, I think the Directorate and the Iranians found common ground: their hatred for freedom-loving souls. If Sam were here, he'd say we're facing the 21st century version of Nazi Germany allied with Stalin's Soviet Union." She turned back to Julie. "Only this time, one faction won't betray the other until what's left of the United States is totally gone."

Julie shuttered. "How frightening." She worked in an ear piece, glancing at Katie. "You know the teaching of *true* history here in the NAC was forbidden. Yet, if one were careful, there were ways to learn the truth."

"I know all about the 'careful' and the 'truth.' I lived it."

Julie sighed. "I made sure my children knew the truth." She paused. "Good thing Denver knows what's going on. Hopefully they can prevent this 'Grand Alliance.'"

"And history repeating itself," Katie murmured, staring blankly at the computer screen.

Thunder rumbled in the distance, rattling the single window and prefab roof. But it was a bright, clear late-autumn morning. Both women looked up, exchanging glances, a familiar dread growing. Thunder rumbled again and again, growing closer with each boom. To Katie, it seemed as if a steel mill's giant stamping iron marched toward them. She rose. "Julie, we gotta get out of here."

Keys jingled outside, and Buster Caldwell burst into the room. "Enemy artillery. Shut it down, ladies! To the shelters, now!"

They pressed the emergency purge and shutdown, and then they sprinted out the door behind Buster. The door automatically closed and locked behind them.

The three were met outside by a crowd of hospital personnel, some pushing beds with patients whose dangling IVs banged against metal trees. Katie and Julie helped gather patients, assisting where they could. The crowd made their way to open double doors built into a low, man-made hill.

Boom. Two hundred yards away, a huge transport truck lifted and exploded. The blast overwhelmed their screams. People covered their ears. The concussion hit Katie like a fist in the gut. Her eardrums popped. Flaming debris rained around them.

Two soldiers stood near the entrance, trying to keep order as people shoved inside.

Katie halted in front of a soldier. "What about the people in the camp!"

"Don't worry about them, ma'am, just get inside."

Katie turned, bolting for the camp, but Buster blocked her path, grabbing her arms, jerking her back. "Missy, we can't do anything for them. Now get inside!"

"But the kids! They're killing their own people!"

Boom. A tree top exploded in the distance. Deadly wooden daggers sprayed everywhere.

"I know!" Buster shouted in anguish. He shoved Katie to the shelter. "But we can't do anything out here but get killed. Now let's get inside!"

Reluctantly, Katie turned, with Buster behind her, making sure she headed for the bomb shelter. The two were the last ones in, and a soldier slammed the heavy steel doors. Katie and Buster made their way down a long rubber ramp. Muffled explosions rocked the ground. Dangling overhead lights rocked, and earth trickled down between wooden ceiling beams. The shelter was a good thirty feet below the surface, and yet the artillery barrage was still felt, causing terror and testing the nerves of those inside.

The corridor opened into a vast chamber. Shouts from doctors and nurses echoed, and people scrambled in unknown tasks. The controlled chaos overwhelmed Katie. For a moment, she stood in shock, unmoving, not knowing where to turn. Buster had vanished from her side.

"Come with me, honey." A woman in blue scrubs grabbed her arm, hustling her to a cluster of patient-filled hospital beds. Halting at the first, the woman took an IV bag from another scrub-adorned woman and placed it in Katie's hand. "Just hold this up until we can locate a tree." The first woman glanced at the woman who had been holding the bag. "Nurse, go assist Doctor Winston."

"Yes, Doctor."

Doctor and nurse disappeared, moving to other patients. Katie glanced down to the patient in the bed. A man lay unconscious, with his head and chest bandaged. Blue camo pants covered his legs—a NAC soldier. She was helping a NAC soldier, the enemy whose army was shelling a hospital and innocent civilians outside. Her chin tightened, and she had the urge to toss the IV bag down and stomp on it. Instead, Katie swallowed, looking away, keeping guilt and hatred in check. After what seemed like hours, but was only minutes, a man relieved her, telling her she was needed across the room where patients were being moved from hospital beds to cots.

With help from another woman, Katie eased a patient from a hospital bed onto a padded cot. All knew why the beds needed emptying; they would get filled outside.

It wasn't until someone shouted for help outside that Katie realized the shelling had stopped. She finished her task and rushed up the corridor with the others to the open doors. The doors were packed with civilian personnel trying to get out.

A moment later, she squeezed through and side-stepped out of the way. Katie paused, gazing at the hospital. "Jesus..." A wall and part of the roof had collapsed. Flames licked roof joists. The communication room where Julie and she had worked only minutes earlier was now a smoldering crater—a direct hit. Was it a lucky shot, or had the listening post been targeted? Katie didn't believe in luck. She was sure the com-room had brought on the attack. Her superiors knew that placing the communications station next to a hospital could endanger civilians; she had voiced it. But they insisted that by making it as innocuous as possible, it would be safe. Katie's chin tightened. If the enemy knew the exact location, why kill civilians? She knew the terrible answer.

Agonizing screams and wails from across the road broke her thoughts. Julie ran past, catching Katie's arm. "C'mon, they need our help!" They sprinted to the refugee camp. Anyone with two arms, two legs, and who could still walk, poured into the camp, or what was left of it.

Julie and Katie paused just inside, aghast at the carnage. Scraps of tents, personal belongings, and body parts were strewn everywhere. The open field where the refugees had camped was now a smoldering, pockmarked moonscape. Nary one tent stood. At their feet, lay a child's arm. A small hand still clutched a hairbrush. Julie covered her mouth, standing in shocked silence. Katie leaned over and vomited. There was no doubt that the refugee camp had also been targeted.

Someone touched Katie's shoulder, and she turned, facing a tall, lanky man. "ZZ, what are you doing here?" She paused and looked behind him. He was alone. "Is your family okay?"

ZZ only stared.

December 2, 2050. Summerville, South Carolina

Five giant helos, Joint Transport Craft called JTRs, hovered over the abandoned mall parking lot. The helos began descending. Twin rotors kicked up a dust storm. No sooner had the choppers touched down than a large ramp dropped from the rear. U.S. soldiers in full combat gear charged out, running for a two-story building on the mall's north end. Seconds later, Humvee IIs rolled down the ramps, speeding to the rear of the same building. Grim-faced .50 caliber top gunners trained their weapons on buildings across from the mall.

Gripping an M-8 battle rifle, Sam slowed to a trot, then halted, glancing to the weather-worn sign above the open entrance. He could just make out the faded, rust-streaked words, *BARNES & NOBLE*. The words spoke to a generation long past.

A young soldier paused nearby, his gaze following Sam's. "What was this building, sir?"

"A bookstore."

"A *book* store?"

"Yes, a bookstore." Combat boots crunched on broken glass as Sam, along with other soldiers, stepped through the wide-open entrance, the double doors long gone. "You remember books, don't you, Private?"

The private, with his weapon aimed down, followed in behind Sam. "Yes, sir. But I didn't know they sold books in stores like this."

Sam glanced back. "Well, they did, until everything went digital crazy." He paused, stepping around a broken countertop. "All the good that does us now, with satellites down, digital systems crashed. It's a black and white world now, Private."

Sam stepped aside and began waving an arm. "Let's hustle, men. We have a war waiting on us!" He turned to an approaching sergeant, a man of around thirty. "Have the men fall in and take a head count. I'm heading upstairs to find our new C.O."

"Yes, sir."

Sam turned, stepping for a spiral staircase across the room. No sooner had he started up when two soldiers trotted down. One was an older man that he recognized: Lieutenant Colonel

Hall, the man that had sworn him in. Hidden behind him was another soldier. Sam backed up and snapped to attention.

Hall paused then stepped to Sam. The older man shook his hand. "Congratulations, Lieutenant Moore, you made it back to hell. I'd like you to meet your new Company Commander." The colonel stepped aside. "I think you two are acquainted."

The soldier behind extended a hand, and Sam's eyes widened. "Rob!"

"Sam!" The two shook hands and patted each other on the shoulder. Rob backed away, giving Sam the once over. "Jesus, man, just look at you now. You look like you could whip a whole platoon of bad guys."

"Not hardly." Sam felt flush as he eyed his friend and mentor. Although Rob seemed genuinely happy to see him, something in the man's tone seemed troubled. Perhaps it was the strain of combat.

"Sam, the medical camp that treated you a few months back was shelled day-before-yesterday. The tent city is obliterated. There are heavy civilian casualties." Rob paused. "The hospital took a direct hit."

The colonel stood silent, eyeing both soldiers.

Sam felt as if spear had stabbed him in the chest. He finally choked out the words. "All those people..." He stared at Rob. "Katie...is Katie—"

"Katie's missing."

"Oh, God," Sam breathed. He swallowed, gaining some control. "So, there's nothing left of her—"

"Excuse me, Colonel," Rob said and touched Sam's arm, leading him into a commons room. "Katie made it through the shelling."

"Make it quick, men," the colonel said, stepping past the two. "Fields, I want to see you and Captain Wilson at battalion headquarters in ten minutes with a complete inventory of your companies."

"Yes, sir," Rob replied. He turned back to Sam. "One of Katie's co-workers was with her when she disappeared."

Sam halted. "What do you mean?"

"This co-worker is Julie Frisk. Ring a bell?"

"No."

"Anyway," Rob continued, "she and Katie had taken shelter during the attack. Afterward they headed to what was left of the tent city to assist when this tall, thin man approached Katie and called her by name."

Sam's brow furrowed. "And?"

Soldiers began unfolding a couple of tables nearby. Rob and Sam stepped away. "Apparently the two were acquainted because she called him by name, too." Rob paused, gauging Sam. "She called him 'ZZ.'"

"Zack Zhimmer!"

"You know this guy?"

"Hell, yes. He's a close friend. We taught together back when we were in Perchance. He taught science." Sam blinked, a jumble of emotions buzzing through his cranium. "Katie met the Zhimmers while I was out of it. Last time I saw ZZ was the night before the ambush. He's a family man. Figured he and his family had moved on to a safer area by now." Sam paused, staring at a pile of decaying, empty bookshelves. "Wonder what he wanted with Katie?"

Rob shrugged. "Well, neither of them have been seen since. I knew you were coming in this morning, so I contacted that co-worker, Frisk, for recent news. She went by Katie's room this morning...nothing's changed. Her personal things are still there." Rob shook his head, eyeing Sam sympathetically. "I don't know what to tell you, man."

"It doesn't make sense."

"I would've done a more thorough search for her, but with shit happening all around and dozens missing after the attack..."

"I understand," Sam said, nodding, "you can't spend all your resources for one person."

Rob pushed back his helmet, staring in thought at a crack in the wall. "She is a U.S. government employee with a high security clearance and a valuable skill. If that man she was talking to had not been a friend of yours..." He glanced to Sam. "I'd say kidnapping was a possibility."

Sam could only stare, trying to digest everything. Kidnapped by ZZ? No way. But maybe Katie and ZZ...did the two have something going he didn't know about? Why else would she have left with him? And why now? Perhaps they were kidnapped together? Sam shook his head. He must find ZZ or Haleana and find out what in the hell was going on. It would be like finding the proverbial needle, but he had to try. A twinge of jealousy moved through him. Katie seemed to genuinely miss him and looked forward to his return. Then he recalled his recovery in the hospital and how she had gone silent for two straight weeks. Could this be a repeat? Only this time, with another man? Maybe Katie didn't have the guts to face him, to tell him it was over, so she eloped with his close friend. Some friend. Rob touched Sam's arm, breaking his thoughts.

"Help Sergeant Luna round up Alpha Company. Have them fall in here in this commons room, Lieutenant."

"Yes, sir."

Rob sighed. "You heard the Colonel. He wants to meet with me and the new Bravo Company commander. I'll return, ASAP."

Sam nodded. His mind was numb.

Rob read the look on Sam's face. "We'll get to the bottom of this, Sam." Rob hustled away.

Sam swallowed, forcing his thoughts to the present. "Sergeant Luna," he shouted, "let's fall in over in the Commons."

"You heard the Lieutenant—Alpha Company, let's move!"

Sam tightened his helmet's chin strap, with his gaze on the American flag patch on his right shoulder. How did he arrive at this moment, a nation at stake, and yet, all he could think of was Katie? With all the scurrying around him, he still felt he were all alone, singled out, and placed below the level plane to catch whatever hell spilled over. Sam said a silent prayer and rubbed gloved fingers over the body armor on his chest. His fingers couldn't feel the new cross or the Christopher that Katie had given him, but he knew they were there. Jaw tight with determination, Sam stepped to the platoon.

Rob returned an hour later and called a meeting with all platoon leaders and senior NCOs. In a meeting room just off the commons, Sam stood with three other lieutenants, four platoon sergeants and a first sergeant. All had weapons slung over their shoulders as Captain Rob Fields addressed the group.

"Okay, listen up." Rob shot a quick glance to each man. "Bravo Company is staking out this place. Charlie and Delta arrive tomorrow. They're to keep roads cleared and help Twentieth Infantry prevent a NAC troop breakout from Charleston's western flank."

A large man wearing a 1st lieutenant's bar stood next to Sam and spoke up. "So, Charleston is surrounded?"

Rob nodded, glancing at all the men. "Yes. Intel believes there's only a brigade force of enemy left in Charleston, if that."

"Over two-thousand tough ones, Capin'" Sergeant Luna said, grinning dryly. The stocky Latino pushed back his helmet. "The panty-waists surrendered long ago."

"Or they're dead," another soldier added.

A young lieutenant stepped up. "Sir, what's *our* mission?"

A chorus of voices jumped in.

"Shh!"

"You don't wanna know."

"Never ask that, sir."

"No, *never* ask that."

Sam couldn't help but smile, recalling mission planning with Rob and Buck back in his guerrilla days. The most dangerous job was always mentioned last. He glanced to the officer. "Lieutenant Morgan, it's considered bad luck to ask what your mission is before it's given."

Rob looked on in amusement.

"I..." The young officer stammered, glancing around. "I didn't know. Hell, hope I didn't just jinx it."

Rob stiffened at the words.

Sam eyed the younger man. He couldn't be past twenty-five, with a lean frame, but he carried his gear well. Intelligent eyes shone from a face that had seen little sun. He cleared his throat and patted the soldier on the shoulder. "Don't worry about it, Morgan. We make our own luck."

The men grew quiet, gazing at Rob expectantly. Rob nodded. "We've been given a special mission."

"Naturally," Sam murmured.

Rob ignored the remark. "Alpha Company is assigned a recon-rescue mission."

Another lieutenant spoke up. "*Recon*-rescue? What the hell is that, Captain?"

"A civilian with a U.S. top-secret clearance was recently captured. We need her back."

Sam did a double-take. Heart thumping, he stared with incredulous eyes at Rob.

"*Her?*" someone queried.

"She must have pictures of a general," another voice offered. A few chuckles drifted.

"She's a gifted communications specialist," Rob added. "This civilian is also a linguist."

The large lieutenant tilted his helmet and gave a disgusted sigh. "Oh, that makes it different."

Rob gave the man a hard look. "Lieutenant Jenson, can you speak Farsi?" Rob glanced around and shouted. "Anyone here speak Farsi?"

Silence filled the room.

"Hell, I'll even settle for Arabic."

Men shifted, glancing down and away.

"That's what I thought."

Sam eyed the large-framed officer. Damon Jenson was a good four inches taller than Sam's six-foot, and maybe fifty pounds heavier. He was an athletic man but with a condescending streak in him that rubbed most the wrong way. Sam's jaw tightened, and he nodded to the big man. "You were outta line, Jenson."

The man gave an exasperated sigh then glanced to the captain. "Sorry, sir."

Rob waved it off. "Forget it." He looked around. "This woman was monitoring top secret communications between Iranian leadership and the NAC Whitehouse."

The young lieutenant, Morgan, nodded to the others. "My last assignment was communications in Denver. Denver suspected there was something up between NAC leadership and Iran. We just weren't sure what. And with limited computer ability to translate, try to find someone on our side who can speak Farsi? Good luck."

Sergeant Luna glanced at the young lieutenant. "Terms of surrender discussed?"

Morgan shook his head. "No." He paused. "Can't say anything more except that we think the NAC and Iranian leaders are in bed together."

"That figures."

"An alliance?" someone offered.

"You gotta be kidding!"

"That explains those Iranians in NAC uniforms," another added.

Sam glanced to the men. "Notice they were always officers?"

"Okay, men." Rob slapped his hands together. "We'll have plenty of time to discuss the geopolitical implications later." Rob looked around and spotted the folding table one of the men had brought in. He and another unfolded it, and then he unsnapped his vest and worked out a map. "God, I miss satellites." He spread the map out on the table and touched a finger to a black dot in the middle of a circle. "There, gentleman, is our destination. We think the woman is being held there."

The soldiers gathered around and leaned over. Sam grinned. The word **Perchance** was circled in red.

Rob glanced to Sam, and Sam nodded. "We have to move quick," Rob said. "Hopefully, she's still there." He refolded the map and stuffed it back into his vest. "We'll meet back in here after chow. Let's say nineteen hundred. Get the platoons ready. We move out at zero-five-thirty."

"Yes, sir," a chorus of voices replied.

As the soldiers filed out, Sam waited for Rob, and the two stepped down the corridor together. Their gear slapped their sides. "Thanks, man."

"Don't thank me," Rob said. "This wasn't my idea, although I did volunteer Alpha Company."

"What makes you think Katie is in Perchance?"

"In our CO meeting with the colonel, he told us he'd received a communiqué that this Zhimmer fellow was spotted cruising toward Perchance with a woman that matches Katie's description." Rob drew up, allowing others to pass. He lowered his voice. "Katie must know some important shit. Sam, those orders to find her came straight from Denver."

"So, you were serious about the U.S. government wanting her?"

"As a heart attack."

Confused, Sam shook his head. "I don't understand. What's going on here?"

"I don't know how else to put it, guy, but... there's still that million-dollar-bounty on your head."

"You think Katie defected and will try to draw me in to collect the reward?" Sam blinked in disbelief. "That's crazy, Rob, and you know it! Katie risked her own life to take down the Directorate. Why would she throw all that away? I'm sure there's a Directorate death warrant out on her, too."

"Well, it's not important what you or I think, Sammy. It's what our bosses think."

Sam ran a hand over his jaw. "This is just so out-of-character for Katie to willingly return to the belly of the beast." He glanced to Rob. "There has to be a reason." Inside, he quivered. *Yeah, she had a reason...another man.* He must consider it no matter how hard it hurt. Did Katie run off with one of his trusted friends? He'd heard about that happening to soldiers. Sam stared past Rob, cursing himself for falling for Katie. Didn't he learn from her ignoring him for all those weeks back at the hospital? Shouldn't that have been a subtle message about her emotional stability?

"Guess we'll find out soon enough," Rob said, patting Sam on the shoulder. "Now let's get some chow. The mess hall is across the parking lot. I understand it's in an old IHOP."

"An 'I-what?'"

"I'll explain on the way. Let's get some hot food while we can."

An hour northeast of Summerville, on a cold, cloudy morning, the military convoy, made up mostly of HUMVEE IIAs, rolled cautiously through what had been known as the Frances Marion National Forest. Company Commander Captain Rob Fields and three other soldiers rode in a 4x4 Utility Recon Vehicle—*FURV*—at the head of the column. The FURV was based on early 21st century SUVs, was diesel-powered, lightly armored, quick and agile, and could go places a HUMVEE couldn't. The platoon leaders, all lieutenants, also rode in a FURV at the head of their respective platoons. Second platoon leader, Lieutenant Sam Moore, sat upright in the passenger seat. Private Nolan Deider was behind the wheel. In the back seat was the radio telephone operator—RTO—Corporal Lance Steagal.

"This is my old stomping grounds," Sam said while glancing around. He nodded to his right. "Our old base camp was about five miles that way."

"So, it's true, sir, that you really were a guerilla fighter?" the young private asked.

Sam looked to the soldier steering the vehicle. He couldn't be past twenty and reminded Sam of a former student. "It's true. Even though sometimes I felt I was in a waking dream." He stared out a window to the forest beyond. "Make that a waking nightmare."

"So, you've experienced real combat?" Steagal asked from the back.

"Yes." Sam paused. "And worse…"

The soldier in back shifted in his seat. "Worse, sir?"

Sam gave a subtle nod. "Yeah, worse."

The radio crackled. *We're coming up on civilian evacs on foot, maybe a couple of dozen, heading the other way on both sides of the roads. Let's slow it down.*

Deider slowed, and the convoy crawled along. The soldiers gazed in pity at the sad lot, hunched with over-stuffed backpacks, some pulling wagons. Sam's jaw tightened, recognizing the looks on their faces. Despair and hopelessness are sad companions.

Sam did a double take. "Jesus Christ! Turn around! Turn around!"

Deider swung the FURV to the left. "What is it, sir!"

The radio buzzed. *What the hell's going on back there!* came Rob's urgent voice.

Sam pointed, frantic. "Pull up past that woman. The woman in the dark coat!"

The private shook his head, easing past the pathetic crowd. The people began stopping, unsure. Sam looked at the woman as the FURV crept past. She glanced at him and halted, staring. "It's her!" Sam shouted. "Get on the horn, tell the Captain we found a person of interest."

"Yes, sir," the corporal in back replied with radio mike in hand.

The FURV crept to a stop. Sam reached for his rifle in the weapon holder and bailed out. "You guys stay put." Slinging the weapon over a shoulder, he jogged to the perplexed woman. Other civilians began gathering around, and the whole convoy ground to a halt. Sam drew up in front of the woman. He removed his gloves and clipped them to a pocket. "Haleana?"

The woman's gaze moved up and down, taking in his battle-dress. There was apprehension in her voice. "Sam...Sam Moore?"

A scraggly teenage girl that Sam barely recognized stood at the woman's side, staring at the soldier in front of her. "It's Sam, Momma!"

The woman hesitated, the backpack slipping from her shoulders, and then sobbing, she threw her arms around Sam. "Oh, God, Sam..."

"It's okay, Haleana." Sam gripped her. "Where is ZZ?"

She released him. "So, this is about him?" she asked, hurtful. "Look at us, Sam. Look at us! We're forced to live like animals, and the first thing you ask is about my damn husband. Don't you want to know about his family?" She waved an arm. "Just look at all of us. What's happened to this country?"

Sam swallowed hard. Had he abandoned his own kind? No. If he had wanted to do that, he would've gone to Texas with those families. Yet, he felt guilt for the group's wretchedness. If he had stayed with the Zhimmers, would it have changed things? *Yeah, sure would have.* He'd probably be dead by now. And they would still be just as wretched. Sam cleared his throat. "I'm sorry, Haleana...sorry that you think that I don't care."

The woman's gaze softened. "And I'm sorry, too, Sam. It's just that...that I...we...don't have control of our lives anymore. There's nowhere to go, no place to turn."

"Haleana, you guys still have me."

"Do we? I mean, look at you. You're a soldier. You're part of another world now."

"I won't abandon you. You and ZZ were there when I needed you." Sam gripped her shoulder. God, it was boney. "You and ZZ are the only family I have left."

Haleana shook her head, sighing in resignation. "I'm not sure where ZZ is. And it's getting to the point that I don't care. He left about three days back, said he'd be back the next day at the latest." Her voice picked up. "Then the NAC army came, stole what little food we had, and kicked us out of our camp, and then..."

"Haleana, calm down. It's going to be all right."

A FURV rolled to a stop nearby. Rob and First Sergeant Luna climbed out. Weapons in hand, they marched over. "What do we have here, Lieutenant?"

Sam glanced to the two soldiers. "The man Katie left with, Zack Zhimmer? This is his wife, Haleana."

Rob shouldered his weapon, and Luna followed suit. "Do tell."

A crowd gathered as Haleana eyed Sam. "Sam, has...has Katie made it back yet?"

Rob gave a start. Sam only stared. "No, and that's who we're looking for, Katie, and ZZ." He paused. "Have you seen Katie at all lately?"

"No," she said, shaking her head. "Not since the hospital when you were injured and in a coma. Katie and I became friends during that time. She cared a lot about you, Sam."

Rob glanced to the soldier next to him. "Sergeant Luna, would you tell the convoy to take five and that everything is okay. We'll be rolling in a few." He glanced to the sad crowd gathering around. "And feed these people."

"Yes, sir." Luna hustled back to the FURV.

Sam caught Rob's eye and nodded. Rob shrugged, returning the nod.

"Sam."

Sam turned, and the teenage girl grabbed him, squeezing him. Sam ran a hand over her dark, tasseled hair. "We'll find your father, Jenna."

"Don't leave us,," Jenna sobbed. "Momma needs you. We need you."

Rob looked the other way, silent.

Sam glanced around, looking for her brother. "Where's Taylor?"

Haleana's chin tightened. "It's just Jenna and me, until ZZ gets back."

Jenna stepped back. "Taylor's gone."

Sam's brow wrinkled.

"Outbreak of cholera," Haleana said coldly. "Taylor didn't make it. Our son passed away in early November."

Sam's eyes closed. "I'm sorry..."

Rob stepped away, nodding to Sam. "Lieutenant, a word please?"

"Yes, sir." He glanced to Haleana. "I'll be right back, and I need to know *exactly* what this deal is between ZZ and Katie, okay?"

Haleana nodded. Sam glanced around to the activity. A large military truck had pulled out from the convoy's rear and was parked on the opposite shoulder. People were lining up as two soldiers distributed boxed rations.

The two officers halted out of earshot. Rob eyed Sam. "I know these people are friends of yours, and I'm sorry for their loss, but, Sam, please don't get any ideas. I just want to remind you, we do have a mission here." He paused. "Colonel Hall had reservations about bringing you back here for this very reason. I convinced him that you would put your men, your mission first."

Sam's gut twisted. Less than twenty-four hours back and he was already at war with himself. He nodded. "You can count on me."

"I know." Rob slapped him on the arm. "Let's hear what she has to say."

The two returned to Haleana. Rob stood to one side. She hadn't moved. Her daughter, Jenna, had already hustled to a line for rations.

Sam tugged on a chin strap, working off his helmet. In spite of the chill, his short hair was damp. "Haleana, exactly where were ZZ and Katie heading, and why?"

"ZZ received word through the Underground that Katie's parents were arrested up in New York. Her younger brother, James, hid out with friends, and made his way down here, to Perchance, looking for his sister, Katie."

Sam swiped a small towel inside his helmet, recalling a year ago Katie telling him about her family up north, and that she had a younger half-brother. "That kid would be maybe, eleven or so? Kinda young to be traveling like that isn't he?"

"ZZ didn't say how he got to Perchance. Just that the boy was staying with the Yarboroughs."

"I know them," Sam said. "So, ZZ and Katie headed to Perchance to get her brother?"

Haleana nodded. "That's the gist of it."

Rob glanced first to the woman then to Sam, but he remained silent.

Sam worked his helmet back on. The chin straps dangled. "So, the Underground found ZZ but couldn't locate Katie?"

Rob broke in. "Her government clearance kept her, how do you say," he air quoted, "'hidden' from outsiders."

Sam nodded, with his eyes on Haleana. "But ZZ found her."

"Sam, we knew Katie had been working there. ZZ decided to check it out."

Sam shook his head. "Just can't figure out how a kid can make it over a thousand miles to Perchance, but can't make it the other sixty miles to Charleston?"

"Does seem strange," Rob added.

Haleana nodded in agreement, addressing Sam. "I asked ZZ about that. He said getting from Perchance to Charleston was the most dangerous part and you, Sam, should go with Katie to get the boy, but with that reward on your head, it was too dangerous. And then we found out that you had joined the U.S. army and were away on training, so you were out of the picture." Haleana paused. "ZZ said that since you and he were close friends, he owed it to you to help Katie."

Sam again shook his head. "I can't believe Katie would just disappear without telling someone and then willingly return to Perchance, knowing Tipton is still there and, I'm sure, looking for her, too."

The three stood silent. Sam glanced to the convoy. Several soldiers milled outside of vehicles, some smoking.

"Sam," Haleana continued, "ZZ has been acting strange the past couple of months. Even before Taylor's death. Part of it is the stress of how we now live but, but he just hasn't been himself for quite a while."

"Maybe he thought he let you and the kids down," Sam said.

"No, there's been a strain on our marriage the past couple of years." Haleana looked away. "He was due back yesterday at the latest." She glanced to Sam with pleading, heartbroken eyes. "You don't think that Katie and he..."

"Ran off together?" Sam murmured. He had wondered the same thing.

Rob cleared his throat. "The couple was spotted near Perchance yesterday. If they were eloping, they sure wouldn't go there."

Sam and Haleana nodded in agreement.

Rob glanced to Sam. "We have to move out."

Sam tilted his helmet, glancing to the bedraggled woman.

His heart wretched for what her family had been through. Yet, at the moment, there was little he could do. Empathy worked through him; both of them had perhaps lost someone they had loved and trusted. But he was a soldier now. "Haleana, I gotta go."

She threw herself into Sam's arms, clutching him and whispering. "I don't know if I'll ever see the children's father again. Jenna and I are all alone."

Haleana sobbed, and Sam comforted her as best he could. Inside, he screamed. To see a woman, a close friend, once so strong now on the verge of a breakdown was almost more than he could bear. He stroked her tangled hair. "Head to what's left of the refugee camp near Charleston. It's chaotic there, but it's the only place around. And you being a nurse, they'll snap you up...give you and Jenna better living conditions." He paused, releasing her. "When I get back, I'll look you and Jenna up, get you out of there, get you a decent place to live."

"I've got to stay with this bunch," she said, "they need me."

Jenna had returned with two MREs under an arm. She handed both to her mother. She turned to Sam. "You're leaving?"

"Honey, I have to."

Jenna stepped to him and wrapped thin arms around him. "Don't forget about us."

A lump rose in Sam's throat. He hugged her back. Then he gently pushed away lest he lose it. "I won't forget my friends, I promise." Sam stepped away, waving, as he and Rob headed back to the FURVs.

The two forlorn figures waved back faint-heartedly.

"Do you believe her?" Rob asked.

Sam took several steps before answering. "I believe she believes that her husband is involved in some scheme, and he's not coming back." Sam swore inside. These were his own people, and he was abandoning them. He had all this hardware, men, and almost limitless resources, and yet he had never felt so helpless in his life. He kicked at the ground. "Shit!"

"Suck it up, Sam." Rob gave Sam a quick glance. "Welcome to soldiering."

32

Katie shifted in her seat, glancing to the driver next to her. "Is this your cart?"

"It is now," ZZ replied. "I got it on the cheap a few days back. Carts are now a dime-a-dozen."

Katie stared out a window into the gathering dusk. "You'd think people would hang on to their only means of escape."

"You know you can't get far with a cart, even a full charge will only get you maybe a couple of hundred miles or so. And, of course, that was the government's plan all along, to limit travel." ZZ glanced to Katie then back out the windshield. "With evacuees driving from camp to camp, most of the carts out there now have dead batteries, and good luck on getting a charge."

Katie pulled her coat tighter. Her always suspicious nature somewhat eased. Still, if Zack Zhimmer had not been a close friend of Sam's, she would never have come along.

"Exactly how old is your brother?" ZZ asked, quickly changing the subject.

"He turned eleven last month." Now it was Katie's turn to change the subject. "I just can't believe you'd leave your family in times like these to help a near-stranger."

"We're not 'strangers,' Katie. We learned a lot about one another those few weeks Sam was out of it."

Katie sighed. "Yeah, maybe."

"Besides," ZZ continued, "we should be back by morning at the latest. Haleana and Jenna can do without me for one day."

"I'm sorry about your son. How awful."

ZZ's grip on the steering wheel tightened. "Thanks. And that's another reason I'm doing this. When I heard that a boy the same age as my son was in trouble, well, no way could I ignore it." Steering around a gentle curve, he glanced to Katie. "And that boy is a brother of my best friend's girlfriend."

"Never said I was Sam's 'girlfriend.'" *Yeah, right,* she mused, *that's why I'm carrying his child.*

ZZ winked at her in the gathering dark. "Come off it, Katie. When he was in the hospital, we had to bring you a cot because you wouldn't leave him."

Thirty more minutes passed, with zero traffic on the highway. No military, civilian, nothing. She recalled escaping from Charleston and from those two morons on this very road back in early February, when this all started. *God*, she thought, *that seemed like a lifetime ago.* She glanced to her government civilian uniform and her U.S. ID. Oh, crap! She removed the lanyard and stuffed it in a pocket. "I can't believe I didn't have you drop me off so I could change and let someone know where I was going."

"I told you that if we left immediately, I'd have you back by midnight, your brother with you." ZZ paused. "With all the chaos in that camp, I may never have found you again."

Katie nodded, and the two remained lost in their thoughts for several miles. Katie broke the silence. "You know the back ways into Perchance?"

"Sure do. But I heard that a lot of the NAC army that had surrounded Perchance has disappeared."

"Where did you hear that?"

"From a couple of deserters."

Katie gazed straight ahead, watching the headlights break through the gloom. "That whole NAC army needs to desert. Americans fighting Americans—it's unnatural." She shook her head. "It's not right. God is punishing us again for past transgressions."

ZZ made no comment. With one hand on the wheel, the other on the gearshift, he stared out the windshield. "So, Sam's in the U.S. army now? Wow, unbelievable."

"Well, believe it." The disappointment then anger she had felt with Sam upon his joining had morphed into resignation, a sort of finality. Could she live with the loneliness while he was deployed? She wasn't doing very good at the moment. Katie wanted to be with Sam, start a life with him, but now, what of *her* career, her plans for the future? If she were a soldier's wife during peacetime, she would have to follow him all over creation, never settling at one place long, never growing roots. She chided herself, acting as if the war were already over and won by the good guys. Would they even live long enough to see it through? Katie glanced to her belly. What about the future for that life, which she now carried?

"Where's Sam stationed?" ZZ asked, breaking Katie's thoughts.

"It's confidential, except to say that he's across The River."

ZZ eyes widened. "The River! Really?"

"Yeah, really. And he's due back any day." She glanced at ZZ. "That's just another reason that the timing is all wrong. I need to be there when he returns."

ZZ glanced to the dash clock. "Unless he comes in within the next four hours, you'll be there, Katie."

Katie missed Sam tremendously—his eyes, his voice, his gentle touch—the way they made love. Those two weeks they had lived together before Sam left now seemed like a dream. Would she and Sam ever be in sync?

"Across The River..." ZZ murmured. "I'd give *anything* to cross the Mississippi. And I would never come back." He glanced to Katie, "Haleana and I hope to cross into the Western Alliance soon."

"You and a million others. I'd go too except..." Katie paused, giving a loud sigh.

"Except what?"

"I have obligations here." Katie glanced to ZZ. "You're right about Sam and I being together, ZZ. Sam and I are tied together, our lives interwoven in some bizarre play. I'll never up and leave him again." She started to tell ZZ of her pregnancy but thought better of it. At the moment, the fewer who knew, the better.

"Sounds like marriage on the horizon."

Katie chuckled dryly. "I just hope Sam's not married to the army. I don't believe in plural marriage."

The cart turned left off the paved road. They wandered down a caliche back road another twenty minutes then halted at an old, wooden bridge. ZZ killed the engine, and the two climbed from the cart. Turning his coat-collar up, with flashlight in hand, ZZ stepped cautiously onto the heavy, gray boards. Katie paused at the bridge's edge.

The flashlight beam moved here and there as ZZ inspected the ancient structure. Dark holes appeared where boards had rotted away. "Except for a few places near the edge, it looks solid enough, at least for a cart." The bridge spanned fifty feet over a shallow creek ten feet below. ZZ slowly walked across. Satisfied, he hustled back.

"Papa had said to use this bridge only as a last resort," Katie said to the approaching teacher. "You sure it's safe?"

"We'll have to take a chance. Even without satellites, the NAC army has had plenty of time the past few months to discover the hidden routes."

Katie stared at the bridge. "They probably took one look at this bridge and said 'Forget it.'"

ZZ remained silent.

Katie hesitated. Something just didn't feel right; this whole trip seemed surreal. "Tell you what," she began, "give me the flashlight, I'll walk over, and you can pick me up on the other side." She glanced into the dark shadow of a steep bank dropping away on her right. "I don't feel like going for a swim tonight."

ZZ wavered, and then he handed her the flashlight. "Good idea."

A few seconds later, Katie stood on the opposite side, and the cart rolled up to her. A gull-wing door lifted, she climbed in, and they disappeared into the murkiness.

There was no traffic. Even though there was a curfew, most folks still left in town chose to remain behind locked doors, not risking an encounter with deserters or the pissed-off soldiers sent to find them. Katie glanced at ZZ sitting behind the wheel, with no seeming care in the world. He drove as if he were on a leisurely evening drive. Wasn't he afraid of them getting caught? "You said that my brother, James, was staying at the Yarboroughs'?"

"Yes."

"Do you know where they live?"

"Sure do."

Katie fidgeted. "Then why aren't we heading there?"

ZZ glanced at her. He swung the cart right and stopped. "You'll find out soon enough."

At that moment, a heavy military truck pulled up behind them, bumping them.

"Do something, ZZ!"

"I am. I'm getting a ticket outta here."

Out of nowhere, a Humvee shot in front of them, blocking them. The cart was trapped.

Soldiers bolted from both vehicles, surrounding the cart, with weapons trained on the two inside.

"ZZ!" Katie screamed. "You got us caught!"

"I'm not caught," ZZ looked over at her, "but *you* are."

"James was never here!" Katie's eyes widened in realization and horror. "What have you done!"

A voice boomed from outside. "Everyone out!"

Gull-wing doors swung up. ZZ casually climbed out. Katie unbuckled her seatbelt, but before she could move, hands reached in and jerked her out.

A soldier shoved her to the front. "Get over there with him. Hands up, both of you!"

Surrounded by a dozen, heavily armed NAC troops, the two stood with hands in the air, helpless. ZZ was expressionless, while Katie glanced around, trembling with fear and rage.

"Step aside," came an authoritarian voice. The soldiers parted, and a man dressed in khaki pants and waist-length leather coat strode up. A rucksack hung from one shoulder. "Nicely done, Mr. Zhimmer, nicely done!"

"Thank you, Mr. Tipton."

The man halted in front of the pair. "Both of you may lower your hands."

Staring at the man, Katie eased down her hands. Hatred overtook fear. Although she had never met Jonathon Tipton, she knew exactly who he was and what he was capable of.

"Well, my dear," Tipton began, scrutinizing the woman. "We meet at last. Your reputation has preceded you."

Katie remained silent.

"And I must say," Tipton continued, "'nicely done' to you, also." The commissar swept his hands. "*You* almost single-handedly destroyed your country."

ZZ cleared his throat, interrupting. "Mr. Tipton..."

"Yes, yes, of course." Tipton tossed ZZ the rucksack. "It's all there, one hundred thousand. And I've included a travel pass, papers, all signed by me and those higher up. It should get you through the checkpoints."

Katie's eyes blazed. "A hundred thousand! You sold out your friends, your soul, for a lousy one hundred thousand dollars?"

ZZ gave a sick grin. "That's one hundred thousand *U.S.* dollars, and no, I only sold you."

In the blink of an eye, Katie punched the former chemistry teacher in the face. Blood spurted from a broken nose. "You low-life bastard!"

Soldiers moved, but Tipton raised his hand, stopping them. The soldiers stood by as Katie rained blow after blow on the man. ZZ raised the rucksack, attempting to block the punches. Katie kicked him in the groin. ZZ doubled over, groaning. As Katie stepped in to kick him again. Tipton spoke and soldiers moved in, grabbing her.

Katie struggled, kicking and screaming. "Damn you to hell, Zhimmer! Damn you to hell!" She suddenly went limp. "How could you do this to your people, your friends? We trusted you! I trusted you!" Head down, with a soldier on each arm, she wept quietly.

Tipton's jaw tightened, and he gave Zhimmer a hard look. "I think it's best you leave now." He glanced to another soldier. "Please move a vehicle and let him pass."

Zhimmer wiped his bleeding nose on a sleeve. Blood oozed from a split lip. "Thank you, Commissar, for everything." He tossed the rucksack into the open cart door and began climbing in.

"Mr. Zhimmer."

Zhimmer halted, gazing back to the commissar.

"I've rescinded the reward for Moore." Tipton paused. "And I never want to lay eyes on you again."

Zhimmer nodded. "You won't, sir." He scooted in behind the wheel, the door lowered, and the cart hummed to life. The Humvee in front eased away. The cart made a U-turn and disappeared into the night.

Tipton removed his glasses and rubbed the lenses with a handkerchief while scrutinizing Katie. "Have you had dinner yet?"

Katie lifted her head. She remained silent. The loathing in her eyes was her only reply.

"Take this woman to my quarters."

"Yes, sir," came several replies. Soldiers half-dragged Katie's limp form to the nearby Chinese-made Humvee and stuffed her in the back seat. Soldiers climbed into vehicles. After a moment, the Humvee moved forward, followed by the truck.

Katie sat upright, with a soldier on either side. Her rage slowly passed, replaced by awareness and cold calculation. If only Sam were here. Sam had to be there, outside somewhere. Hopefully he would come looking for her.

If she lived long enough.

Jonathan Tipton stood near a stove, eyeing the Spencers' granddaughter sitting at the kitchen table. If it weren't for the leg shackles, she would look as if she were only a visitor who had dropped in for tea. He gauged her for several, long seconds before speaking. "I'm having Italian tonight. Spaghetti. Thanks to your friends, I'm afraid that's all I have to offer. Supplies are running a little short these days. But that is only temporary. Things will soon be back to normal." He paused. "I would like for you to join me."

Katie stared up to the older man. "No, thank you."

Dressed casually, Tipton stood over a pot of boiling water, working in pasta. "Surely, you'll have a cup of tea with me."

The woman shook her head.

"Perhaps something stronger?"

Katie remained silent. Her somber eyes were icy.

Tipton shrugged, returning to the boiling pasta. "Suit yourself."

Tense seconds passed. "Why don't you just get it over with?" Katie asked. "Or are you going to talk me to death?"

"What do you mean?"

"I mean," Katie said flatly, "my execution. Let's just get it over with."

Tipton stirred a nearby pan of spaghetti sauce. He was indeed lucky to have this food. He glanced over to the woman staring at him. He admitted, it was hard to read what lay behind those dark eyes. Hatred, yes he had read that, but nothing else. But the hatred was expected. "My dear, Ms. Spencer, you are worth more alive than dead. If you are executed, *I* certainly would not be the one to order it."

Katie swallowed again, taking in the sparse kitchen for the first time. "I will have a glass of water."

The commissar nodded, stepping away from the stove. After drawing a glass of water, he stepped over to her and placed the glass on the table in front of her. Yes, she was attractive, he admitted with reluctance. Yet, Katie Spencer was appealing in a different way, a way he had seldom seen, and certainly not for the last few years. And after her display this evening, she had something few ever received: his grudging respect.

Katie tilted the glass. As she drank, her eyes never left him. She replaced the glass. "Thank you."

"You're welcome," Tipton replied, returning to the stove.

"What are you going to do with me?"

Tipton stirred the boiling pasta, remaining silent. Steam rose, fogging his glasses. He wasn't sure himself. *Indecision* had been alien to him. But now? The Spencer girl certainly could be used as a bargaining chip. Would she draw in his true target, Samuel Moore? He hated admitting that even his abhorrence for Moore had slid to the back burner as personal survival took its place. Tipton sighed. He was tired inside. He was tired of living off animosity, loathing; antipathy for others can only get one so far. Look where it got him now. The commissar of what?

"It must be hard being this lonely," Katie said.

The lid clattered on the stove and his fork dropped into the pasta.

"Not having a friend in the world..."

What was he even doing conversing with this traitor? Tipton gingerly fished out the fork from the boiling water, and then he turned to her. "At least I know who my friends are." He stared at the fork thoughtfully. "Although I will say, even I didn't think Zhimmer had it in him."

Katie cleared her throat. "Being a commissar, I'm sure you consider treachery a virtue."

With his back to her, he stiffened. She was trying to goad him. Didn't Spencer know she was playing with fire? He could have the guards outside simply drag her away, never to be seen again. "'Treachery,' as you call it, is a useful tool."

Strained seconds passed. "Why am I here in your quarters?" Katie asked.

Tipton used one of his favorite weapons: silence.

Katie stared. "You must know the United States Western Alliance is winning. It'll be over soon. And you know what they do to war criminals. If you think the price on my head was high, try laying a finger on me. There will be no place on this earth you can hide. And I'm not talking about the government coming after you."

Tipton strode toward Katie and loomed over the sitting, shackled woman. He felt his neck swell. "You—" He raised his hand as if to strike her, but instead he stabbed a finger in her face.

Katie glared back defiantly.

After a moment, he turned and strode stiffly back to the stove. What had gotten into him? He couldn't believe he let someone get under his skin like that. Was he getting soft? There had been a time not long ago that he wouldn't have given one twit what that girl said; she was beneath him in every way. Arguing with that...that rebel only elevated her to equal status. Yet, as he stirred spaghetti sauce, he cringed inside. Part of her words were true; the war was not going well for the North American Commonwealth. Savannah and Jacksonville were now under U.S. control. Charleston, for all practical purposes, was lost. That traitorous Western Alliance Army was slowly but assuredly rolling up the East Coast from south to north.

Tipton turned off the burner and replaced the pan lid. If the NAC's new Persian allies don't enter the fray soon, all would be lost. And then what would happen to him, a Commissar Colonel? It could get really ugly; the retributions against the Directorate would be horrific. Acting humanely now might lead to lesser charges if he were caught. But he had no intention of getting caught. If the NAC fell, he would simply skip out and start over with a new identity, perhaps even in one of those western provinces. One thing his years in the Directorate had taught him was to always have a backup plan. He was a realist and believed in stacking the deck. He already possessed several false identifications.

"So, Mr. Commissar," Katie asked snidely, "again I ask, what are you going to do with me?"

His thoughts broken, Tipton faced the woman at the kitchen table. "By rights, you should stand trial for treason. There are a dozen other charges that could also be tacked on, including murder." He paused, watching Katie shake her head in disbelief. "But as for now, you are my guest."

Katie nodded to her shackled ankles. "Yeah, right. You're hoping to use me to lure in Sam Moore. He's your real target, isn't he?"

Tipton ignored the comment. Yes, recapturing Samuel Moore had indeed been an ambition that kept him going. In his darkest days, the vision of Moore in chains, rotting away in a cell, filled him with great joy, even more than seeing Moore swinging from the end of a rope. Once Moore was dead, the hatred might stop, and that could take away one of his few joys in life. But with Samuel Moore in prison, the hatred could gleefully fester. He could visit Moore when the mood struck, torture his mind, constantly reminding Moore who had won.

But now, all those glorious dreams of revenge were on the verge of evaporating like summer rain. Tipton reached for a colander. He paused, glanced around the kitchen, and audibly chuckled; just look at him now. The once-powerful, respected Commissar Colonel now hardly more than a commoner, a lonely old man with no family, no friends, and making spaghetti—spaghetti! He sighed. Even the capture of the once-hated Samuel Moore now held little attraction. Why did he even pay Zhimmer for the Spencer girl? Was he grasping at straws, hoping that the capturing of a dead enemy's granddaughter would bring back the thrill of the hunt?

Tipton's shoulders sagged. He carefully poured steaming pasta into the colander, allowing it to drain. Now, he was reduced to cooking for himself. Well, he should be happy. He, at least, had food. Most in town were on the verge of starvation. He wondered how could the people in this town be so miserable, yet still so proud? Tipton dumped the pasta back into the pot. What he hated most was life. Not just the life he now lived, but the way he had lived life itself...so many regrets...he choked inside. No! No! He had no regrets.

"I heard you tell Zhimmer that you called off the reward for Sam Moore?" Katie asked. "Why?"

Ignoring the question, Tipton carried a steaming plate of spaghetti to the table and took a seat across from Katie. "Are you sure you won't join me?"

"I'm not hungry."

"No, I suppose you aren't. If I were in your place, food would be the last thing on my mind." Tipton tucked a napkin into his open collar and reached for a fork. "Well, if you'll excuse me, I am famished."

"I can't believe you paid one hundred thousand dollars for my capture just to have me here to watch you eat spaghetti."

Tipton swallowed, dabbed his lips, and smiled. "It does appear that way, doesn't it?"

Katie shifted in her seat. Chains rattled. "I ask again, why do you—"

"You are a bargaining chip, my dear." The commissar poured himself a glass of wine and glanced at her. "You're invaluable to the U.S. regime. I know about your linguistic skills. A native-born Commonwealth citizen who speaks fluent Persian," his gaze shifted to hers, "priceless. The Directorate was foolish in not giving you membership and then employing you in the state department. Perhaps things would've turned out differently. But here you are."

Katie's chin tightened, and she looked away.

Tipton took a sip of wine, replaced his glass, and sighed. "Your skills still make you valuable to us."

Tapping fingernails nervously, she eyed the older man. "You hand me over to your bosses, *you* throw away *your* chance for a conditional surrender." Her tapping stopped. "Or your escape. Am I right, Commissar?"

Tipton chewed silently, scrutinizing the woman across from him. He tilted his wine glass, washing down the pasta. Replacing the glass, he dabbed his mouth with a napkin corner. "I can see why Moore would want you around...give him a little class. You are a very astute young lady." He paused, nodding. "And I grudgingly must commend you and that teacher for pulling all this off. Yes, it appears there's more to Moore—no pun intended—and you than I first thought." And, indeed, Katie Spencer did have his admiration. If he were perhaps twenty years younger and in another time. "Are you sure I couldn't interest you in a glass of wine?"

"No..." Katie lowered her eyes. "No, thank you."

Tipton watched pasta curl around his twisting fork. What was he to do with her? When the war began, his sole purpose in life was to capture Moore and the Spencer girl together, have Moore hang in front of her, and then turn the girl over to the authorities. However, like everything else as of late, *need* took precedence over *want.* To his alarm, his plans were reformulated seemingly before his very eyes.

Tipton lifted his fork. *Change*...change had reared its annoying head once again and to his dismay, the concept was making itself at home. Later, to accommodate the latter and to satisfy his *want,* he believed he would simply allow Moore to rot in prison. But now... Tipton chewed silently. Change had consumed what was left of his former self. He recalled Leonard Spencer. He'd become just as archaic as that old man. He, a once vaunted and feared commissar, was becoming only a caricature of himself. He had to do something quick before the laughing started. He would rather die than suffer the laughing.

Tipton swallowed and reached for his wine glass. Killing or capturing Moore no longer held the importance it once did. Nothing seemed as important as it once was, and for that, he was sorry.

Knock-knock-knock. Tipton took a quick sip, replaced his glass on the table and glanced to the door. "Enter."

A soldier dressed in blue camo, with a weapon slung over a shoulder, stepped into the room. He spied Katie, did a double-take, and then he stepped across the room to the small kitchen table, halting a few feet away. "Mr. Tipton, may I have a word with you in private?"

"Certainly, Major." Tipton glanced to Katie. "If you'll excuse me?" He tossed the napkin near his plate, and the two entered a narrow hall. "What is it Major Pevy?"

The major, in his mid-thirties, removed his helmet. "Delta Company's second and third platoons have been gone all day for what should have been a four-hour mission. They still haven't returned."

Tipton's jaw tightened. "And you couldn't raise them on the radio?"

"No, sir. No word from them at all." The major paused. "We checked the barracks. All their personal gear is gone."

Tipton shook his head, swearing softly. "More deserters..."

"I'm afraid so, sir. They're surrendering in mass now. Whole units at a time."

"And this location is not yet even threatened."

The major shook his head. "I guess the men heard about the East Coast cities falling, and then when the enemy took Charleston, it was just too much, too close."

"Some military we have," Tipton murmured sarcastically. "What's our troop strength around here?"

"We're down to about quarter strength, maybe three hundred."

The commissar gave a disgusted sigh. "What do you suggest, Major? And surrender is not an option."

The soldier's gaze hardened. "Surrender? Not at all, Mr. Tipton! I'll shoot the first son-of-a-bitch who says we ought to surrender. For now, the enemy is not moving this way, but..." He pointed to the dining room. "With her here, that may change." He paused. "What's so special about her other than her being the one that started this war with her lying broadcast?"

Tipton rubbed his face, remaining silent.

"You're still hoping to bring in that damn Moore, aren't you?"

"Don't take offense, Major, if I tell you it's none of your business."

The major's eyes narrowed. "Well, I'll let you in on a little something, Mr. Tipton. If that WA bunch learns their leading-lady is here and wants her back bad enough, we no longer have the force in Perchance to stop them."

Tipton swore silently. He couldn't believe it had come to this. He eyed the younger man. "Are you saying we retreat?"

"That's an option I would strongly recommend."

Tipton wrinkled a brow thoughtfully.

"Valor is one thing, Commissar. Stupidity is another." The

major pointed down the hall. "That woman in there is the WA's Joan of Arc. At least that's what the U.S. believes. They may risk a rescue."

"You're not saying that I should turn her loose, are you? Not after paying one hundred thousand U.S dollars."

"No, sir, I am not. Either we send her on to Central City, or we retreat with her in tow, or," the major hesitated, "ransom her back."

Tipton had given thought about the latter, but that would come much later as his *personal* passkey. "Let me sleep on this, Major. Nothing will happen tonight."

"Yes, sir." The soldier donned his helmet. "I've been a soldier for fifteen years, Commissar, and I've never seen morale this low. Our mission was to defend the crossroads. It turned out to be a non-factor. For the life of me, I don't understand what you see in this shit-hole of a town, anyway. No disrespect, Mr. Tipton, but we never should have been deployed here to begin with."

Two months ago, Tipton would have bitten off the soldier's head for questioning his judgment. He worked off his glasses and rubbed the lenses on a shirtsleeve. "This is my home, Major."

* * *

The early morning cold rain whipped across the road, glistening off the dark-blue Humvees and three-axle heavy trucks as the NAC army made its way out of Perchance. Dark, rain-laden clouds skidded across a wintery sky, casting a foreboding pall.

In spite of the weather, hundreds of citizens lined the way, taunting, giving obscene gestures, and booing. Some clapped while spitefully waving small American flags. The spectacle was not a goodwill send off, but a good riddance demonstration of defiance.

Sitting in the back seat of the lead Humvee, Tipton glanced to the crowd and sniffed. "What a bunch of ingrates." He knew that no matter what, he would never again see Perchance. Still, even with the rude outpouring, part of him was dejected. He hated to admit that the quaintness of the community had grown on him. And now his last memory of this town...

Katie was seated next to Tipton, with her cuffed hands resting in her lap. She had been allowed to shower but had to throw on her now soiled old clothes. She gazed to the crowd outside. "Do you blame them? I witnessed the NAC's so-called 'goodwill' toward these people. You were an occupying army. You guys treated the citizens like dirt, stealing everything they had."

Tipton continued staring out the window. "You don't know that."

"I lived here last spring, under your nose the whole time."

Tipton jerked around. "I don't think so. That would've been too risky on your part. I don't believe you're that daft. We would've found you."

"But you didn't. I was here when you hung my grandfather."

"Your grandfather was a terrorist. He was responsible for the deaths of at least thirty-five soldiers." Tipton cleared his throat. "He had a trial, was found guilty of treason, and legally executed."

"He was a patriot given a show trial. The outcome was expected." Katie paused, glaring at the man next to her. "*You*, Mr. Tipton, killed him. And you might as well have killed my grandmother, too."

Tipton shrugged, unfazed. "Suit yourself." He leaned forward. "Major, what unit did you say we were joining up with?"

The same soldier that had visited Tipton's home the night before sat in the front passenger seat, studying an old-style map. He was now the senior ranking officer. "Fifth Brigade, sir. They're in Columbia, waiting for us." He glanced out to the rain-soaked countryside. "With this weather, it may be dark before we arrive."

Tipton nodded and leaned back. Katie's last words haunted him. How many deaths was he responsible for over the years? He had lost count. It was his job to make sure there were no insurrectionists running amok. Executions were something he never dwelled on. Although, lately, those condemned souls were implanting a conscience in him. There were nights he needed medication to get any rest.

Tipton glanced to the girl next to him. Once they reached Columbia, he would be forced to hand her over to the authorities. Someone had contacted the Directorate Commissioner, his boss in Central City, alerting them of his captor. Late last night, he received a Directorate communiqué. He was to hand over Katie Spencer to the OIS in Columbia. Directorate leadership was anxious to get their hands on her.

Katie shifted in her seat, and the armed soldier on her left eyed her suspiciously. She glanced to the Commissar on her right. "What's going to happen to me, once we get to Columbia?"

"I already told you. You'll be escorted via rail to Central City. You'll be interrogated, perhaps given a chance to renounce your cause, and if you're lucky, pardoned."

"But not freed."

Tipton laughed out loud. "Young lady, you'll die in custody." Katie gave a start, and he waved a hand. "You won't be executed. At least I don't believe so. You're much too valuable alive. And I'll put in a good word for you, tell them you surrendered on your own." He scrutinized her. "You needn't mention that a 'friend' stabbed you in the back. It won't help your case. Eventually, if you prove your worthiness, you may even live a life of luxury, but you will always, *always* be monitored, twenty-four-seven, three-sixty-five, for the rest of your life."

Katie sighed. "A virtual prison."

"You could say that."

Tipton didn't tell her that if the NAC lost the war, and that seemed very likely, she would never be released to the enemy. Katie Spencer would cease to exist. *Another soul to add to the growing list, huh, Jonathan? Do you really want this as your coup de grace as you go down in flames? No, on second thought, you won't go down in flames. You'll simply be tossed into the dust bin of history and forgotten. If you hand the Spencer girl over to your bosses, your legacy will be erased, as you had tried to erase others.' You thought you were respected. I've got news for you, Mr. Commissar of nothing. You were **never** respected. You were hated, Jonathan—feared and **hated**! And that will be your legacy.*

Tipton reached a decision so decisively that he visibly shook.

Katie glanced at the older man. "What was that about?"

Tipton eyed her silently. After a moment, he leaned forward. "Major, I need to interrogate my prisoner once more before we reach Columbia. Privately. This will be my last chance to gather information before Central gets hold of her."

The soldier gave him a perturbed look. "You want me to just stop the convoy and..."

"Yes, please." Tipton glanced to Katie then back to the major. "I noticed that some of the smaller vehicles in back of the convoy only had a soldier or two in them. They could double up in other vehicles for a while. When we stop again, the prisoner and I will return up here."

The major gave an annoyed sigh. "A reminder, Commissar, this is my show now. I have orders not to let the prisoner out of my sight."

Tipton's eyes narrowed. "And may I remind you, Major, that my evaluation reports weigh heavily when it comes time for promotion of field grade officers."

The major's jaw tightened. Hesitating, he reached for a radio mike and spoke. The convoy crept to a stop on the deserted highway. Within seconds, a small truck-like vehicle, similar to an early 21st century SUV, pulled alongside the larger Humvee.

The major glanced to the commissar. "There's your ride. Don't be long, and don't hold up the convoy."

Katie began protesting. "What are you doing! I'm staying in here!"

Tipton shook his head impatiently, put a shoulder to the door, and stepped out into the rain. "Come on, Spencer, get out. Let's go. If I wanted to harm you, I have had plenty of chances."

Two soldiers climbed from the nearby truck and began walking back to locate rides. Tipton glanced to the empty, idling truck. He reached in for Katie.

She kicked at him, screaming. "Let me be!"

"I'm losing patience," Tipton replied.

A soldier jerked the struggling woman out of the vehicle and nodded to the truck. "Want me to get her strapped in, sir?"

Tipton stepped around the vehicle to the two. "No." He scrutinized Katie for a long moment then turned to the soldier. "That won't be necessary. She's decided to come peacefully."

Katie stilled, cautiously eyeing the older man. "What are you going to do?" she growled.

The soldier released her. Tipton reached for her arm, escorting her to the passenger side. "I'm trying to save *both* our lives," he murmured.

Katie stared. Then she slowly climbed into the passenger seat and strapped in. Tipton looked over the vehicle's roof to the soldier about to climb back into the Humvee. "Tell the major that I'll be in the convoy's rear," he shouted. "I don't want to hold things up."

The soldier nodded. Within seconds, the lead vehicle lurched forward and the convoy began its slow trek northeast.

Tipton silently watched the half-mile convoy slowly roll by, waiting to take his place at the tail end. After fishing out a key, he removed her handcuffs. He tossed them and the key on the floor.

Katie rubbed her wrists, gazing at him, incredulous. "What do mean, 'save both our lives?'"

The last vehicle crawled past. Tipton swung the truck in behind and matched the convoy speed at a blazing twenty miles-per-hour. "My timing has always been impeccable," he began, "and I sense that *now* is the time for a change."

Katie continued gazing at the commissar. "And me?"

"I haven't decided. But one thing I can tell you is you're *not* going to Central City."

"But you said—"

"I know what I said," Tipton shot back. He eased off the throttle. The distance subtly grew between them and the vehicle in front. "Listen, young lady, if the Commonwealth loses this war, the Directorate will put you out to pasture, permanently."

"I can't believe you're doing this," Katie murmured. She shook her head in disbelief. "Commissar Tipton growing a conscience?"

"Let's not get hasty." He glanced at her through rain-speckled glasses, with a hint of a smile on his lips. He gripped the wheel, again, reaching some great conclusion. The vehicle in front disappeared around a curve. Without warning, Tipton spun the wheel, making a U-turn.

Katie's eyes widened. "What are you doing!"

Tipton nailed the throttle, and the two were thrown back in their seats. "I'm taking you back to your people."

"Unbelievable. I would never in a million years have guessed this of you."

The truck sped down the highway, distancing itself from the convoy. Both Katie and Tipton nervously checked outside mirrors. There was no pursuit. The commissar glanced to Katie. "I'm hoping that by returning you, little Ms. Spencer, I can get a pass to places unknown." Tipton chided himself for spilling to her his newfound dream.

Katie gazed to the older man. Her dark eyes held a new light. "Sounds like you're surrendering."

"I wouldn't call it that. I only wish to start fresh, began a new life."

"Well, you told me you couldn't guarantee my safety, and now, I'm saying I can't guarantee yours." She glanced to Tipton, and for the first time in days, she smiled. "But I'll put in a good word for you."

They laughed.

The radio crackled. *Commissar! Where the hell are you going! Get back here with that prisoner!*

The commissar glanced at Katie and buried the throttle.

Sam stared out the window of the idling FURV, windshield wipers squeaking a steady cadence, and thankful he wasn't out in the rain. It was near noon. The day was cold and dreary, so there was still plenty of time to get wet. Misery was a companion hard to shake.

The radio squawked. *Nighthawk Two, over.* In the back seat, Corporal Steagal keyed the mike. "Nighthawk Two, go."

Papa said it's your turn to pick up the pizza, over.

Private Deider, who was behind the wheel, and Steagal glanced at Sam. "Let's do it," Sam said. Deider shoved the gearstick, and Steagal clicked a hand-held mike. "Nighthawk One, Nighthawk Two heading to the drive-through. Over."

Roger that. Out. Posted on the north side of Perchance, Sam's mechanized infantry platoon began rolling forward, with his FURV in the lead. The other three platoons checked in. Perchance was now surrounded by mechanized U.S. Army troops, who began cautiously creeping forward.

Deider worked a gloved finger under his helmet, wiping off sweat, and addressed no one in particular. "Heard that scouts ran into a few civilians who said the NAC army pulled out early this morning."

Sam nodded, staring keenly ahead. A few hours back, when Sam learned of the enemy army leaving, he should have been elated. A citizen reported to the scouts that it was rumored that a female prisoner was being held at the Commissar's quarters. The men backslapped and high-fived—"there's our girl" several commented. Then, almost in the same instant, his heart sank when he learned the Commissar's quarters were abandoned and that Tipton, and Katie, most likely went with the army. Sam had to force his personal thoughts down. Soldiers' lives were now at stake, depending on what he did or didn't do. "Could be a ruse. They could be out there, waiting for us to enter town, catch us from behind, cut us off, and close in." The men nodded. A fourth soldier in Sam's FURV manned a single .50 caliber in an enclosed, armored turret. The ominous sound of a heavy bolt being pulled back echoed.

The seven-vehicle convoy crossed over the Santee River. Sam glanced at the very spot where this had all begun, over a year ago. If he had tossed that shortwave radio into the river, would he be here at this moment in time? He wished Leo could see him now. Who would have thought that he, a school teacher and former Directorate member, would return to Perchance as a Lieutenant in the *United States* Army? *God, it is amazing,* he reflected, *where life's convoluted paths lead us.*

The platoon frequency in their helmets crackled. *Lieutenant, we have a NAC FURV coming up fast on our six-o'clock!*

Sam spoke into the mike hanging from his helmet. "Fire warning shots." He turned to the RTO in back. "Put this on company."

"Yes, sir." The large radio in back came alive, and the whole company was now able to hear the communiques.

A heavy .50 caliber thundered. Everyone within five miles could hear it. Asphalt spat in front of the rushing FURV.

It slowed, but it's still coming. Wait, two NAC Hummers are closing in behind it. My God! They're shooting at the first one!

"Form a front!" Sam shouted into the mike. "I want those vehicles secured and prisoners taken, if possible!"

The Humvees in Sam's platoon spread out, training .50s calibers on the in-coming NAC vehicles. Soldiers scrambled out, taking positions behind the trucks.

NAC machineguns hummed, peppering the FURV heading toward Sam's platoon. *Boom.* The FURV's fuel tank exploded, lifting the rear end. The vehicle swerved wildly. It hit the ditch hard, rolled over one-and-a-half times, and came to rest on the driver's side. Flames engulfed the vehicle's rear, licking toward the front.

Rat-tat-tat-tat... The platoon's heavy machine guns opened up on the remaining two vehicles.

Boom. One vehicle exploded, an orange fireball lifting into the rainy sky. The second made a quick U-turn, speeding away. Bullets bounced off its armored tail.

Soldiers were already around the overturned FURV, several with aimed weapons, while others held fire-extinguishers, lathering the enemy truck in foam.

Outside his Humvee, weapon in hand, Sam shouted to the RTO still in the truck. "Tell the Captain we've secured two of three enemy vehicles, the third got away."

The soldier grabbed a mike. "Papa, Nighthawk Two, over..."

Sam sprinted to the FURV on its side. The flames were almost out.

"Get me out!" a woman screamed from inside. "Get me out!"

Sam's insides froze. He recognized the voice. Two soldiers

were already on top of the overturned vehicle, with pry bars wedged inside the door jam, working to free it.

"Katie!" Sam shouted, racing up. Adrenalin pumping, he slung his rifle over a shoulder, leaped onto a tire, and jumped to the door. "Katie!" Surprisingly, the passenger window was still intact. Sam peered inside. He couldn't make out detail, only that a person coated in blood was clinging to a seat back. "We'll, get you out, baby! Don't panic! Stay calm. ZZ and your brother in there?"

"No! It's just me and Tipton. Sam, oh, Sam, the seatbelt release is jammed!" Her voice wavered. "I hurt all over. I'm afraid for our baby." She glanced down. "And the Commissar's hurt bad, Sam. He needs help more than me!"

The Commissar? Our baby? Sam stared, too stunned to move or even speak.

A soldier eased Sam away. "Excuse me, sir, but I need to be right where you're standing."

Sam blinked, roused into the present. "Someone get on the horn, tell Captain Fields we've procured the pizza. Mission accomplished."

Men pushed on pry bars. A creak sounded, and the door popped open. Sam and another soldier reached inside. Katie's face was blood spattered. She held the seat in a death-grip. "Easy, baby," Sam said, "I'm coming inside to cut you lose."

Katie gazed up, wide-eyed. "Anytime is fine with me. And we have to get Tipton to a hospital."

Handing his rifle to a nearby soldier, Sam began to shimmy inside the open doorway.

"Baker is smaller, sir," a soldier said. "It might be easier if—"

"I got it," Sam replied, disappearing inside the cab. He craned his neck, seeking a foothold, when his gaze landed on the commissar. The limp figure was strapped in, but his left side was jammed against the door, his left arm twisted under him. Blood pooled on cracked window glass. Sam crouched on the console's side, worked off a glove, reached down, and touched Tipton's neck, feeling for a pulse.

"Oh, God, I pray he's alive. He helped me, Sam. We were trying to get away."

"There's a pulse...barely." Sam worked his glove back on. "Let's get you outta here."

Several pairs of hands reached in. "We've got her, Lieutenant!"

"Okay, baby." Sam wedged a knee against Katie's thigh,

taking weight off the seat harness. He pushed the seatbelt release: nothing. He drew a dagger from a boot sheath. "Here goes." He began sawing. A mixture of rain, sweat, and blood trickled into his eyes, stinging them. The material was military grade and tough. A long, agonizing minute passed as Sam sawed away. When the blade was almost through, he glanced up. "Okay, you guys, pull her up!" Sam made one last slice, and the belt ripped away but was caught on one of Katie's arms.

Katie winced, groaning in pain.

"Hold on up there!" Sam shouted. "She's hung up. Let go of her left arm." Hands released Katie's left wrist. Sam instantly felt her weight. "I've got you," he said calmly. "Everything will be okay."

Katie nodded. Her breathing was heavy. With her help, Sam looped the seatbelt over her arm and freed her. She thrust her hand back up, and several pairs of hands grabbed her arm.

Sam sheathed the dagger and pushed. "Okay, let's get her outta here!"

Soldiers tugged, and Katie scrambled out as Sam steadied her from behind. He clambered out the door after her. "The driver's in pretty bad shape."

"We'll have him out in no time," a soldier said, disappearing inside the wrecked FURV.

A soldier handed Sam back his weapon. He checked the action, slung it over a shoulder, and hopped down. A combat medic was already at Katie's side.

Sam tugged off his gloves as he stepped up to her.

The woman collapsed into Sam's arms, and he gently cradled her, aware of her injuries. "It's okay," he whispered, "It's okay." Katie quietly sobbed as Sam ran his fingers through her hair, consoling her. "You gave me quite a scare, lady. Next time, let someone know where you're going. We have a whole freakin' army out looking for your ass."

Katie pushed away, smiling through the tears.

Sam wiped sweat from his chin. "Where's your brother and ZZ?"

"James was never here. ZZ tricked me and turned me in for a reward."

"What the—" Sam stared in disbelief. His heart almost stopped. No way...and yet, here she was. He had gravely, fatally misjudged character. What other fatal mistakes had he made?

"I'm sure that despicable bastard is not going back for his family," Katie continued. "I'll fill you in on it later."

The medic stepped up. "Let me look her over, sir." He took

her elbow, "come with me, ma'am." He escorted her to another Humvee. Sam followed behind. Radios squawked, and men prepared to move out. Another team checked out the destroyed NAC vehicle, searching for survivors. Only charred bodies were found.

The rain had let up as a medic eased Katie into the open rear door where she sat, facing Sam. "Sam—"

"Katie—"

They spoke simultaneously.

The medic reached into a first-aid pouch. "Excuse me, sir, but I need to ask her a few questions."

"So do I," Sam replied. He glanced to the medic. "Just one question, Specialist, and it's something *you* might need to know."

The medic nodded.

Sam turned to Katie, nodding to the overturned FURV. "When I was up there, I heard you shouting something about 'our baby.' What did you mean by—"

"I'm pregnant." Katie looked up, scrutinizing him. "We're going to have a baby."

Sam flinched as if slapped. "Yes, indeed, we have a lot of catching up to do."

Whatever the medic had in his hand, he dropped it back in his pouch. "Yes, ma'am, I did need to know that. I was about to give you an antibiotic."

Katie smiled weakly, never taking her eyes off Sam.

A commotion came from behind. Several men worked the commissar from the overturned, scorched NAC truck.

Concern moved through Katie's face, and she started to rise.

The medic placed a hand on her. "Just stay put, ma'am. We'll take care of your friend." He wiped an alcohol patch over her cut face. "We'll get you fixed up."

"I'll be right back," Sam said. He jogged to the overturned vehicle. By the time he got there, they had Tipton on a stretcher. He was conscious, but groaning and coughing up blood.

"Get him on his side," someone shouted. One of the soldiers that pulled him out turned to the medic. "His back is soaked in blood. Looks like he took a round." He nodded to the NAC vehicle. "Cheap Chinese armor."

The medic leaned over Tipton. "Don't see an exit wound. Let's get him ready for transport."

With a man on each stretcher end, they hurried over with their load to where Katie and another medic stood. Katie held an ice-pack to the back of her neck while a medic tied it in place.

Sam walked next to the stretcher, gazing at the prone figure of Jonathan Tipton. Blood streaked his face, but that's not what held Sam's attention; Tipton had lost so much weight that he hardly recognized the older man.

The commissar's eyes fluttered open. He began struggling. A soldier placed a hand on his shoulder. "Take it easy, buddy. You'll be all right. You're in good hands now."

Tipton's eyes focused, and he struggled to speak. "The girl..."

Sam laid a hand on the older man's shoulder. "Katie's okay, Mr. Tipton. She's okay, thanks to you."

The group halted at a Humvee, setting the commissar's stretcher on the ground. Tipton's eyes searched the soldiers. "I recognize that voice. Moore...Moore, is that you?" Blood frothed through his lips.

A medic leaned over Tipton. "Don't try to talk, sir. We're going to get you to a hospital."

Katie stepped to Sam. They gazed down at the injured man. Sam kneeled to where Tipton could see him. "I'm right here, Mr. Tipton."

The commissar's eyes fluttered, struggling to focus. "A soldier? The uniform looks good on you, boy. Take care of Ms. Spencer." He finally noticed Katie. "I'm sorry about your grandfather," he wheezed, "please forgive me." He paused, struggling to breathe. "I ask for forgiveness in all I've done, but...I fear it's too late..."

Soldiers cleared a place in the Humvee as others reached for the stretcher. Sam held out a hand, halting them. "It's not too late, Commissar." He took off a glove and placed his hand on Tipton's shoulder. "We forgive you, if that's any consolation, but we're not the ones you need to ask. And thank you for taking care of Katie. You did the *right* thing by returning her. We'll forever be in your debt for that."

Katie kneeled next to Sam. She reached for Tipton's hand, squeezing it. "Jonathan," she murmured, "you *are* a good man. You took care of me."

Sam's eyes widened.

Tipton coughed. Blood oozing from his lips. He forced a smile. "If I had a daughter, I would want her to be like you."

Katie squeezed his hand She glanced up to Sam, tears welling.

"Take care of the girl, Moore, or I'll have you arrested for neglect."

Before Sam could reply, Tipton began a ragged coughing fit and convulsed.

A medic shoved Sam away and leaned over the commissar. "Cardiac arrest!" A medic's assistant shoved a needle into Tipton while the medic started CPR.

Katie covered her face. Sam wrapped an arm around her shoulder and led her away as the men frantically worked to save Tipton's life.

After a couple of minutes, a medic stepped over to the couple, addressing Sam. "I'm sorry, Lieutenant. We did all we could."

"I know you did."

The medic glanced first to Katie then to Sam. "Was he a friend?"

Katie nodded. "He helped me escape from the enemy."

"Let's just say he was a former colleague of mine," Sam added, "and we'll leave it at that."

Sam believed his past was now completely, finally dead. A strange melancholy settled over him. His thoughts went to ZZ, and he glanced back to Tipton's covered body. Betrayal and decency...such a thin, gray line the two walked on. Well, he had a million questions to ask Katie, but now was not the time.

Sam released Katie, eyeing her. "Feel all right? I mean, from the roller-coaster ride?"

"Right now, I'm fine. Ask me again in the morning."

Sam escorted her to his FURV, giving orders to troops along the way. He eased Katie into the backseat then stepped over to a soldier, the oldest man in the platoon, directing traffic.

Platoon Sergeant Michael Cepsecke was forty but could run circles around most of the guys half his age. He was a couple of inches shorter than Sam but a solid twenty pounds heavier He was also one of only a handful of soldiers in the company who had seen combat. Not only was he a father figure to the younger enlisted, but also a mentor to several of the junior officers. Sam was the sergeant's supervisor and considered him a valuable asset. And he wasn't above seeking the sergeant's advice.

"Sergeant Cepsecke."

The sergeant waved an arm at a passing Humvee, which halted in a column behind others. "What can I do for you, sir?"

"May I have a word with you?"

"Certainly, Lieutenant." He waved the last vehicle past, and speaking in his helmet mike, ordered back the team that was checking out the destroyed NAC vehicle. He turned to Sam. "If it's about those two knuckleheads that kept firing after the cease fire..."

"No. I'm sure you'll handle that in your own way."

The sergeant scrutinized Sam from under his helmet. "Then?"

"Did I do the right thing here?"

"What do you mean, sir?"

"I mean," Sam hesitated, "my orders almost killed two innocent people."

"Suppose that FURV had been packed with explosives, Lieutenant? That *has* happened before."

"If those NAC Humvees had not opened up on it, I would've ordered that FURV destroyed."

Cepsecke gazed at Sam with keen blue eyes. "But those Humvees did, and you didn't." His solid jaw tightened. "My old man once told me, 'you buy your ticket, you take your chances.'"

Sam nodded.

"I've found that in this business," the sergeant continued, "you can't afford the luxury of the second guess. You dwell on the second guess, sir, and if you survive the war, you'll find yourself sleeping under a bridge somewhere, scrounging metal for shelter, begging for a few sheckles so you can keep the demons away."

"I already have a boatload of demons, and I don't need anymore."

Cepsecke gave an understanding nod. "You did the right thing, Lieutenant. You did exactly what I would've done."

"Thank you, Sergeant. Your opinion means a lot. Just thought I'd ask."

"Sir, by you sharing your concern with me, it tells me that you'll do just fine." He paused. "We've only served together a few weeks, Lieutenant, but I know a good officer when I see one. And I'm looking at one now."

Sam felt his face flush. "Thank you for the insight."

"Anytime."

"I'll get Captain Fields on the horn and see what our plans are now that we've got the girl."

"Yes, sir."

Sam headed back to his FURV.

35

It didn't take long for word to spread throughout Perchance that a United States Western Alliance Army was camped just outside of town. Rumor spread that the gunfire they heard was the U.S. defending the town from a humiliated NAC army bent on revenge for the degrading sendoff. That evening, the town's mayor—who was recently freed from custody, along with several town officials—paid a visit to Alpha Company's camp, presenting a hastily constructed key to the city to Captain Rob Fields. Fields had set the record straight about the gunfire; it was only two vehicles chasing a third with an escaping prisoner inside. But it didn't matter to city officials; they'd already made up their minds that Alpha Company was the hero of the day. Knowing he'd be recognized, Sam laid low, not wanting a distraction from the accolades the town had bestowed upon Alpha Company.

With Katie Spencer secured, and Charleston now completely in U.S. hands, Alpha Company's new short-term mission was to secure the crossroads in Perchance. The next morning was brisk but sunny when Alpha Company rolled into town. Red, white, and blue banners hung overhead in several places. And, for the first time in decades, full-sized American flags were openly displayed. The Stars and Stripes, along with the old South Carolina palmetto state flag, fluttered in a stiff breeze from a pole on top the boarded-up courthouse. Everyone that could, turned out. Shouts of encouragement and cheers welcomed the troops as the convoy made its way to the soon-to-be-opened courthouse.

Katie sat in the backseat next to the RTO in Sam's FURV. She would leave for Charleston that afternoon for a short debriefing and proceed to what remained of the refugee camp. The convoy slowed as it neared what was left of the gallows, part of which had been torn down and used for firewood. Sam and Katie stared grimly at that metaphor for a police state and what would happen to the entire North American continent if the U.S. failed in its mission. Suddenly, a smile spread over Sam's face. Hanging from the now-darkened propaganda marquee in the middle of town was a banner reading **GOD BLESS AMERICA.** He'd hated that marquee. Sam always suspected that patriotism to the USA lay just under the surface, waiting for a day like today to explode into joy. He imagined scenes like this were happening every place liberated by the United States.

* * *

Three hours later.

Sam's past surrounded him. Rob felt for him, giving Sam the afternoon off to sort things out, and to spend private time with Katie.

Sam eased the FURV to the curb and climbed out. He wore gray camo with a holstered .45 fastened on his hip. Katie stepped out from the passenger side, adorned in clean jeans, work boots, and a light coat covering a man's flannel shirt. Red scratches covered her forehead and face.

Sam worked off his helmet, tossed it into the FURV, and stared in shock at the cement slab that had once been the Spencer's home. Katie looked on in pain and disgust. He glanced around, the breeze stirring his short hair. "Girl, they sure did a number on those houses. There's not one brick left."

Katie reached for his hand. "They shackled papa and made him and granny watch, while the bulldozers crushed everything in front of them." The two strolled up to what had once been the old couple's home. Neighbors' homes on both sides and across the street were also bulldozed.

"They even took out the trees," Sam commented, pointing to a crater where a stately magnolia had once stood. "Geesus...look at the track marks. They're everywhere."

They stepped reverently onto the slab. Katie pointed to a place just off to the left. "That's where you and I had tea last Christmas." Her grip on his hand tightened.

Katie studied him, and in spite of the sorrow of the place, she allowed a smile. "I love you, Sam."

Sam blushed, returning her gaze. "And I love you, Katie."

The couple stepped here and there, Sam searching the slab. "Where was the cellar door?"

"Right behind you."

Sam noticed a square of fresh cement. "They cemented the cellar?"

"Yes," she said, nodding. "The monsters left nothing..."

Sam had left his old backpack in the cellar that fateful day he was arrested. In that backpack was the photo album the Spencers had given him, including his birth-father's unopened letter. There was also well over a million dollars stuffed inside that pack. "Once this damn war is over, I'm coming back here

314

with some heavy equipment to open up that cellar."

"Are you thinking about the photo album or the money?"

He gazed at her, astonished. "Both. How did you know?"

"Granny found your backpack."

"Really? What did she do with it?"

Katie shook her head, shrugging, and then she tugged on him. "Come on, there's one more place we have to visit before I leave." She released his hand. "We'll have a lifetime to explore our past...and live the future."

Katie's last words were not lost to Sam, and he smiled as he stepped to the FURV. "I want to rebuild this place."

"So do I," she agreed.

Ten minutes later, the FURV halted under an awning next to several tarped gas pumps. They were at Michelle's old dry-goods store. Sam stared at the boarded-up windows and the plywood-covered entrance—all so forlorn. He shook his head silently. Katie tossed off the seatbelt. "We need to get inside."

"Now?"

She climbed out and stared back to Sam. "Yes, now."

"Why now?"

"I'll show you once we get inside."

"If you say so." He punched a button on the dash, and the FURV's armored tailgate swung open. Sam stepped from the vehicle. "Let's see what we have in stock." Rummaging around, he came up with a heavy pry bar and a small sledgehammer.

Within seconds, the plywood panel covering the door was off. "I'm surprised this place isn't padlocked," Sam said, reaching for the door handle. It was locked.

Katie dangled keys from around her neck. "Look what I just happen to have." Sam stepped aside, and Katie pushed open the door.

Sam stepped to an outside window. "I'm sure the electricity is off and we'll need light." Sam didn't want to admit it, but he was also anxious to get inside.

Within minutes, plywood sheets on the ground, windows uncovered, Sam stepped into what had once been Michelle's pride and joy. Katie had already disappeared into the gloom inside.

A musty smell, mingled with the familiar scent of leather, filled his nostrils. Even in the dim light, he recognized the surroundings, and recollections of his old life rushing back. Now, the shelves were completely bare. He paused. This place was sad, forsaken. It reminded him of his mother's old home his last days there. The store was a living thing, and like every living thing, it needed love, care. This archaic building missed its owner, but it still yearned for life.

"Sam," Katie shouted, breaking his thoughts, "come here."

He followed her voice, tripping over an empty cardboard box, and drew up, spotting her in the dim light two rows over. She stood staring at him, smiling. He instantly knew why.

"Do you know what happened here?" she said, casually strolling up.

He grinned. "This is where we first met."

"A lifetime...a world has passed since then." With her arms folded, Katie paused in front of him, gazing up. "You were such an arrogant ass that day."

"Me? Well just excuse the hell outta me! You were the smart-mouthed Yankee that started it."

Katie fell into his arms. Sam wrapped his arms around her petite form, cradling her.

Slowly, he dropped to a knee, taking her hand. "Katie, will you marry me?"

Caught unaware, she could only touch her lips. Her gaze searched his. Tense seconds passed. "I don't know. You being a Directorate guy and all..." She placed a finger on his collar. "Where's that little gold triangle?"

"At the jewelers, getting polished." Sam held her hand, smiling. Butterflies rose as they did that day over a year ago, when he had first laid eyes on Katie. His eyes glistened, and a lump rose in his throat.

Katie squeezed his hand. "You passed." She bit a lip. "Of course, I'll marry you, you egotistical—"

Sam rose and crushed Katie to him. Her body arched to his, their lips met, and they kissed passionately.

"Don't start something you can't finish, Lieutenant," Katie whispered, breathless.

"Oh, I'll finish it, just not here." He nibbled her neck. "I can't believe I'm going to be a father."

"Well, believe it. Around six months from now, we will be parents." Katie eased away, touching a finger to an eye. "So, when is this marriage going to happen?"

"ASAP."

Katie raised a brow. "Like?"

"A soon as Alpha Company returns to base."

"Is that the old mall you were telling me about last night?"

Sam nodded. "Rob said that if there's no action here, we'll be relieved in a week or so. I'll round up an army Chaplain or a preacher. And you look around yourself for the same." He paused, noticing the strange way Katie gazed at him. Then again, perhaps it wasn't strange at all. "What do you think? Too fast?"

"No..."

"I'm sorry I don't have rings yet, but I'll get them."

"It's okay, Sam," Katie said softly. "It's okay. We'll get those later."

"Katie, I think deep down, it happened to me like it happened to your grandfather with your grandmother."

"What do you mean?"

"The moment I laid eyes on you, I knew I was going to marry you."

Katie laughed and sobbed at the same time. "Moore, you are so full of it."

"'Why, Katie, whateva do you mean?'"

They laughed.

Katie touched his arm. "Come on, there's something I need your help with."

"What is it?"

"I'm not telling, so quit asking."

Sam thought he knew and prayed silently, fighting down elation.

The couple made their way to the back of the store. They halted, staring at the floor. "Do you want the honors," Katie asked, "or do you want me to?"

"Let me, ma'am." Sam reached down, pushed aside a rug, and tugged on a metal ring. A trapdoor rose. Darkness yawned in front of them. Sam turned to Katie. "More books?"

"Um, not exactly." Katie peered into the blackness of the basement. "Hope I can find what I'm looking for in the dark."

Sam clicked on a flashlight. Its bright beam pierced the darkness. Grinning, Sam handed her the tiny, tactical light. "Ladies first."

The two descended the stairway. The beam flashed over empty bookshelves. Katie halted at an empty bookcase. "You grab that end, and I'll grab the other."

"What the—?"

"We'll go your way." Katie set the flashlight on a nearby table and grabbed the bookcase end. "Okay, now!" Katie pushed, Sam pulled. The bookcase, while not heavy, was bulky. "A little more," Katie said, puffing.

Sam panted. "What's behind here? A safe?"

"Yes. Okay, hold it!"

Sam made out something shiny in the wall. The flashlight beam illuminated it; a wall safe was there all right. He felt giddy, afraid to get his hopes up.

"Hold this," Katie said, handing him the flashlight. She knelt and began twisting the combination lock, stopped, then reached for the handle. *Click.* The door opened on the first try. Katie reached in and worked out something wrapped in plastic.

Sam leaned over, holding light to it. It was his photo album.

She handed it to him, grinning. "I believe this is yours."

He held the album in quivering hands and felt a lump in his throat. "Didn't think I'd ever lay eyes on this again."

Katie reached back into the safe, coming out with a bundle wrapped in a plastic garbage bag. "Here's the rest of your money." She set it on the nearby table. "Should be a million-two inside."

Sam blinked, shocked. "I kissed all of this goodbye long ago."

Katie gazed at him. "We had to use some. I hope you're not upset."

Sam shook his head, speechless. Once the war was over, with this, he could help others rebuild their lives, starting with Haleana and Jenna. And there would still be plenty left over for Katie and him...and their child.

Katie patted the sack. "Some money went to the underground to buy weapons, ammo, and supplies for the cause. And granny still needed treatment."

Sam reached out, touching her cheek with the back of his hand. "It's okay, baby. It was money well-spent."

Like a feline, Katie moved her face against Sam's gentle touch. Then she closed the safe door, spun the dial, and rose. They scooted the bookcase back over the wall safe, and then they made their way upstairs. Sam carried the sack of bundled money, under Katie's arm was the photo album.

After placing everything in the FURV, Katie help Sam reinstall the wooden shutters and plywood over the door to discourage looters. They climbed into the FURV, gazing wistfully at the old dry goods store.

"One day, I want to reopen that store," Katie said.

Sam nodded. "I like that idea."

Katie reached over and placed a hand on Sam's. "I'm looking forward to our life together."

Sam punched a button, and the FURV fired up. "And I like *that* idea even more." He shoved the gearstick, and the FURV disappeared around a corner.

* * *

One week later.

Late at night, Sam sat on a cot in the NAC-built army barracks in Perchance. Morgan, the young lieutenant from Denver, and he roomed together. The room sat empty now except for their two cots, gear, a portable radiator heater, and a wooden crate Sam had scrounged, which he now used as a nightstand. Morgan oversaw guard duty that night, so Sam was alone.

He studied a memo in his hand. Seems Zack Zhimmer's body was fished out of the Mississippi River near Vicksburg yesterday. Sam's fingers skirted the paper. Tentative cause of death pending an autopsy appeared to be a pointblank shotgun blast to the chest. "That'll usually do it," Sam said out loud. He sighed, shaking his head. He had genuinely liked ZZ. The man had been like an older brother. Even though ZZ had betrayed *everyone*, Sam had mixed emotions and still found it hard to hate the man. War...war does that, revealing the inner-self. Perhaps a self you didn't know existed. Some who appeared dependable, strong of character, as ZZ had seemed, may end up only a shell of what might-have-been. Sam gave a subtle nod, deciding that ZZ was another casualty of war. His true sorrow was for Haleana and Jenna. Sam would try to assuage their loss as best he could. After a reflective moment, he tossed the memo onto the nearby crate-turned-nightstand. It landed near a faded, brown envelope. Hesitating, he reached for the envelope.

Written on the front in faded cursive were the words *Samuel Wainright*. Sam swallowed, fished out a penknife, and gently swiped the top of the envelope. He didn't notice his hands shaking until he worked out the folded, single sheet of yellowed stationary. On top of the paper was the U.S. Marine Corps seal. In the upper, right hand corner was written *26 OCT 26*.

Sam's eyes moved down...

Dear Sammy,

Son, if you're reading this, you know I'm not there. I wanted more than anything in the world to be with you and your mother and watch you and your little sister grow up. Guess that isn't going to happen. Mommy did tell you that you are going to have a baby sister, didn't she? I know you and "Sissy" will take care of Mommy.

I pray that you never have to see war—ever. There is a lot of pain and suffering all around. Even though I'm not there with you, the war may be over, and the good guys have won. If we lost, you may never read this, or if this letter does find you, it may be in the distant future. I fear greatly for our nation, Sammy. If we lose this great struggle, the country I grew up in and loved until my last breath may no longer exist. In that, I pray I'm wrong. I pray you will grow up to enjoy the freedoms we once took for granted. Sammy, one last thing to remember: <u>DO NOT EVER TAKE FREEDOM FOR GRANTED</u>.

I have to go now. It's almost lights out, and I still have to write Mommy. I love you, Son, and I wish I was there to tuck you in. I hope to be home soon and watch you grow into a man.

Love Always, Daddy

Sam sighed. The paper shook in his hands. "I love you too, Daddy." He reverently folded the letter, tucked it back into the envelope, folded the envelope twice, and stuffed it into a pocket on his backpack. Glancing to his watch, Sam chuckled in poignant irony; he had ten minutes before lights out. He stared into the shadows. Then he buried his face in his hands.

November 15, 2053. United States Joint Strike Base, Charleston, South Carolina.

At dawn, Sam opened kitchen drapes, allowing the autumn sun to brighten the room. In a nearby vase, orange and white chrysanthemums caught the sunlight and radiated their innocence. He stared at them, reflecting. His thoughts meandered back...back to when and where it all started.

Sighing, he turned and paced the kitchen floor. Tennis shoes made a soft *thump*. It was a quarter-to-eight in the morning, and he had finished a two-mile run an hour earlier. He snorted; it felt strange wearing something normal, like sweats. Sam paused, glancing to the woman at the kitchen table. "I want you and the kids to go to Aransas Pass like we've discussed. Mark and his uncle will meet you at the train station in San Antonio and drive you on to *the house.*"

Katie sat at the kitchen table. Steam rose from a cup of breakfast tea. She gazed at the cup, eyes unfocused. "Any chance you'll be joining us soon?"

With his eyes on his wife, Sam paused. His jaw tightened, and he remained silent.

"Just thought I'd ask," Katie murmured. She glanced his way, met his gaze, and regarded him in somber thought. "This is a lot sooner than we had planned."

"Baby, by spring it may be too late. We can't risk getting caught in a flood of refugees."

"I know. Westbound traffic has already picked up since *the* election."

"More reason for our family to head for Texas while we can."

"Mommy!" A brown-haired, two and-a-half year-old girl bolted into the kitchen, halted at Katie, and tugged on her robe. In her hand was a toy airplane. "Evan won't let me play!" Her words were surprisingly articulate for one so young. A dark-haired boy exactly the same age as the girl scooted into the kitchen, lunging for the tiny airplane in his twin sister's hand. "It's mine! Give it to me!"

Katie sighed her impatience. "Emma, Evan, what have daddy and I told you two about sharing?"

Sam looked first to the children then to their mother. "That is his personal airplane she's holding. Emma has her own things she doesn't share."

"Well," Katie began, "I'm sure he didn't want it until he saw Emma with it. Besides, Emma's not going to crash his 'personal' plane into the dog food, then try to feed it to Sonny." Sonny was the family's two-year-old German shepherd.

Sam had to chuckle. Life was never dull with two-year-old twins. How he would miss them and Katie! He knew Katie suffered in his absence, too. He hadn't been back three months from his year-long deployment to Indonesia, and now he and Katie would be separated again. But this time, it was different. *He* wasn't leaving, at least not yet. Katie, the children, and Sonny were. Sam reflected on how they arrived at this moment, their country, once again, poised for suicide.

The North American Commonwealth had surrendered to the U.S. Western Alliance in the summer of 2051 and ceased to exist. Iran signed an armistice with the U.S. shortly thereafter, pending a final treaty. The Directorate was dismantled, and its leaders were imprisoned. The country was reunified once again under the U.S. Constitution, but in name only. Over a generation had passed since the country was whole; it would take more than a couple of years to heal old wounds, restore trust. Central City once again became Washington D.C.; however, Denver would, at least temporarily, remain the nation's "legislative" capital. The NAC president, Robert Henshaw, along with the vice president, were forced to abdicate. They were pardoned, in a gesture of goodwill. A month later, Henshaw's body was found hanging from a rafter in his Vermont home. Officially, it was recorded as a suicide, but most believed it was an assassination by the former Directorate. The president of the U.S. government's Western Alliance in Denver became the first President Pro-tempore of the new United States, until national elections were held a year-and-half later, in November, 2052.

That election took place a year ago. Everyone assumed the nation would elect the well-known Western Alliance governor of Arizona, Kellie Myerson. She was Jewish and known as "The Iron Lady," a firebrand who believed in U.S. Constitutional law and enjoyed popularity on both sides of the river. Then, out of nowhere, a relatively unknown, Rashad Emani, emerged as the winner of the first *United States* presidential election since 2024. In January, 2053, Emani took the presidential oath and became the country's first president of Arabic descent. Anticipating federal backing, American Middle Eastern political groups declared Sharia law in several northern and eastern cities with heavy Middle Eastern populations. Although the president called for peace and understanding, he failed to denounce Sharia law. Riots broke out, blood flowed in the streets, and National Guard units worked with local police to quell the violence. People fled cities where Sharia law was enforced. Those who approved of Sharia law filled the void.

A massive, historic demographic shift was now occurring. To Sam and others, it seemed the opening salvo of a rerun of a nightmare. And he wasn't the only one alarmed. His unit was placed on alert last month. And now, it indeed appeared the nightmare was looping back.

Sam had graduated from U.S. Army Ranger school a year ago. He could not tell his wife that his unit clandestinely now took orders, not from the brass in Washington D.C., but from Denver. The former Western Alliance was covertly reforming, mobilizing, anticipating the *final* countdown. Their battalion commander told company commanders that the last thirty years was "an ice cream party" compared to what may lie ahead—an "American Armageddon," the colonel had called it. But Sam would never tell Katie that even if he were allowed to. Yet, he knew she knew. The final curtain call beckoned, a part of destiny. Sam believed only divine intervention could now stop that rush to American extinction. Every day, he prayed for his country's deliverance. If it meant his men and he would be one of the Lord's dispensable tools in delivering their country from its madness, then so be it.

"Okay, kids," Katie said, breaking Sam's thoughts, "run along, and be nice." The twins scampered away. She stirred her tea and took a sip. "Sam, I just hate leaving this job. I mean, I just made news program director."

"I know, honey."

"And that kind of position, especially in this economy, doesn't come along often."

"And you worked your ass off to get there."

"Do you think if I just take an early leave of absence...?"

Sam hesitated. "If the scuttlebutt is true, there might not be anything to come back to."

"Always the glass half-empty with you. You're just so encouraging." Katie gave Sam a tart look. "And I hurt enough already." Katie scooted away from the table and rose with a groan, laying a hand on her swollen belly. "I guess our son will be a native Texan."

Sam leaned an elbow on a kitchen counter. "Appears that way."

Katie tightened her robe sash, reached for her teacup, stepped over to Sam, and paused. Both hands cradling the cup, she gazed up, scrutinizing him. "I know you can't tell me everything, but are you referring to 'nothing to come back to' as in flat, glassy, and glowing in the dark?"

Sam looked away.

"Sam!"

He remained silent, focusing on an American flag refrigerator magnet. How long would the Stars and Stripes last before bleeding to death? "I can't say anything else," he said as they locked eyes, "and neither will you."

Katie placed her cup on the counter, staring past Sam in disbelief. "And Texas will be safe?"

"Well, at least safer than here. That's why I insist you and the children go there, ASAP." Sam knew better than to *order* Katie to do anything. That was like beating a brick wall with a plastic bat.

"And you'll be here, at ground zero?" Her dark eyes flashed, and she waved a hand, furious. "Now just how in the hell am I supposed to deal with that!"

"I didn't say I would be *here*." Sam reached out and gently cupped her chin. *So soft*, he thought. "Sweetheart, you know as much as I want to, I can't say..."

She reached up and caressed Sam's hand. "I know, baby, I know. I just thought that with you a now a major and your battalion's second in command, you could shed some light."

"Girl, you're in charge of a news department. You probably know more than I do."

"A jillion rumors fly. Ninety-nine-percent are just rumor or wishes." Katie shook her head.

"I won't be going overseas this time."

She looked up, hopeful.

Sam cleared his throat. "I hate the word 'deployment,' especially when it's used to describe dispatching troops within our own borders."

Katie turned away, distraught. Sam eased up behind her and wrapped his arms around her now-large waist. "We have two hundred twenty-two acres of land with a house, a well, a generator, and everything's paid for," he said. "All near Aransas Pass, five miles from the coast, like you wanted. It's ours, free and clear. You picked it out, Katie. Said you loved that old Victorian house, said it had character, was a 'home.' We'll still have the salty scent of the sea breeze in the evening." He paused, holding her even tighter. "That house will be our home from now on. I'll come to you as quickly as I can, you know that."

"I know," she whispered, snuggling deeper into his arms. "I know."

"We have friends there. You and the kids will be okay. You said you trusted that former student of mine from Texas, Mark Thurmont. You recall he's the one that gave us a heads-up to the property. Said it had belonged to his great aunt and uncle at one time."

"He said we were like family to him," Katie murmured. "That made me feel good. He went on and on about how you took care of him and the other kids, and how they owe you for their freedom. I remember him saying that with us owning that house, it's like the house would be back in the family again."

Sam released Katie, stepped to the kitchen bar, and took a swig of lukewarm coffee. "Well, it's ours now. If you recall, Mark said the house was a survivor of Hurricane Harvey back in the late teens. Tells you how good that house was built. Still, with its age and all, I know it needs work."

"Lotta work," Katie said. "Lotta work. Um, Texas, our new home..."

"I've put in a transfer to Corpus Christi Joint Base," Sam began. "That's less than an hour from Aransas Pass. Of course, until what's about to happen is over..." He shook his head in resignation. Morose silence settled over them.

Suddenly, tiny arms gripped his legs. Sam reached down, hoisted each child into an arm, and crushed them to him. He pecked first Emma then Evan. "I love you, and I love you."

"You said you loved Sissy first, Daddy," the little boy said. "It's my turn to be loved first."

Emma stuck out her tongue at her brother.

Katie chuckled, shaking her head.

Sam rolled his eyes. "Okay, we'll start over."

The End

About the Author

Jay Chalk is a twenty-year veteran high school teacher of government, U.S. history and English. He's the author of several novels, two of which are speculative fiction, and he's currently working on a third, hoping to tie them into a possible trilogy. He lives in East Texas and when not teaching or writing, he's flying or playing the guitar.

www.twitter.com/jay_chalk